DARK SWAN

J. M. IVIE

Dark Swan
Copyright © 2022 by J.M. Ivie

For information contact :
J.M. Ivie
www.authorjmivie.com

Paperback and Ebook cover design by Franziska Stern
Hardcover and interior design by J.M. Ivie

First Edition: July 2022

10 9 8 7 6 5 4 3 2 1

For my friend, Josh Langlois—
Whose love for this book breathed fire and stars and dreams into its
very pages.

LEVELS

ORDER OF THE VARENT
Wielders of the ethereal magic

Jinn

Furie

Fae

Sun Lord

COURT OF OURIA
Wielders of the terrestrial magic

Sphinx

The gods

Elves

Banshee

SYNOD OF THE DEPRAVED
Wielders of the mystic arts

Daemon

Leviathan

Numina

Midnight Traveler

THE COVEN
Wielders of the lesser magic

Leprechaun

Unicorn

Merfolk

Lesser faery

THE UNKNOWN
Wielders of the untested magic

The Stars

Mother Earth

Father Time

The Emberfang

The Changeling

PART ONE
MERIS

My fingers sought the ring, though I knew full well I wouldn't find it on the chain about my neck. How did I become like this? How had I fallen so far?

"Meris."

A pinch at my ear sent spikes of pain through my left jaw. I whipped around, almost smacking Lady Gathbred. Her brow furrowed, reminding me of the last time I'd annoyed her. "You're dazing."

The pulse and roar of anger slipped through my veins. "I'm sorry," I said, voice taut with the barely-contained rage, "it won't happen again."

"See that it doesn't."

I grimaced, forcing the meek, submissive attitude I was supposed to have. Would it be so bad? Would telling her off be so terrible? I was to leave and be employed under Mr. Brackenridge come the next week.

But there was no telling what Lady Gathbred would do, so I bit my tongue, tasting blood as we descended the cobblestone path and weaved under the footbridge leading to the castle. In the corner, three slave children ate their measly scraps by a muddy divot, and my stomach curdled. How many diseases were in that puddle?

"Dirty beasts," Lady Gathbred snipped.

"Someone needs to help them."

She turned to me, thin brows shading her glassy eyes, and I regretted that I'd spoken out of turn. "Give a six-pence to a beggar and he will beg for more. If you're so concerned, *Meris*,"—she wielded my name like a weapon—"you can take your week's wages and buy them meals. I'd love to see how self-sacrificing you are when it comes to your own money."

I sucked in a wavering breath, and the invisible weight on my shoulders became a mound of iron. The children stared at me from their begrimed spot; brown eyes dulled by the sun, hair unkempt, skeletal arms clutching rotting fruits and molding bread. But it wasn't their position that reminded me of my younger self. It was the wide-eyed hopefulness.

My stomach dipped as I turned and entered the treat shop. The dung-scented air was replaced with the smell of chocolate and sweets. Luxury and wealth surrounded me, mocking me with what I'd failed to do for those children. Every step made the floor boards creak and groan. Perhaps the place was as worn as I was.

As battered and used.

I approached the counter and slowly eyed the sweets on display. Their decadence came in such stark contrast to the world outside. To the poverty mere feet from the bakery door. "I'm here for the Yeodo treats." My voice wavered as I glanced at Lady Gathbred behind me. She preened her silver-gold hair, waiting for me to finish the task.

"The Yeodo treats?" asked the confectioner, tilting his round, dark head to the side.

"Yes, I ordered them special two weeks ago." I'd handed him a sickeningly large sum of money, so he should remember. If he didn't have them, then I'd be doomed. Lady Gathbred would demand the money back—money I could never hope to return, no matter the new job I *might* have after that. "Please, tell me you have them."

"Ah!" The confectioner mumbled something before vanishing into the back room. A moment of cold, unwelcoming silence hovered over the area. "Here we are," he said, reappearing with a small basket.

"Excellent." Lady Gathbred flipped the towel off the treats to inspect them. They were redder than my hair and as round as the midnight moon, with white filling and edible glitter. A sickly-sweet berry scent wafted from the basket and caused my stomach to make obscene noises in the relatively empty establishment.

We exited the shop and walked the length of street again, this time in relative silence. Lady Gathbred's heels clicked along the pavement toward the rows upon rows of townhouses outside the market like taunting nails on a chalkboard.

She released a long sigh, stopping before a townhouse which looked to be three times older than her. The rusty windows were fogged by mildew, giving the home the appearance of being haunted by a less-than-benevolent spirit. I sometimes forgot we visited her ailing friend every week. Her Aether-bound duty, Lady Gathbred had said, though I knew it was because the lady who owned that house had no heirs and a hefty inheritance to give away if she ever decided to pass. "I will return soon. Keep the treats safe."

Disgust lodged in my throat. Of course I'd keep them safe, I don't know how I'd pay her back if they came to be ruined. Relief flooded my body as her pink frock vanished into the townhouse. I was alone for a moment and could breathe. I could slump if I felt so inclined...

"Ah, if it isn't Meris Vahla."

Flakes of anger slipped from my veins as I spun, facing Chester Gathbred. His pristine, fawn-brown hair was the same color as his neatly pressed coat and vest. I'd forgotten how sickeningly handsome he was, with eyes so dark they appeared like a void sky against his tanned skin. The smell made my breath snag—the faint hint of tobacco and whiskey sending me into a memory I desperately wished to avoid.

Fingers grazed my neck, looping around the fragile golden chain. "You don't need this do you?"

I averted my gaze.

"Silence?" he asked, too close for comfort. My limbs locked up, my mind lifted and levitated into white-hot panic. "You know, you weren't ever this quiet when we were together." He looped his arm around my waist, tugging me closer to him.

Sickness sat at the base of my throat, ready to lurch upward. We'd been close once…with the wind in our hair, his arm wrapped around my waist to steady me as we rode his speckled mare across the mist-cloaked field.

"Ever want to come back?" he whispered into my hair. "You could become Lady Chester Gathbred before the sun goes down."

"No." I practically jumped from his grasp, feet landing unsteadily on the crooked street.

"No?" His grin sharpened, pushing memories of the past upward. My lungs constricted every manageable breath. "You're still a servant to my house. Aren't you supposed to do what you're told?"

He reached his hand out to touch my hair, again.

He touched my hair, fingers undoing my necklace.

I took a step back, pressing flush against the wrought iron fence. Every reply, every stabbing remark I could muster, faltered on my tongue, resting in the buzzing nothingness within my mind.

"Do you expect a better offer to come?" he asked, tipping his head to the side. "Anyone else would break you like a prized mare."

I didn't fight my frown. "I'm not an animal."

His features darkened, slithering with indignation likened unto a man who'd never been told no. "You'll end up becoming a wife to an old man, caring not only for his dozen children, but his own needs. Do you want that?"

Panic spread through my veins, stabbing my nerves and unsettling my soul. Of course I didn't. But after what he'd done? I couldn't trust him…I couldn't be with him. "Leave, Chester."

With another wicked smirk, he reached a hand and seized the basket.

"No!" I jumped toward him, clawing at the air in a pathetic attempt at reclaiming the stolen goods. "Give it back!"

"Why is this basket so important, Meris?" He spun out of my reach, laughing.

He spun out of my reach. "This ring isn't important, is it? You'll get a new one from me."

"Give it back."

Tears choked my breaths. "I said give it back."

He pulled the cover off the Yeodo treats. My stomach dropped. "What if I ate one?"

"Please…" My mourning call was barely audible; the sound lodged in my throat, choking me. "Please don't."

"Marry me."

I wanted to throw up. He wasn't going to give it back, no matter how much I begged or groveled. Not unless I agreed to marry him. And that? That wasn't an option I wanted to entertain. So I stood and remained as silent as the grave.

"Okay." He grabbed a treat in his long, thin fingers and took a bite. "So… so tasty."

I froze. In his movements, a solitary object had come free from below the collar of his shirt. My ring. No longer thinking about the treats, I jumped in one last attempt to get back that which was stolen. My fingers brushed against the metal.

The world flashed, and I stood in a place other.

I scanned the surrounding forest. It was winter. Fangs of ice tore into my skin; my teeth chattered. My clothes were in shreds, and my bare feet sank into the wet, cold snow.

Another hallucination?

Though this one was far more vivid…

The moonlight coated the trees in a yellowy haze before it drifted behind the clouds. This—this was different. The way the mist fell along the dead earth, wrapping misty tendrils around the barren trees and shrubs, made my stomach clench.

I shuffled forward, my body aching below the weight of winter. The smell of wet bark and the caress of forgotten time sank into my lungs, coating my tongue in iron. Wind howled through the forest like a wolf, beckoning the golden moon to show itself once again. A shiver crawled up my body as it reappeared. That beautiful moon, drenched red.

A tribal drum pounded in the distance, slow and hypnotic. The red glow bathed the forest floor, and the snow became stained crimson.

Numb shock overtook my body.

It was blood. Blood coated the aspen bark, the rocks as it dripped from the moon.

The tribal drum became a voice; a voice chanting something I couldn't place. *Meris. Meris. Meris.*

I crumbled to the ground. My knees wailed as they crashed against the rocks. I looked, my hands now drenched in red. I tried to scream, but my voice caught in my throat.

Wounds peeled open from my right arm from an invisible force.

The world shattered, and I was living the same moment—the same heartbeat. I hadn't moved. I was still reaching for the ring. Chester danced out of my reach, careening his body and throwing his foot out, snagging my ankle.

Pain pounded into my knees as I hit the ground. My palms tore against the pavement. A hand grabbed my neck, forcing my head down, and the skin along my brow shredded against the rough gravel. I gasped, torn between fighting him off and giving into the surging panic. What had I seen? What was that world?

I still saw the blood and heard the voice.

"You *disgust* me, Meris," Chester whispered through gritted teeth. "I'm the best you will ever have, and yet you reject me so casually?"

I gasped a breath, fighting the tears clawing upward as I staggered to my feet and inspected the blood coating my hands. My face burned.

But the pain was nothing compared to when Chester Gathbred dumped the entire contents of the basket onto the gravel and stomped on them with the heel of his boot before he wiped the mess of it on the torn hem of my dress. "I know the price of those treats," he said, voice low and serpentine. "I also know you won't be able to pay my mother back anytime soon. So, when you're ready, come to me, and I will help. Or maybe you should wither…either outcome would bring me joy."

I wanted to scream, though nothing came out but a pathetic whimper.

"You're just a woman, Meris." He kicked the basket for good measure, sending it skittering down the lane. I tried to speak, opening my mouth only to have the words freeze at the tip of my tongue. The world around me flipped, turning upside down and spinning, thrusting dizziness into my body. "Don't think yourself capable of more than you are." And with that, he walked away.

My muscles quivered. Heat rushed through my body, pounding on my heart. It was enough to make me want to tear him apart limb from limb.

But I couldn't.

I was *just a woman.*

2

The crumpled paper weighed heavily in my hand, and I traced the official seal depicting a winged woman. Not only had I been fired with no hope to find work thanks to the Gathbreds, I had to pay the fine before the end of six weeks or be sold to Chester, who'd already offered a price for me. How convenient for him.

"You know I hate to lose," Chester said, smiling as the firelight flickered across his cheeks. I watched as he moved the chess piece and took a rook from his opponent. He was winning, and I was so proud of him.

I touched his hand, but he moved it away.

My heart stuttered.

I blinked away the memory, fighting to keep my tears at bay. If I didn't pay before that date, they'd come for Mae, sell our home, and hunt me down like a criminal.

A chill ran over my body as the thought slithered through my mind. Quickly, I shoved the envelope in my dress pocket and opened the gate to our cottage. It was one of the only things we owned.

I shuffled down the path, dreading the conversation ahead of me. A numb sting panged through my stomach, coursing through my veins like a shock of guilt. In a way, I suppose it was guilt. Perhaps I should've accepted Chester's offer and saved us the trouble.

I wanted to curl up in a corner and cry. Cry until I felt nothing. Cry until the pain inside tore me apart. There's no way I could pay them back.

Even if we sold everything, it would only be a drop in the bucket.

And I couldn't ask that of Mae.

Upon reaching the door, uncertainty and fear of what would happen when I stepped inside curled through me. Mae would be so disappointed. She worked so hard, weaving and weaving until her hands were ruined, and I went and wrecked everything.

I opened the cottage door and found Mae on the sofa. Her gray hair was matted in places, and her eyes were sunken in. Our struggle to make ends meet had worn her down.

"Meris?" She blinked, gripping the ring that hung from the chain around her neck. I remembered begging her to be rid of it when I was a child. I shivered, remembering at how afraid I was of the eye-shaped gem in the center. The eye which only glinted in the darkness. Watching, as though it was alive.

If she would've sold that, we could've lived comfortably. But neither of us could part with the rings…not for want of money, nor for love.

She still didn't know Chester had stolen mine six months before.

Hesitantly, I walked to her side.

"What happened?" She touched the scrapes on my face before turning my hands over and looking at them.

"I—" I bit at the hateful words in my mouth, reining them in and keeping them to myself. If she knew Chester had done this, no force on earth would be able to keep him safe from her ire. As satisfying as that would be, I didn't wouldn't have been able to bear watching the guards haul her to the Iron Keep. "I fell." This excuse—the lie—sounded too familiar. A lie I'd told two years ago.

"Fell?" She frowned, regarding me with that aged, all-assessing gaze. "Well, I'm glad you're alright." A sigh escaped her lips, then after some moments, she looked into my eyes again. "Are you alright? You don't look well."

I shook my head. It was impossible to fight the tears now. I pulled the letter the officer had thrust into my trembling fingers from my pocket and gave it to her. "I...I ruined Lady Gathbred's Yeodo treats. I need to pay her back."

"Oh, Meris." Steadying herself, her hands gripped the edge of the rickety chair. She looked ready to faint. "What will we do?"

"I don't know." I turned my attention out the window where the night curled shadowy fingers over the horizon, blotting the lingering wisps of daylight into absolute nothingness.

Mae's pale hand gripped my own, wrenching my gaze from the night-soaked world outside to her watery blue eyes. "Let's pray to Aether. I..." She squeezed my hand, kissing the scrape on my thumb as though that would fix all the trouble. "I can't lose you."

My wavering voice would have betrayed me if I spoke, so I remained silent. Though we weren't blood related, Mae had been a mother to me, and I owed her for what she'd given me. I owed her, and I needed to make this right.

But how could I?

Tears streamed down my cheeks, and I inhaled a sharp breath, scrambling to order my thoughts. If Julna were there, she would have known what to say...how to help me in a way that only a sister knew how.

Finally I said, "What if we left? What if we fled?"

Mae's laugh was mirthless. "Meris, we can't. They would find us and do worse than..." The words ceased, and she fell into silence.

Go, that little voice said inside. *Go, Meris.*

Mae weaved her fingers through my hair, gently braiding a small strand. She'd done this since I was an infant, braiding whatever hair she could while I told her stories. Silly stories, usually... about princesses and women with wings, and men made up of magic and a land of pure daylight and autumn. "Tomorrow is a new day. Come. Bring me to my room and I will tell you a story to wash the fears and heartache away."

— ℂ —

I looked down at Mae. Somehow in her sleep she looked younger. Her skin almost had a glow to it, and a smile played at the corners of her mouth. I brushed a strand of coarse, gray hair from her face and rose from my seat.

Tears continued to sting my eyes as I walked across the cramped living space to my room. It was small, barely large enough for the bed and shelf I'd crammed in.

The glint of my reflection in the mirror gave me pause. A bruise had begun to bloom under the angry red wound where my brow scraped the gravel. Not a good look on my already desperately thin body.

There was nothing healthy looking about me.My hollow cheeks were blotchy from the sun, and purplish bags hung from under dulled brown eyes.

I wanted to spit at my own reflection. There was nothing to love in that. Nothing to be proud of. It was honestly a wonder why Chester even wanted me. With a resigned shake of my head, I peeled off my overclothes and plopped into my bed without bothering to wash.

I was too tired.

Too tired of being a mess up, an *object* people thought they could claim and use.

After what happened with Chester, I should've believed happiness was a fantasy, and that darkness would be the only thing to reign.

The memory of what Chester and I once were drove knives into my heart.

I was too tired.

— ⟨ —

Dreams flooded my mind, and the weight of it all nearly made me choke on my breaths. My room was as dark as the Reaper's scythe, carving the promise of death and torture into my skin. Gooseflesh flared along my bare arms. I couldn't distinguish the hour, nor could I quiet the hammering of my heart.

A clock ticked somewhere in the house.

Tick... tock. Tick... tock.

Something flitted in the corner of my eye, bright and unearthly, and I turned to face it.

Nothing.

My door hissed open with a delayed creak, groaning on its rusty hinges. Now slightly ajar, a faint light emanated from the hall, pulsing and throbbing like a heartbeat. I slipped from my small, rickety bed and stepped slowly toward the door.

There was nothing in the short hall outside my room other than an array of moonlight speckling the wooden floorboards. If there was an intruder, I didn't know what I would do. I fumbled to the left, trying to stay in the shadows of the corridor in case someone was there. Perhaps this was where I died, slain in my own home in the middle of the night, with only the clicking laughter of leaves to bid me farewell. My fingers brushed against the cast iron pan hanging on the wall.

I yanked it up and held it. What was I doing? I couldn't stand up to an intruder.

I avoided the creaking planks and slipped farther into the main room, my pulse thick in my throat.

Again, there was nothing. A death-still quiet overcame the house, and not even the aggravating ticking clock made a sound. The moon was clearer there, shining bright beams onto a solitary book in the corner.

A book I'd never seen before.

After scouting every corner of the house, assuring myself there wasn't another soul in sight, I snatched up the strange volume and slipped back into my room. I fumbled for the matches in the dark, barely able to strike them and light the candle. Warmth from the flickering flame spread over my face as I inspected the book.

This was definitely not my book. The ornate cover was a combination of gold and emerald, weaving into an ivory circlet in the middle of the leather. There was a latch, yet no key. But it didn't matter. The jewels alone were worth more than my debt.

The book shuddered in my grasp; the coils of gold pulled away from the edges, twining into the emerald. Panic spread over me as I tried to grab the jewel, only to have it vanish below the leather.

Magic? Or madness?

I placed the candle back on the small table beside my bed.

Clank.

There, below the candle, was a key.

My insides twisted. This must be a dream.

I laughed, shaking my head. Most *definitely* a dream. And, if it was a dream, then I shouldn't be troubled with the outcome. So I took up the key and unlocked the book.

The air whooshed from my lungs. Words, delicately written on the paper, read: *Run, Meris.*

I slammed the book closed.

Rolling over, I pulled my sheets up to my chin, trying to fight the chill working its way below my skin.

Foolishness. Fantasy. Madness. I was losing my head.

I shot from my bed. Something nagged at my insides, begging me to open the book. Chanting. Ringing. *Pounding.* If there was a chance that whatever is in this book could help, then I would take it. I'd rather be called raving mad than be sold, or worse, marry Chester Gathbred.

I picked up the book and flung open the once jewel-bound cover again.

Run, Meris.

Page after page after page after page. *Run, Meris.*

Unease jarred me, and I hugged my knees in a futile attempt to calm myself. Who would put a message like that in a book? Was it a cruel prank sent by Chester to somehow get me to run to him? No, that wasn't possible. The cover was magical—so it must be a magical book.

I stayed awake until my eyes hurt and the sun began to show over the horizon. I barely registered throwing on a pair of worn brown trousers and a wrinkled yellow shirt.

"Meris?"

I spun around, and Mae stood at my door, brows knitted tight together as she asked, "What are you doing?"

I sucked in a breath, putting on my best smile. "Just getting ready for the day."

She nodded slowly before looking out the window. "I'm going to see if the butcher still wants to buy our cow."

My heart sank. "But—"

"No buts." Mae shook her head. "I'll return before nightfall. I wish to inquire about other places... we will need to work together on this."

I nodded and she took her leave. If I didn't return before the time ran out to pay up...

Mae. What would they do to Mae? Would they sell her? Work her to death?

That was not an option. Either I'd return and give myself up, or I'd return with something to show. Even if it wasn't not by way of this mythical book, I had a better chance of finding a job outside of this hellhole.

Aether. They'll hunt me down.

But I had six weeks.

Six weeks to pay up.

Without much noise, I slipped out of the house and walked down the main road. The book was tucked in my pack along with a map. If it was right, then I needed to run.

If it's wrong... Well, I didn't want to know.

3

The early morning chill wrapped its arms around me in a breathless embrace as fog rested along the ground like a veil. The skittering of squirrels along the trunks of sprawling oaks and the music of the forest wren danced over my ears. Between the delicate breeze and lively chorus around me, I felt almost…safe.

The forest path spread like a villainous snake, curving and twisting between dark trees and foliage. Was I really taking advice from a book? Was all this even real? Was it my way of avoiding a problem? Shaking my head, I traversed the winding woodland path, plunging deeper into the tree line. I'd tried to avoid the spiderwebs knitted across the road, but ended up swatting at the fine silk threads the little creatures had wove throughout the night. Perhaps it was cruel to ruin what they created, knowing full well it's their only source of food. Somehow, I could understand the spider more.

Oh, quiet, Meris. You're going insane.

With a sharp breath, I recentered my thoughts, reciting what I'd do if I was able to get out of the bind I was in. Best case scenario, I would find Julna and return to Mae, and we would live far, far away from the torment we grew up in.

I ground my teeth.

That encounter with Chester yesterday had sifted up too many memories.

It hurt to think about what happened—what was taken from me when I was young. So, instead, I focused on my surroundings; how my shoes sank into the soft earth, the cold that enveloped me, the sun as it rose. Pink streaks of morning mingled with the palest blues and softest oranges. I'd always loved sunsets and sunrises. Only in those moments did I feel safe.

I released a breath and looked behind me. What was I even doing? Had I become a lunatic?

I laughed. Maybe I had. Maybe I'd finally cracked.

Why hadn't I just stayed home and tried to get another job there? Why did I have to be such a—

I stopped. A small, white creature bobbed its head at me, long ears twitching ever so slightly in the morning light. A rabbit?

Its large black eyes locked with mine, and it angled its head. Such a simple gesture, one I was certain many creatures did, but this one seemed to speak with its body.

I inched closer to the small creature, unsure of what I was actually doing. Something drew me to it.

It broke into a hopping dash.

I ran after it, propelled by curiosity.

The forest thickened; jagged rocks and fallen limbs blocked my path, keeping me trailing far behind the creature. The spring air swirled around, causing sweat and shivers to roll down my back. Somehow, despite the times I'd slipped, I kept pace. The scent of mold, moss, and wet earth mingled with the cold wind burning my lungs. The spring foliage covered in dew made the ground wet and slippery.

My feet hit something, and I lost footing. Numbness rolled down my legs as I skidded into a tree, hissing as pain seared through my shoulder. Every inch of my body throbbed, angry and swelling. Perhaps I shouldn't have started running after the rabbit like that.

I sucked in a breath, holding my arm, and stood.

The rabbit practically floated in front of me, regarding me with silent consideration. How could an animal look so *human*?

"You're *late*."

I blinked as a void opened in my mind. "Did you... talk?"

The rabbit stared, its black eyes settling into mine. A pocket watch dangled around its slender neck, ticking ever so gently. The sound was distinctly magical, resembling the ticking I'd heard before I found the book. "*You're late,*" it said again, mouth unmoving, voice pulling from everywhere.

A resounding snap cleaved the air. The earth tore under me, screeching like a hungry beast, opening into an abyss.

I fell.

My heartbeat became non-existent.

Finally, for the first time in years, I screamed.

PART TWO
WEEK ONE IN YAMIRA

4

I ce tore through my body as I dropped into the obsidian-hued pool below. My limbs were limp as water pulled me under. Black coated my eyes; frost seeped into my flesh. I pushed against the freezing water, trying to recenter my body.

Everything burned from the cold, driving icy claws deep into my marrow. I swam as fast as I could to the surface, taking a lungful of painful air.

I couldn't see anything aside from weary shadows cast by the specks of a winter moon. The shuddering darkness coated the bark of the trees in a layer of doom and uncertainty as I struggled out of the water. Where was I? How did I get there?

Aether.

I stepped and my feet hit ice—no, snow. The crunch was so loud it could wake the dead. Or, perhaps the silence of the forest made sound deafening. The crisp air smelt of icy-rot and winter storms, pulling pieces of shattered memories from the recesses of my mind. I inhaled, but my lungs burned. Everything *felt* frozen… even my insides.

Where was I?

I strode forward, my legs stiff, cursing the Aether as I began my walk through the bitter-cold world around me.

The muted light of the white moon drenched everything, yet the land seemed alive. Despite the chill wracking my body and the shadow-kissed ground below my feet, I was at ease.

Where did the rabbit creature go? How did I end up here?

A weight heavier than an anvil dropped in my heart. This wasn't home... this wasn't anywhere near home.

A rumbling howl cleaved the air, tearing into my nerves. My insides squirmed, and I pivoted my body. Two eyes, unblinking, pierced the veil of darkness; the shade of uncut jade, dripping with intentions unspoken. But within my bones I knew. I knew the stare reeked of death and torment.

My breath snagged in my throat.

I needed to move, to walk away. The thundering beat of my heart throbbed in my ears. One. Two.

Snap!

Time stilled.

It saw me... Aether above, it saw me!

I ran. I ran as fast as I could.

My knees burned. A pinch formed in my calf. The cold bit at my lungs as I took in sharp breaths, careening through the ever-growing and ever-expanding forest.

The beast barked and lunged.

I spun, crashing into a dark stone wall. My head pounded. My body ached. The monster was on me in a second.

Claws drove into my back. Pain seared through me. The biting cold penetrated the wounds, digging deeper than the beast had. Hot tears spilled from my eyes.

Another gash.

A loud yelp cracked through the forest. My bleary vision kept me from seeing anything clearly.

"You," said a voice—accented and haunting—reminiscent of a memory. "You are hurt?"

I blinked, but the tears froze in my eyes. "Please..." I croaked, "help. I will give you anything."

Warm hands slipped around my neck, keeping me from falling onto the icy snow. I gasped, my throat closing and burning.

"You shouldn't make those sorts of promises with me," he said, his voice a wisp of a shadow. Somehow, the tone alone eased the pain in my back.

"Just help me." I didn't have time for this. I could barely breathe.

"If I help you," he said, the pain dulling. "You must help me."

"Deal."

He hissed a breath, and something stung the palm of my hand. The attack was no more than a fleeting memory as the world slipped out of grasp.

— (—

I jolted awake. The room was soaked in a warm, golden light. Shadows lapped at the flickering candlelight and fire, wrapping the area in a still quiet. My head throbbed. I was close to collapsing again, but... this place. I needed to know where I was.

I breathed in through my nose, and the delicate smell of sandalwood and cedar wafted into my nostrils. The pounding in my head didn't get any better when I sat up. The room spun like a top, and I nearly lost my footing in reality—whatever reality this was.

I swallowed. Everything was foggy as I tried to piece together what had happened to me.

I was attacked. Wait—

Bandages wrapped around my torso, and some of my thigh.

A monster attacked me. My garments were gone, and only a thin robe and blanket covered me. Where was I? Who did this?

A loud clink echoed to my left, and I yelped. Folds of dark fabric appeared, wrapping around a figure. Slowly, the figure became visible, his body appearing from a vapor.

A man stood before me, his face nothing more than shadows.

"Who are you?" I barked, pulling the blanket up to cover me completely. I squinted into the dark, trying to make out his features.

"Your... language." His voice drew shivers up my arms; deep, wistful, foreign. "Forgive me if I do not speak it fluently. The longer I speak with you, the more I will speak it better."

"What do you mean?"

"You're in my land." He paused, as though considering how much he should tell me, then drew closer. "I have not seen one of you for... too long." A pang shuddered through my chest when he came into view. He was beautiful. His hair, so dark it nearly swallowed the light, fell over his forehead in delicate waves. And his skin... how could a man have such glowing copper skin?

He seemed human enough despite appearing from nowhere, and looked barely into his thirties. When his eyes locked with mine, I froze. They glowed like a kaleidoscope of hues; magenta and indigo catch the cool blue light of the moon and the orange of the fire. Thick, dark lashes matched the angled brows just above his hooded cat-like eyes.

"Where am I?"

His smile stoked something deep in my stomach... Beautiful, cruel, and ominous—as if a thousand schemes hid behind the grin. "Yamira, specifically the Crimson Plane." He paused, his looming figure standing still as a statue. "Do you know it?"

I shook my head. Who was this strange man? "How did I get here?" I asked. The flames crackled loudly as he walked toward me, causing the floorboards beneath his feet to release a breathless sigh.

"I brought you here." He tilted his head to the side, as if trying to make me remember the scratches on my back and the pain. "Do you not remember our deal?"

"What happened?"

The man gestured to my body. "It was merely a Loogaroo." He said it like the beast was just a pest, not like it had been shredding me.

"What is a Loogaroo?"

The shadows in the room contorted, transforming into the beast I'd seen in the woods. I nearly screamed, but the man held a finger up to his lips. Did he just...shush me? "A creature who hunts during the full moon, desperate for blood. I often have to deal with them traipsing into my lands from Eira's Stars-forsaken territory." He offered a smile that couldn't be mistaken as anything but condescending. "You were delirious. I've done my best to make you comfortable."

I leveled a glare. Delirious *indeed*. "Where are my garments?"

He tipped his head forward, his hair tumbling about his forehead in a feathery motion. "In shreds. The creature tore through much of your shirt. The wounds were deep, but will be healed soon, so long as you stay within my palace and allow me to tend to them."

I scowled. "I'm not staying here."

He tilted his head to the side, as if what I said wasn't clear enough. "Would you rather the wounds fester? I am sure there are several diseases which could have been transferred—"

"I need to go home."

The man laughed, but the sound came out bitter and hollow. "Home..." he said, voice low and weak. He held up the book I'd stuffed into my satchel, and I stifled a gasp. "You were on a journey, were you not?"

"It's none of your business."

"Humor me." The man flipped through the pages of the open book as he leaned against the side table by the bed. "If you told me of where you were going, perhaps I'd know how to get there."

I bit my tongue. Maybe if I explained it to him, he would let me go. "I was looking for a place to make my family's life better."

"Why not live here?"

I looked away, knowing such a life was a dream for the disturbed. Barely a second in and I knew this place was brutal, cruel, and untamed. "No. I can't live here."

"Well," he said, "in that case, you can leave." He paused, fiddling with the tassels on the bedpost. He was letting me go? My heart somersaulted, leaping into the air and spinning. "Once you have paid me back."

Time stilled. I should have known there would be a condition. "What?"

"Paid me back. You'd said you would give me anything." He grinned, and suddenly I realized that heat from earlier had nothing to do with attraction. It was pure, unfiltered anger. "You will remain here, in my home, and pay me back for saving you from the Loogaroo, and from freezing."

I sat higher, gripping the robe tight around my torso. "But I didn't ask you to save me!"

"No, if I remember correctly, you begged me to save you." He didn't even bother to look me in the eye.

"How long do you plan on keeping me here?"

He shrugged, vanished in a cloud of black and purple mist, and reappeared, sitting on a chair. "Why do you want to know?"

"How *long*."

Again, he shrugged. Was this a game to him? "Several months, give or take."

"I don't have several months!"

The man tilted his head. "Why is that?"

A lump formed in my throat, making it impossibly difficult to speak. "If I don't get back before six weeks is up my..." I took in a shaky breath. "Mae—the woman who's *raised* me—will be forced to pay for my wrongs. I don't have time."

The man stood, straightening the coat that obscured his body from view. "We will see, then." His slash of his white smile was all I saw before the folds of his garment faded away, and he vanished along with it.

I wanted to cry.

I wanted to scream.

Most of all, I wanted to kill that grinning monster.

5

My fingers were practically chunks of ice by the time the creature returned. As he appeared, something hissed, as if the air was being devoured into a hollow in the atmosphere.

"I'm going to freeze," I barked.

"I sometimes forget how ill-equipped you creatures are to the cold." He picked at the straps on his coat, the fabric rustling against the ankles of his leather boots. "I had to prepare your room."

"I'm *not* staying here."

He made a sweeping gesture, and the muted colors in the room shattered into gentle hues of orange and yellow. After a moment of mumbling to himself he said, "No, no. This arrangement won't work at all. Not like I hoped. Not like I'd planned."

"Excuse me?"

He waved his hand, seeming to ignore my question, and an outfit appeared on the bed. "Dress yourself. I will return in a few moments and take you to your chambers. We can discuss the details at a later time."

He turned into a shadowy mist and vanished.

I'd about had it with this… *thing*. Whatever he was.

I stood, nervously wrapping my blanket around my freezing body. A shiver slid down my spine, like fingers stroking the length of my back. Goosebumps flared over my flesh, and I did my best to calm myself. I grabbed the trousers, barely paying attention to anything aside from the coiling frustration building in my chest. When I slipped them on, I almost smiled if not for the scandalous amount of leg that it showed. The tight fabric around my ankles tapered upwards into billowy pants with two slits that stretched up to mid-thigh. They were much different than what I wore back home… comfortable, and made of silk.

I slipped on the blouse, pleased to find it of similar material. The shirt tightened around my waist and wrists, while the flowing material gaped open in the back, allowing breathing room for my wounds. It was so different, and nothing like I'd ever seen or worn before. Certain I was immodest wearing it, I tried to see if there should be more layers.

After failing to find any other pieces to the outfit, I slid my feet into the slippers and combed out my hair. Sticks and dirt clung to my damp red locks. I looked so pale, so tattered and worn. It was worse now that the world around me was brighter, more vibrantly beautiful, than back home.

I was out of place in my world, and now I was out of place here. Maybe there was a tribe of skeletons I could join and attempt to blend in. Or maybe there was a graveyard with the undead stalking through a withered forest, meandering their way, never finding the rest of death. I'd belong with them, I think.

I growled as I fixed my slippers, trying to dismiss the thoughts worming their way into my mind.

The creature reappeared, his figure encased in mist. "You look decent. Glad to see you're wearing clothes."

"If you call these clothes."

"I do," he said. "If you have a problem with them, I can take them back and you can walk around in that robe."

I released a low growl. "You're a pig."

"If you're going to try and insult me, at least try and make it something I don't take as a compliment. Pigs are rather intelligent creatures." He chuckled, holding out his hand. I didn't take it. "I'll show you to your room."

"I can walk fine on my own."

He grinned. "Yes, but I'm quite lazy and do not wish to walk up four flights of stairs and cross the ridiculously large foyer. I'd rather just mist us up."

A laugh escaped my lips. "Well, I don't mind the walk. So, I'd rather do that."

He groaned, eyes narrowing on me like an accusing arrow. "I won't beg."

"And I won't budge."

Like a viper, he snatched my hand faster than I could react. Stardust and fog exploded around me, and dizziness washed over my head in waves. A half second, and we are standing in a new room.

I swallowed a breath, reeling around until I faced him. "Out!"

His eyes widened, as though I'd just insulted him for going against my wishes.

I balled my hands into fists, taking a step away from him. Trying to push away the feeling of his skin meeting mine. "I said out, you... *faery*!"

He grimaced. "I'm not a faery. What do you think those are?"

"I don't care. You need to leave me alone."

"You will eventually have to learn how to work with me, you know." He shrugged, walking toward the door. "I'll leave you be. But next time you try to insult me by yelling my race, creature, I'm a jinni."

I looked his way, scowling. I didn't know what he said, but the way he said it... it sounded familiar. "*Out.*"

He bowed, a mocking gesture. "As you wish, my *goddess*." And he vanished in a cloud of star-specked mist.

I stifled a frustrated scream. How did I find myself in these situations?

Rocking back on my heels, I spun and took in the room. The large bed was plush, as if made of a cloud, beckoning me closer and into its silky sheets. The red and white bedding tied into the rest of the room. The floor was pure white marble, glittering with what appeared to be iridescent diamond shards. The curtains, lively and open, were red and sheer, allowing the sweeping autumn wind to flood the chamber. The walls... I couldn't even explain the color. They were something between gray and white, like a stormy sky filled with mist.

My back reminded me of the wounds, and I laid on the bed. The ceiling twinkled and ebbed, as if the galaxy was within my reach. Could I touch the stars that drifted and darted back and forth?

What matter of place was this?

I must have lain here for over an hour watching the stars flit and flutter and shift. Someone knocking on my door jarred me, and I sat up, suddenly dizzy from the simple action. "Yes?"

Please don't be the jinni.

"I have food for you." He entered the room, arms folded behind his back.

I peered over the bed, fully facing him. "I'm not hungry."

"Funny, I thought you'd be hungry."

"Then you thought wrong." My stomach roared in protest to my stubbornness. I really shouldn't be like this—but it was hard to allow this entitled creature any leeway. I'd already lost my freedom to him, I'd not lose this even if it was a stupid thing to fight over.

His voice was saccharine, dripping with honey-soaked sympathy. "Really?"

Another grumble from my empty stomach. "I'm *not* hungry."

There was nothing but silence. I wondered if he was even listening, or perhaps he was considering if I was actually telling the truth despite my protests. After a moment, he looked up, his eyes an eerie mixture of blue and amethyst. "Are you saying you aren't hungry, or that you aren't hungry for the food I offer?"

A small grin crept its way onto my lips. "I won't eat anything you give me."

"Fine." His voice sharpened. "Be difficult. It's only harming you." And he vanished.

Anger radiated through me, and my back erupted with heat. I wanted to hurtle through the window. Maybe the frigid wind would cool me off. I shook my head.

I did need to eat, though. Despite my protests, I knew I'd need to find food. And so, slipping from the bed, I inched out of my room. My stomach pinched, and the cramp of hunger became almost unbearable. I had to find the kitchen.

I walked down the obsidian pillared halls, tracing the whorls and spider-like designs painted into the columns. I blinked away my surprise, trying to take everything in without imploding. How could a monster own such a beautiful house? The black marble floor lit up with a vibrant blue light with every step I took. My footprint lasted for a second, then vanished. I bit my lip, pressing the tip of my foot to the floor before spinning in a circle. The floor kept the pattern, and I suppressed my excitement. With my hunger forgotten, I glanced up and down the hall. I could lay down for a moment and soak this in. Julna would have been angry with me if I didn't. Honestly, *I* would be, too, if I didn't explore.

I sank to my knees and pressed my palm against the floor. A galaxy burst around my hand, glittering with iridescent diamonds. I twirled designs, giddy as the little stars gravitated to my finger.

The stars hummed against my legs, flitting and dancing closer to me. Morning light speared into the hall through the bevelled glass windows, waltzing with the little celestial bodies. A chorus of chimes ensued, mingling with the fresh autumn air, and soared through the corridors with magic and wonder on its wings.

I stood, curiosity piqued, and marched down the hall. What exactly was a jinni? I'd never heard of one up until he'd said the word, but something in the back of my mind poked and prodded, telling me I'd heard of it long ago.

After what seemed like an eternity, I managed to find the kitchen. The buttery sunlight swept in, delicately brushing its rays along the white marble floor. I sneaked into the pantry. Was it just him here? I hadn't seen a single soul.

The remnants of potatoes and meat wafted through the clean atmosphere, curling threads of hunger and desire into my veins. My stomach cinched painfully. I searched, and not even a crumb of food could be found. Where in the Aether's name did he keep everything?

A faint yelp resounded in the doorway behind me, and I turned. A girl, with hooves for feet and skin as blue as the afternoon sky, stared at me. Her eyes were gold and glowing like the sun. Amidst her long, fluffy mane of white hair, a single alabaster horn protruded from her head. It looked dipped in glitter and tears, like the shells which lady Gathbred kept locked away in the gallery. "I'm sorry," I said. "I didn't know anyone was in here."

The blue skinned girl cocked her head to the side, the remnants of tears staining her cheek. Was she crying? Was she alright?

"You look starved." Her voice was magical, and my heart skipped a beat at the purity in her tone. "I'll get you food."

I nodded, unable to speak.

She almost galloped away, coming back in seconds with a plate of food, placing a fork and knife down. "When was the last time you ate?" She pulled a glass from a cabinet, filling it with water. "Did Setizar not bring you any food? Cruel monster. Though I suppose I can't fault him, he forgets to eat his own meals most of the time."

Setizar... was that the jinni's name? Or was it someone else?

She gestured to a seat, and I nestled myself onto the stool at the kitchen island. She placed the water in front of me, smiling.

"Thank you." I looked at her. "Well... he offered."

She laughed. "Oh? And you didn't accept?"

"Are you surprised?"

The girl shrugged lightly, and I considered that a dismissal. "Setizar means well. Honestly, he's frazzled. It's been a long time since—" She stopped herself, as if saying more would be bad. "Have you enjoyed your stay so far?"

"No. I want to go home."

"I can understand," she chirped, tiny, purple lips spreading to reveal a vibrant smile. "I promise I will try to make your stay here as pleasant as possible."

I stared at her. Her blue skin shimmered in the morning light, as if silver dust rested below the layers. "What... are you?"

She tilted her head again. "What do you mean?"

"I mean..." I bit my lip, torn between clarifying and running. "I mean, what kind of creature are you? I've never seen anyone like you."

She smiled, eyes brighter than before. "Oh! Well, I suppose there's not many like me out there where you're from. I'm a unicorn."

I'd nearly spewed my water. "What?"

"A unicorn. Do you not know what those are?"

"I do, but...but, unicorns are horses."

She blinked, her face unmoving. After a moment, she erupted into a fit of giggles. "Oh, that! That is the funniest thing I've ever heard!" Her laughter was like chimes in the wind. "Is that what legends have said?"

I nodded, almost ashamed of my response.

"My dear, forget everything you know. Nothing here is like what you think."

That could lead to the answers I needed. "What's a jinni, then?"

The unicorn's sunshine eyes fluttered, looking toward the hall. "We," her voice was barely a whisper, "we don't speak of the jinn. Setizar is the last and only jinni."

"Why don't you talk about the jinn?"

She leaned a blue elbow on the counter, tiny lips puckered slightly. "Setizar gets upset when we speak of them."

Somehow, I wasn't satisfied with that answer. "What's your name?" I asked, taking a bite of my roast. It melted in my mouth, making my eyes roll back into my head. Aether, this was amazing!

"Cerie," she said. "Yours?"

"Meris," I managed through a mouthful of food.

Cerie laughed, plucking a few things off the counter and placing them in the sink.

"Are you the only servant?"

Cerie nodded. "In a way. I'm his housekeeper, and the only other living creature here aside from him. Sometimes Setizar hires others to aid me in the work, but the palace keeps itself up."

"Keeps itself up?"

"Of course. Setizar designed it to clean itself so he wouldn't have to see too many creatures." She smiled, shaking her head. "I tell him he needs to get out more, honestly he keeps himself locked in his room or the garden most days."

"Why do you work for him?" I grumbled, shoveling food in my mouth.

Cerie turned to me, pressing her lips together and fighting a smile. "He's really a gentle, caring creature. You'll learn to love him as I do."

"I doubt that." I laid my fork down, my back beginning to burn again. "He's holding me hostage even though he knows my family is in danger. I —" I shook my head. "Thank you, Cerie. I think… I think I'm full. You've been very kind."

Cerie nodded, her hair tickling the sides of her face. "Very well, my lady. If you wish, I can direct you to places which would greatly entertain."

I only wished to leave. "Please," I said, managing a smile. Perhaps she could show me something useful. Like a way to escape.

Cerie stood and gestured to the door. "This way."

6

I followed her through the halls, and my heart thudded against my ribcage. "What—"

"The ballroom." Cerie threw her arms wide, spinning around.

The floor was a giant glass mirror, twinkling and reflecting the tawny sunlight flooding through the open archways. When I stepped on the floor, ripples appeared. It shuddered below my feet, and I leaned down to touch it. It was cold against my finger, rippling again and causing the ground to appear as a glistening lake. "Water?"

"Not quite, but you're close." The clean autumn wind cut through the open window and rustled her white hair. "It's enchanted. You can dance for hours and your feet won't hurt." She thrust her hoof hard into the floor for emphasis, and I watched as the violent ripples spread from corner to corner. "I haven't the slightest idea of how it works. You'd have to ask Setizar, since he's the one who comes up with these sorts of strange things."

I swallowed my awe as I looked outside. Sunlight quivered through the crimson leaves of the maple trees, shedding shattered light into the circular ballroom. The domed ceiling above boasted several chandeliers, the crystal-like prisms refracting thousands of rainbows on the white walls.

"You should have seen this place eighteen years ago," Cerie mused as her layered green gown fluttered around her knees. "Setizar wasn't always a hermit. He used to throw parties, and everyone would come. Ah! And the ceiling was illuminated with stars. You should have seen it."

"What happened?"

Cerie's eyes flickered in my direction, cutting through the crisp air with a hesitant gaze. "I cannot say… I was away when it happened. If you wish to know, you must ask Setizar."

I grunted. I didn't particularly *want* to speak to him, but I wouldn't say so out loud. At least not in front of Cerie.

— ☾ —

I'd seen almost everything as we rounded the hall and entered the last corridor. "What about over there?" I asked, pointing to a set of stairs that spiraled up toward a long corridor. The ominous darkness paired with the gradual click-click of the grandfather clock beside me caused a pulse of dread to spear through my veins.

"The east wing?" She shrugged. "It was in the process of being remodeled, so you shouldn't go up there."

"Why not?"

Cerie looked up at the spiraling stairs that vanished into the obsidian black hall. "Setizar banned anyone from entering in case a hazard would befall them. It's been years, but I distinctly remember he said it's very unsafe."

"Do you know why he hadn't deigned to repair it?"

She shook her head. "He hasn't repaired many things."

She brought me to the library, and I'd told her—politely, of course, since she wasn't the monster holding me hostage—I'd like some time alone. She'd agreed and excused herself. I could laugh, especially since I was making my way to the east wing. Adventure surfaced on my tongue, and the same giddy feeling I got when I smelt fresh coffee or caramel cream fluttered in my stomach. Something about the place made me want to explore it; to uncover every secret tucked away in its cavernous body. I reached the black onyx stairwell, swallowing the breath lodged in my throat as I gazed at the darkness above me. A shiver crawled across my spine, digging into my skin.

This seemed familiar.

The beat of my heart mingled with the rush of wind howling through the halls, pulsing like the stroke of massive wings. I winced at the cold hitting my face as I ascended, trying to realign my thoughts. Off limits indeed...and definitely not under construction. Something important must've been up here if that jinni was so intent on no one entering.

And that important thing could possibly help me escape.

It seemed as though an eternity passed before I finally reached a large hall with various doors lining the shadow-kissed walls. Wrought iron beams curved into the ceiling in the shapes of membranous wings, weaving slowly into feathered ones. Beasts, like tigers, were carved from starlight and frozen in the dark marble floor as if they were suspended in time. Was the floor hiding another world below my feet? I breathed in, reaching the end of the corridor. The door here was different from the rest. It was filled with—mystery. The air was cold, and a chill ran up my back, gripping me around the waist.

I shoved the door open, stepping into the freezing chamber. Hickory wood floors, shadow-lined stone walls, and massive windows three times taller than me.

A large chandelier hung in the center of the room, glinting like eyes in the dark of a forest. A ghost of wind winnowed through, upsetting the crystals. I followed the sliver of spiraling sunlight illuminating a mirror hanging on the wall. It was simple, far from ornate, yet it was the only thing in the room aside from the chandelier.

I approached, biting my lip. The mirror reflected my pale skin, nearly the same hue as moonlight. My reflection... it looked different. I looked different. My ears pointed ever so slightly, and my nose had a gentle slope instead of the slight crook after I'd broken it. Even my sharp features looked smoothed.

What was I seeing?

"Hello," my reflection said.

I gulped a breath, trying to stifle the scream clawing up my throat.

"What... are you?" My voice cracked.

My reflection tilted her head, bright red hair rippling down her white neck. "I am you. And you are me."

"No. You're something different."

My reflection smiled. "I'm Tatum, if you must know my name." The voice slithered into a deep rasp, the figure no longer a reflection of my own but as black as a starless, stormy night. Vermillion-hued eyes emitting soft tendrils of red smoke latched with mine. The form shifted, turning into a man. "You want answers, I see."

I nodded.

"A question," Tatum said. "And for a price, you will get an answer."

"How do I know your answers are true?"

Tatum yawned, rolling his neck. "Alright. Your first question I will answer without fee. Make it something simple: something you know the answer to."

I looked at him sideways, and his eyes flared a little brighter, solidifying into pupils and irises. Still, they held the same unearthly red hue. "What's my name?"

Tatum flashed me a cutting grin. "I said a question you know the answer to, *Meris*."

My throat tightened. "What?" Despite the cold chamber, I was warm. Heat throbbed in my veins, shooting up and down my body like waves of fire, curling into my gut with burning claws. My pulse spiked as my scowl deepened. *Meris*. How did he know my name? "We are done here."

Tatum pouted, his figure slumping. "Shame. I thought we could have some fun." He shrugged. "I will see you again soon."

"Don't count on it."

Tatum tipped his chin upward, and a coil of darkness slithered over my neck. "When you decide that you need me, come back here and chant my name."

— ☾ —

I stalked to my room; my heart beating faster than a prized stallion. I shuffled down the star-floor, my bones groaning as I ascended the second flight of stairs. Scaling the four flights up to my room was agony. If I could, I would mist like the jinni did.

My mind was a web. I was caught between logic fighting for purchase amid the chaos of this new world, and the questions festering deep in my bones. I didn't need to think that the mirror man knew anything. It was probably lying and had heard my name about the house. Trying to get me to make whatever sick deal it had in store for me.

Still…

I shook my head, turning onto the third flight.

I slammed into something dark, warm, and smelt of cinnamon and autumn winds. Stumbling a few steps back, I braced myself against the wall.

"Going somewhere? Or leaving somewhere?"

The jinni. His eyes looked like the sunrise of an early morning, speckled with the still lingering stars.

"Just… back to my room," I hedged, worried he'd somehow discovered my little excursion.

He sighed, gently placing a hand on my back. Something deep inside wriggled below his touch, as though ants were crawling across my organs. "Walking all the way?"

I nodded, unable to pull myself away from him. *Magic.* Magic had likely rooted my feet to this place.

"Want a hand?"

I ignored the protest of my aching joints. "No."

He shrugged, sliding his hands into his coat pocket. "Fine, have it your way." And he vanished in a cloud of mist.

Annoying jinni.

I entered my room, slammed the door, and whimpered. My back still burned, but it had become more of a numb afterthought. I walked around, then decided to inspect what was in the armoire. I opened the doors, and garments flew out. With stifled curses, I attempted to shove them back in. After several failed attempts, I groaned and lay on the bed, defeated by fabrics.

"If I had known you'd be so messy, then I may not even have made that deal with you."

I looked at the jinni, standing amid all the clothes. "Can't you ever just leave me alone?"

"I realized something," he said. "You never told me your name."

I scowled, keeping my eyes on him.

"Remember, we will be working together. You'll have to at least tell me what to call you, otherwise I will have to make up a name for you. I can be very creative."

I ground out my words. "My name is Meris Vahla."

He smiled, a glittering gem of a grin that made my stomach twist. "Meris…" The way my name fell from his tongue sounded like chimes. Or perhaps he was perverting it… using it for his own vile purposes.

"Now, leave me alone."

The jinni smiled. "Do you not wish to know my name?"

"I already know your name." I lifted my chin. "Cerie told me."

He misted, reappearing at my bedside, and angled his aggravatingly perfect head to the side as he asked, "And when did you have a chance to speak with Cerie, Meris?"

I bit the inside of my cheek. "I wandered."

"Into the kitchen?" he asked. "Is that where you had gone?"

I stifled a growl, the sound gurgling in my throat like a yawn. "Yes."

His eyes flicked up and down my body. "Very well." He straightened, slipping his hands into his coat, and said in a callused voice, "Did Cerie show you around the palace?"

I nodded tightly.

He looked at me again, his eyes lingering on something on my face. "You will be healed in no time." With that, he vanished in a cloud of purple and black mist.

— ☾ —

Cerie popped her head into my room a half hour later, her bright eyes locking with mine. "Setizar said to come see you…" She trotted into the room, pulling open the curtains to allow the autumn air to flood in. "Also, he says you are to be in the drawing room tomorrow morning."

"Why the drawing room?"

Cerie shrugged quickly, shuffling over to the armoire and fixing the clothes that fell out. "Who knows with him."

I sighed.

"I need to check your wounds," she said. "Has it been comfortable? I tried my best."

I nodded, comforted by the fact that Setizar wasn't the one who undressed me and put on the bandages. Perhaps I should've been nicer when I first met him and not made so many assumptions.

Cerie tottered into the lavatory, returning with gauze and a vial of glowing orange liquid. I slipped off my shirt, and she began removing the old bandages.

"So, when can I explore the land beyond the castle?" I tried to look at her in hopes she wouldn't guess what I was up to.

She paused, her eyes narrowing on me. "Yamira is no place for you in this state. It's barely a place for us." She dabbed the orange liquid on a towel, making the white material look to be drenched in honey. "There's plenty to be afraid of, but if I were to list them, it would take all day. The most you need to worry about are the ogarak. If they were to find you, there would be issues."

"The what now?"

"The ogarak. They are…" She trailed off, her gaze hazing over. "They have plagued our lands ever since the Silver Queen separated the realms. Before then, they were allowed to eat the human's cattle at their own risk. Now we have to deal with them... and since the Season Guardians are weakened, we subjects are at greater risk of dying."

"What do the ogarak look like?"

Cerie breathed in, gently cleansing the wounds. "Let's just say they look like red lizards with horns and very sharp teeth. Oh, and wings."

I swallowed the lump in my throat.

"Now, the greater threat than ogarak, are the leviathans." Cerie pressed the rag to my wounds, cleaning the cuts with care. "They're the ones you really need to worry about, even if you're with Setizar. They practically match him in magical stamina and speed. I can't describe what they look like much since the leviathans can shift their forms, but mostly they appear like the jinn. That is why it is especially dangerous to go outside without Setizar."

"What can *he* do?" I asked, my fingers trembling.

"After the Silver Queen's curse, not much. But to be frank, they're afraid of him. Jinn are not to be trifled with, and he's been around this long for a reason."

I sucked in a breath, gripping the sheets to stifle my cry as Cerie continued cleansing the wounds. "So, why are they so dangerous?"

Cerie pressed a little harder in my wound, and a cry escaped my mouth. "They eat creatures. After they torture them, of course," she said, shuddering. "I've seen what they are capable of."

My breath caught between an inhale and an exhale. I looked at her, unsure of what to do. Unsure of whether I should've felt safe or frightened. Cerie finished wrapping my wounds, and I slipped my shirt back on. "Why doesn't Setizar, you know, destroy them?"

Cerie's expression dropped. "He can't." She looked out the window. "His power is chained."

"Chained?"

She nodded.

Air hissed beside the bed. "What are you two talking about?"

I looked, finding the jinni standing beside me.

"My lord, what are you doing here?" Cerie asked.

His expression lightened, and he angled his head left. "I need to speak to you about something."

She nodded. "Understood. Good afternoon, Meris." She bowed and trotted over to the jinni, placing her hand in his.

"Afternoon," I said to the cloud of mist and magic.

7

Golden sunlight warmed my cold face, waking me gentler than Mae on my birthday. I yawned, squinting at the morning rays dancing along the glittering floor. If I weren't being held captive by a creature from another realm, I might've stayed a bit longer in the sheets, curled into the plush pillows. Begrudgingly exiting the plush territory, I stood on the cold marble floor and dressed myself. They were the same clothes Setizar had given me last, but it didn't make much of a difference, I doubted he would be able to tell.

I really shouldn't be in the habit of calling him by his name, though. That seemed far too personal for a creature who'd set his mind to hold me captive.

The grogginess wore off. There was something last night…I'd thought I'd heard screams, but something had kept me weighed down in sleep. As if I'd been cast under a spell of some sort.

Or perhaps given a sedative?

I slipped from my room, trying to shake off the feeling that I'd missed something important. That *someone* had kept me from that knowledge…

I trailed my fingers against the slick opal banister as the scent of night mist and citrus filled the air. It was just as grand as the rest of the palace. The ornate pillars stretched high and braced the deep blue domed ceiling. Gold symbols, charts of the stars, and images of sundials and clock faces were painted within the layers of sky-like heaven above. Everything had life, glittering and glowing, ebbing and flowing—breathing with magic. I followed the hard curves of the wall, tracing the swirls etched and carved into the stairwell.

Shadows lapped away at the light as I stepped onto the level below. My skin must've shown against the dark walls and onyx pillars like a sheet of white snow.

The jinni's image flooded my mind, inciting a groan. Even his taunting face was showing up now. I'd love to smack the smile from his cocky face.

As if my thoughts summoned him, the demon appeared. First his too-white smile, then his face, then his folds of purple and black garments.

"You're late…" he purred, like he were some sort of feline.

You're late.

That rabbit's voice seemed to replace his—layering reality with a recent memory.

"You might break something walking down these stairs," he said.

I looked at him. His copper skin and midnight-dark hair, sharp features, and curved grin. His magenta eyes appeared blue and specked with golden stars, like the ceiling above. He stood about four steps away, blocking my route down the next flight. "What are you doing?"

"Waiting for you… at a healthy distance, of course," he said. "Where have you been?"

I crossed my arms. "Avoiding you."

"That's a full-time job, I wonder how you will get anything accomplished." He mimicked my posture. Was he mocking me?

"I am just waiting for the day you trip and fall over that cape you drag behind you."

"I can remove it if it bothers you."

I fought my scoff. "No, thank you. The less I see of you the better."

He laughed and motioned to my outfit. "Why haven't you changed?"

"Because this is all I have."

"No it isn't." He scowled. "You have an entire armoire of clothes."

"I'm sure they will be revealing and disgusting."

He shook his head. "Later, after we have eaten, you should inspect the armoire instead of tossing them out in a fit of rage."

His hand slipped into mine, dragging goosebumps down my arms, and we misted into the dining hall. Light collected around me, and I blinked against it.

"You could at least warn me!" Cerie said from somewhere to my left.

"Sorry." The jinni bowed, a smirk curving the corners of his mouth. "I will send a rose and beg your forgiveness."

"Make it an apple," she said. "And grovel. That's the only way I will forgive you."

"I'm sure you would love to see me on my knees, Cerie." He grinned. "But alas, I bow only before my bed."

"You worship your bed, you lazy beast."

Setizar draped himself into a chair at the head of the table, his posture languid, as though he didn't have a care in the world. "I light a candle in ceremonial servitude before I dive into the silken sheets."

Cerie rolled her eyes, tapping the table. "Would you like breakfast, or would you like to go back to sleep?"

"Breakfast," we said in unison.

I sat opposite to the jinni, fidgeting idly with the napkin set in front of me. Silence stretched between us as Cerie prepared breakfast in the kitchen. I wanted to ask about last night: to know if the scream was real, or if I had imagined the whole thing.

His eyes snapped to mine. "Something on your mind?"

I slumped. Perhaps my face gave more away than I expected. "What happened last night?"

He stiffened. "What do you mean?"

"I heard screams," I said, unsure of if I should have even brought it up.

The jinni placed the book on the table, the subtle thump of the leather jarring my insides. He pressed his fingertips together, eyeing me dutifully. "A fae was brought to my gate. She'd been poisoned by the local Elven tribe who think poisoning a random forest dweller, dumping them at my palace door, and waiting and see how long it takes for Cerie to heal them is some sort of entertainment." His eyes lingered on mine as if trying to gauge my reaction. It didn't help that his eyes were pools of ever changing magic. A blush creeped over my neck and cheeks, and I diverted my gaze. What was wrong with me? "The elves are just that way. Lazy, irresponsible, and useless."

"You couldn't heal her?" I asked, mustering up the steel to look at him once more. "You have all those potions and stuff—"

"Those potions didn't heal you, Meris." He leaned back, his sunset eyes looking more like an early morning sunrise. "I've been healing your wounds. At least, whenever I *can*. You're a bit skittish, and I've had to get creative. However, poison is out of my wheelhouse. Only unicorns can cleanse a body of poison. But sometimes the poison is too far into the victim's bloodstream, or there is too much. Cerie has had to deal with the death of several creatures…"

I looked in the direction of the kitchen. How can Cerie deal with that on her shoulders?

"Tell me," I whispered, directing my eyes back at him. "Tell me everything I need to know about the world."

The jinni waved his hand idly in the air, as if my question was something he needed to swat away. "There isn't much you need to know since you aren't going to leave the palace without me. The only things you need to know are: do not exit the gates. Do not enter the maze. And never, under any circumstances, enter the east wing."

My stomach dropped. "Alright." I swallowed the fear creeping into my throat.

He smiled, assuring me he's fallen for my feigned meekness. "Good. Glad we can agree."

8

If the east wing is as 'forbidden' as the others, then I needed to know what lay in the maze. And I have quite enough time to locate the maze. I scurried down the hall, the only evidence left were my footprints. Well, for as long as the little floor stars glowed. I tried to remember Cerie's instructions on how to find the garden—which I'd learned bordered the gate to the maze.

I stopped at the edge of the mezzanine. Honeyed light danced with the glistening sapphire floor through gold-tinted, beveled windows. Little clouds moved through the marble below like the star floor above. If I were to name this palace, I would've named it the Palace of Midnight and Sun. The upper portions of the place were reminiscent of the night sky, and below was a warm spring day. As I descended, every stair was colored slightly differently. A sunset, spilling into the blue marble.

Though I shouldn't have been surprised, I still was when the blue floor glowed yellow below my feet. Part of me wanted to open every door and explore, but I needed to find the garden before my absence was noticed. I needed to know what the jinni was keeping from me, and if it could help me find my way home.

A chill worked its way under my skin, and a hollow of emptiness formed in my stomach.

Julna would've loved it here...

Every day was a little harder to bear thinking I'd never see her again. I couldn't do that to Mae.

I slipped down the halls in search of the garden. The wide crystal doors cast fractured rainbows on the floor, and I groaned as I pressed them, my sparkling red slippers hitting—

A gasp snagged in my throat as I opened the door.

It was autumn. Flowers bloomed around me, and birds fluttered in the cool air. Lavender flowers, roses, and gardenias had spread themselves everywhere, swaying to a silent song in the crisp breeze. An arch of ivy separated the sections of the garden, like magical gateways to other lands.

Perhaps they were... I'd never know.

With a deep breath, I weaved through the many areas of the ever-growing beast of a garden. Trees and vines reached toward me, brushing their gnarled limbs against my clothes, making me slow my pace.

A looming hedge stopped me in my tracks.

The maze.

It stood before me like a sentinel of darkness and mystery. Something within beckoned me forward... beckoned me to enter the tunnel of hedge and green. Shadows twisted around the iron pillars that held the gate.

A gate which was locked.

I cursed. Of course it was locked. Why had I expected it not to be? In my agitation, I kicked the door.

It opened without pause.

I entered the area, shuffling forward nervously. My feet sank into the snow... *Snow.* I must've stepped out of the enchantment that held the garden in a state of autumn.

The shadows eating away at the corners and snow made my skin crawl. I continued down, weaving my way through the maze. At least there was fresh snow. I could have been able to follow my footprints back. It was cold. With teeth chattering, I cursed as the sun dipped behind the clouds. The temperature dropped once more, sending rolls of shivers up and down my spine.

How could I even survive this? I shook my head and pushed onward, refusing to go back.

The wind howled through the elongated bushes and tickled my nose with the smell of ice and rotting bark. My arms ached. My insides quivered.

A light caught my eye.

A glowing iridescent light came around the corner, lining the green leaves. I stumbled toward it, my insides screaming for me to halt—to turn back.

But I didn't. I only listened to the chant luring me toward the heart of the maze.

I entered the area, gasping on the frigid air. My bones balked with every step. There was a fountain in the middle, with water suspended in frozen droplets.

I ventured toward it, lungs raw. A mist of breath clouded the air. Why was the jinni so set on me avoiding this area?

I reached out, ready to touch it.

Talons gripped on the ledge of the fountain, and a hiss reverberated in the air. "Who are you?"

I screamed, stumbling back. A woman stood there, skin pinched and wrinkled while her thin white hair floated around her head. Her hands were like the feet of a crow, and her eyes—they were two gaping hollows where eyes should be. Her mouth curved upward like the beak of a bird, baring rows of razor teeth.

"You are beautiful, and so young…"

I scrambled to my feet, only to have her snatch my arm.

"Let me," she crowed, chomping at the air like a beast. "Let me drink of your youth."

I kicked her, my foot meeting leathery flesh. She released me, and I ran. I ran even though my lungs burned and my throat turned to cotton.

Careening left, I slammed into a pillared hedge, busting my bottom lip. Dazed, I stumbled to my feet again, tasting blood. She could be behind me, waiting and watching for her moment to pounce. Sickening heartbeats pounded in my chest as I darted and weaved through the obstacles of dark-

ness and hedges. My footprints from earlier tracked a path in the snow...
and made a perfect circle back to the fountain.

Hedges and snow and shadows spread around me, undisturbed by my
heavy breaths. Where was the hag?

Her cackle echoed to my left, and I ran down a different path, only to
wind up back where I started.

Again.

And again.

And again.

My lungs burned, my feet were numb. My fingers were ice.

I skidded to a stop. She stood before me, a picture of an undead
corpse. "Where do you think you're going?"

"Out," I said, breathless.

"Ohhh." She licked her lips, tongue black and decayed. "Even your
voice is like music."

I stepped back, and she stepped forward. Her shadow wrapped around
me, and I fought the chill.

She grabbed my arms, fingers digging into my skin like barbs. "Don't
worry. I will use your youth. It will not be wasted—"

Please. Someone... anyone! I shouldn't have come here.

There was a crack of thunder in the air, and the temperature lifted.

The hag screamed, her claws cutting into my flesh before she was torn
away. Her angered shrieks echoed around me, clawing at my ears.

"Hagitha." Setizar's voice was tinged with mild amusement. Did he
come to save me? "I thought I told you not to play with my things."

I looked up, his black-cloaked body standing between me and the creature.

"She wandered into my maze, Setizar." She smiled, a grotesque thing
like a swelling blister. "You said if anything steps into my maze, it is
mine."

"You didn't like that peasant I sent last time?"

"He tried to kill me."

"Ah..." The jinni looks at me, a scowl forming on his brow. "Pity. I put so much faith in him, too."

She hissed.

"Meris, this"—he inclined his head to the hag—"will cost you."

I nodded.

A slash of a white smile was all I saw before he turned back to her. "What will it take for me to bargain her off of you?"

The hag laughed, black-gummed grin spreading. "Come back tonight, Lord of the Crimson Plane. Or should I remind you of the consequences of breaking our deal."

"No need, *Grimhildr*." The jinni grabbed my arm, not acknowledging the scratches the hag left behind. "We will speak again soon."

We misted from the garden, reappearing in a room of white and gray.

I whipped my head around, scowling. "What do I owe you?"

"You imbecile!" He clenched his fists, throwing off his coat before falling into the nearby chair. "Do you have any idea what that was?" He scowled, as if finally registering what I had done. "You went into the maze."

I swallowed the lump in my throat.

His shoulders fell, and I finally understood where we were. My room. "How many seconds into the hour were we when you decided to disregard my warnings?"

I looked at him, crossing my arms. "I can do what I like."

"That is painfully obvious." The jinni dropped his gaze to the scratches on my arm before drifting back up to my busted lip. "Let me tell you a thing or two about Yamira, Meris." He stood. "One. You do not leave my palace without someone with you. Death will surely hunt you down if you step foot outside the gardens." He leaned down, lips nearly grazing my ear. Somehow, I was rooted where I stood. I couldn't move. "Two. Fear the Reaper. He may be a legend where you are from, but he lives. Which is why you never make a bargain with anything." His fingers wrapped around my injury. "When you make a bargain, your soul is bound by the deal. You were lucky it was me who came to your rescue in the woods and not one of the others... or the Reaper."

"I wouldn't say I was lucky."

He pressed his thumb against my wound, and pain slipped up my arm. A warning, I assumed. He clicked his tongue, lightening his touch. "Now, hold still."

I stifled a gasp as warm magic caressed the red marks left by the hag.

"A Grimhildr's claws infect." He looked at me. "If I were to allow this to sit, you would turn to stone before the hour is up. If anything other than a powerful, cunning jinni tends a wound like this, the process would be sped up. You would be stone in seconds."

My heart was already hammering too rapidly in my chest to be of any good. My breath was too ragged. What was this? "Do you often refer to yourself in such a manner?" I asked, trying to get my mind off the way his magic felt along my skin.

"I suppose it depends on who you ask," he said, withdrawing. The wounds quivered, then vanished. "Some would say I'm the most clever creature of them all, some would say I'm far from that."

"And who would say you're not?"

He flashed me a devilish grin before he ran his thumb gently over my lip. Heat spread over the cut, then the dull throbbing was gone. When I found his eyes, there was something in them. Cold...distant...uncertain. "You'll find out soon enough."

I looked at him, and the magic which stuck me to the ground vanished. "Well, now that you're done, you can leave me alone."

"No," he said. "Not if you intend to break the rules again."

I rolled my eyes.

"You think I'm joking?" He folded his arms behind his back. "I would assume you would be more grateful to me for saving you."

"I wouldn't need you to save me if you would just let me go."

He shook his head. "I just explained how the magic works. You cannot be released until you pay your debt."

"This is ridiculous! How do I even pay off these debts?"

"Stop doing dumb things, and stop making bargains."

"I wouldn't—"

"I know," he raised his hand. "You wouldn't 'need to make the bargains' if I just let you go." He raked a hand through his hair. "Believe me, if the situation were different, I would have saved you without a bargain."

"What's so different about this situation? Why did you do this to me?"

He looked at me, shaking his head. "Never mind." He faced the window. "I just need to keep an eye on you now." He waved his hand, and a silver bracelet appeared around my wrist.

"What's this?"

"A leash, love." He lifted a brow, grabbing his coat once more. "Consider that a warning." And with that, he was gone.

I looked at the cuff, gripping it to pull it off... but it clamped tighter. And I became just a little angrier.

— ☾ —

I sifted through my armoire, unable to forget the way his magic felt...

I kicked the door. What was wrong with me? I should've been able to stand up against this creature better than I was.

I bit my newly-healed lip, suppressing all the rage and desire inside. I breathed in, blinking. "Okay, we are going to have a talk, Meris," I said, pacing around the room. My fingers tingled with warmth and heat, spreading over my back. An itch festered between my shoulder blades, and I fought the urge to scratch it. "You're okay. He's handsome, and magical... it's new and different, and you're just reacting like a normal human." I looked at myself in the mirror, nodding. "Now, let's go over the facts. One!" I pivoted, stripping off my garments. "He kidnapped you and is holding you prisoner." I pulled out a similar outfit to the one I was wearing, with a red sheer collar and sleeves. "Two, he locks himself up here in a castle with creepy creatures roaming his lawn." I stopped, knowing full well that wasn't in the least bit normal, whether you were from another world or not. "Okay. That is worthy of both two and three." I adjusted the sleeves of my shirt. "Four! He…" I looked at my arm, examining the un-marred skin, remembering what he'd said to the hag in the garden. "Four, you are a *thing* to him." I clenched my teeth, facing myself again in the mirror. "And you, Meris… you are not a thing."

9

I walked through the halls and down to the drawing room where I should have been earlier. The door swung open and light flooded my vision.

"I thought you'd never arrive," the jinni drawled from the other side of the room.

"I contemplated not coming," I said, idly fingering the bracelet on my wrist. "But I'd hate to *inconvenience* you."

His eyes locked with mine. "You've already inconvenienced me quite a bit."

"What did you want me here for?"

"Well," he pointed to the shelf, "would you be a dear and pull that red book down for me, please? It will help me explain everything."

I wanted to spit at him. But, I knew if I wanted this nightmare to end, I'd have to work with him. I walked over to the shelf and reached for the book, placing it down on his desk.

"Eighteen years ago a dangerous creature was unleashed on this land." I fought my eye roll. He opened the book and blew on the pages. The words flew from the paper, spinning around the room and bleeding ink until my surroundings were enveloped in darkness.

A figure emerged, cloaked in mystery and shadows.

"We know her in Yamira as the Silver Queen. None of us can remember who she was or if she still walks among us, though we assume she left this world the day the last furies fell." The jinni stepped through the figure, reducing it to dust. "But, before she left, we were cursed. She stole much of this world's magic, locking it away in a box and sealing it with the blood of a furie. The only way to open it again is by someone with furie blood. This is why I need you."

I leveled him a glare, not understanding what this had to do with me.

"This world is filled with dangerous creatures." Setizar picked the book up and snapped his fingers. The world shunned the shadows, and sunshine once again filled the chamber. "The kind that would use your skin as parchment and your bones as toothpicks. Magic here may seem chaotic, but I assure you it has rules and boundaries." He turned the book around, showing me the words written. The symbols shifted, changing into something I could read. "I am of the jinn, meaning my kind, furies, sun lords, and fae are all in the same order."

I looked at the line. *Order of the Varent. Wielders of Ethereal magic.*

"What's this?" I asked, gesturing to the bottom. *The Unknown. Wielders of the untested magic.*

"That, is the magic none of us here in Yamira have tested. It's raw and unknown."

"Then what's the Changeling?"

The jinni sighs, angling his head. "The Changeling is one of the first magical creations, the creature who gave us our magic. It was torn apart by the Stars for being too powerful. The Stars then created the jinn, the gods, and the numina. When the creatures intermingled, their magic created the other races. There was chaos when creatures and humans began to harm each other, stealing magic and abusing it. So, the Stars did one last thing, one thing to balance it all. They removed the power to take magic from the creatures and created the furies, the only creature able to absorb magic and give it to others. The furies kept peace, until the Silver Queen struck."

"Do you think the Silver Queen is the Changeling?"

His grin spread, glimmering with pride. "We have our suspicions. But it's likely she's another furie."

I cleared my throat, glancing down at the pages again. "What's the difference between this," I point to the line below, *Court of Ouria, Wielders of Terrestrial Magic*, "and Ethereal?"

The jinni slipped a small glass orb in my hands. "The best way to describe the difference is this orb. The orb itself cannot be manipulated by me, since it is of terrestrial make. Only those within the Court of Ouria have a chance to change its shape, size, and material." He snapped his fingers, and stars illuminated within the glass. "But within? A void filled with the magic of the cosmos? That is my domain."

"How does it work?" I traced the words, not completely understanding.

"I can mist, as you know. But my range is limited. Void magic is more complicated to grasp... it is what I just showed you. It stems from an idea or desire."

I chewed my lip, reading on. It appeared that both furies and fae could do the same things, just to a different extent in some ways. Though, fae walked the line between both Ethereal and Terrestrial. Jinn, it seemed, were at the top of the food chain.

I looked up at him. "What happens when you use your magic? How does it work?"

Setizar flashed a smile, and I hated how my insides warmed at the sight. "Magic is... it's like muscle." He held out his hand, and I placed mine in his. There was a gentleness to his motions...the way he traced his fingers across the slope of muscle on my forearm. "The more you use it, the easier and less strenuous it becomes. Trust me, I've had days where my magic is sore, and it hurts to exert myself in any way to use it. This is the case with anyone who uses magic." He stood, warmth leaving as he retreated from our close contact, before slipping his hands into his coat pockets and looking out the autumn-kissed window.

"So, how do I fit into this entire thing?"

He grinned, crossing his arms across his chest. "You're a furie. This means you are the only one who can open the box and return the magic to this realm."

I almost laughed.

"Something funny?" The jinni scowled, leaning his head to the side.

"You're insane." I mirrored his movement. "I'm only human."

The jinni leaned in, his fingers lacing together. "That's what you truly think?"

The star-blanketed hallways seemed to flicker a few shades darker. Something like the chiming of bells, muted by a winter wind, cleaving through the air like a death song. I fought the shiver slithering along my body. "How do you know? I've never had any magic, and I never will."

"You think I don't know a furie when I see one?"

I shifted in my seat. "Do you think I don't know what I am?"

"You may believe that you're a human, but given enough time here in Yamira, you will once again come into your true form."

"Once again?" I laughed. "You don't know me."

His eyes flickered. "I think I know you better than you know yourself."

"And I think you're a lunatic. This whole thing is ridiculous! Release me from my debt since you're obviously out of your mind."

He barked a laugh, his shoulders slumping as he leaned into the chair. "Then I will add this. If you don't show any signs of powers by the next full moon, the summer solstice, then I will release you from your debts and allow you to go free. Until then, you must promise to try and at least be helpful."

I ground my teeth, words buzzing in my mind. "Deal."

— ☾ —

I followed the trail out into the garden, examining the flowers. Shadow-black roses twined themselves along the birch arches, accompanied by silver-ringed irises and orchids as colorful as sunset. The wind howled through the sky, casting an eerie feel over the garden.

Despite the array of birds singing and the sound of a bubbling brook nearby, the garden was eerily silent. The wind crying through the orange skies made me uneasy. I couldn't place it. I should be at ease here in the open atmosphere, but I only felt caution and dread.

Perhaps it was the conversation I had with the Jinni in the study earlier. *No wonder he's a hermit.*

"Meris."

I turned to see the Jinni standing in the arch of the doorway, his hands in his pockets. A few birds quieted at his voice, and I found myself wondering if he's the source of my discomfort. "Yes?"

"Enjoying the garden?" He took a few steps toward me, his black shoes gliding across the vibrant grass. "Find anything that has piqued your fancy?"

I tried avoiding eye contact. He stood there, looming over me like a shadowy specter. "No."

"No?" He almost sounded offended. "Not even my white lilies?"

"Or the black roses."

He smiled, snapping his fingers. A single black rose appeared in his hands, his eyes limned with light. "So, you enjoyed the rose... interesting."

I tried to protest, but he'd caught me. I *did* enjoy the look of the rose.

"Flowers are said to be mirrors to the soul." The jinni spun the rose between his fingers. "The type, the color... everything. It says something about the person."

"What does a white lily mean?" I crossed my arms, lifting my head to look at him better.

He grinned. "Many things."

"What does a rose mean then since you're obviously skirting that subject..."

He released a laugh, and my heart stuttered at the sound. The sound that crawled across my mind and brushed against my skin like the soft fur of a feline. "Be more direct, my love."

"I am not your love." I took a long step backward.

An amused twinkle glinted in his sunset gaze. "A rose has many mean-
ings as well. It can be anything from innocence, to passion, to love." He
looked around the garden, though I hadn't missed how he'd looked at me
when he'd said *passion* and *love*. "Did you not see the other roses?"

I hesitated, but looked where he pointed. Dozens upon dozens of other
roses peppered the area. All colors, all types, all sizes. How had I missed
them?

"But, the black rose..." He dipped his head, pressing the rose to his
lips before taking in a breath. "The black rose means rebirth."

10

I followed the gentle slope of the hall toward the mezzanine. Other than the few rooms I'd explored, I hadn't opened many other doors. "So," I asked the empty hall, my voice mocking me as it ricocheted through the corridors. "Why am I here? What reason is there for me to be here?"

Nothing but the distant sound of chimes and wind answered me.

The sheer curtains moved gently as the breeze swept in through the wide, open windows, beckoning me to look out into the starlit twilight.

I didn't have time to wait for an answer to come to me. I needed to find it. The jinni was completely out of his mind thinking I was anything other than human. I just needed to wait two weeks. Two weeks and I would be on my way back home. But what would I do? How would I explain this to Mae? I groaned, slipping my hands into the pockets of my pants. I'd never worn pants before, and the feeling was still new.

I drifted into a room with walls taller than that in the ballroom. The glass ceiling allowed the shimmering light of the stars and moon to shine in on the vines twining themselves around the white onyx pillars. Willow trees rested in various places of the room with leaves that looked like illuminated emeralds.

Glowing flowers fluttered open, sending the aroma of jasmine and lavender fluttering around me, caressing my nose with the scent of forgotten memories as I walked farther in. Something about this room had me questioning my reality. Perhaps this entire situation was some strange dream.

I must've had the plague. The thought of Mae hunched over my dying body and doing her best to help me made my heart twist.

I stopped, spotting a circular pool in the middle of the solarium. The water was so blue I could almost lose myself in it. The bottom looked like the moon above me, pulsing with a gentle white light.

Beckoning. Enticing me into its waters.

I breathed in, and the floral scents only drew me closer to the pool. I dipped my fingers into the water. Something pure and crystalline pounded into my veins, washing assurance over my nerves. Curiosity consumed me and I stripped off my clothes.

Folding my shirt and pants, I dipped my feet into the pool first, then realizing it wouldn't be a shock, I jumped. The water rushed around me, shimmering and dancing on my skin. It caressed my body like folds of fabric, inviting and soft. Blue, gold, silver, and iridescent water glimmered, enveloping my pale arms. It eddied and swirled in a delicate dance with moonlight.

I leaned my head back and closed my eyes.

It was like swimming through a pool of starlight and childhood dreams.

My mind drifted to warm summer days spent near the river with sugared lemons and cold water and laughter. The memory of my sister's big brown eyes, limned with wonder and excitement, resurfaced. Her eyes sparkled like the water. Had I ever heard a voice like hers? It sounded like the chirp of a bird in the early morning as the sun began to rise; so pure and full of life, quivering with love and joy... of magic and secret promises.

We were so happy.

I pulled my head up. I gasped, trying to take in the cool air. Warm water trickled down my face.

I was... crying?

The tears fell. Prompted by the memory of what I used to have... the happiness long lost in the abyss of misery.

I swam to the ledge of the pool, grasping the lip in desperation. I couldn't stop the tears. I couldn't stop them. No matter how hard I tried, they continued to pour. I was already longing to see Mae again. I wished I could have done something else... wished I could have helped her.

Helped Julna.

A hand touched my shoulder, and I'd nearly let go of the ledge.

Cerie knelt by the side of the water, her sun-bright eyes glimmering. "This place is peaceful, isn't it?" she asked, sitting cross-legged at the lip of the pool. "When Setizar built it, he said it would heal sorrow and only bring good memories. Somehow, this room has the opposite effect. The more at peace, the more the happy memories flow, the worse you feel."

I nodded, unable to see her clearly through my tears. "Why is it still here, then?"

Cerie pulled her hair out of her face, tying it into a bun. "Because no matter how much it hurts, the good times and happy memories shouldn't ever be forgotten." She pursed her lips. "Sometimes coming here can help, to an extent."

I pulled myself out of the water. "I can't ever be happy..." I looked at the pool, the ice on my heart melting and turning volcanic. "It hurts too much to be happy."

Cerie placed something warm over my shoulders. "I know."

I tugged at the fabric. A towel. She'd given me a warm towel. Had she known I would be here?

"Remember, this is the one place in the whole castle which Setizar will never step foot. If you ever need to escape him, come in here. The pool is where the magic is strongest, so just walking around the circumference of the room this will be less...potent."

I nodded, tugging the fabric closer. "Why did he have to make this room to begin with? And why does he avoid it?"

Cerie tugged her legs close to her chest, propping her chin on the space between her knees. "He loved someone long ago. She and he... they were meant to be. You could tell. She told him that a pool of happiness was something she wouldn't mind having."

"I agree." I laughed through the tears. "If it wasn't so painful, I would have enjoyed it."

Cerie's laugh was somewhat soothing, dismembering my sorrow slowly. "That's exactly what he said when he finished it."

"What happened to her?"

Cerie's body stiffened. "The war happened to her. When the Silver Queen attacked—" She stopped, words seemingly frozen on her tongue.

I think I knew what happened next.

"Anyway." She sniffled, drawing the back of her palm up against her tiny nose and rubbing. "He obsessively built this after she had been gone, as a sort of memorial to her. When he finished, he said he would never step foot in here again without her. And that is what he has done for the past seventeen years."

I tucked my wet hair behind my ear. "I'm sorry that happened." I meant it. No matter who you were, losing someone you cared so deeply about is something no one should have to experience.

"We all are." Cerie looked at me, her eyes glowing. "We miss her..."

"You knew her?"

Cerie whispered, "She was my best friend."

A stab of pain lanced through my chest, as if her broken heart was mine to bear. "I—I'm sorry."

"Don't be." Cerie stood. "It wasn't your doing." She looked toward the moon-drenched window. "It wasn't anyone's doing."

I nodded, but heard the words unsaid in the magic-thick air.

It was the Silver Queen.

11

Fire burned around me.

The forest was engulfed in flames, as though readying to singe the heart of the world. The heat licked my skin, piercing my flesh with fangs of fire. Ash coated my throat, chalking my lungs with acrid heat.

A woman stood before me, her eyes the shade of burnt amber and smoldering nightmares. "My dear…"

My heart halted. Why did this woman look… familiar? Something about her—I couldn't place it. She filled me with fear, and yet comfort.

I wanted to speak, but I couldn't. I never could speak in my dreams. I couldn't respond. I couldn't ask her who she was or if I knew her.

Why couldn't I feel my heartbeat? It was as if I'd died. The heat around me was the only warmth I felt.

Smoke covered the forest floor, twining black tendrils around my body. "Don't you know?" The woman moved her thin arms in front of her, clasping something in her hands. "My dear, don't you remember?" She held it out to me.

My beating heart rested in her palm.

Thump.

Stop.

Thump.

Stop.

Pain pierced my chest—a knife drawn in and down my breastbone.

Thump.

Stop.

Thump.

Stop.

It spread to my back, radiating pain everywhere. I screamed—a pitiful, muted scream.

Thump.

Stop.

I gasped for air, trying to breathe. My vision was bleary. Dawn sunlight drenched my room in hues of pink and gold. My heart—

Thump.

Thump.

It pounded against my palm. My back tingled, my fingers buzzed. I pulled my body up, leaning on my elbows. The silk sheets slid below my legs as soft as rose petals, grazing my skin with velvety kisses. The floor rejected the light, as dark as midnight. Shadows lingered in the corners, holding onto the night. Smoke, like in my dream, tugged at my nostrils, as if it was real. This place... it was messing with me.

There was a gentle rap at the door. "Come in?"

Cerie popped her head in. "Hello, Meris!" She placed a small tray near my bed. "How're you feeling?"

"Much better." I looked at the tray, raising a brow. "What's this?"

"Porridge with fresh berries." Cerie offered me a grin, but I was nevertheless confused. This was one of my favorite breakfasts... I always asked for it every birthday—

Wait.

"What is today?" I jumped out of bed, looking out the window. "How many days have I been here?"

"You've been here three days now."

My pulse kicked up. "Mae—"

"I'm sure she's alright," Cerie crooned, shaking her head. "Why is it important to know what day it is?"

I inhaled, my heart racing faster than before. "My birthday is coming up. I've never not seen her on my birthday before."

My bed creaked. "How old will you be?"

"Eighteen."

She made a small noise—a gasp or a sob, I wasn't sure—and I turned to her. "Are you alright, Cerie?"

She looked up at me, a small smile playing at the corners of her mouth. Tears. There were tears in her eyes.

"Cerie?"

"Meris." She exhaled, her thin blue fingers pinching at her white dress. "I'm fine. I'm just a bit emotional today, honestly. After the whole incident with the elves and all." She paused. "That reminds me!"

She scampered to the armoire, throwing open the doors. "Setizar asked me to help you pick out a few outfits."

"What?" Ice and panic pinned me where I stood. "Why?"

Cerie's arms vanished within the many folds of multi-colored fabrics. "You're going somewhere with him, actually. He needs to introduce you to the other three lords. Aurel, Eira, and Lhysa. They are the rulers of Summer, Winter, and Spring."

I shook my head. "Why do I need to be introduced to *seasons*?"

She pulled out a blue dress-like garment, though instead of a skirt it was loose pants. "They're lords *of* seasons. And we need them if this plan to return the world to its former state is going to work. If you want, I can give you a quick overview of our magic system and how it works?"

"The jinni and I have been over the magic stuff." I crossed my arms, raising a brow. "Or should I keep a handbook with me?"

"You can't possibly remember everything he told you, can you?" Cerie scowled. Why was she doing this? Something strange—a dark shadow of emotion—flitted over her face.

"Of course I can."

"Good." She smiled, returning to her former demeanor. "I'll pack your bags. You leave in one hour."

"Wait—" I hurried to her. "An hour?"

"Yes. Since you said you already know the magic system, I don't think there is much need for delay." Cerie dipped her head, her hair sparkling in the dull morning light. "Enjoy your food, I'll finish packing."

— ☾ —

I didn't know what to think of myself. The dress-pants outfit, whatever I should call it, revealed more than I'd ever been comfortable revealing before. It dipped into a sharp V just below my collarbone, allowing the sunlight to dance over my exposed skin. Despite being uncomfortable, somehow the garment felt right. The deep blue fabric shimmered slightly, catching my eye every time I walked past the mirror. Thankfully, Cerie had left my hair alone, aside from the few glowing orange pearls which pinned it out of my face.

There was a gentle knock on my door.

"Come in," I said, knowing full well who it would be. I wanted answers before we left.

The jinni walked in, his dark hair combed back. Every cut and curve of his face was on full display as he strolled into the room. His hands were in his pockets, that billowing coat of his resting on his shoulders. "You look beautiful, Meris."

I dipped my head, not wanting to say anything just yet.

"Do...do you not like it?"

"Why would I not like it?" I snapped.

"Well—"

"I do like it." I kneaded my temples. "I like the whole thing."

A small smile pulled at his lips. "Then what's the matter?"

I leveled a glare at him. "I just want to know where you're taking your thing?"

He scowled, as though not making the connection to my ire with his earlier comment to the hag. "What?"

I returned his look with one of my own.

"Meris..." He drew his hand down his face. "Never mind. Come along, I have our carriage waiting."

"Carriage?"

He nodded.

"Can't you—mist?"

"I like to arrive in style. And honestly, I can only mist so far." His eyes softened, and the piercing magenta sunset dimmed. "We will be riding for a few days, reaching the border between the four seasons. They have responded, the lords we are meeting with. We will be meeting in the town of Nightmore."

He held out his hand, and this time I took it. Mist and stardust encircled my body, spiriting us outside where a carriage sat ready.

I followed Setizar, relaxing as the warmth of day wrapped around me. Was it truly autumn here?

"The weather likes to change. It's mostly crisp, shudderingly so," he said as if he could read my mind. "It doesn't change much here."

"Is it ever summer?"

"Only in Aurel's plane." The jinni tilted his head, revealing the tight, sharp edges of his face. "I do have one question, Meris." He aided me in stepping up into the coach. "What do you see yourself as?"

"What?"

"We are about to go somewhere very special. What do you see yourself as, Meris?"

"A...woman?"

He chuckled, his shoulders rolling forward slightly. "Alright, well, put that aside. What do you want to be?"

"Strong…" I said before it even truly registered in my mind.

That whimsical smile returned. "Strong? How so?"

"I want to be able to…to help myself, for once."

His eyes flickered into the shade of the autumn leaves around us. "Well then, you are a warrior. I shall address you as Lady Meris, and you?" He tilted his head back, revealing his merciless jawline. "You shall address me as Lord of the Crimson Plane."

I lifted a brow, grinning. "I think I'll stick with calling you a jinni."

He broke into a laugh. "It was worth a shot."

12

We stopped at an inn after hours of riding. At least the carriage wasn't unbearable.

I shoved my feet back into my slippers as a pinched breath escaped my lips. The jinni would probably be upset if I didn't hurry in. Not that I would've minded watching him get a bit ruffled. That, honestly, would be far more amusing than anything else. I laughed, clutching my bag in my hand. It was heavy—heavier than I'd thought it would be.

I shuffled out of the carriage, spotting the impatient jinni leaning against the door of the inn, one ankle hooked over the other. His long purple and black coat seemed to gobble the light of the orange lantern. The place looked more like a manor than an inn, sprawling, red brick wings and large white windows emitting a soft, orange glow. Was everything this pretty here? Autumn leaves speckled the still-green grass, following a pathway of flagstones that weaved below the canopy of red maples and orange-leafed willows. Cinnamon and cloves drifted into my nose, filling my insides with memories of cider and cozy blankets.

Memories I *knew* I didn't possess, but felt the tangible assuredness of them, nevertheless.

"You ready?" the jinni asked, holding out his hand. "I can take your bag."

I tugged it closer, smiling. "No. I'll carry it. I'm fine carrying my bags."

The jinni slid his hands into his pockets, grinning. "Very well." He tilted his head to the side, his eyes roving over me for the briefest of seconds. "We have two rooms adjacent to each other."

I groaned. I wanted to be on the other side of the building. "Fine. What level?"

"It's a bit of a jaunt." He flashed me a smile before slipping a note into my hand. "Would you like help?"

"No."

"I will let you have at it then." His smile was villainous, bordering the look between sadistic and wicked. "Top floor. Up *five* flights of stairs. You ready?" And with that, he vanished into thin air.

Great. Now I knew what that look was for. It wasn't invasive, it was calculating, as if he were guessing how long I could climb without toppling.

Shades of redwood and maroon bombarded my vision, accompanied by the honey-hued lights of the chiming chandeliers. I followed the carpets down the hall. My arm already ached. I placed the bag down for a second, peeking at the note he'd given me. There were so many strange symbols; things I couldn't understand.

How did he expect me to follow this note?

I hissed a breath, snatching my bag again and plodded toward the first stairwell. The stairs seemed to last forever. I stepped up, thinking it would be the last, only to find there were more.

And it was only the first staircase.

I finally reached the top, my legs already aching. I wasn't used to hauling heavy items up stairs. Groaning, I began the trek up the second flight, my joints burning and repulsing the exertion.

Step.

Step.

Step.

My legs hurt.

Step.

Step.

Placing my bag next to me, I leaned against the wall. How would I make it up to the top level? I needed to work on my strength. I was weak...

A hollow sound formed in the air around me, and cool mist licked my arms.

"My offer still stands." The jinni leaned against the railing.

Tempting. I could just give my problem to him and be done with it. But that would be too easy, and I already needed to work on getting stronger. "No. I can do this."

"I know you can," he said, still leaning against the railing. His right foot hooked over his left, black hair embracing the golden light of the stairwell. "But I am asking if you *want* to."

I pushed myself up, snatching the bag. "I want to do this. How will I survive if I don't try to do things that make me feel uncomfortable?"

"Be careful." The jinni lowered his gaze, taking a step toward me. "Yamira is no place to try new things. You could be hurt...or worse."

"Why are you so concerned over my wellbeing?" I asked, trying to make sense of him.

His eyes flickered, and something akin to sorrow and pain surfaced, but the look was fleeting, replaced by a devil's grin. "Because if you die, I will have trouble completing this plan of ours."

I rolled my eyes, stepping up the third flight. "You mean this plan of yours."

The jinni trailed behind me.

"So," I looked at him. "I found the pool room the other day..."

His eyes burned into me. "What possessed you to go into that room?"

"It's beautiful," I said. "I couldn't leave it be, even though it was painful."

He stood beside me, eyes focused ahead. "Alecto, my—" He paused, shaking his head. "She wanted that room." Something painful stabbed through his voice, cutting into me as he spoke. "She would have been furious if I didn't finish it."

"What exactly...what happened to her?" Cerie didn't say, but I had a hunch.

"The Silver Queen stabbed her in the heart. There wasn't anything to be done." His back went rigid. "I know this world is confusing to you, Meris," he exhaled, stopping at the top of the third flight, "and nothing really makes any sense. Give it time, it'll all come to you."

I nodded. "So..." Chalk coated my throat. "Tell me more about the furies. What are they, exactly? Since you claim I'm one."

His eyes found mine, amethyst and glowing with pain. "The furies are a race of immortal creatures. When they are killed, they simply are born again."

"Then," my stomach hardened, dropping like an anchor to the bottom of the sea, "why aren't there any around anymore?"

"They were spirited away by the Emberfang, a creature of the rift. The Emberfang stole them away, sealing a gateway with furie blood. We don't know where it is."

"So, if we find the gateway, we find more furies?"

"You'd have to find it, Meris."

"But I'm not a furie. I'm just a helpless human from Inder."

A smile appeared on his face. "Then, since you're so helpless, will you allow me to help you carry that bag to your room?"

I laughed, shaking my head. "I'm not going to let you have your way."

"At least I tried." He slipped his hands into his pockets again, keeping silent all the way to the top of the last flight of stairs.

— ☾ —

I sat on the edge of my bed and stared out the window toward a lake below. The water danced with the moonlight, a beautiful melody of darkness and wonder. Stars twinkled overhead, winking angelically through the bands of shadow sky. In the distance the song of an enchanted traveler lifted into the air. The woeful tune of the violin tore into my heart, reminding me how far I was from home, and how alone I was.

I supposed that was something the jinni and I had in common: we were both alone. And we had both lost someone we loved.

13

I hadn't slept much, afraid the horrors of the past few nights would come back and haunt me once more. I supposed it did either way, since I'd laid awake and thought about it. I sat up, still not used to the comfort of the beds in this realm. My silk nightdress felt so good, unlike those scratchy cotton dresses I wore to bed before I'd arrived in Yamira.

That was one thing I would miss when I left.

I yawned, peering out the window toward the honey-hued world outside. Small insects flew in the beams of gold light scattered between the crimson oak leaves, dancing to the melody of birds. Pallid pink and lilac hues graced the sky above the autumn forest, welcoming the new day with a budding countenance.

An eddy of wind curled through the underbrush, lifting fistfuls of leaves into the air before sending them skittering onto the ground. Some pushed against the window, making the sound of crinkling paper tossed into a snapping wood fire. It was a hollow sound, crunching and dead, but still it created a peacefulness within me that I couldn't place.

I closed my eyes, listening to the sweet trilling and warbling songs of birds as they danced in the morning dew, calling out into the world without a care.

A crack resounded from behind me.

"So—"

I turned, throwing a pillow at my intruder.

The jinni dodged the projectile, raising a brow. "You're supposed to be dressed and ready."

"Get out!"

"I expected you to be ready."

"I expect you to knock. Now *out*!"

He raised his hands in a gesture of surrender. "Fine. Be ready in a half hour. We need to eat still, and I don't want to be late; that's Eira's thing. She would be mad if we're later than her."

"Who—" I stopped. She's one of the rulers? I should've taken notes. "Never mind."

Setizar flashed a shameless smile. "Breakfast is being served in the hall." He fiddled with a loose string the bedpost's tassels. "If you dress and prepare in fifteen minutes, I'll be your servant and escort you to the breakfast room."

I wanted to retort, but remembered I'd agreed to try and be helpful. Leaving on time today was something we both wanted to do. "Alright. I'll be ready in a minute."

The jinni's smile was the last thing I saw before he vanished in a cloud of shimmering mist.

— ☾ —

My hair was still wet when he returned. I had my bag packed, my bed made, and myself dressed and ready for the day.

The jinni paused, looking at me for a moment.

"Something wrong?" I lifted my head, shifting my weight.

"You need your hair to be dry. It's rather cold this morning."

"I can only do so much with a towel," I said. "I'm not magic."

"But I am." He smiled lightly. "Here." He vanished and reappeared behind me. I jumped, and he took a step back. "Meris?" He tilted his head, confusion washing over his features.

"I...I don't like anyone approaching me unexpectedly from behind like that." I fought a shiver, my heart pumping wildly.

His features darkened. "I will remember that, then." He held out his hand, looking into my eyes. "Do I have permission to use magic on your hair?"

"I don't care," I said, fighting the tightness in my chest. It was hard to breathe.

His hands weaved through my hair, gentle—unobtrusive. The starlit pool surfaced in my memory. The smell of autumn mountains and books. Sunshine through orange leaves, and a dance between two lovers.

"There." The jinni released my hair. "All dry."

I sucked in a breath, steadying my shaking nerves. "Thank you."

"Shall we go down to breakfast together, or will you be taking the stairs again today?" Setizar asked, one brow arched.

Despite myself, I laughed. "I think I've had enough stairs for one week."

"Very well," he said, the corners of his lips curving upward. "My lady, if you would do me the honor?"

I placed my hand into his outstretched one, and we misted from the room. The aroma of freshly baked bread, simmering berries, and cinnamon filled the air. There was no doubt that we'd entered the dining hall.

"I think I know what you should try," Setizar mumbled as he pulled out a chair for me. "There are these fluffy rolls dipped in cinnamon and sugar."

"A...a cinnamon roll?" I raised my brow.

"Yes." He grinned, focusing his attention on my fingers as I tugged the corners of the napkin. It was a pensive look, something that seems so unlike him. "Alecto—" He stopped. A twinge of *something* shot through my veins. "She loved them, and I haven't had one in years." His eyes shuddered to the hue of wine and night mist.

"Are you sure we should have one?" I didn't know why, but I felt guilty. "I don't want it to—"

"Of course." He smiled, a forced thing limned with grief. "She always said to never deprive any creature of a cinnamon roll, and if I ever did, she would have my head."

I couldn't tell if he was being serious or not. Not until he broke into a contagious grin, his usually lighthearted and devilish demeanor returning. Somehow, the annoying jinni I knew was much more familiar than the sorrow stricken one who sat in front of me seconds ago. "She sounds like she was an amazing creature."

He looked at me, and a mixture of chilling aloofness and cradling warmth settled in his face. I couldn't make sense of him. "She is."

A waiter approached the table, a tray in one hand bearing two cups of steaming water. "Courtesy of the Owner." He placed the cups down. "Tea?"

"My usual," the jinni said. "And for you, Meris?"

I blinked. "I don't know."

"She will have the green tea, then."

The waiter snapped his fingers, and two teabags appeared in the cups. "Anything else?"

"Of course." Setizar leaned his head back, his copper skin and dark appearance complemented by the surrounding area. Was it his goal in life to be aesthetic with everything? "Two cinnamon rolls and two bowls of porridge."

"Any toppings on the porridge?" The man looked at me, his eyes sinking into slits.

"Berries?" I asked. "Fresh berries?"

The man nodded and released a somewhat disheveled grunt before exiting the room.

"Now that we have breakfast settled, I suppose I should fill you in as to what will be happening." Setizar leaned his elbows on the table, raising his brow. "We will be meeting with two very powerful beings, and one annoying one."

"You and two others?" I chirped.

He broke into a wide smile. "You think yourself a jester, do you?"

"I'm learning from one."

"I'd think you'd laugh more if I was any good," he whispered.

"You're more irritating than funny."

"I see you still need to learn more about comedic timing." He cleared his throat, returning to the topic at hand. "These creatures keep the balance between seasons, so I need you to be on your best behavior while I discuss the plan with them. They need to trust us, to believe that we won't turn on them and steal the magic for ourselves—"

"You mean yourself. Remember, I don't have magic."

He groaned, rolling his neck. "Without their help, completing our mission will be very difficult."

"You haven't really explained the mission."

"You will learn all about it during the meeting. That is why you must remain on your best behavior."

Before he could say another word, the waiter returned with our food. He placed both bowls down, accompanying them with a plate with two brown buns with a white glaze over the top. "Enjoy."

I felt the jinni's eyes on me, his words echoing in my mind. The mission, the whole reason I was here was because he thought I was a furie, and that I could help him get his magic back. It reminded me he wasn't human—he was a creature, my *captor*. I felt at ease around him, but the warning echoed in my mind to not trust anyone.

I should know better than to start trusting someone.

"Go on," he said, pushing the plate a little toward me. "Try it."

I pulled the plate closer by my fork, the glass screeching as the metal glided across it. "These aren't going to kill me?" I asked as I stabbed the bun and twisted off a piece.

"Not in the least. I'm the last being to want you dead, Meris. You need to at least give me that much trust."

I chewed the inside of my cheek, trying to pick apart his words and sense any lie woven between them. Assuring myself I would be fine, I took a bite. His eyes watched me eagerly as I put it into my mouth.

The sugar… the cinnamon. Oh, *heaven*!

"This!" A smile I couldn't contain lifted my lips. "I love this," I said through mouthfuls of the bun. "You know," I mumbled, pulling the plate closer so the whole thing was in front of me, "it's unfortunate he didn't separate the things, since I'm going to eat them both."

Setizar laughed, leaning back and watching me. "So, you like it?"

I nodded, closing my eyes. "I've never tasted anything better."

His voice was tinged with bitterness and sorrow, though joy coursed through his tone as he said, "That makes me happy."

14

The entrance to the city was an arrangement of vibrant colors. Despite being midday, the sky was the deep indigo of a moonless night speckled with stars. The buildings were ornate, with reaching banisters carved like whitewashed bones out into the checkered streets. Purple scarves billowed behind women dressed in tight fitting corsets, knee-high petticoats, and silver-plated boots. Men wore top hats of varying sizes and shapes.

I stepped out of the carriage. "Where are we?" I asked as the fresh autumn breeze drifted through the orange forest surrounding us.

"The heart of Yamira, a place which exists outside our rules. It was governed long ago by Megaera, but she hasn't shown herself here since long before the Silver Queen." The jinni pointed his chin to the wrought-iron gate, carved like dead vines and encased in shadows. "Stay in the light. Wherever the shadows linger without the flicker of flame to banish, don't trod. Remember," he touched my shoulder, "you're a warrior. Not a woman. Not a human. Not anything but a warrior."

Though I was confused, I nodded.

He said a few things to the carriage driver, directing him to where we'd be staying, and turned back to me. "Come along."

I followed him without a second thought.

Creatures half my size with delicate butterfly wings fluttered just above us, while round orbs of white light floated in the dark alleys.

A faun stood to our left, waving his hands in the air and shouting, "A ride through the skies! Wish to fly? Now's your chance!"

I stole a glance at the price: *One important memory.*

"Does something interest you?" the jinni asked, standing beside me. "Ah, the flying carriage. It's a fun thing to do if you don't mind parting with some important memories."

I nodded, chewing my lip. The craft—a sleek black carriage-like thing with whorls of gold painted on the doors—was roofless, with a cozy red-velvet seat big enough for two people to ride. "How do you fly it?"

The jinni grinned. "It flies itself. Guided by magic, of course."

I fought a smile. Thoughts of the open air surrounding me and the crisp feel of the wind weaving cool fingers through my hair bombarded my mind. "It would be fun to do, you know?"

"Take a ride?"

"Yes. Sort of." I looked at him, carefully assessing if he's up to mischief. "It would be fun. I wish I could fly—to see the world from the sky."

He stared at me for a long moment, his eyes revealing nothing. "Perhaps one day you will."

I managed a smile. It was odd when he suddenly became soft and sentimental, looking at me as if he'd known me since the dawn of time. However, I got the feeling he was telling me not to make this deal. Not to trade an important memory.

"Well!" He clapped his hands. "I must be off to be sure the meeting is still on. I will send for you once everything is settled and I'm certain our arrival will be perfect. The town is a very safe place, so you are free to wander wherever you please. Just don't trade your soul, or heart, or anything remotely valuable. Avoid the fortune tellers, they're all con artists." He released a sigh, glancing back at the magical sky carriage ride. "If you want anything, speak with me before making a bargain. It's a dangerous thing to do here."

"Alright."

The jinni smiled, obviously pleased with himself, then proceeded to

tap the cuff on my wrist. "I'll find you in about an hour." He vanished before I could reply.

Alone, I turned and trudged off into town. The faces which turned to
look at me were a variety of shapes, colors, and, in some cases, faceless.

A creature blocked my path, nothing but a monocle and mustache visible on his face. The town glittered to life behind the monocle, assuring me
he was indeed completely transparent. His top hat was as tall as the walking stick he had in his white gloved hand, which he took off and bowed.
"Care to enter the library?" he asked in a lilting, cut-glass accent.

"N-no—"

"Ah! Who's this?" A man appeared from around the corner. His body
below the sharp suit looked to be made of branches, twigs, and knotted
vines. His head was a pumpkin, with two sideways triangles for eyes and
jagged points for a mouth. That wasn't even the strangest thing. His
pumpkin head was on fire. He swept into a bow, his gash of a smile widen-
ing. "Care to tell us your name?" he asked in a bemused tone.

"I'm...I've gone mad."

"Oh?" he said, his voice carrying through the clove-scented air like a
giggle. "I like mad people. All the best people are mad."

"You—" I shuffled back.

The pumpkin man stopped in his prancing, angling his head and taking
me in. Recognition fluttered over his face, and he asked, "What are you?"

"Jack," said the invisible man. "You don't just ask someone what
species they are."

"I didn't ask her *species*, Libby." Jack grabbed a fistful of fire from his
head, twining it between his spindly fingers. "She's in Nightmore now. I
was asking what she sees herself as, obviously."

"For all things—" Libby drew a hand over his non-existent face.
"You're such a pain."

Jack snickered. "I do try."

I had to brace myself on the fence behind me.

Jack threw me a pensive glance. "Don't let him fool you, he loves me."

The invisible man clicked his tongue. "Love covers a multitude of sins, but it does nothing to aid you in gaining some brains."

Jack's smile vanished, and I half expected Libby to apologize. An eerie silence settled over the world, washing my nerves in tight waves of anticipation. Perhaps they'd have it out right there. Perhaps they'll demand the other apologize for their actions and words...

"I can show you around town, if you like," Jack said, ripping me away from my own mental wandering. "I'm an excellent guide!"

"If you accept his offer, beware!" Libby gestured to Jack. "He's hotheaded and is apt to cause nothing but trouble."

I swallowed and nodded. "Thank you, but I think I can find my own way."

They bowed, though Jack looked less than happy to say his farewells before they vanished within the crowd of creatures. I didn't waste a single second before setting off again.

"Potions! Elixirs! Companions! Sold for the small price of a memory!"

"A slip of conscience is all that's needed to buy my wares, don't listen to that fellow!"

"Mine are far better!"

"No, no, you just charge more!"

The voices slashed at my ears like claws. A building off to the side, with 'fortune teller' stenciled on the outside in gold letters caught my attention. I slipped inside.

Pink smoke swirled through the room, sweeping up a maelstrom of glitter in its heady body. It smelled like berries and tonka beans, resting a heavy scent of caramel in my nose. Small ornaments of origami dangled from the ceiling, caressed by the vapor.

A male with a bulbous face and body turned to me. His skin more blue than a summer sky, clothed by layers upon layers of pink, gold, and emerald garments. "Welcome to the *Calla Tapir*, the one stop emporium of curiosities and remedies. What can I help you with today?" He put a strange pipe to his lips and inhaled before expelling glittering pink smoke.

"I just came in here to escape the crowd."

The creature smiled, gesturing to a purple armchair. "Most do. Come and rest yourself. The town can be quite agonizing." He took another drag, and his eyes drank me in, hooded and lazy. "For a secret, I can tell you your future."

"Why a secret?"

"Secrets are far better currency, my lady. Men have bargained their souls to keep them hidden."

I inhaled, coughing the candy-sweet smoke clawing into my throat. "What kind of secret?"

"One that you would rather no one knows."

My face burned red. What sort of secret would I rather people not know? What one thing would I like to keep hidden? Chester's name surfaced, and I turned my head. I couldn't tell him that. I couldn't release something so dark. The memory—the secret I've hidden from everyone.

He took another long drag, expelling the smoke into impatient rings. Waiting. Waiting for me to reveal this thing inside.

Tears stung my eyes. "How does the secret exchange work?"

"You place your hand here," he gestured to a gold mirror —"and think of the secret. The exchange is painless and immediate. No returns."

"Do I also get to keep it? Or does it…disappear?"

"Of course. It's a secret, dear one, not a memory."

I stepped forward, glancing at the mirror. A jolt of guilt spiked through me. I knew what I could exchange.

I placed my hand against the cold glass, closing my eyes. I remembered heading up the stairs and seeing the creature called Tatum. His glowing red eyes, his shadowy form, and the words he'd spoken.

A second later, I stepped away. The blue man smiled wide, yellowing teeth gleaming. "That's a beautiful secret." He scratched his swollen chin, the fat jiggling and shimmering. "Here is your future: You will find your purpose. Denial of becoming anything other than what you are will be your constant, but you will embrace it soon enough."

I groaned. Right, I was conned… This was what Setizar had warned me about. "Thanks," I breathed out, underwhelmed. "I'm going to go now. Thanks for letting me crash here for a bit."

He bowed his head, though he looked a little more alert, a little more awake than before. "Pleasure was mine."

— (—

I kicked a bone-white rock on my way down the street. I couldn't seem to make heads or tails of this place. I wanted to go home and lay in bed.

Home.

I didn't have a home here. I just had a room. I fought the urge to scream curses into the sky.

My stomach growled, pushing against the walls of my abdomen. I wondered if there was anything here I could buy…

"Meris."

I spun, seeing the jinni standing there behind me. "What?"

"We are going to have lunch. Aurel and Lhysa have already arrived."

I shrugged, but since I was hungry, I could put up with him for a bit. "What are we eating?"

"Anything you like."

"I could use a sandwich and some tea."

"I'm certain that's available." He smiled, extending his arm for me to take. "I only ask one thing: please, be careful when speaking during this meeting."

After the day I'd had, this weird jinni was the least of my worries. I looped my arm around his. Would he figure out I disobeyed and gave a secret away for a fortune? He did say that fortunes in this realm weren't good. Schooling my features to look as passive as I could, I resumed our conversation, sifting up some irritability. "You said that already. Why do I have to watch my words so closely?"

"Aurel is a touchy, dramatic creature. If you antagonize him, he will begin to reciprocate. Anything can be seen as antagonizing, so be careful."

I nodded.

We walked through the streets, heading toward a small eatery off the corner by the library.

The doors swung open, and a ruckus greeted us. Loud clattering of plates, scraping of silverware, and heated words rang through the air.

"Lucky for us," the jinni whispered in my ear, directing me to the side, "we have a room reserved. We don't need to hear this. Well, not as much."

My stomach hardened. But once we entered the room, my gaze shifted to the two other occupants. A woman with skin as dark as mahogany and eyes the hue of a starless night stayed seated, while the man with long, golden hair rose. He was gorgeous, the living personification of the carved gods in the gardens of the Gathbreds. Eyes of purest silver sliced in my direction as his smile split his golden beard.

"Setizar." The man bowed mockingly, his muscles tightening in an impressive display. "Who is your companion?"

"Her name is *Meris*," the jinni said flatly, drawing out my name to a sharp point.

"And what is she?"

"Wouldn't you like to know." His eyes sparkled. "Now, shall we get started?"

Tension bracketed the man's mouth as he made a gesture to the seats beside him.

"Good to see you, Lhysa." The jinni dipped his head. "How are things in Spring?"

The woman lifted her chin, dark eyes sliding from Setizar to Aurel. "Sunny and cool, unlike in Summer where everyone is roasting like a prize chicken at a feast."

The jinni chuckled and looked at the golden-haired man, shadows wreathing those pink-orange eyes. "Aurel, are you not going to defend yourself?"

"No," he said, crossing his arms, shrugging off the insult like an un-wanted coat. "I prefer to wait for Eira to arrive before I say anything else. Wouldn't want my beautiful comebacks to go unappreciated."

"Speaking of Eira," the jinni looked around. "There's been too much snow piling into the Crimson Plane. The maze is absolutely arctic. I need to ask her to tone it down."

"Why don't you just call your sector Autumn like everyone else?" Aurel groaned. "And maybe you'll get your blasted leaves to skid back up to the north. I hate how my people have to keep raking up that mess."

"Speaking of things that annoy," Lhysa snapped, her lips pressed into a flat line as she glared at Aurel. "It's getting so warm that the flowers have begun to wilt and in some cases burn. You need to go and check those summer runes you have at your borders."

"Do you know how much work that is?"

"I do," she said. "If you don't check them then I will have to send you a *bill* to create more runes."

Aurel growled.

"How much would it cost to make one? Seven important memories will do. I'm sure you have dozens upon dozens to shed in all your four-hundred years of existence."

"I have possibly four, and no more. Either you'd have to find a differ-ent form of payment, or someone else will need to give up their memories to make your precious runes." Aurel shed his casual demeanor and re-leased one last feral smile. "It would be a shame, a real shame."

Before Lhysa could snap back, the door opened and the room dropped to a frozen temperature, as if winter itself had begun to stroke my bones.

"Ah!" Aurel stood. "Eira. It looks like you're fashionably late, as usu-al."

The woman wore a dress as green as the forest floor, crafted from what seemed like withered vines. Her slanted eyes found mine, one as dark as midnight and one as icy as a winter frost. "I haven't missed you, Aurel."

She settled into a seat with the grace and manner of a queen. "Lhysa."

"Eira," said the dark-skinned woman, her brow quirking up. There seemed to be a strange rift between these two. One exuded warmth and comfort, while the other was hewn from the frost and bitter ice of unforgiving winter.

"Setizar." Eira tilted her head, ignoring the pointed stare from Lhysa.

"Eira."

My gaze bounced between the four beings in the room, unsure and worried of what might happen. The clanking of forks on the glass, the sound of plates clinking, and the smacking of food created a chaotic melody that I wanted to escape.

Aurel's voice cut through the noise. "You don't look yourself, Alecto. Is everything alright?"

I blinked, a hum buzzing in my ears. What did he just say?

Aurel dabbed his mouth, as if he hadn't said something jarring.

"Aurel!" Eira hissed. "Why did you say that?"

"Don't you think she bears an uncanny *resemblance* to Setizar's long lost love?"

I went to stand, my temper rising. It was enough of a bother to have to sit there, like a formal prisoner and listen to their bickering, let alone be pulled into one of their blasted conversations.

However, before I rose, a hand touched my arm, giving me pause. "You're here, Aurel," the jinni drawled. "You can't think she will be alright when your presence is absolutely suffocating."

Aurel flashed teeth at him. "I didn't think the fossil could speak so of a *human*."

"I'm pretty sure you would confuse a fossil with art on any good day."

"Only between you and a pile of feces do I have a problem distinguishing."

"Perhaps you should study art." The jinni picked at his nails. "You're obviously missing the masterpiece in front of you."

Aurel dipped his head, loading his next barrage of attacks in his figurative bow. "I think you're abstract art painted by a monkey."

Eira groaned. "Here we go again."

"What?" I asked, completely lost between their argument and Aurel calling me Alecto...

Eira stabbed her fork into her food. "It's like watching two toddlers bicker over a new toy."

"Well," Lhysa rolls her shoulders, "if you would contain your never-ending winter to your plane, we wouldn't need this meeting."

Eira's nails dug into her palms. Shadows writhed between the corners and cracks of the walls. The echoes of the past and future mingled together in the room.

Lhysa fidgeted with her headband, moving the flat gold disks between her fingers. Every movement seemed to be searching—as if she was digging for comfort or a remark within the plates of metal along her forehead.

"Lhysa," Eira crooned as a predatory smile worked its way onto her face, holding the promise of malice within its pearly cage. Clearly this wasn't a tone she donned daily. Her ice-blue eye caught the lamplight of the room, and she smiled, looking more like a winter lioness than a woman. "You don't enjoy the cold I shovel your way?"

Lhysa's mouth flattened into a disapproving line. The shadows of night roiled, but none touched her, repelled by the glowing aura of light from her figure. She sat like a goddess of old, her gaze filled with silent and fresh-awakened fury toward the Lady of Winter. "Neither the snow nor heat that has invaded my lands has been pleasant—or beneficial. I suggest you take the necessary precautions when dealing with the weather."

"I don't think I need to do anything with the weather, Lhysa. You need to accept that winter is the more dominant season in Yamira."

"I do believe summer has Winter beat, Eira." Aurel grinned, tossing his long hair off to the side.

"Oh for the love of—" The jinni raised his hands. "Can't we get along?"

"Says the lord of the weakest season."

The jinni lowered his gaze, finding Aurel's. "But it is by far the most wonderful season. I dare say, everyone travels to the Crimson Plane. It's romantic."

"Like you would know. You're still hanging on to Alecto's memory."

A sound like the crack of a whip snapped around us. The room filled with mist and shadows. A darkness draped over the jinni's face, and his usually casual demeanor shifted. For the first time since I'd arrived, he was angry. "She's worth hanging onto." His voice was a little less graceful than a hound's bark, underlaid with tones of flickering, kindling rage.

"It's your fault she died, stuffed up jinni." Aurel's words seemed to spear through Setizar. The mist sunk back into him, replaced by a mournful gray light.

Silence washed over the room.

"You're right, Aurel." He looked up, eyes swirling from a sunset into gray and blue. "It should have been me."

Lhysa coughed, raising her voice. "Well, there must have been another reason we were gathered here, Setizar. Unless your plan was to have us bicker for hours, I think we should hear it."

I thanked the Aether for her. The room became less tense, and the mood shifted lightly. Lhysa was a pillar of life; light wanting to burst forth behind the darkness of her eyes.

Aurel was different. *Something* different.

But between them all, it is Eira who I was most cautious about. Frigid in presence and face. Her one eye seemed to shift between a deep blue and powder color, twining the shifting snow between the lines of her iris, eclipsed by her raven pupil. Every instinct in my body said to run. To get away from her.

But Setizar laid a hand on my arm, as if sensing my want to flee. "First things first, are we going to come to an agreement over the season borders?"

The three at the table looked at him, raising their brows.

Eira cleared her throat, sliding those eerie blue and black eyes my direction. "There is no coming to an agreement, Setizar. We simply cannot."

"I think we should!" Aurel shot to his feet. "I am tired of the leaves."

Lhysa nodded. "I'm tired of the hot weather."

The jinni's smile returned. "And I am tired of the snow. So, Eira, either you agree, or there will be a bit of a tussle on your hands."

Her eyes narrowed, and she clicked her tongue. Apparently she wasn't used to spending time around her equals—or perhaps just other people in general. "I'll speak to my sister."

"Do tell the North Wind I say hello," Aurel said.

"Her name"—Eira ground between clenched teeth—"is Feng. Remember that." The room dropped more than four degrees, sending frost crawling up my arms.

Aurel swatted the air, and the chill alleviated. "Well. If this matter is not fixed before the harvest moon, I intend to come beating on your front door with my entire army."

"If you can get past my sister without her ripping you to shreds, self-righteous sphinx." Eira inspects her nails.

"Indeed, Your *Highness*." Aurel dipped his head, rolling his lips between his teeth. "I'd love to catch up with the banshee."

A verbal fight ensued once more.

I shoveled the food into my mouth, unsettled by the current conversation.

"What if we don't come to an agreement?" Aurel drawled, looking at Setizar with unnerving calm.

"Then the seasons will just grow more and more intense and out of control." The jinni gestured to the room. "We are already so disoriented by the runes we must have made. I have an issue with Eira's Loogaroo pouncing onto the Crimson Plane without heeding boundaries."

"The water Wraiths are swimming down the rivers and disrupting the townspeople," Lhysa added.

"The western side of my territory is being overrun by springtime. The winter plants are dying." Eira shot Lhysa a glare. "Thanks to your season."

Setizar sighed. "We can only do so much with our magic."

"Especially since yours is so limited," Aurel remarked.

"Thank you for the *insulting* reminder," the jinni growled, hissing a breath between his teeth. "Either way, I think I have more important things to tell you." Setizar looked at me. "I'm certain you are wondering why Meris is here."

My heart stuttered a beat.

"Yes, you have a few things to explain," Eira snipped.

The jinni nodded, bracing the palms of his hands on the table. "She's a furie, though she personally doesn't believe it."

The room stilled.

"If her powers can manifest, we can use her to open the Box and return this realm to what it is supposed to be. I happen to believe the Box is in the human realm, as was told to us."

"You're basing this off here-say." Aurel coughed. "We aren't certain where the Silver Queen put the Box."

"Have we, in all these years of searching, found it here, Aurel?"

He crossed his arms. "Well, even if it *is* on Inder, how are we supposed to get it?"

The jinni's eyes slid to me. "That's another reason why we need her. She came from the other world. If she could find the Box, she can bring it back, and we will get the chance to set things right."

"What if she decides to stay on Inder and not return?" Eira scoffed, lifting her brow. A question that was possibly on everyone's minds. "She doesn't seem happy to be here."

"Incentive." The jinni smiled, though a muscle pulsed in his jaw. What was he *truly* thinking? "If she finds the Box, returns it and helps us, then I will give her the things she wishes most." His eyes slid to me. "Sound reasonable?"

My nails bit into my palms as I clenched my fists. This is what I searched for—something life-changing. I would be able to find Julna, help

Mae, and have my revenge on the Gathbreds. "Sounds like we have a deal."

— ☾ —

I asked if I could try some of the treats in the shop, mostly to escape the havoc in the room, and to my surprise, Aurel accompanied me. "So," he said. "Setizar found you and now you're his prisoner?"

I nodded.

"Oh," Aurel almost growled. "That's unfortunate. He's a brute."

"How long have you known him?" I asked.

"A long time. *Too* long."

"So, you don't like him?"

"Don't like is an understatement." Aurel arched a brow. "We don't get along... haven't for years."

"Why?"

He shrugged. "Bad blood. We were once close, but when he fell in love with Alecto, that drove a wedge between us. You see, love triangles can be a tricky thing. And they chose each other in the end." Aurel's eyes locked with mine. "How unfortunate you landed in Autumn. Had you landed in Summer, I would have invited you for tea."

I laughed. "Tea makes everything better."

"That and oysters."

I scrunched my nose. "Those always smell awful."

"Ah, I cannot say they don't." He placed a hand over his heart. "However, what they lack in smell, they make up for in taste."

I laughed again. "I wouldn't know. I've never actually eaten one."

"Never?" He looked at me sideways. "Never *ever*?"

"Nope! Not in all my seventeen years of life."

"Seventeen…" he said, looking me over. "Has it really been that long?"

I stopped. "What?"

"I'm sorry." He smiled, not easing my questions at all. "I got a bit lost in my thoughts. What were we talking about? You being unable to have tea with me, correct?"

I smiled. "It is a shame…" I said. "I would have loved to have been able to have tea with you."

"It's never too late." He bowed and pulled a card from thin air. "Tea? Tomorrow morning in my rooms at the Palace ala Veranda?"

My smile grew, knowing what that would do to the jinni. "I'd be delighted."

— ☾ —

It was nice having a break from the bickering, even if it was for a moment to grab dessert. "So… you're a sphinx?" I asked, patting the sides of my lips to make sure I'd cleaned every last bit of chocolate.

He grinned, a beautiful pearlescent smile against his golden skin. "What do you think?"

We paused at seeing a familiar figure standing outside the door. The jinni leaned against the banisters, arms crossed. "Enjoy your dessert, Meris?" His eyes snapped to Aurel. "How unfortunate *he's* here."

"Likewise," Aurel said in a sing-song voice. "It's been nice going this time not seeing you."

"When will you go back to being a statue?"

"When you stop breathing."

Setizar bowed. "That'll be a long time."

"Don't forget tea, Meris." Aurel snatched my hand before I left and placed a kiss against my knuckles.

The jinni's irises appeared dipped in blood and obsidian. "Agonizing sphinx."

"Self-righteous Jinni." Aurel picked his nails. "Still alone, I take it?"

"As you said, I haven't been able to let Alecto go." The jinni's demeanor turned into something dark and unwieldy.

"Try and move on, Setizar. Why don't you ask that pretty little unicorn—"

"Back off, Aurel."

"Perhaps I should speak with Cerie, I'm certain we would have a riveting evening, the both of us."

Setizar fisted his hands. "Cerie has made it clear how she feels about you and your flirtations. I suggest you don't even try anything, or so help me—"

"What are you going to do?" Aurel stepped toward him, cutting his threat short. "You've always been weak."

Setizar's eyes flashed with something, shattering from the frightening red and eddying into magenta and blue once more.

Aurel didn't relent. He seemed far too riled up to even think about stopping his barrage of attacks on the jinni now. "How are you even going to find love after all this time? What has that done to your heart?"

An invisible dagger was thrown through the air with those words, making it painfully clear it stabbed whatever emotions the jinni had within him. "I won't be like you, Aurel." Setizar finally released whatever darkness was roiling around him, allowing it to scatter among the thousands of shadows within the city. "You're far too cowardly to actually *try* and win anyone's heart."

"And at your rate you'll never find anyone," Aurel said. "Look, Meris hates your guts."

Setizar flashed him a deadly smile, making me certain he'd gone mad. "I've given her no reason to like me." With that, he grabbed my arm and pulled me into the room. My heart roared in my chest, pounding and pounding until it felt like there would be no escape.

15

After the meeting, the jinni said I could explore the town some more while he discussed the details of locating a place where the rift between worlds was most likely to exist. Somewhat disgruntled I couldn't participate in the discussion, I wandered aimlessly through the streets of Nightmore.

A small alleyway led toward a pathway overgrown by vines and ivy. Something about it called me into its dark abyss. The jinni's words resurface, warning me not to enter the shadows.

But the beckoning was stronger, the question of what lay beyond the veil of darkness begging to be answered. Tentatively, I began walking, ambling lightly down the shadowy path. The farther I went, the darker and thicker the air became. Anxiety wrapped fingers around my lungs, suffocating the clean breaths out of me and inserting soot and grime in its place.

I spotted a pale, purplish light just a few yards away. I couldn't quite see the ground, but I could make out the indistinct lines of a cobblestone path. Beautiful music washed over the thick air as I stepped forward, pouring out from a wagon-home illuminated by an unsettling green lantern barely penetrating the black. It was so dark here...

Everything was shadowed, and the light did nothing. Women whispered near their homes, hiding between the slivers of light and obsidian dark. Why were they hiding?

Young children, with skin the color of midnight and eyes the shade of poppies, darted between trees and shrubs. They looked like Tatum. Women with hair as green as spring grass looked at me with cautious gazes.

Where was I?

"Who's this?"

The voice was parroted by three others asking the same thing. It was a hollow, eerie sound, and my blood froze.

A man, with hair as long as mine and as white as snow-capped mountains, stood between me and my hasty retreat. Three others, who looked like mirror reflections, joined him.

"I'm just leaving." I stepped to the side, but my movements were matched by the man's.

"You aren't leaving."

The others chimed in, "No, you're not."

That frightful chill stroked my spine, dragging icy fingers along my skin. "I wandered from town, I really should be going."

The man's smile was sharp and canine, revealing wolfish fangs. "We want to get to know you."

The other three echoed him as they did before. "*Indeed.*"

I swallowed back the trickle of fear pushing against my heartbeat.

One behind me drew a sharp fingernail—or claw—along my neck. "Come play with us."

"Yes," they mirrored, "*play.*"

I couldn't breathe. "You want to play?" I looked at each one. Their teeth, as sharp as razor blades, flashed at me in bared smiles. My stomach tightened and I tried to relax my shoulders.

I could do this. "I have a game for you boys." I pushed my toes out of my heels, hoping the darkness concealed my movements. "I call it—" I snapped my foot up, grabbed the shoe, and slammed the pointed heel into the temple of one of the creatures. Blood spurted on me and my arm, staining my lavender sleeves maroon.

I ran.

I ran before they registered what I'd done.

I slammed into the corner of the street. Behind me, three of the creatures were in pursuit. The slick road bit into my feet like fiery fangs. I tried to keep my balance as I darted through the alley and onto the main road. My pant leg snagged on a post, slashing into my skin. I tore it free before a creature could grab my neck.

I screamed.

My legs burned. My breath came in ragged, sharp intakes.

But they were still behind me.

Their panting breath, snapping jaws, and muscular haunches were too close for comfort. A whistle rang somewhere. I didn't stop. I needed to get somewhere safe.

The corner of the street was sharp, and I almost tumbled. Thankfully my pursuers were having just as much trouble.My shoulder scraped against a rough building wall. Everything burned. A howl cleaved the air behind me, joined in by two others.

I chanced a look over my shoulder. The creatures were something between wolf and man. My heart beat madly, drowning my senses in a thick veil of thunder. I needed to get to the tea room.

The uneven ground became worse as I slid into another alley. Fear gripped my heart, squeezing air from my lungs. The world blurred. I needed to stop. I needed to *breathe*.

Another howl echoed closer, and I knew I couldn't. There was no stopping. Not yet. Not until I was back at the tea room.

Was I even going to be safe? Would the jinni protect me from these monsters, or was I hoping for something that was impossible? Would he hand me over to them for punishment?

I skidded to a stop. The doors swung open and I barreled inside.

The wolf men were on my heels, smashing plates and scattering customers.

I ran into the back room where the Seasons had remained, and the look on the jinni's face darkened three shades. "What's wrong?"

The sound of the men clawed into my ears, and I stumbled forward.

"The girl!"

The other two parroted him as before. "The girl!"

The jinni stood, slid his hands into his pockets, and cast those burning eyes on them. "What girl?"

"She struck one of us!" Said one, pointing a finger at me, and the other two agreed.

"Oh?" The jinni's eyes flicked to me. This was it. He was going to hand me over, and I'd die. "You know she isn't a girl. She's a warrior. As far as I can recall, anything not human in Nightmore is protected by the laws of magic."

The three growled, and one lunged, only to thud into a wall of Setizar's magic.

"Leave. You don't belong here." His shoulders tightened, and his face was a series of hard lines. "Or I will skin you three and use you as bathing room mats."

I swore one of them whimpered.

16

I hissed as I stumbled into the washroom. The scratches burned, my feet felt like they were four times their size, and the gash on my leg was still bleeding. The apartment Setizar had rented was large, and though he was barely a few steps away in the adjacent room, I felt alone. I slipped out of my dirty clothes and soaked in the bath. The warm water caressed my body with soothing gentleness, smelling faintly of lemons and lavender.

After my soak, I did my best to wrap my wounds before I put on the red outfit set on my bed. I assumed Setizar had placed it there for me at some point. The pants were billowing, tightening around the ankles and waist and matching the long sleeved top. Now clean of blood and grime, I released a relaxed breath. A band of galaxies moved beyond the window, dancing with the stars and planets of the universe. Everything reminded me of Julna. The music bubbling up from the town was soothing, and I could almost hear my sister's sweet voice.

I breathed in, and a tinge of citrus and winter frost swept into the room.

I couldn't help it. I swayed with the song, clasping my hands against my heart. It thudded against my palms, as if still remembering what had happened earlier. Shoving the thoughts behind me, I *listened*. I needed to listen.

My feet carried me around the room, moved by the song in the street as if a thousand angels whispered into the darkness, caressing the night with words obscured by shadows. The twinkling stars were chimes in the tune, making the sound I assumed glittering diamonds would make in a secret cave.

I missed my sister. I wished she were with me... if only to see this place. She'd always dreamed of magic and powers, of beauty and the world beyond, of the mysteries of life and death. She seemed to want to know it all. I wanted to get back to her.

I ceased my dancing, a tear rolling down my cheek like a cry in the darkness, alone and beating with wings unheard.

"Well," the jinni muttered, leaning against the doorframe and pulling me back to the moment with alarming dexterity. "All washed?"

I wanted to glare at him—or at least reprimand for being so rude and tactless in entering my room without knocking—but I simply nodded.

He gestured to the chair, and I sat, crossing my arms. I was ready to be lectured. I'd disobeyed the rules he'd laid out earlier, and therefore I expected a proper tongue-lashing.

He stood, slid his hands into his pockets, and looked at me. The accusing gray and lavender in his eyes twisted my heart.

"Meris," he said, his tone low and soothing. "Roll up your right pant leg, please."

I swallowed my retort, trying not to make an already uncomfortable situation worse. Perhaps he deserved a proper knock aside the head, but now wasn't the time. I lifted my pant leg and he knelt, wrapping warm fingers around my ankle and propping my leg on his knee while he unfurled the bandage.

"This is a nasty cut," he whispered, eyes flicking to me for a half second before returning to the wound. He pulled a small vial out of his coat, and in mid-air, a cloth appeared from mist and shadow. "You'll have to take it easy for the next few hours while it heals."

I nodded. Where was the lecture?

He poured some of the vial on the cloth before pressing it gingerly to the wound. I hissed, gripping the chair. "I'm sorry." His eyes widened, and I realized—I realized in that face, in the quiver of his lashes—he wasn't a creature who derived any pleasure from pain. "I'll try to be gentler."

I shook my head, reeling from his reaction and my own traitorous heart. It fluttered, beating with wild frenzy in a way I'd never felt before. "It just stings a little."

He angled his chin. "I don't often tend wounds, so please... let me know if any of this hurts." He returned to cleaning the cut, fingers illuminated with white.

But there wasn't any pain.

"How is there no pain?" I asked as he pressed the cloth deeper into the wound and there was nearly no feeling whatsoever.

Setizar remained silent.

I chewed my lip, watching him. His dark hair covered his brow, and I couldn't see his face. Bronze skin peeked out from his shirt, unbuttoned at the top, revealing the delicately cut muscles of his chest. I swallowed the lump in my throat, tracing a curling black tattoo just below his collarbone with my eyes.

He wrapped my leg again, better than I did, and fixed my pant leg. "All better?"

I nodded, though my insides were as hot as summer. "Thank you."

A grin swept over his mouth, changing the gray-lavender of his eyes to deep blue, indigo, and magenta. "Would you like to go somewhere with me?"

"Where's my lecture?" I asked. He responded by summoning a pair of slippers and sliding them on my feet. "Where are we going?"

"Is that a yes, then?" He offered me a wide smile. "Because I won't take you unless you say you want to go."

I groaned, narrowing my gaze. Where was he taking me? Was I going to be sacrificed to a god? No, he needed me. Also, he didn't seem to want me hurt, otherwise he would've kept my leg in the same shape of disrepair. "Alright. I want to go."

His smile gleamed like pearls in starlight. "Then, my lady, allow me to take you to the destination." He held his hand out, a flicker of mischief lighting his eyes.

"Can I trust you?"

"You probably shouldn't."

I bit the smile snagging at my lips, but it was useless. I slipped my hand into his, and we misted from the room.

— (—

The mist evaporated as the world cleared, revealing the looming gateway.

Beside the jinni sat the flying carriage. "What's this?" I asked as the attendant opened the doors.

"You said you wanted to fly." The jinni gestured to the carriage.

There was a stuttering pulse in my throat. "What did you have to pay?"

He swatted the air, though a pained thread streaked through his eyes. "It doesn't matter."

"The price was a precious memory—what memory did you exchange?"

He smiled, any hint of pain and regret vanishing. "I don't remember. That's the thing about that type of exchange, you won't remember what you lost."

I swallowed, watching as he took a few steps toward the carriage.

"Don't just stand there, Meris. I didn't give up a memory that was likely very precious and very invaluable for you to not enjoy yourself."

I barked a laugh and took his outstretched hand. Once the door closed, the attendant waved at us, and a thousand sparks of glittering light erupted around the carriage. We lifted, weightless, with only the nipping wind below and the celestial sky above.

My fingers dug into Setizar's arm as the carriage rattled and ascended.

The world spun, gently swaying from side to side. Fear clenched a fist around my heart, sending it tumbling forward into terror. I squeezed my eyes shut. I was going to fall.

"You aren't going to fall," Setizar whispered as though reading my thoughts. His arm looped around my shoulders with an assuring tightness. "Open your eyes, Meris."

I did so, though half-committed. Ribbons of dusty starlight wrapped around us, tinged with shimmering mist and pallid moonlight. The scent of jasmine flowers and white sage, mixed with sea salt and wonder, filled my lungs and lifted stars into Setizar's sunset eyes. I realized I still clung to his arm, and embarrassment washed over me in waves, crashing against the walls of my emotions like whitewater. Without a word I pulled my fingers from him, separating myself from his warmth.

Yet, the lingering feel of his arm resting behind me and his hand on my shoulder stayed, demanding to be revisited. Desire settled on the tip of my tongue, like salt and sugar.

The flying carriage jolted forward, and I found myself seeking Setizar's arms again. "Aether!" I squinted at him. "What did you do that for?"

"Apologies," he said. The insincere grin on his face said otherwise. "It's been awhile since I rode one of these."

I huffed, pushing away from him once more. "Don't do that again... I want to peek over the edge."

With trepidation as my rope, I peered over the glossy black door beside me. We were much, much higher than I'd thought. The lights of the city looked like tiny fireflies winking at me from below. Every building was lost in an indigo hue, void of any other color, masked in a veil of mist and blue. No sound aside from the rushing wind and the chime of magic could be heard.

Magic. I could hear magic.

It sounded like delicate, tiny chimes. The way glitter looked was the way the magic sounded, pure and ethereal. Galaxies, stars, and lights of unknown entities graced the heavens above. It was as perfect as a watercolor, brought to life by the delicate, bleeding strokes of the gods. "This is... gorgeous."

I couldn't see him, but I knew he was smiling. "It is. There's no other place like Nightmore. No amount of money or coin will ever buy this feeling—the wonder inside. Only a ride in the night sky can cause this."

I reached up, touching a low, lonely cloud. It felt like mist and moved like shadows. "I never want to come down."

There's something mournful in his voice when he said, "You were born to chase the stars, Meris."

I glanced back at him. His eyes were on me, though a crystalline tear seemed to gleam in those star-kissed irises; a secret hidden below the hue of a dazzling sunset.

Before I could ask, before I could even breathe, a technicolor star streaked by in the ultramarine sky, leaving a trail of fractured rainbows in its wake. As quickly as it had appeared, it vanished.

"Make a wish." Setizar lifted his chin, pointing to the still lingering ribbons of color in the sky.

"Really?"

"Really."

I breathed in and looked around. Could this really be possible? I'd seen many things, but nothing like what I'd seen and experienced in the past six days. There'd been magic and horror, beauty and ugliness, yet everything was balanced. A strange mixture of wonder and tangible familiarity let me know this was real. I closed my eyes. "I wish—" the words halted in my throat. What did I wish for? What did I really want? "I wish that everything will be alright. That we all get what we want, and what we need."

I looked at him again.

My heart stuttered. His catlike eyes smiled, and somehow, it broke my heart. What lay behind that gaze? What things were running through his mind that can make him smile without his mouth? "That's a beautiful wish." He leaned back, closing his eyes and embracing the night air eddying around us. "Let's hope the Stars listen."

I laughed. "The Stars don't answer."

"They do, sometimes, they just prefer to listen and not speak." He smiled, looking at me for a brief moment before winking. "Shall we continue flying?"

I nodded, chewing my lip. "For as long as we can, please?"

He bowed his head, moonlight and magic catching in his raven hair. "As you wish."

17

I'd dreamt of swimming in a pool of starlight and memories, and morning had come faster than I'd wished. If I could've stayed asleep a little longer, bathing in the wonder of the dream world, I would.

After shuffling lazily out of bed, I changed my clothes and inspected my wounds. Healed. Every single one.

A small smile lifted my lips. I went *flying* last night! I sat beside Setizar and we talked… we spoke as equals, as… almost as if we were friends. He wasn't as rotten as I'd first assumed, I supposed. Certainly he didn't wish me harm, and even went out of his way to see me smile.

But what if it was a ruse? What if he was using me?

I shook my head. It would be over once he realized I wasn't a furie. But how would I explain everything to Mae? I still had too many questions.

Slipping out of the bedroom, I took in the large space the jinni rented. Much like the room, it was gaudy and luxurious. Mahogany furniture wrapped in red velvet, side tables accented with gold, and a massive ivory fireplace added to the decadence of the area.I drew nearer, breathing in the oak burning and basking in the comforting heat reaching toward me. I wasn't cold by any means, rather, the fog that veiled the city of Nightmore brought with it the autumn air that made everything seem magical. And I wanted nothing more than to soak up every element surrounding me.

A note sat on the mantle, addressed to me. The handwriting was achingly familiar, as if I'd seen it before in some distant dream. Gently, I took the cream note from the marble mantle and opened it.

Meris,

I must attend to a few things this morning in the city. If something is wrong, tap the cuff about your wrist three times and I will find you. I trust I can leave you alone for the time being, though. I doubt you will find trouble so early in the day. I may be underestimating your abilities, but please don't try and prove me wrong. It would be nice to go throughout our day without a near-death experience.

If you're hungry, enjoy the fruit. It's on the counter.

Forever yours,

Setizar

Chewing my lip, I closed the note and placed it back where I'd found it. The thoughts of the fruit Setizar mentioned made my stomach growl, and I meandered into the kitchen. A bowl of white apples, silver raspberries, and golden pineapples rested on the edge, drawing me in with their potent, sweet aromas. As soon as I grabbed the glimmering ivory apple, there was a gentle tap at the apartment door. Fear shackled my nerves, tightening my muscles. Who could be calling? Perhaps it was Setizar, or a message from him? Should I answer?

Come on. I could open the door... this city was safe now. Rolling my neck, I tried to release the tension in my back. It tingled, as if two invisible fingers caressed the space between my shoulder blades.

I opened the door only to find a small, red-headed man standing there. He bowed, nearly touching the floor with his forehead, and handed me a card. "Lord Aurel has requested I escort you."

That's right, Aurel had said he'd invite me to tea. Yesterday I was so much more assured about going and dining with him, now I felt uneasy. Was it because of the time I'd spent with Setizar?

Oh, come on. I couldn't let him keep me from having a good morning.

I bowed to the small man. "Thank you for coming to get me." He held out his hand, and I had to stoop to shake it. "What's your name, sir?"

"Blarney McCoppertop, Ma'am!" he chirped. "Leprechaun of the first coven."

"What?"

"What?" He tilted his head to the side. "Oh! What's a First coven?" He tugged at my arm and we walked. "Magic wielders. I only know a little, so I can't graduate to the second coven."

"No—" I stumbled over my words. "I mean... you're a Leprechaun?"

He chuckled. "What else would I be?" He looked at me, eyes brimming with curiosity. "I am a form of faery, ma'am. I cannot think that you would have supposed I am anything else."

I swallowed. "Of course." My head was spinning with questions, but I kept quiet, allowing him to escort me the rest of the way to the Palace ala Veranda.

The walk didn't take us very long before we entered a cozy street. The eastern wind wrapped warm fingers around my neck, carrying with it the scent of honeysuckle. The building did look like a palace, with its tall alabaster walls, towers, and turrets. Ornately designed iron crestings curled over the steeply pitched gables just above the arches of the windows. Blarney opened the door, leading me through the redwood halls and stained-glass soaked corridors.

"Do you work for Lord Aurel?" I asked, barely able to keep my eye on the leprechaun. The gorgeous assortment of color flooding in from the windows danced with the flickering lamplight, splitting my focus.

"No, no. He's a friend. I owe him much," Blarney said, stopping at a door. "We have arrived."

My heart stuttered as I laid eyes on the lovely spread. Small cakes, tea, sandwiches, fruits like the ones in the apartment, and berries were placed on the table.

Aurel stood and bowed. His white outfit suited him, like an angel or otherwordly specter coming down from the heavens for a luncheon. "I was half expecting a rejection letter."

"I'd reject you in person, sir."

He smiled and pulled a chair out for me. "Enjoy being locked in your chambers?"

"Not in the least... but, it's safer." I gave Blarney a nod of thanks. "My escort was nothing short of pleasant."

Blarney's cheeks blushed bright red. "Oh, my lady. You do flatter me!" He tipped his green hat. "Do enjoy your tea. I will be back when you summon, my lord." With that, he tottered off.

"Pleasant fellow, isn't he?" Aurel smiled and sat across from me. "I apologize for the spat between Setizar and I earlier. I acted like an infant."

I laughed. "You were both dealing low blows." My thoughts swirled into the conversation, to the heated words tossed between the two creatures. "What did he mean? When he said for you to turn back into a statue?"

"Oh..." Aurel scratched his neck. "Honestly it's not that big of a deal. A Grimhildr got to me, and I turned into a statue. I was stone for a good many years before it took twelve jinn to turn me back. One of them died in the process, so he's been... salty about that."

I nodded, remembering the Grimhildr in Setizar's garden.

"Turn to stone from the claws of a Grimhildr, you don't usually come back. I was lucky, plenty of other creatures haven't been."

A thick cord wrapped around my heart. How many creatures had been subject to the Grimhildr? "How long have you been here in Nightmore?"

He poured tea for himself, regarding me over the steam. "A few days. I wanted to visit some of my past romantic partners."

I nodded slightly.

"You know," Aurel began, tapping his spoon against his cup. "You scowl."

"I what?" I blinked, trying to recenter my thoughts.

"You scowl." He smiled, his amber skin shimmering in the moonlight. "Were you not too thrilled when I mentioned my *friends*?"

I almost coughed out my drink.

Aurel leaned back and sipped his tea. "If you weren't opposed to the idea, I might ask if you'd like to be another *friend* of mine. Of course, you would be different. There's fire in you—"

"So!" I straightened, refusing to allow what he'd said to phase me. "What can you tell me of the Silver Queen?"

Aurel grinned. "There's not much we remember of her. We don't know why she stole our magic, or why she hasn't come back. We're waiting for the day when she returns to finish the job."

"Is there anything you can remember aside from that?"

He nodded. "We believe Inanna is connected to her somehow, but we have yet to find out how."

I breathed in a lungful of the sweet air. "Who's Inanna?"

He shook his head, that familiar grin vanishing. "A daemon with enough military power to tear the realm to its core. She will often ask us if we know where to find the Changeling, and if our suspicions are correct…"

"That the Silver Queen is the Changeling?"

He looked out the open balcony, his eyes shadows. "We assume so, but we cannot be certain."

"Do you think there could be a way to reason with the Silver Queen?"

His next words were biting. "No. She hurt Alecto… hurt us *all*."

"What can you tell me about the Box that Setizar wants me to retrieve?"

"You're quite the inquisitive type, aren't you?" He offered me a melancholy grin, rolling his neck.

"I like to know as much as possible."

"Well, the Box is sealed by furie blood, specifically Alecto's blood. The Silver Queen stabbed Alecto and used the blood on the knife to seal the Box." His words were a whisper, a stumbling assortment of barely audible vowels and consonants, "We don't know why she did it."

"There's a lot of things you all seem to not know when it comes to this Box. Even if I *am* a furie, which I highly doubt, how do you know that just any furie blood can open it?"

"Let's just say, we have a hunch it'll work."

I rolled my eyes. Unbelievable.

— ☾ —

Aurel said he'd meet me in his rooms after I used the lavatory down the hall. As soon as I finished up and freshened my face and hair, I followed the little glittering map he'd given me. The paper was plain, with the blueprints of the hotel scribbled in gold. A small firefly appeared on the paper, flashing its way to the room where I was to go. I knew where I was thanks to the glittering gem inked on the paper. It moved when I did, and I figured out the map quickly, arriving at his rooms in no time. The doors were slightly ajar, and I tapped on the wood.

"Come in, Meris."

I entered.

He was sitting in the center of the room, long blond hair pulled back into a messy knot, while his eyes focused on the canvas in front of him. He'd ditched his shirt, and every chiseled edge of his torso was on display, etched by shadows and light. Tattoos swirled along his muscled arms, depicting a battle of some kind. He wiped his hand on his trousers, smiling at me. "Come, come!" he said, waving me over.

I shuffled toward him, and he tugged my hand. I nearly fell onto his lap, and my skin heated as it brushed against his. "Sorry," he muttered, placing one hand on my waist to help balance me. The mere touch seemed forbidden, and something I'd already thought far too much about. "You're lighter than I thought. Actually, this is a better view for you." He turned me a bit, hands resting on my hips as he angled me toward the canvas. The water...the water moved. The sun danced off an iridescent ocean where mermaids swam. A mighty sea-faring vessel with black sails cut through the waves, a magical ship on its own accord. I leaned in, trying to read the name stenciled on the side. A faint 'M', but other than that, I couldn't make out the rest. "It's beautiful."

I felt his grin. "It's a lost art... you have to love it to make it come alive."

I turned and looked at him, realizing just how close we were.

"Meris?" Aurel smiled and rested his hand on my shoulder. "Mind if I paint you?"

"M-me?"

"Of course!" He pointed to the couch. "There's something about you that begs to be captured. I wish to paint you and watch you come alive in an image."

"But...," I looked him in the eye, "you said you have to love something to—"

"Well I don't exactly hate you, or feel neutral about you." He laughed, poking my nose with a paint-covered finger. "Come on." He stood, grabbed my hand, and pulled me over to the couch. Now closer, I could better make out the tattoo on his forearm, something that seemed of ancient make. It was beautiful; a mixture of feathered swirls easing into a pyramid. An eye rested where the pyramid peak should be.

"What does the tattoo mean?" I asked, sitting where he placed me.

"It's homage to my homeland," he said and turned, gesturing to the metallic wing design on his muscled back. "You'll have to allow me to take you to Summer someday. I can show you the palaces, especially the river which shines like molten gold across the green fields."

"Sounds beautiful." I looked at him, truly looked at him. He was a man crafted from gold and sunshine. I didn't know why Setizar said what he'd said about him.

Aurel grinned and patted my knee. "Now, sit there, and look like yourself."

I laughed. "And what does myself look like?"

"Absolutely stunning." He winked and settled back into the seat.

A blush crept over my skin, but that little voice bubbled up. *He lies. You know you aren't.*

"You," Aurel interrupted my thoughts after he changed the canvas, "remind me of a shining desert star. Fiery. Beautiful. Angry. Hostile." He looked up at me. "And determined."

I wrangled my unraveling nerves.

"You may not see it, Meris. But…" He blew on the canvas, silver eyes locked with something there. "You will soon see you have power. Something only some of us can dream of."

I looked at him, unsure of what he was saying to me. "Well, then, hopefully you will be around when I figure it out."

He dipped his head in a half-committed bow. "Of course."

— (—

My heartbeat wasn't there. Nothing pulsed in my body.

Another dream?

Fire blazed on a lonely mountain, lapping at the black sky with red-hued fury. Pain radiated from my back, grinding at my muscles with agonizing slowness. The taste of iron stung my tongue, rabid in its intensity. Blood dripped from my chest.

"What have you done!" someone yelled. A scream cleaved the air, followed by the hiss of metal over metal. "No, no, no!"

I tried to look up—tried to look anywhere aside from the gaping hole where my heart should've been. Blood dripped, falling from the wound.

A crunch, followed by swift, riving pain, echoed in the smoke-licked heavens. I tried to scream, but silence was the only thing that escaped my lips.

"I will get you back for this!"

My eyes snapped open.

I looked around, my heart pounding. The room was a blur of yellow and moonbeams, stitched together by corners and tapestries.

"You must have been tired." Aurel looked at me from over the canvas. Right. I was still laying on the couch. "Rest well?"

"How long was I asleep?"

"Oh, twenty minutes?" he said. "You were saying something, and when I looked up, you were fast asleep."

I nodded. "I suppose I'm a bit tired." The dream crept up into my mind, sending uneasy shivers up and down my spine.

"Have nice dreams?" Aurel smiled at me, but something lined his grin. Something I couldn't decipher. "I hope my room offered a reprieve."

Why did I feel so uneasy? What was it about his presence that shifted? Warmth and the reassuring grasp of a summer day had been overwhelmingly present until then. Now there was the illusion of that warmth, but below it was an iciness. "I should probably get going." Could that dream have had anything to do with him? The thought nearly made me panic. "Thank you, you've been so kind."

Aurel nodded, the cruel curve of his grin and the glint in his silver eyes reminded me that I shouldn't get too friendly with him... with anything in this world. "Thank you for allowing me to paint you."

18

The ride back to the Crimson Plane was quiet, and the jinni kept glancing at me.

"So, mind telling me where you wandered off to this morning?"

I blinked. Maybe he knew? Maybe he followed me, and *he* was the one who'd put that awful dream into my head. "Not particularly."

"Why not?" He raised a brow, angling his head. Something in the gesture settled my nerves. He was like a curious kitten trying to decipher the meaning of a sunbeam. Somehow, that made him a little less frightening. "Because you went somewhere you weren't supposed to, perhaps?"

I groaned. "I didn't—"

The snap of the carriage wheel cut me off, and I tumbled forward into Setizar. He grunted as my elbow rammed into his stomach. A sheer prick of pleasure coursed through me, a horrid combination of sadistic glee and karma. Perhaps being a bony woman did have its benefits after all.

However, my elation melted away as cold reality crushed the happiness of payback. The world tilted, and we tumbled to the right, cracking and snapping echoing through the air. A horse's screech cut through me, followed by the sounds of wolfish howls.

The carriage finally toppled, and Setizar and I fell into the autumn peppered woods. Setizar misted us out of the carriage's drop. The wooden sides splintered at impact, and I curled into a ball.

Then, the woods fell silent.

Not even the wind whispered.

My heart beat so hard my stomach curdled. I was dizzy from suddenly misting with Setizar. It wasn't a planned mist. It was chaotic, frantic...

A flicker of rage surfaced on his face as he scanned the surrounding forest. "Meris," he whispered. "Grab my hand."

I nodded and clutched his outstretched palm tightly. Fear formed in my heart as we misted from one end of the forest to another, tumbling into partially melted snow. I could see the beads of sweat forming on Setizar's brow after the fourth mist.

He stopped, his voice hoarse. "There," he said, pointing to a snow-covered cabin ahead of us. "It's small, but it'll work until morning comes around."

Something like a string of yarn knotted around the tip of my stomach and yanked. An indistinct, numb pulse of electricity shot up and down my body. "You're not well..."

He looked up at me. His face was ashen and void of its previous coloring. I helped him up the steep slope and to the cabin door. The howl of wolves shrieked in the distance.

Somehow, I knew I wouldn't be getting any sleep that night.

— ☾ —

The fire's gentle warmth spread through my frozen body. Despite my clothes being damp, I had no intention of removing them and drying them as Setizar had suggested. He'd peeled off his agonizing coat, which was wetter than my own clothes, and now sat near the fire with his velvet, black shirt, half unbuttoned, and his coal-colored trousers. His eyes were closed and his head was tipped back.

"So, why can't you summon help?" I asked, shuffling closer to the flickering flames.

Setizar sighed and rolled his shoulders forward. "I'm drained." His eyes finally opened and he looked at me with blazing sincerity. "Remember the muscle thing I told you about?"

My heart stumbled a beat. "So, how much magic could you use right now?"

"Barely enough to mist us out the front door." His shoulders slumped. "I've never been this worn out before... I suppose it's been a long while since I've exerted this much magic in such a short period of time."

I settled down on the ground, looking up at him. "Feeling human?"

His mouth opened, then shut promptly afterward. He waited a moment, then said, "Well, I don't like being without my powers." He breathed in, the fire flickering and illuminating those razor-edged outlines of his face.

"Well," I scooted closer to him. "What would you do if you had to be without them for long?"

"Why do you ask?"

"Just curious."

"Curiosity is dangerous," he whispered. "I've never given it much thought, honestly."

I fought the shiver stroking my spine and shoulders. The eerie chill of darkness and cold enveloped me. I wanted to change my clothes, to get into something warm and dry. Instead, I was dressed in wet, weather-beaten garments. I needed to turn around and dry everything, but I needed to get warmer and dryer to even move. I groaned.

Setizar eyed me in concern. "Too cold?"

"No." I shifted stiffly, cursing myself for the delayed reaction. "A little."

Setizar laughed. "How about this?" He sat up, leaning his elbows on his knees and looking into my eyes. "I can give you the shirt I'm wearing and you can use it while your garments dry."

Somehow the thought of any of that made my stomach harden. My body felt like a mix between a volcano and an iceberg. Shivers and unrelenting heat flowed through me.

A smile danced on his lips, as if he knew what the offer would do to me. "I'm only keeping the offer active for as long as that pink hue remains on your face."

The heat became almost as unbearable as the cold.

"Okay," he leaned back. "Don't take my offer. It's far more entertaining watching you shiver and cower by the fire."

His words sounded as unbelievable as he'd seemed when I'd first arrived. "Fine," I ground out.

The smile that hid a thousand secrets returned to his face. He slowly— oh, so slowly—unbuttoned his shirt. I looked away. I couldn't feel comfortable looking at him.

He handed the garment over, and I muttered my thanks. "Can you..." I looked around the tiny cabin with no privacy. "Close your eyes and don't look behind you."

"A demand?"

"Yes," I hissed. He turned around with a dry chuckle, and when I saw his eyes were closed, I shucked off my wet clothes and replaced them with the dry shirt. It was just long enough to cover me, but still showed far too much leg than I'd ever shown before. Pulling down the hem, I sat next to the fireplace again and cleared my throat.

"Well." He looked at me, and released a nearly imperceptible breath. "Warmer?"

I nodded. The shirt smelled of him, of autumn spices and sugar. It was warm from his body as well, easing the cold from my skin.

"So, feel like telling me where you went this morning?"

I looked back at him, taking in the hard, tight planes of his body. He was perfectly muscled, and in all the right places. The hint of the tattoo I'd seen yesterday was in full view, and now looked far more mysterious. Four jagged lines curved up his collarbone and tapered along his shoulders like wings. The ink was as black as midnight, yet it glimmered in the firelight with a blue sheen. What could it mean? Aurel's tattoos meant something, could his? I was certain it wasn't a fashion statement, since he always wore several layers.

As he leaned farther from the fire, and the tattoo began to lighten, ebbing away and vanishing altogether. Did he make it appear? Or was it heat which caused its appearance?If heat was the cause, then why had I seen it the other day?

He crossed his arms, and I looked away. It was like a small, fuzzy animal moved around in my stomach.

Finally, I lifted my head. "I think I'd like to keep what I did a secret. Since you have yours, I'd like to have mine."

A smile tugged at his lips, reminding me how much I enjoyed seeing it, although I was generally in an annoyed mood when it appeared. "Of course you do, Meris."

I bristled a bit at his tone and swallowed the jagged insult I wanted to throw at him. "Tell me something about yourself, *Setizar*."

"Is this a way to get to know me, or simply find my weakness?" A roguish gleam lit his eyes.

"I guess you'll have to figure that out." I returned his smile, which in turn made his bloom into a beautiful, glittering thing. The same smile he'd given me on the flying carriage. "I'm fine with anything, even if it's a harmless secret."

"Secrets are rarely ever harmless, love." He tilted his head, narrowing those cat-like eyes, as if he were digging through a satchel trying to find a story to tell. "I stole a magical ornament from Eira when I was younger. Let's say, she was very upset with me."

"Why'd you take it?"

"I took it because I could. And I knew she'd get deliciously angry."

I laughed. "And what did she do?"

"She declared war." He shook his head, a melodic chuckle surfacing. "Good times."

I smiled, looking to the ceiling. "When I was twelve, my sister dared me to race the local boys down by the woods. When I beat them, they got mad—" I stopped myself. That was the first time Chester and I spoke... and the beginning of what I thought was to be forever.

"When I was young, barely twenty, I didn't show signs of power," Setizar began, his tone low and calming. "My parents, both powerful jinn, weren't pleased. So, they took me to a place called Redrim, hoping the lord of the place would be able to tap into my 'potential'." The way he said it made me wonder what happened. "They didn't know that he had... ulterior motives, and that he planned on killing me instead of helping me. But nevertheless..." His eyes flicked to me. "It worked. My powers came rushing in, and if I didn't run out of stamina, I would have brought the cursed place to the ground, leaving only rubble and ash."

"What did they do to you?"

His breath was loud as he inhaled. "Things only conjured in nightmares, Meris. The scars   from that day are gone by magic, but somehow..." His hand pressed against his side, and a ghost of an expression flitted across his face. "I feel like I'm still bleeding. I never want to go back to that place, or sit in the dungeons below the catacombs of the old palace."

His words twisted my stomach. My feet moved on their own, and I pressed my hand against his heart. His skin was warm against my cold fingers. I didn't even know why I did it, or what I planned on saying. But the words came out, like a cup that was too ready to tilt and pour. "If you're bleeding inside, does it make you feel better if I feel the same way?"

His eyes kept contact with mine.

My heart was rabid in my chest. "Some scars never stop bleeding." I removed my hand, inching back to the fire. I swallowed. The memory dug into me, and the panic renewed. Tears stung my eyes, and my body became numb.

"Meris," Setizar's voice cut through whatever took over me. "What's wrong?"

"Nothing." I stifled my sobs, though they didn't ease.

"Meris..." The tone was soothing, coursing over my bones and settling a warm hand over my fluttering heart.

I could've been smarter. I shouldn't have been with Chester that day.

Or, I could have…

I shook my head. Perhaps I deserved what happened.

Setizar took my hands in his, warming the frozen tips with his heated palms. "Show me your past, Meris."

"Why?" I could barely see him through the web of tears. "Why do you want to know? It's ugly…horrid."

His body was rigid under my fingers. "It may be ugly, it may be horrid, but it's a wound, and wounds will eventually heal, but only if you allow yourself to clean it."

A skittering sob cascaded down my throat.

"I can't."

He found my gaze, and a gentle smile appeared on his lips. "Then I won't push you to tell me."

An hour passed before I finally crawled into the measly bed after changing back into my now-dry clothes. There was no bedding, no blankets, no pillows, and I was shivering.

Setizar still sat on the floor by the fireplace.

My gut was a series of ribbons, and I cursed myself for the thoughts willing themselves into my mind. "Setizar," I called to him. "You... you going to sleep?"

"Yes."

"On the floor?"

He looked at me, eyes a striking amber in the light. "Yes."

I didn't push the subject. "Okay, goodnight then." His eyes lingered on me, and I couldn't help but feel guilty. "We can trade. You get the bed and I get the floor."

"Nope."

"Please?" I pressed my palms together, pleading. "I feel bad."

"You don't think I would feel bad?"

I groaned. "Well." I patted the mattress beside me, issuing a layer of dust to explode into the air. After a moment of coughing and swatting the dust away I said, "What if we shared?"

His laugh rumbled my chest. "Just go to sleep, Meris. Don't worry about me."

"You sure?"

Something glimmered in his eyes as a sly smile quirked his lips up-ward. "I don't want to give you the opportunity to choke me in my sleep."

"I would rather use a club," I said. "But, since there are none here in the vicinity, I suppose you're safe."

He stood slowly, taking a few steps toward me. "I don't want to make you uncomfortable."

"I—" I swallowed. "I think I'd feel safer with you closer." As if on cue, the distant howl of wolves shattered the night sky. "Just don't get used to it."

— (—

The fire flickered to death, and only the smoldering embers remained. A damp chill settled over me, thrusting ice into my veins.

"You're shaking the bed." Setizar poked my spine, as if he could press a nerve and make me cease.

"I'm cold."

"So am I, but I'm not rocking the bed like a bloody rabbit with fleas."

I turned over with a grunt, ready to say something. My breath stilled as his sunset eyes emitted gentle waves of light between us. The warm glow caressed the ebony locks askew over his copper skin. Was his hair as soft as it appeared? Was his skin warm...

I berated myself for the thought, and the unsettling tingle rolling along my fingertips.

His smile was strange, familiar and unraveling. "Well, if you're so cer-tain I'm not as cold as you, then you should get closer. Perhaps the heat from my body could warm you?"

I recognized the taunting, teasing lift of his voice. "Maybe I'll keep shivering and drive you mad all night?"

"Maybe I'll turn into a cat and curl up atop the embers."

I grappled with the thought, watching him carefully. "You can do that?"

A heady laugh escaped him, and he rolled onto his back. "No, but your face was worth the tease."

I kicked his leg before laying on my stomach. "If you could turn into a cat, I'd pet you. But, since you can't, I guess I won't."

"I'm sure there's a spell or two which could bless me with a second form..."

"If you could refrain, I'd be grateful. Besides, you'd probably still be smiling as a cat, and I don't want to see that."

Again, a gentle laugh escaped him, curling into the air with autumn mirth. Setizar's arm brushed against mine, and just the brief second of contact left me wanting to get closer...

Stop it, Meris. I shouldn't be thinking those things about him.

I sucked in a breath, wrestling to control my unsteady nerves and traitorous heart. "So, what does that tattoo mean? The one on your chest?" I shifted slightly.

His eyes slid to mine, his fingers tapping the plane of chest visible from his shirt. "It was a blessing from Alecto. You see," he turned, facing me, "she burnt me once, and felt so horrid afterward that she gave me the same magic of the furies—or, shared it with me at least. So, whenever I get close to fire, the symbol will appear. Not only a symbol of what the fire cannot do, but the bond that Alecto and I shared."

I reached out, breaching a dangerous line. The closer my hand got to his skin, the clearer the tattoo became. Curiosity pushed me forward, guiding my heart and mind, urging me to do what I wouldn't have done before. I loosed a few buttons... then a few more, until I slipped every last one from its place.

"Meris, what are you doing?" Setizar's voice was rasping, spiking with uncertainty and trembling with question.

I swallowed my hesitation and pushed the garment back. Every curve of the tattoo was on display now, glimmering with starlight. His skin was warm and smooth below my fingertips as I glided them over the ink. "Why does it appear now?"

His eyes searched mine, flickering into the shade of a twilit sky. "Because your soul is made of fire."

A laugh threatened to slip from my mouth. However, I kept my hand pressed against his chest, enjoying the feel of his heart beating against my palm. Like a lifeline I didn't know I needed. "There's no fire in my soul, Setizar. There's nothing in me that is even close to that."

His hand covered mine, warm and assuring. What was the feeling I had when he was near me? Why didn't I wish to run and hide?

"Meris." He tightened his grip, emphasizing his words. "I can't convince you of what I see. But, know that you are much more than you think you are."

— ☾ —

The cold winter wind howled through the cracks in the cabin, fluttering in and sweeping against the hardwood floors. Sleep wasn't coming for me, not tonight.

Setizar moved a little, and I realized he couldn't seem to sleep either.

"Is something wrong?"

"It's the air," he said. "There's something amiss in the air. I don't know what…"

I faced him, my body aching from the cold. "What's wrong with the air?"

His chest rose and fell as he took a breath. "Darkness. There's whispers in the darkness."

An eerie quiet settled over the cabin. There was no wind. Setizar sat up, the bed creaking from his movement. Groaning wood cut through the atmosphere like nails dragging along chalky pavement. An unearthly shiver rolled up my spine.

The place smelt of mildew and fire, mingled together to create a chorus of smoky uncertainty. Again, the taste of iron surfaced on my tongue, like in the dream earlier.

"Don't move," Setizar whispered, standing. Rings of mist curled around his throat, as if they had life of their own and wished to choke him. The temperature dropped. Everything stilled.

The door to the cabin splintered. Debris clattered onto the floor, and three wolves entered, six foot tall, standing on legs which looked too human. Their fur was patchy, showing pale-gray flesh under the woolly pelt. "Give us the girl," said one, pointing a claw at me. "And you will live."

"No," Setizar growled, flicking his wrists. Mist rolled into the cabin, slithering up his body like snakes. Two short swords appeared out of the haze, coalescing from the cloud around his palms. "Do you think I travel without weapons?"

"Do you think we travel alone?"

A chorus of howls resounded. I dared not move.

"You are not a fighter, Jinni. We don't believe you will make it out alive."

The tallest wolf sneered. "Perhaps the Changeling can return upon your death."

Setizar's eyes changed, shifting into the color of fire and rage. "I'll give you one chance. You can leave peacefully and live."

A hollow growl erupted from the wolf-man's throat. "We don't want your mercy!"

He pounced.

His claws were met with Setizar's steel, but it wasn't enough. The other two were on him, and three others barreled through the windows.

I was standing now, my heart beating harder than a drum and wilder than the beasts in the cabin.

A rogue hand reached for me; claws curled and hunting for blood. I ducked under the bed as claws grazed the cuff on my arm. A hollow scream escaped me. Multiple hand-like claws tore my pant leg.

A loud thump followed the whimper of an animal. Blood seeped onto the floor.

Another claw flung under the bed, and I narrowly evaded it. A long nail appeared beside me, flaking with rust and algae. I grabbed it. Instinct took over. The crunch of flesh and muscle vibrated under the nail. A loud howl followed, and blood dripped from the creature's hand.

I rolled out from under the bed, firmly gripping the bloody nail. Reflexes and adrenaline spurred me forward. Another creature lunged at me, and I thrusted the measly weapon into its eye.

Setizar crumbled in the corner, his body covered in blood. I didn't know whose.

Hands grabbed me from behind, and my back erupted with pain. Something inside my breast swelled and burned. It began in my veins, in my pulse, in my innermost being.

It exploded. Everywhere... *everywhere*. Fire bursted from my fingertips, reaching out and catching the entire cabin ablaze. Nothing was safe. Nothing aside from Setizar.

I screamed, and the fire grew hotter. Brighter. Whiter.

My back shattered. My spine snapped. But there was no pain. Only an unfurling relief amidst the screaming.

And all fell silent.

Like a mirror enveloping the frozen flames, everything stilled. Setizar's face was a mixture of horror and awe. Every flicker, every ounce of flame, vanished. I stood, stumbling back. My heel dropped into something hot and slick, like tar. I spun, yanking my foot out the charred remains of a creature. My stomach heaved, and a bitter tang surfaced on my tongue.

What did I do?

What did I just become?

PART THREE
WEEK TWO IN YAMIRA

20

Everything inside me was an empty void. *Drained* of something. Setizar's arms wrapped around me, his warmth spreading over the frigidity of my body. He cursed. Was this a dream? "Stay with me, Meris."

Darkness blanketed the world. "What's happening?"

A coil of pain ebbed through me, tightening in my back. The world was black as pitch. Setizar called me, but I wasn't sure from where.

Where was he? Where was I? I tried to move, but my body was a pillar of ice.

Glimmers of gold and red sputtered to life. A woman with red hair, much like my own, stood to my right, her entire figure clad in armor.

Another woman, with hair like honey, was to my left, dressed in a slip of garment mimicking a robe. Shadows crowned their foreheads and dropped veils about their faces.

"You're so close," the red-head said. "You're so close. You only need more time. Trust the jinni."

The blonde breathed out, her voice a whisper in the wind. "Remember, in the end, he will not steer you wrong. He will keep you safe."

Their voices, like a memory long lost and surrendered to time, came barreling back. Who were they? Where was I?

Another voice cut through the sky. "Trust nothing the jinni says or does."

"No," said the blonde. "Trust him."

"She speaks lies," said the disembodied voice. "Trust no one. You can't even trust yourself."

My eyes were heavy again, and the figures dissolved, yelling something I couldn't understand. Words I couldn't make out. Warmth was over me, and I moved a little, thanking whatever gods were listening and opened my eyes again.

A warm fire flickered close to the bed where I laid, licking the shadows from the hearth. Was I in a cottage? Trying to clear my somewhat bleary vision, I pushed the patchwork quilt off. The door to the left was ajar, and an old woman stood over a large cauldron. My heart stumbled. Was she planning on eating me?

I fumbled out of bed, but my legs were weak and unstable. I fell, and glass from the far corner of the room clattered and crashed on the floor as I tumbled.

My back was so heavy, weighed down by an unknown force. I tried to stand, but I couldn't. I rolled on my side, now feeling like a muscle projected from my back and was being stretched too far.

Wings. A pair of white, membranous wings projected from either side of me.

I screamed.

The door flung open, and Setizar waltzed in. "Aether, Meris! What are you doing on the floor?"

"What are these!"

He offered me a blank stare, confusion wrapping over his features. "Wings. What else would they be?"

I tried to lift myself, but failed as the wings held me down.

"You need to think about the wing muscles."

I growled. "Get them off me!"

"I can't," he said, throwing his hands in the air. "You need to do that. I have no power over your wings. You summoned them, you need to remove them."

"I don't even—" Tears stung my eyes. "What happened to me?"

"You tapped into what is within you, Meris."

"What. Am. I."

His brow rose, and he walked closer. "First, you may want to put something on."

I looked down, seeing my tattered clothes, torn from the beasts and singed by the fire. "Help me up."

"So demanding." He reached his hand out, and I grabbed it. "I've told you what you are. You're a furie." He steadied me as I stumbled into him.

"I need you to explain everything."

Before he spoke, the crone entered the room. She was exactly as told in fairytales. Old, raggedy, and missing some teeth. There were warts on her long, beak-like nose, and her eyes were slightly bulging from below the droopy lids and heavy bags. "I doubt the jinni will be able to tell you much, dearie." She dipped her graying head and smiled. I wished she wouldn't do that. Her smile looked like a hole in a rotten plum.

"Alright. Why am I here? How can I get rid of these wings?"

She cackled and sat on the small wooden chair beside the dresser I'd nearly toppled. "You were once in this world, before the fall of the furies and the closing of the portals."

"And how long ago was that?"

"Oh, about…seventeen years?"

I scowled at her, and Setizar chuckled.

"The only reason you were able to enter our world, dear, is because you are a furie."

I blinked. "I thought the only reason I'm here is because of the white rabbit."

Setizar and the woman looked at me. "The white rabbit?" Setizar asked.

I nodded. Was it me, or did his voice sound hoarse?

The woman shook her head. "You must hurry, jinni. It appears you have very little time."

"I know," Setizar's eyes fell on me. "We have work to do, Meris."

— ☾ —

I did my best to get comfortable in the small hut with my gigantic wings.

"What are three things you want most in life, Meris?" Setizar was in the corner, his eyes fixed on me. The memory of the voices came flooding back. Should I trust him as the two women said? Or listen to the faceless woman and trust nothing?

Should I even listen to the people in my dreams?

The firelight cast languid shadows on his face, drawing sharp lines along his cheekbones. He looked more like a weapon then, with his razor-edged features and eyes like amethyst-blended rubies.

"Meris?"

I blinked, realizing he'd been waiting for my answer. "I want my sister back," I said. "I want to become someone who can't be hurt."

"And the third?"

That same fire coursed through me, and I looked down at my arms. Every vein glowed vivid orange. "I want revenge." I looked up at him again, the world blanketed in a strange red hue. "I want it more than any-thing."

Setizar's eyes flashed with something I couldn't discern, clearing the hut of the eerie glow and returning it to normal. A shadow of emotion slithered over the room, and I fought the shiver stroking the inside of the wings. "Then let's work with that," he said. "Let's start by trying to find your sister." Setizar stood, straightening his shirt.

"What about your powers? We're far from the Crimson Plane, aren't we?"

He smiled, a crooked, beautiful thing that made my weak heart putter. "You've been asleep for nearly two days. My magic is rather relaxed now."

· I looked at him. Something was missing from his words, but I couldn't seem to pin-point it. "Well, if you need me out of bed, you need to help me get rid of these wings."

Setizar misted from the doorway and reappeared beside me. "Those beautiful, white and majestic pieces of membrane?"

I sliced him a cutting glance.

"Fine. We will find out how to remove them—for *your* comfort." He sighed dramatically, and I had the feeling that he didn't want the wings to go away.

I nodded, and he brushed his hand over the large plane of skin on the right wing. It felt the same as if he were gently stroking my shoulder.

"Look," he said into my ear. His breath was warm against my skin, and I fought the urge to melt into him. Instead, I turned my attention to what he was looking at. There, on the wide plane of my wings, was a handprint, glowing and tinged with red stardust. Setizar's handprint. "Humor me?" He continued to brush his palm along the wing, and everywhere he touched, the wings changed into an image of a sunset-limned cloud. Mist shuddered over the tips, swirling into the air. The wing twitched. "Want me to do the same to the left wing?"

I nodded. I wanted to feel this same lightness in both wings.

"The furie were a race of warriors," he began, gently caressing the remaining planes of flesh-colored wing left. "They were dedicated to vengeance and retribution. They punished men for their crimes against the natural order by taking the stolen magic away. Warriors from birth. Angry, jealous, and endless in their destruction if the situation demanded. No one wanted to mess with furies. That is, until the Silver Queen wrought darkness and shadows. As the last furie fell, and her blood spilled on the earth, the Veil was created, sealing away the furie realm from our own."

"Who was the last furie?"

He paused, his thumb gently caressing the wing bone. There was something longing in his silence, something deeply wounded and haunted. His eyes dimmed, slicing through the warmth with frigid want. Finally, he said, "Alecto. She was the last."

My heart lodged in my throat.

Setizar brushed his finger against the curving bone at the tip of the wing. "When magic is severed from another realm, illness spreads to those who once possessed it, and magic dwindles from us. This is why we must reconnect the worlds. A heart cannot beat without a body, neither can a body live without its heart. Inder is Yamira's body, and Yamira is Inder's heart."

"This seems to be more complicated than just seeking this fabled Box and giving it to you."

Setizar smiled and gently smoothed the wrinkle between my brows with his thumb. "There's always more than one layer to every story." He stood and looked at the wings. "Looks like we're done. How do they feel?"

"As light as an afternoon sky."

"Good." He rubbed his palms together. "We have work to do. Try to tuck them in, we need to take this outside."

21

The woods outside were something out of a picture book. The willow trees covered the lush grass, their limbs dancing in the breeze, and leaves sang like luminous green gems in a wind chime. It was dark until we stepped into the center of the clearing. Vines covered with glowing, magical flowers opened at Setizar's presence; the entire wood sprang to life. The small, bubbling waterfall off to the right erupted in blue light, as bright as the noonday sky. Even the leaves of the trees appeared as lit lanterns of green light.

A breath escaped my lips. "It's so...beautiful."

Setizar chuckled. "I think the forest likes you."

"What?"

"It opened." He gestured to the world around. "This is a glimpse of your power—a visual hint at the beauty within you."

"I thought..." Something swelled in my breast as nature glowed around us. "I won't complain."

Setizar turned, looking at the two new limbs protruding from my back. "I can attempt to help you learn to fly, if you'd like?"

I nodded. "What should I do first?"

"Try to open and close them. Strengthen the muscles."

I complied, beginning the exercise. "So," I asked, already slightly strained from moving my new limbs. "If all the furies died—"

"I know where this is going," he said. "You're wondering who your parents are."

I nodded again.

"I can't say." He angled his head away, averting his gaze. "But perhaps you will find out soon."

I couldn't quite pinpoint it, but somehow I knew Setizar wasn't telling me everything. "You're leaving something out," I managed. "What aren't you telling me? Why am I just now finding out what I am, after all this time?

"Time is often a messed up creature, Meris." Setizar crossed his arms. "Not everything needs to line up."

"For this it does."

"Why are you so suspicious?"

"I didn't say I was." I stopped moving my wings, and the tips dragged across the soft grass. "I'm saying things aren't making much sense to me, and I have a feeling you know why."

"Suspicious." He smiled, lifting a finger in the air. "Remember, Meris, nothing is as it seems here in Yamira. Trust nothing, not even yourself."

His words mirrored what the women in my dream had said. I couldn't help but feel ill at ease with the strange similarity between their words. "Can I trust you?"

"What do you think?" A smile, strewn of mystery and the unknown, played on his lips. Something unsettled me... something he knew. Why didn't he just tell me?

Confusion washed over me in waves. Where did the knot begin and end? "Alright, what do we do now?"

He rolled his neck. "We try and figure out how you can retract the wings. The furies have the ability to fold their wings back into their body using magic. You'll have issues keeping the wings in at first, but after a while it'll be natural."

I groaned, trying to recenter my thoughts on my wings and not the empty hollow in my chest. "So they may just pop out at times that I don't want them to?"

"Here." He grabbed my hand, running a finger down the bracelet on my wrist. The metal vibrated, shifting into crystal. For half a second it stopped, then it moved again and changed color, from clear to ruby. "It will help, I promise. You'll be able to focus better with this on your arm."

I closed my eyes, willing the limbs into my body. My back ached, threatening to derail me by the pain. But I kept thinking, willing, *hoping* the wings away.

Visions of strange colors flashed before my eyes, beings with similar wings wreathed in starlight and sunshine. Some were frozen in time, moving as slow as liquid amber. Their wings were as clear as glass, trapping thousands of tiny suns within, while others were masked in twilight and fire.

A woman clothed in black with a smile like blood replaced the images; blurred… but her grin lingered like a festering wound.

"Good." Setizar's voice cut through my vision, yanking me back

I opened my eyes. "Are they—gone?"

Setizar nodded. "This is just the beginning, Meris. You need to learn much more than you think. Come, we'll begin with your combat training. You're a furie, so this won't take very long. You're born to fight and wield a weapon. You are a weapon, Meris. Let's go and sharpen you."

A weapon. Was that what he was after? A honed warrior to do his bidding?

I shook the thought away, letting it roll to the ground. There was no hesitation. No thought. Nothing holding me back. I nodded and we faced each other.

"You need to know one thing before we start." He pulled that starstrung sword from the abyss beside him. "I'm not an easy opponent. I don't teach simple. I will hurt you if you don't learn, just remember that." He smiled. "But, you must return the favor. Don't hold back, go for the kill."

"*What?*"

He threw a sword my way, and somehow, I caught it. "Neither of us will die if we use these weapons, it will just hurt more than fire from the underworld."

I laughed. "I don't know how I feel about this."

"You'll learn quickly."

He began teaching me basic defense methods: the proper way to hold the sword, the best places to strike, and how to find where my opponent would be most vulnerable.

After the basics, I told him I was ready.

Perhaps I was a bit overzealous.

He swung his sword, and I barely managed to block him. He struck again, switching the sword in his hand and sliding the weapon along my side.

I hissed in pain, but—no blood.

I spun and blocked, and he smiled.

I didn't register him moving and clipping my foot with his blade. I yelled and struck him with all my might. Useless. Utterly useless. He'd blocked me without even a half thought. Just... reflex. I groaned and thrust again, cleaving the tranquil forest atmosphere with my chaotic weapon. He didn't even blink before he blocked me again.

"Remember," he said, brows pinched tightly. "You're a furie, Meris. A weapon. A creature crafted for warfare and destruction."

I groaned. "How will *that* fact help me?"

He stepped closer, placing his blade under my chin. The cold metal bit into my skin, freezing my jaw with its cold point. "Trust your instincts and don't think too hard. I saw what you did to those wolves back in the cabin. I want that rage, that fire. You need to release it."

I hissed. "That was an accident."

"It was *innate*."

"How?"

"You were born a warrior, Meris." Setizar lowered his weapon, stepping closer. So close I could smell the hint of autumn mist on his shirt.

"You're more powerful than you think, more of a threat than you can even comprehend. Trust your instincts. That warrior within you is rearing and ready for battle, don't hold her back."

I popped my neck, meeting his gaze. Sapphires dipped in amber. How could one fall into his eyes and see an amethyst night one moment, then a gleaming sunrise the next? "So," I said, fiddling with the weapon in my grasp. "Don't think, but I also need to think?" I raised my brow. "Sounds like a contradiction."

"Stop talking and fight. Let's see if it's a contradiction."

I lunged at him, and before he could block, I used my feet. My wings open, holding me in the air while my heel connected with his chest.

He stumbled to the forest floor, though he deftly blocked my second attack.

His sword found its mark in my heart, and I screamed. The pain lasted but a fleeting moment, before it was replaced with kindling rage.

"Again, Meris."

I ground my teeth as blood roared in my ears.

We did the same dance, the same routine, again and again and *again*.

Finally, I managed to knock him to the ground, his sword clattering inches from his hand. I lunged forward, my red-kissed wings spreading like a harbinger of death. My sword pressed against his throat. "Like that?" My voice shifted into something altogether unfamiliar, strange and foreign. Something filled with confidence.

He smiled, labored breath mingling with my own. "Yes." He lifted his neck a bit, allowing the blade to bite into his skin. "So, what do you do when you get someone in this position?"

I paused.

"You should probably slit my throat."

"But—" I blinked. My heart stuttered a beat. "I can't."

Pain erupted in my side, and turned to see Setizar's sword buried in my stomach. He removed the weapon, and again there was no blood or wound. "Hesitation will get you killed, Meris. Don't hesitate. It doesn't matter who your opponent is. If they try to kill you, you need to be faster. You need to kill them first. Their life is all that matters to them, and your life should only matter to you. The winner is the one who lives."

I nodded, but somehow, I couldn't bring myself to accept what he'd said.

— (—

I fell into bed, my back a series of tight, pinched knots. I looked out the small, round window off to the side. Barguet—the crone—was in the other room cooking. The faint scent of curry and eastern spices were divine, and after the training I'd done with Setizar that afternoon, I was starved... and tired. Mostly tired. I wasn't sure if I could conjure the energy to go and eat. Was there a type of magic I could use to make the food just appear in my stomach?

That would be nice.

I groaned and rolled over, forgetting my wings were still out. It took too much thought to keep them tucked away and inside my body. Maybe one day I would be able to control them without much thought like Setizar said, but somehow I knew it wouldn't be for a while. I took another deep breath, smiling at myself. I'd practically beat Setizar today, so I'd count that as a victory.

The swords, despite not leaving any injury, felt just as bad as I'd assumed real ones would. I didn't want to meet my end with that amount of pain flooding my body, and it was a pretty good incentive to not do anything foolish that would get me killed.

Well, good incentive not to get stabbed, at least.

22

The wind from the morning rolled in and fluttered through the window, banishing the shadows into something less familiar. Something darker and unusual.

"Meris," Setizar said, his face obscured from view in the darkness of the corridor. "We need to hurry and return to my palace. We still have some time before Cerie sends out a search party looking for us."

I laughed, willing my legs from the bed as Setizar grabbed a cape and pulled the dark purple garment over his shoulders. With a fluid motion, he slipped the hood over his head, looking far more like a rogue than the pristine lord from a few days ago.

"You better hide those wings."

It wasn't like I hadn't tried already. Still, I chewed my lip and concentrated as hard as I could. Energy slipped from my body, and pain erupted in my back. In a heartbeat, I felt so much lighter, though the pain in my head increased. "So, what do we do now?"

"We keep our heads down. The fastest way is through the Forest of Memory. Here." He held out a red cloak. "You might want to put this on."

I paused, and our spar resurfaced, bubbling to the surface with questions. "If it came down to me and you," I said. "If what we wanted—or needed—conflicted? Would you fight me?"

"Why are you asking this?"

"I am saying that, if I stood between you and what you wanted most, would you kill me?"

His eyes settled into mine before he released a heavy sigh. "No."

"Why?"

"Because." He leaned closer, his fingers lifting my chin. His eyes were like the magenta nightfall kissed by the still-lingering pink of sunset. "Because what I want—" He stopped. "Because what I want died seventeen years ago. I'm only doing what I must so the worlds we know don't fade from existence."

My heart stumbled. Head buzzed as if a thousand bees attempted to get into my ears. "Setizar."

He tilted his head, pointing to the door. "Come along, Meris. We only have so much time before we're home."

— ☾ —

After what seemed an eternity of walking, we stood in the middle of a flowing meadow. The hills rose like fresh baked bread, covered over in bright green grass peppered with amber-leafed trees. I breathed in, and the air had a faint scent of salt and sea. "Where are we?"

"Near the border of Autumn and Summer. There's an ocean that way." Setizar exhaled, turning to get a better look of the surrounding area.

"Is it a big ocean?"

"Large. Endless, even. Aurel keeps track of what goes on there, though, making sure his little minions don't get too rambunctious."

I leaned forward, taking in another deep breath. "I'd like to see it one day."

"Maybe you will. But it's a dangerous place."

"Really?"

"Pirates. Mermaids. The Reaper, too. They tend to keep to the Summer realm."

"Pirates. In Yamira?"

"You'd be surprised how vast Yamira truly is, Meris. Now, enough fantasizing about Aurel's drab domain, let's find our home. We shouldn't be too far away now. The only issue will be not getting distracted."

"Wait!" I grabbed his coat sleeve. I needed to know one thing before we continued. "About what you said earlier—"

"I said a lot of things, to which thing do you refer?"

I growled. "You know what thing, Setizar."

He closed the gap I didn't know had formed between us. "It means what it means. I won't ever lay a finger on you, Meris."

"That's not what I'm talking about. And even if it was, you *stabbed* me with a sword."

"An enchanted sword that wouldn't truly hurt you. I want you prepared for whatever will come your way. You don't think it hurt me to inflict that pain?"

"You seemed to enjoy it."

"I didn't." He groaned, running a hand through his hair. "I don't want to see you in pain. But that temporary pain that I had to inflict... I know it'll do you good."

I huffed. "Then, what did you mean when you said—"

"Meris." There was no hesitation. "Alecto is dead, and nothing I do would bring her back. The furie I knew is gone."

He paused, frozen in the warm summer air surrounding us. I met his gaze, now as blue as the sky with a tinge of green swirling in their depths. His eyes were like this world... ever changing their hue, making him as unpredictable as anything. I hated this feeling... this ache in my chest. "Glad we got that cleared up."

He smiled, yet somehow it looked lonely. *Sad.*

I couldn't allow myself to care, though deep inside, I did.

— ℂ —

We stopped under an apple tree, plucking the fruits and devouring the sweet flesh. "I've not had an apple since I was seven!" I tore into the red fruit again.

"They're better in Yamira. The air is pure and magic fuels the tree. You're tasting magic."

I laid my tired body on the grass, and just as my back hit the ground, my wings tore through my shirt, flopping out on either side of me and smacking Setizar in the face.

I laughed.

"You're a menace," he said, clicking his tongue.

"Thank you, I try."

Setizar threw the core at me, and I watched as it landed pitifully far from his intended target.

"You have a horrible aim. Should I really be taking lessons from you?"

Setizar barked a laugh, scratching his neck. I had so many questions to ask him, things I'd been wondering. But, somehow it didn't feel like the right time. He looked calm, happy here in the meadow.

I sat up, hugging my knees. My forearm scraped against the buckle of my calf-high boots. "How much longer until we get back to the palace?"

Setizar smiled, his thumb trailing the bone of my wing. He seemed fascinated by them. Honestly, I supposed I was, too. Once I became used to seeing them, I liked them a lot more. "Not much longer. You'll be sipping raspberry tea and eating more than apples and stew before nightfall."

23

The late afternoon sun drifted low beyond the red mountains, obscuring our path with shadows. Vines weaved through the crimson-leafed sourwood trees, their flowers illuminating the branches like small orange stars.

My ankles hurt, and my back burned from the strain of my still-open wings.

"I'm warning you, Meris." Setizar looked at me sideways, still adamant about the topic that had commenced a half-hour ago. "Your wings will start sprouting feathers."

"And I doubt it." I raised a brow.

"All furies have feathered wings."

"What if I'm different?"

"You'll believe me when you wake up to feathers on your bed." Setizar chuckled, running a thumb over my left wing. "It's been so long."

"What?"

He folded his arms, taking a step away from me. "Been so long since I've seen furie wings."

When did my heart start beating like a broken windup toy? It hurt. It ached. "Alright."

Setizar's eyes burned into mine like fire, as if he wanted to say something to me and wouldn't. I wanted to ask him, but somehow the words caught in my throat.

The gates to the Crimson Plane were in view, rising over the tree line. The iron-wrought bars were sealed tight, clamped together by golden clasps. But once we neared, the gates swung open on their own. The echo of autumn chimes winnowed in the air like sparks from a magic spell.

"Meris." Setizar smiled. "I'd like to do something."

"What's that?"

He took a sweeping bow, snatching my hand in his. "I'd like to throw a ball in your honor. Your birthday approaches soon, does it not?"

I blinked. Had I told him my birthday was soon? "Yes… it does."

"What day?"

"Next week, on the longest day of the year."

He clapped his hands together. "Perfect."

My heart somersaulted, stumbling to a stop. "Why would you throw a ball in my honor? It doesn't make sense."

The garden wound and twisted, meandering under red-spotted archways and rose-encased paths. "Because, without you, none of what we're trying to do would be possible."

— ☾ —

Starlight dripped through my window like raindrops against glass. Blues and reds flooded my vision, splitting the room into a mingle of ice and fire. I flipped on my side, wings stretching oddly. I needed to remember why I was here and not let myself get pulled into the magic.

I sat up, kneading my temples. Somehow, between the current of travel and change, I'd become confused. I didn't know what was real or how to feel anymore. Was this even real? What if I'd fallen into a hole on my way to Yeodo and I was dying? Perhaps I hit my head and all of this was a hallucination.

I pinched my arm.

Pain.

Well, that certainly felt real. But then again, so did the sword.

Moonbeams spread light into my room, washing the red blankets with soft light, turning them a shade of maroon. My floor embraced the shadows; corners vanishing with the darkness.

I slipped out of bed, wings dragging across the floor as starlight twined against the edges of my new appendages. Why couldn't I be normal? Why couldn't I have had a normal childhood? Couldn't I go back to summertime, sitting by the cold water and eating candied lemons?

I froze.

Wait? When did that happen? When did Julna and I sit by the riverside and eat sugared lemons? As far as I remembered, there wasn't a river where we lived.

But there *had* been in that memory. When I was in the water, I'd remember that. And I knew for certain that I was with my sister.

I needed to get her back. It was still my goal. Save Mae, get my sister back, and finally live a normal life.

Reaching into my armoire, I pulled out a shirt. All my shirts had been open backed for the most part, though this one was a bit more scandalous, with only a tie around the neck and waist to keep the garment together.

After I'd finished tying the shirt, I opened my door. Moving through the hall where the small stars followed my footsteps, I made my way to the east wing. It was time I paid Tatum a visit.

— ☾ —

The arches heading to the room sent shivers up and down my bare back. That familiar feeling of someone standing there, reaching a hand around my waist and gripping tight, rekindled.

Was I really going to meet with Tatum?

I shook my head. I needed answers… answers which no one had been willing to tell me. And likely wouldn't.

I stepped into the room, and I swallowed the mounting fear trembling in my throat.. "Hello?"

A tapping sounded next to me in the mirror. *Tatum*.

Tatum smiled, his face nothing more than shadow, but his eyes glowed amber. "Meris. Finally come to make a deal?"

"Depends." I picked at my shirt, trying to keep calm. "Can you give me answers?"

"Of course."

"I don't want cookie cutter fortunes, Tatum. I need actual results. You know, that I can trust?"

"Fine." He leaned against the mirror, looking into the distance. "Let's start with things you don't know."

"Which are?"

Tatum picked at his nails casually. "Honestly, it's rather stuffy out there, don't you think? Why don't you come join me and we can talk over tea?"

The mirror swung open, and he stood there. Nothing changed aside from the fact that I could see the contours of his face. "I don't know."

"I swear, you will be able to leave whenever you wish." He dipped his head. "This is merely for comfort."

I gritted my teeth and stepped one foot into his home beyond the mirror. It was eerily similar to the room I was just standing in, except warm, cozy, and fully furnished. Tatum's hand wrapped around my arm, but it was a ghost of a touch. I barely even felt him guiding me forward. "I see you've been able to summon your wings. What else have you learned?"

"Not much." I kept an eye on him. "This just happened."

"Of course it did. You've been reunited with magic for the first time in many, many years." Tatum sat on a paisley armchair, twirling his finger along the design. "So, nothing happened? Nothing out of the ordinary aside from your powers?"

"Why are you asking?" I took a seat across from him. "Should something else have happened?"

Tatum slipped a watch from his pocket, flipping the face and checking the time. "I'm only asking the prudent questions before I go on." He braced an elbow on the armrest, propping his chin on his fingers. "Well, let's start with the basics. What is it you want to know?"

There were so many things I wanted to know. "Why am I here? Why am I seeing things, remembering and dreaming things I never saw before?"

"That's a complicated question." He straightened his slouched posture. "Listen—"

I stood, my veins igniting red. "It's the only thing I want to know. Why am I here?"

Tatum's nails dig into his chair. "Fine. What a pathetic thing to waste your wish on." He waved his hand, the mirror changing from door to an image. "Before I tell you what it is you wish to know, you must know the price you have to pay for this."

I nodded.

"I'm trapped in this small space, have been for many, many years. I wish to see the world. You're going to offer your services."

"Fine. That's fine."

"Don't you wish to know how you're doing that?"

"Sounds pretty cut and dry. Now tell me what I want to know."

He flashed his teeth. "Demanding." He kicked his feet up on the ottoman, looking me up and down lazily. "You're here for the purpose of reuniting magic to this world. And what you're seeing are images of your past. The life you once lived here in Yamira. Typically, furies have an ornament—usually a small piece of jewelry—with them to help them remember everything when they're reborn, but you don't have that." He slid poppy-colored eyes to me, brow furrowing. "I'll throw another wish in there, because that one was silly."

My pulse thickened. What do I want to know? What one thing do I want more than anything in this world? A smile and a chiming laugh pounded into my mind. "Where's my sister?"

He angled his head.

"Julna, I want to know where *Julna* is."

A grin spread over his features. What could that smile mean? "*Julna.* Well, that is an interesting name for her. She lives in Yeodo. You need only mention her name and you will be able to find her. The next full moon the door to the human realm will be ready to open and you will be able to walk through. Beware," Tatum lifted one finger in the air "seek not your sister, but the Box. Return only with the Box, and leave Julna there. Your return must happen within two days of exiting the gateway, otherwise it will close and you'll be trapped in the human world with no way to return."

"What happens if I don't return to Yamira?"

"Then you'll have a very important question left unanswered." Tatum grinned. A darkness tinged with pain fluttered over his smile.

"Which is what?"

Tatum stood, his fingers brushing against the mirror. "Who I was to who you once were."

24

"M eris."

Head pounding, I sat up, squinting my eyes to try and find the source of the rummaging. Setizar stood by the shelf, thumbing through the books. "What are you doing?"

"It's nearly the afternoon." He pulled out a book, flipping through its pages. "Has Cerie not come to wake you?"

"What's going on?"

"Unless you want to be eaten by an ogarak in, oh, twenty minutes, you must prepare yourself. I have to go to Redrim, and you need to blend into the staff."

That word… it… I couldn't pinpoint it. It sounded familiar. "Where is Redrim? Didn't we just arrive?"

"We did." Setizar crossed the room and pointed to a page in the book he pulled from the shelf. "But the time has come to give Inanna an offering. Hurry and recite this, would you?"

I looked down at the jumbled words, ciphered into a breathing alphabet.Suddenly, they shifted, becoming something legible. A spell? "Why do I have to recite this?"

"It'll suppress your powers. We can't have Inanna figuring out you're a furie. So, please… do this?" He pressed his palm against my cheek, as if… was he anxious?

I nodded and began to read.

"Bear the magic with the wings—
Conceal within me those things
Of magic with glint and glow,
Below the shadow of my skin
May they hide there within,
Hide my wings, hide my power
Hide my magic within my body's bower
Keep unseen that which is borne
Till I should wish them return."

My back burned, piercing my skin like thousands of needles and shooting into my bloodstream. Fire, as hot as magma, burned in my stomach with a vengeance. Then it puttered out, as though ice-water had been thrown on smoldering flames.

And just like that, my back lightened and my body felt weaker. "Is it done?"

"Yes." Setizar looked me in the eyes before weaving his fingers through my hair in slow, deliberate movements. "You need to not move, alright?"

I couldn't move. Instead, I was frozen between shock and my rabid heartbeat. Magic swept over me, grazing my head and neck in soft, soothing strokes. "What are you doing?"

"Putting a veneer over your hair. I can't have Inanna asking any questions in case she sees you somehow."

"What are you even—"

"I don't have much time to explain. Just remain quiet, don't draw attention to yourself, and don't ask any questions."

He pulled on my hand, handing me the loose-sleeved outfit I'd worn when I'd first arrived, though this time black as midnight. As soon as the fabric was placed in my hand, he misted from the room.

I supposed I needed to put it on, and I didn't have much time.

— ☾ —

Setizar reappeared five minutes later, his entire appearance altered. He was no longer clothed in that strange cloak, but a fitted black suit with sapphires adorning the tips of the lapels. His shirt was buttoned—mostly. He left the three top buttons undone, perhaps from lack of time or just his style choice. It really made him look different. Not like the half-crazed jinni who kept himself tucked in the library, but a ruler. Someone who would cut you down with a simple look should you disobey.

Despite the extravagance, however, he looked exhausted. His eyes were a muted magenta, staring into mine. "This will be interesting." With a sweeping bow, he extended his hand. "Meris, your hair looks stunning, though I do prefer the red."

I frowned. "Why'd you make me a blond?"

His eyes lit slightly. "Curiosity."

I placed my hand in his—magic coursing over my fingers as they grazed against his skin. "You like blonds, I suppose?"

"I've always liked the way their hair looks." He grinned. "Though Aurel ruined blonds for me forever."

I couldn't fight my smile.

"Now, try and blend in. Look natural. If you can, stay in this room. Don't leave. Don't trail after me. We need to be careful."

"What—"

He turned and left the room.

I clenched my jaw, following him down the hall. "Setizar!"

"Meris, get back in the room."

"Not until you tell me what's going on." I crossed my arms, narrowing my eyes. "If you think I'm—"

A thundering hiss filled the air, and a dark abyss opened in front of us. A woman flanked by two creatures.

Ogarak.

The word filled my mind with a reverberating echo, clicking into place without hindrance.

Setizar took a few steps backward, turning his back to me to face the creatures. His fingers found my arm, and he pushed me behind him.

"Setizar—" I choked on my words, tightening my grip on his hand. He squeezed back, gently, as if reassuring me everything would be alright.

"Setizar," the woman said. Her eyes were hidden below a black veil, only showing the snowy skin from the nose down and her blood-red lips. "Who's this?"

"This is Meris." Setizar lifted his chin.

I couldn't place it. Something seemed off...

"Where's Cerie?" The woman looked around. "Aren't you bringing her?"

"You have a habit of hurting her," Setizar said through clenched teeth. "I need her here."

The woman's mouth dropped into a frown. "Pity. I love playing with her." She angled her head in my direction, as if looking me over. "Who's this?"

"A new servant," he said, his voice dropping again into a feral growl.

"Just a servant?" She smiled. "Then you have no objection to her coming along. Since she's just a servant."

My heart was pounding hard against my bones, churning my stomach. The two ogarak flanking the woman were armed to the teeth. Armor coated nearly every inch of their horrible, scaly bodies, leaving only their massive wings unprotected.

"Well, then. We shall be off to Redrim. It's time for the season to change. Summer has fallen in the human realm, so you and the other lords will be my guest for a few days." She looked at me with a danger-coated smile. "I suppose your pet here will get to see what it looks like when a Season lord has to turn the hands of time."

"Meris stays."

The woman grinned, a slash of white teeth framed by red. "*Meris comes, or else you will find her suffering far worse than a day or two in Redrim."

Setizar's body stiffened, and I knew then that her threat wasn't to be taken lightly. And with that, we stepped through her portal of night and darkness.

25

Shadows swirled around me. My head throbbed with ache—as though I'd spun a hundred times in a circle. I nearly fell, but Setizar's arm wrapped around my waist, keeping me on my feet. Darkness and oblivion became tangible, something glazed in red.

My vision cleared, and a palace of maroon tile greeted me like a valley of blood-drenched marble. The red moon shone pale light onto my frigid fingers through the atrium, coating my skin in a dangerous poppy hue.

A metallic smell filled the air like rust and copper.

"Welcome to Redrim, pet." The woman stepped near me, a staff made up of tiny bones in her hand. "I'm Inanna, the *goddess* of this realm."

Setizar's eyes were on me, I knew it. I could feel them burning into the back of my head. Yet, I... I didn't want to show this woman any form of respect. Something in my very soul said not to bow.

No bowing.

No reverence.

"Is your pet broken?" Inanna looked at Setizar. "Why doesn't she bow?"

"Meris..."

Inanna pressed her staff under my jaw, making it hard to breathe. "Bow, creature, or you will break."

"Meris," Setizar lowered his tone. "You really should bow."

I looked her in the face. There was nothing. No eyes to look into.

Nothing laying beyond that venomous smile.

Slowly, I dropped into a curtsy, but dared not look away from her.

"How interesting." Innana looked from me to Setizar. "Should I punish her for taking so long?"

"No!" Setizar moved, his body now in front of me. "Whatever it is you plan, take it out on me…not her."

Her posture stiffened as she took a step closer to him, her fingers wrapping around his jaw. That mere gesture sent orange flames coursing through my body. "Well, in that case," a knife appeared in her hand "alright."

She thrust it into his side. Blood speared from the wound. The slithering sound of the blade cutting through flesh, the drip of gore on the ground…

"No!" Hairs rose on my neck.

Inanna smiled at me, her grin dark. "This is what happens when you hesitate, pet. Next time do as you are told, or fate will be far more cruel."

I pressed my hand against his wound as blood poured from the gash. My heart beat fast… too fast. I needed to help him. How could I help him?

He hadn't made a sound. Not a single sound.

My head was in a haze. "Setizar?"

He looked at me, his eyes a burning shade of sunset. A kaleidoscope of shattered, vibrating hues. "I'll be fine."

Inanna chuckled. "You will be staying in one room. I'm sure you won't protest, since you obviously get along so well."

My stomach was ready to lose strength. Whatever meal I ate last clawed its way up my throat, ready to vault onto the red floors.

"Guards, escort these two to their room. Tomorrow Setizar must be well enough to perform his part of the ritual."

Claws dug into my skin, lifting me off Setizar and yanking us apart. "No!" I pulled against the hands which had me captured. "Let us go!"

"Rest well. You will need the night to recover from your injuries."

I couldn't move against claws wrapped around my waist.

Trapped.

The halls were a blur as we were hauled down the corridors. My eyes couldn't take it all in.

"Meris..." Setizar's voice was something between a scream and a whisper. A fine line of misery and pain. "Stay calm."

I yanked against their hold, fighting as they dragged me up a set of black marble stairs. The icy temperature of the place contrasted to the fiery color of the world around in cruel irony.

The guards threw us into a room, their teeth gnashing as the door slammed behind us.

"Setizar." I stumbled to his side. Blood still slithered from his wound, dripping onto the ground. "What do I do?"

"Help me up?" he ground out, his teeth clenched so tight I imagined the pain in his jaw was overwhelming. "I need you to help me take off the jacket... and the shirt. Aether, this was my favorite suit."

I nodded, lifting him onto his feet and guiding him to an ottoman. "Sit here." He did so with no hesitation. I gently took off his jacket, then unbuttoned his blood-stained shirt. "What do I do next?"

He winced. "Water and a cloth."

I ran into the adjoining lavatory, rummaging through the cabinets before finally finding a cloth. Quickly, I poured water over it and ran back to him. "What next?"

"You need to pour magic into it, Meris," he whispered, his eyes no longer vibrant but dull. Almost gray.

"Stay..." My eyes burned. Tears? Why was I crying? Why was I so worried about him? "Stay with me." Using the cloth, I pressed my palm flat against the wound. "I don't know how to heal."

"Most furies can't do it on their own. But I believe you can heal it. Just think about the wound. Think about it closing—" Setizar groaned, growing limp. "You need to hurry. It's eating up my magic."

"I'm trying!"

Close.

Close.

Close! Please close!

Heat poured from my hand, stitching the wound. White and red light laced my fingertips. It was working!

Setizar's face was ashen, but his eyes had begun to pull light back into their star-strung irises. Shadows and darkness weaved over the blood—the wound vanished.

"Thank you, Meris," Setizar whispered, voice hoarse and grating. "I may need to lay down for a bit."

I grabbed his arm, helping him onto the bed. I understood that 'sore' feeling after using magic. A muscle deep in my soul was exhausted, burning from the strain I'd put on it. The red moon poured an eerie orange light into the room, casting shadows along the contours of his face. Why did he say I was a weapon? Every inch of him was sharp and angled—much more of a weapon look than I was.

He fell quiet.

Every second ticked by like an hour.

Every minute passed was an eternity.

His eyes were so full of worry, that sunset I'd seen when we'd first met replaced by a blazing palette of angry hues. It burned even brighter when he looked at me, so full of this emotion.

I swore I would never forgive Inanna for what she did.

— ☾ —

I wanted to scream. This dream had come back. Darkness swirled around my waist, my legs, my wrists. The darkness, so hollow and cold, bit into my skin like iron and ice. They were hands.

"Meris!" Setizar yelled. Something about his voice was an echo... a muffled noise.

The hands grabbed my shoulders, then violently tugged.

You're being dramatic. Chester's voice cut through the shadows, stripping away my pride. My humanity. *You don't need this.*

A scream finally escaped my lips, and I sat up.

I blinked. The moonlight flooded in, and I breathed. I breathed and breathed, trying to shake the memory. I sucked in the cold air. My heart beat in my chest. Every suppressed memory rushing back like a tidal wave.

He's taken it. He'd taken my ring...my tether. The very thing I needed to remember who I was in this world. And he still had it.

Setizar's eyes locked with mine. "Are you afraid?"

Tears stung my eyes. "Yes."

"Meris..." His brows knit upward as he took a step back. "What happened?"

I shook my head. I couldn't let him know what was behind that door in my heart. No one had seen what was behind that door.

You don't need this, Meris. Again, Chester's voice echoed in my mind. Panic. The walls closed in. All the doors were locked. The darkness swelled. My knees weakened...

I nearly vomited onto the floor.

"Meris," Setizar hummed. "Listen."

I barely saw him kneeling before me.

"Meris. Take my hand." He held his hand to me, his purple eyes melting into worried blue. "What's wrong?"

My tears choked me. My throat tightened. A shrieking hum sounded in my ears. Every aching thump of my heart ground against my ribs. "I'm not... you shouldn't be concerned about me. You were just stabbed."

His eyes flickered a shade darker, twisting with something indescribable. "Don't say that. Don't ever say that, Meris."

"But it's true—"

"No." He squeezed my hand, his words tinged with surety. "Don't you dare think you're not worth something. The Stars created you for a reason, and you're destined for more than you realize."

A pained swelling grew in my throat as I nodded. If he knew, he might change his mind.

"Good." He released an audible exhale. "May I?" he asked. I didn't know what he's asking, but I nodded.

His arms wrapped around me. He was warm, comforting. Tears began to fall from my eyes. I cried. I couldn't help it anymore. The pain tore through me.

Setizar kept a light hold on me, so gentle I could almost break. "Show me your past, Meris," he whispered in my ear. "And I will break its bones so it can never hurt you again."

I wrapped my arms tighter around him. Every ill feeling I had toward him melted away, finally thawed.

"What happened, Meris?" Setizar smoothed my hair from my face.

"He's taken it."

He pulled away slightly. I must have woken him. He was completely disheveled; his shirt was only half buttoned, and his hair was a frazzled mess.

"This boy from Inder," I wriggled from his grasp and laid back down. "He took my ring. I…Something inside me broke when he stole it." I'd never known just how much it meant until I no longer had it. Until it was stolen. "It's his now, and that? That makes me so…"

"Angry." He moved away.

"It wasn't his to take."

"No, it wasn't." Setizar exhaled. "But it is still yours, Meris. A thief does not own that which he stole."

I squeezed my eyes shut. "How do you do it?"

He took up a spot on the bed, near enough to allow me to know he was there, but far enough to give me space. "When the Silver Queen stole part of our powers, I felt useless," he said, weaving his fingers together and resting them on his chest. "Weak."

Weak. I knew that feeling all too well. "You'll get it back… you'll get it all back. I promise."

He twirled a strand of my hair between his fingertips, and the blonde hue shifted slightly to red. "Yet, there are some things I may never get back."

I poked him, trying to get us both out of this dismal conversation. "You're almost charming, you know. When you're not being depressing."

"Almost? Are you implying I'm not?"

"Oh, I'm more than implying."

His chuckle warmed my bones. "If I were charming and pleasant, I'd have much more than just you to deal with."

"And I'm already a handful."

"I need four arms with how much trouble you get into." He closed his eyes, much to my disappointment. I wanted to stare into his eyes a moment longer. I wanted to see the sunset which glimmered there one more time before I fell asleep.

I bit my lip. "Mind... If I ask you something?"

"Why—"

"Because I'm curious."

"Meris, why would I *mind*?" His smile was a glimmering dazzle of magic.

"Am I safe with you? Am I truly safe?"

Setizar's smile wavered. "I swear I won't do anything to you, Meris. And as long as you're with me, no harm will befall you."

I believed him, after what he did for me today—the wound he took for me. I nestled deeper into the bed, and a rush of emotion swept over me. Safety. Was that what this is? I felt... *safe*.

I almost cried.

I'd not felt safe in so long. "So," I said, exhaling. "What deal did you make with the hag?"

"So nosy..."

"Please?"

There was silence, and I'd begun to think he wouldn't answer me. "I offered her some of my youth."

"What?"

He lifted a brow. "That night, I allowed the Grimhildr to take some of my youth in exchange for you being safe. When you saw me the next time, I had a veneer. Horror of all horrors if you saw me with graying hair and wrinkles on my face."

I almost laughed. "You don't have a veneer on now, right?"

"No, I recovered swiftly, but I suffered a drain. That's why I couldn't mist us very far when the carriage toppled." A pause. "I'm losing my magic, Meris. We all are."

A pang of guilt shot through me. "I'm sorry… all that was my fault."

His fingers combed through my hair. "I'd do it again if you needed."

"Why?" I leaned on my elbow. "Why would you do this for me? I'm nothing but a girl who fell through the world's cracks."

His smile was as bright as a morning star, hiding something there between his words and his eyes. "Because you're worth it."

26

A meadow surrounded me, weaving a path through time and space toward a grassy terrain.

Stars dropped from the sky, hovering around me, shattering their pale blue light along the earth. "Where am I?"

The stars sang in reply to my question. The meadow lengthened, expanding toward a lake as placid as a mirror. It was delicate, as though I'd disturb the tranquility of the world around me if I were to touch the surface.

"Dear, dear Meris. Don't look so shocked." Tatum stood in the middle of the still water, his hands tucked into his pockets. His smile unnerved me. What did I do? "You and I used to be quite good friends."

"What are you saying?"

"How do you think I'm speaking to you right now?" He snapped his fingers, appearing beside me. Did he... mist? "I'm in your *head*, you know."

"No."

"Oh, yes." He looked toward the star-lit horizon. "No matter where you go. I wanted to explain it to you, but you didn't give me the chance. Don't say I didn't try to warn you."

Stars shivered, then flickered out one by one.

Sweat dripped down my back, slicking my hair to my head. Was that a dream? Setizar was sound asleep beside me, his chest rising and falling in slow, melodic movements. I needed to ask him about Tatum... no matter what he thought or might say, I just needed to know what I'd gotten myself into.

I reached over, my fingers a hair's breadth away from his skin. His heat rose, mingling with my own. Should I even wake him?

I placed my hand on his shoulder. His body tightened and he spun, grabbing my wrist. Realization sputtered over his features. "Meris? What are you doing?"

My heart pounded like a drum in my ears. "I was..." My chest hurt. His eyes locked with mine, a mystery of beauty and shadow. "I was going to ask you—"

The door swung open, and the glass windows shuddered.

"It's time." Inanna entered, her blood-stained lips parting to reveal her too-white smile. An iron crown, pointed up and down like the fangs of a vampire, rested on her ink-black hair, gripping tight to the veil covering her eyes. "Are you ready?"

Setizar sat up, bracing his upper body on his forearms. "Normally you're a much more accommodating host, Inanna. Whatever has brought this foul attitude?"

Her smile turned into a frown. It was a crooked, twisted thing, bleeding with ill-intent. "You have one hour to be in the sanctum. Don't be late."

"Wouldn't dream of it." He dipped his head, offering her a devil's grin.

Inanna turned her heel, flanked by her two guards, and exited the room.

"Meris," Setizar whispered, his fingers wrapping around my wrist. "Whatever you do, don't show your powers. Don't initiate a fight with any of the creatures here in Redrim either. Ever since the curse, Inanna has gained unimaginable power. There's a law against killing the ogarak, leviathan, and fae, one bound by a magic we cannot undo without our powers returned. But, if you hurt any of the creatures of Redrim, you will be bound to Inanna until the blood debt is paid."

"Why are you telling me this now?" My head was spinning. The air in the room was stale, and I couldn't find oxygen like I could before. It was stiff, plagued by mold.

"Because, if you give her a reason to be suspicious, Inanna may try and prod you, or initiate some sort of fight between you and the creatures just so she can lock you here in Redrim and prod further."

"Just for *fighting* one?" I pushed myself off the bed, catching a glimpse of my blonde hair in the mirror. I almost forgot about the veneer he put on me...

"Yes. Ever since the Seasons lost our reign, Inanna put it upon herself to take charge over us. Her magic rewrote some of the laws, and until we are restored we can do nothing against it." He pulled himself off the bed, slipping on a new shirt. "She used to do our bidding, to remind us when to change the dial of our season for the realms."

"*Realms?*"

Setizar smiled. "Of course. Ever wonder how the seasons change?"

"I mean—" I massaged my temples. "There's more than this realm and Inder?"

Setizar paused, rolling the sapphire button between his fingers. "Of course there is. We aren't the only ones out here, *darling.*" His smile cut through me as the folds of his coat appeared from his mist and wrapped around his shoulders, still bloody and torn from yesterday. "Don't get too angsty without me. I'll be back in twenty."

And he misted from the room.

"Don't call me darling," I said to the air, hoping he could hear my words. I watched the clock in the corner, the small hand slowly ticking by.

One minute.

Two minutes.

Three minutes.

The agony of being alone in this red-drenched world was almost overwhelming. Not that I missed him, I just despised being alone in a place I felt completely unsafe in.

Four minutes.

Five minutes.

Six minutes.

I started pacing, not knowing what to do with myself. I'd fixed my outfit several times already, and I even brushed my hair. Still, I paced madly.

Seven minutes.

Eight minutes.

Nine minutes.

"Where has he gone? Where was he even going?" I peered out the window, looking at a lake of red below. Why was everything so red? Why couldn't it be blue, or some other color?

The clock hand flicked to ten minutes, and someone knocked on the door. "Are you letting me in?"

I groaned, opening the barrier and letting Setizar inside.

He raised a brow. "Miss me?"

"Not at all."

Setizar smiled, his grin shooting through my veins with heat. "Why don't I believe that?" Setizar looped his finger through my hair. "And for the record? I think red is far more suitable for you."

I slapped his hand, scowling. "Eat dirt."

"Feisty today, are you?"

Something was... something seemed off about him. "When am I not feisty?" I crossed my arms, unsure as to what had taken over him.

"I suppose you have a point." His eyes locked with mine. Solid purple? I never saw that hue before. Something must have really come over him. He drew the back of his hand across my cheek—my skin crawling at the gesture. "But, then again, how well do we know each other?"

This wasn't Setizar. "Well," I rolled my lip between my teeth, "we know each other very well. In fact," I grabbed his hand, holding on tightly. "You remember that thing you owe me?"

His eyes narrowed. Confusion swept over his face. "Enlighten me?"

"You know…" I leaned closer. "About the Hag? You said you'd tell me the deal you made with her."

He smiled. "Of course."

My insides burned. If this wasn't him, then who was it? Who could this be? "You know…" I had no weapons. None. I risked a glance at the clock. He should be back soon, if something hadn't happened to him. "Why didn't you just mist into the room?"

He froze. "I didn't want to walk in on you, in case you were changing."

Another lie. The real Setizar knew I didn't bring extra clothes, nor did he ever seem to care. "Of course. It's just, normally you're not early."

"Well, I'm never late either, am I?"

"Depends." I leaned back. Worst case? I'd try and use my powers and hope for the best. "But, one thing I know for sure."

"And what would that be?"

I stilled, my back straight as a needle. "That, despite how many times your eyes change," My heart pounded. My arms were limp. "They're never a solid color."

His smile grew, a feral growl escaping his lips. "Clever girl."

27

My fingers trembled as the fake Setizar walked toward me. He made no noise, He had… no shadow? My heartbeat dragged— sluggish and slow. Pounding. Rhythmic. Uncertain.

My limbs weakened, the bones in my legs seeming to splinter. "Who are you?"

His grin spread, slithering into a savage smile. "Who do you think I am?"

The strange sense of familiarity pulsed through me. "Tatum?"

The reverberating chuckle wasn't the reply I wanted. His eyes shuddered until they glowed and his figure shifted. "You really are smarter than you look. But you're not smart enough. I'm not Tatum."

"Then who are you?" I felt like choking them.

Inky-black hair cascaded down their lithe figure, and their ashen skin turned a dull, lifeless hue. The creature's lips curled inward, writhing with shadows and promises of the unknown. "I'm certain you know better than to threaten me with any form of violence. You should probably stop thinking about it now."

What? "What are you saying?"

"Why do you think my steps are silent? Do I make any noise?" The creature moved again—and again, no noise was made. "I'm not truly here. Like many here in Yamira, you will slip into insanity if you don't keep focused." They looked around the room, dipping their fingers into their pockets.

Water dripped somewhere nearby as metal creaked on hinges in the distance. Screams ricocheted through the still and blood-red atmosphere. The creature looked at me, a crack of thunder pounding in the air as rusted metal poured into my nose.

The light illuminated their features, showing every vessel of blood, every vein, every tendon, every bone below. A grinning skull looked at me, fierce and carving hollow fear into me.

"Why are you here?" I kept as still as I could, knowing if I moved I might do something I would regret.

"Because, if you're not careful, you could very well die. And personally I really don't want to see that happen." Eyes met mine, a fervid shade of violet. "I am Biodru the Emberfang. I'm here to warn you, and I don't have much time. Nothing is as it seems. Everyone has an agenda. Keep no friends, save no family, and make no bargains."

"Then why should I trust you?"

The chime of the bell ripped through the skies.

"Because I have my own agenda, which involves you surviving."

One.

Two.

Three chimes.

Biodru was gone.

Sounds flooded into the room. A thunderstorm, wind howling through the Aether-forsaken hills and mountains, and pained screams bombarded my ears.

"Enjoying the environment, I take it?"

I didn't even hear him appear. Setizar stood, smiling, his amethyst and rose eyes locking with mine. I could see it now. There would be no mistaking his eyes—the gentle expression that fills them. Biodru had a calloused look in the cutting edges of their purple irises, nothing like the warmth that spread over me when I looked into his—

Oh, Aether. What was I thinking? I couldn't do this to myself. Not after what Biodru just said. Then again, how could I trust them?

"It's not my cup of tea here." I breathed out, hoping to expel this nervous energy in my lungs. "How long will this changing season take?"

Setizar paused in his steps, his hands shoved deep into his coat pockets. A new blue coat, a new black shirt. He must have gotten new clothes from somewhere. Where did he go? "It won't take long at all."

Something sounded strange. Was he alright? "What are you not saying?"

"Many things, Meris." He smiled. "But, this? The changing of the season? It's not what it seems. I just need you to stay calm, alright?"

"What do you mean?"

Kindling rage coiled around the room, intensified by the red light drenching everything. He was the only blue-hued entity in this area. "You will soon see."

Not exactly an answer, but the way he said it made my stomach twist.

— ☾ —

The doors opened, hissing along their hinges like starved goblins. I followed Setizar, his coat trailing behind him like flags before a war.

Inanna stood beside a throne, a death-kissed smile spread across her lips and a scepter of onyx in her hand. Her grin was a knowing one, expecting something that would please her.

Below the red obelisk lantern, the other lords sat, eyes void of emotion.

"Are you ready, *Lord* of the Crimson Plane?"

Setizar stopped before the fifth throne, not bending a knee to bow. I couldn't see his face. "I am, *Queen* of Redrim."

Her smile spread, unamused and filled with dark intent, and she snapped her fingers. Two males, with long silk-black hair and skin as gray as death, grabbed Setizar's shoulders. His coat was removed, and he was forcibly guided to the throne.

My stomach became clay, melting and twisting. "What are you doing?"

The two creatures shoved him into the last uninhabited throne. He didn't fight, why did they have to be so rough?

His face was a series of tight, hard lines as the other season lords fell into absolute silence with him. His eyes darkened, dipping into a midnight blue and volcano red.

Inanna turned toward me, sweeping her hand through the air. "The ritual, pet. And to make sure you don't cause a ruckus, my guards will be standing beside you."

Two ogarak grabbed my arms, pulling me away from the throne. "What are you doing?"

Inanna released a breath. "Setizar, you have the oddest choice in females." She took a few steps toward him, wrapping her fingers around his throat. "I hope you've healed from yesterday's little *skirmish*."

"It's not the worst you've done to me, Inanna." Setizar smiled, angling his head to the side. "Honestly, it was tactless, I'm surprised you even did it."

"Shock value, darling." She drew her nail along his cheek, gently at first, drawing her wine-red lips closer. Her nail bit into his skin, causing droplets of blood to pool around the sharp point. "I do enjoy watching reactions."

I pulled my arms. I couldn't let this happen to him.

"Meris," Setizar's eyes locked with mine. "Calm down. Remember what I told you?"

"You're suicidal!" I screeched, pulling again at the two ogarak. Fire pulsed through my veins, burning in my back and neck. "You can't do this…"

Inanna swatted the air. "Troublesome." She drew her fingers down his neck, pulling at the top buttons from his shirt. "Comfortable, *Meris*?" Smiling, she pulled away from him, making a quick motion toward a table.

"It's the price of the season… the price we have to pay for humankind. They don't even know we exist, yet we suffer for them." She pulled out a knife, drawing it across her white palm. "With Mother Earth gone and Father Time missing, it's up to us to move the hands of time and nature. Redrim is the dial, and they power it every quarter."

One.

Two.

Three drops of blood fell onto the table. "Trust me." She looked at me. "This will hurt them much more than it will hurt you to watch."

The blood on the table glowed, pulsing orange. Her hand likewise emanated the same color. Her slow steps toward Setizar pierced my heart with a blade. "Don't do this."

Setizar smiled at me as Inanna drew a symbol against his chest with her blood. The symbol glowed, small veins of light spreading over him.

She did the same to Aurel.

To Eira.

To Lhysa.

A hum of magic replaced the silence. Then, their echoing chorus of pain.

"Stop!" I fell to my knees. "Stop it!"

Inanna was stone-faced, though a smirk lifted one corner of her mouth.

They were in so much pain.

The sky darkened, flickering between red and black. The hall filled with agony; I could feel it ripping through my bones as though I were up there with them. Shadows and light warred, gripping their throats in reply to their torment. Color was draining from them.

From *him*.

This needed to stop!

Stop!

Oh, Aether, make it stop!

I pulled, but I couldn't move. The ogarak's arms were tight around my own, but I couldn't feel them…

"Stop!"

My back shattered with heat.

Wings sprouted from between my shoulder blades—fire bursting from my fingers. My entire body burned, shuddering at the world around me.

Setizar's half-opened eyes widened.

The other lords jolted to their feet.

Inanna was a pillar of frozen shock.

The world fell   silent. No flashing lights, no darkness… just red. An angry beast had cracked open its eyes within my heart like a monster of magma.

The ogarak ran.

"Aether," Inanna breathed, taking a stumbling step back.

I scowled at her, my wings no longer heavy, but light and ready for me to use them. "Let them go."

"She…*her*?" Inanna looked at Setizar, as if ready to pounce.

I wouldn't give her that chance. I vaulted, kicking off from where I stood and barreling to Setizar's side.

The floor below us dropped.

Setizar and I fell into the white oblivion.

28

Cold air pounded pulled against my body, ripping at my wings and stinging my face.

Setizar!

He was falling as well, a foot away in this white nothingness. I gasped, reaching out to grab him. My tendons balked at my attempts, stretching out of proportion. Just a little more—

I flapped my wings, propelling myself forward and grabbing him just as the world flashed blue around us.

Instinct took over and I wrapped my wings around Setizar, pulling him close to my body.

Crack.

Pain shot through my body and ripped into my wings. Ice and fire peeled my skin. We hit the earth below and tumbled down the mountainside.

I lost my grip on Setizar as we rolled down the steep slope. My left wing was limp and bleeding, soaking the snow in red.

"Meris?" Setizar groaned, staggering to his feet.

Hot tears fell down my face, freezing into icicles by my chin. I couldn't move. My body hurt, my wing was snapped.

The world spun, churning nausea in my stomach. "Setizar… are you—" Pain shot through my back and I screamed. Blood continued to flood from my wounds.

"Meris, you need to keep still." Setizar touched his fingers to my stomach gingerly, sending a cool warmth spreading over whatever was there. "Aether!" He groaned, placing his hands on my leg. "You have to stay awake, for just a bit longer, alright?"

I nodded, something else thundering over his voice. Armor... and hundreds of footsteps.

I turned, wincing at the sunlight reflecting off golden scaled armor. A woman led an army of creatures, all coated in silver and gold plates. She raised her hand, wind peeling down the mountain. "Halt!"

I froze, unable to move. Not from fear. I did not fear her, for reasons I didn't know. But the pain had become too much to bear.

Her helmet morphed, dripping onto her shoulders like molten gold, giving way to the tightly braided white hair. Narrow black eyes stared at me, glinting with familiar understanding and curiosity. There was a frigidity about her, a frozen soul lingering under the layers of honey-bronze skin. "Where's my sister?" She looked at Setizar, something lacing her features. "Men, scour the countryside. Find my sister...and that annoying sphinx." Her gaze flicked back to me. "Welcome to the Northern Kingdom, furie."

Pain pulsed through me. I didn't even register her words. "Who are you?"

She took a few more steps toward me, her glittering gold armor clinking as she knelt. Her scowl made me wonder what she was thinking. "You don't remember?"

"What?"

She released a tight breath, her hand clasping my own. "You are safe now and under my protection." She looked back at her army, her face remaining untouched by emotion. "Help them. Be careful, the furie is injured and requires attention."

As soon as the gray fingers of the armored men touched my body, I slipped into unconsciousness.

— ☾ —

"Oh dear," Tatum said through the darkness. "You've really botched it up this time. You could have died if the jinni didn't thrust most of his magic out to heal that gaping tear in your stomach."

I groaned, sitting up. I was back in the meadow. "What else was I supposed to do?"

"Other than not letting your raging emotions control you?" Tatum stood by the water, his hands clasped behind his back. "Honestly, you would have been left alone if you had remained calm and let the ritual be done. Think about all the pain you could have evaded? And now, unfortunately, Inanna knows who you are."

"And who am I?"

He smiled. "That would require another deal."

As if. I groaned, rubbing my temples. "So, what do I do now?"

Tatum turned, his gold-red eyes locking with mine. "You wake up."

I gasped. White light erupted around me, followed immediately by scalding pain. A whimper slipped through my mouth as I tried to sit up.

Red-brown spots speckled the pale-blue bedding. Blood. My wings were stretched out, held to either side of the bed by slings. Spots of flesh glowed with magic. A light blue magic, with heat radiating off the wrapped wounds. It burned—but in a good way. I knew whatever it was, it was helping.

"Ah," a woman said. "Finally awake?"

I turned. It was the woman from the mountain. Her gold armor was replaced by a figure-hugging gold dress made of reptilian skin. "Who are you?"

She tilted her head. No smile. "Do you truly not remember me?"

I blinked. "I've never even met you before."

Her expression flicked between emotionless and uncertainty. "Interesting."

"Interesting?"

She finally smiled. "What's your name?"

This was so strange. "Meris Vahla."

Though her face remained relatively unchanged, her mahogany eyes widened. "Fascinating." Her gaze flicked up and down my mangled wings. "How are you feeling?"

"Like I fell a thousand feet."

This time, her smile was genuine. "You did, if you remember."

"Why are we here? What's your name?"

She grunted a little. "Lhysa opened a portal and sent you here to keep Inanna from getting grabby. I imagine that daemon is having a fit now and has beheaded at least a dozen leviathan." A grin flickered on her lips, as if the thought alone brought her joy. "The leviathan will come back, they always do. There's only one way to kill them..." She trailed off, her eyes glassy. "And my name is Feng."

I didn't ask anything more. She seemed like the type who would get quickly bothered by too many questions.

"How much do you know of Yamira, Meris?"

I shifted, though the radiating pain in my body hindered me from doing much else. "Enough."

"Enough?" Feng looked at me, her eyes narrowing. "Well, then you must be grateful that I found you before something else did."

"Something bad, I assume?"

Feng nodded. "A creature of the Veil. Come." She gestured for me to get up, though she paused. "You're in pain. Hold on." She pulled something out of a dresser near the bed, a small vial of white liquid. "Drink. This will ease the pain for now. Don't exert yourself, otherwise you'll do more harm than good."

I took the vial from her, opening the lid.

"Right now, only Setizar could heal those wounds, but he is gravely lacking in magic. Everyone is. It will take them a day or more to recover."

The potion slid down my throat, gliding through my veins. It tasted like winter snow and left a trail of bubbles on my tongue. The pain was already a numb afterthought. "Wouldn't Terrestrial magic be the ones who can heal wounds?"

Feng smiled, less of the genuine one I saw earlier, but real nevertheless. "You would assume so, but we can't. Only some creatures can, like the jinn and the fae. I suppose if we had a fae healer around, we would be well-off here. Unfortunately the fae are gone, save for precious few."

"What happened to them?"

"Inanna happened." Feng's expression darkened, a deep cut of untouchable emotion. "I was there the day their blood was spilled, when the gates sealed shut and the skies turned red. The day the last furie fell."

My breath stilled, shuddering with the howling wind. My wings still hurt, but I was able to walk without crippling pain. "So, what are you going to show me?"

Feng smirked, tilting her head to the side. That unreadable expression became darker and thicker, like a chorus of cloaked secrets dangling before me. "The Veil."

At her words, a tribal drum began to pound. So faint I could barely hear it. A string of unearthly melodies carved into the sky, pulsing and tugging me. Was it my heartbeat? I was drawn to the balcony, looking toward a forest wreathed in darkness. A black mist wafted from the tips of the trees as red lightning pulsed from within the heart of the woodland. "That's the Veil?"

"As dark and as vile as legends have told." Feng's eyes glassed over, as though wicked memories had taken hold. "It is rumored the Silver Queen created it from a dark magic, like that of the daemon, but far more wicked."

The red lightning struck again, cleaving the atmosphere. "Where did the Silver Queen even come from?"

Feng released a breath, her talon-like fingers latching onto the ledge. "It is said she appeared in the dead of the night after Setizar and Alecto's bonding, tore his power from him and used it to slaughter the jinn who had remained in Yamira." She gestured to the dark forest, though the stabbing pain ebbed through me. Alecto was much more than his love. And he lost everything. "He was only spared because he's the Lord of the Crimson Plane. A creature who brings forth the harvest season."

I watched the pulsing light within the wood, keeping rate with my heart. "So, no one knows where she went?"

"None." Feng closed her eyes, blonde hair whipping in the air.

I couldn't keep quiet, I needed to know how it happened. "What happened to Alecto?"

Feng inhaled, then released a puff of white haze into the sky. "She was killed. Stabbed. The last of the furies aside from her sister, Megaera. They never found either body, but the amount of blood left in the forest let Setizar know what happened to his beloved."

"So if I'm to help, there's more to do than just grab the Box." I paused. Everything seemed so strange. As if I could remember it myself. The deep connection I felt to this—to everything. "I need to find the Silver Queen and kill her as well."

Feng turned, eyes tracking my slow movements. "Setizar is in the room down the hall, nearest to the stairs."

I nodded. "Thank you."

Feng bowed at the waist. "I will be gone for the night. Please, make yourself at home. Eira and the other lords are here as well, so don't hesitate to walk around if you feel the need."

I nodded again.

"Enjoy your stay and relax." Feng smiled, her dress moving. Armor. Her dress shifted into a full suit of armor.

"What are you going to be doing?"

She stopped at the door. "There's no rest for those like me." With that, she strode down the hall and vanished from view.

— ☾ —

I opened the door. A faint peach light illuminated the white room, tinting the crystal bedpost pink. The chime of the hour echoed through the hall, urging me into the chamber. A rug that appeared to be woven from frost and snowflakes rested in front of the blazing fireplace, covering a large part of the glimmering frozen-lake marble below.

Setizar's eyes flicked to me. He was on the bed, his ashen skin starting to turn copper once more. Tatum must have been telling the truth. He used most of his magic to heal whatever injury had threatened my life. "Meris?" His voice rippled through the air, stroking my heart gently. "You look awful…"

"Way to compliment me," I said, trying not to smile. "Glad to see you're well."

"You took most of the impact." He patted the bed beside him, and I took up his silent offer. "How are you even walking?"

"Feng gave me medicine."

He nodded, twisting his arm around my back, avoiding my wings. Holding me as if to assure himself that I was there. "You scared me."

His pounding heartbeat coiled around me, mingling with my own. "How?"

His silence wasn't something I was used to. He always had some response, not this unsettling quiet. He removed his hand, fingers folding together. "What did Feng say about your injuries?"

Again, not an answer. "Basically, they'll keep me comfortable, but you're the only one who can mend them."

He nodded, twisting around, his fingers limned with stardust. "Alright. I can start now."

I smacked his hand away. "Not in a million years. You aren't nearly well enough to do that."

He looked like an injured pup, and I almost felt bad about being so harsh. "You're far more hurt than I am, Meris."

"Your magic is drained! If I let you use it on me, then what would happen?" I shook my head. "It's not happening. I don't know what happens if you exhaust all your magic, but judging from how pale you were, I'm guessing it's not good."

He released a breath, crossing his arms. "Fine."

I settled closer next to him, my wings draping off the side of the bed. "Tell me everything I need to know about Inanna? About the Silver Queen? And... Alecto."

Setizar nodded, his fingers brushing the hair out of my face. "I suppose it is time you know everything." With a sigh, he began. "Before the curse, there were the four sentinels. The four seasons. Spring, Summer, Autumn, and Winter. Only the children from the line of the original sentinels were allowed to rule, and it has been that way since the dawn of time.

"When the seasons change, the lands give the sentinels a boost of power and magic. So they watched diligently for when the clock would turn and Mother Earth to change the season. One day, it didn't happen. So, they waited... and waited. Nothing happened. That's when the sentinels turned to the Changeling. The Changeling worked with the family of Redrim, and it was settled on that day that the sentinels were to turn the tables. I need to give you a bit of a backstory about Redrim, for you to understand it." Setizar gently took my hand, fingers running over mine. "There was a goddess named Hecate. She was too powerful, going as far as claiming to be as powerful as the Changeling. The creatures of the realm became afraid, so the stars stole away most of her magic and banished her to an island that exists within its own time.

"She married the Lord of the land, and the two of them built the empire known as Redrim. After a thousand years, Hecate amassed an army and prepared an assault on Yamira. Let's say it wasn't pretty. Hecate and her family line were cursed. And that curse involved the fact that they would forever help change the seasons. The changing of seasons is painful, and the pain would be a constant reminder to her children of her mistake. Somehow, the pain only reminded the children of the injustice done to Hecate." Setizar paused, his finger twisting a lock of hair. "I don't blame

Inanna for the anger."

Somehow, neither did I.

"Inanna is the most powerful in her line, being a daemon and a child of Hecate's bloodline. She was the one who aided the Silver Queen in the curse."

My heart hammered against my bones. "How long until magic is dead?"

"We don't know. Could be tomorrow, could be another decade. All I know is I can feel it dwindling... the season change is getting worse each year, and I am starting to forget simple magical tasks."

"Find the Box, return to the powers, and we will be able to reverse this curse," I said, and resting my head in the crook of his arm. "So, if we can lift the curse on your people, we can lift the curse on mine. Sounds like a solid plan. Anything new on the portals?"

Setizar shook his head. "We've been rather caught in trouble these past few days."

"I happen to think you're understating the situation."

He laughed. "You could call it that." He turned his head, his face mere inches from my own. His eyes were as bright as an evening star.

My pulse beat in my throat, and my breath felt suddenly uneven and ragged. Oh, Aether. Please. This couldn't be happening... why would I do this to myself? He loves *Alecto*. His heart belongs to her and her memory.

Why did I feel this way?

"Meris?" His voice was low, gentle like the caress of a hand down my spine. "Is everything alright?"

No. Everything was not alright. Sweat slid down my back, building in the most inconvenient places. "Of course."

"Are you certain? You look rather flushed. Do you have a fever? Here let me—"

I practically threw myself off the bed. "I'm fine!" I yelled, a bit too enthusiastic. "I mean, I should probably just go lay down. It's late anyway, and we both need rest."

He nodded slowly. The expression on his face told me everything: he didn't believe a word I said.

29

Water resounded around me, flooding my ears and bombarding my senses. Mountain air swept through the clearing, twining its windy fingers around my hair. Great. I was in the dreamscape again.

Tatum kicked my side, jolting me from my rest. "What was that for?" I shouted, leaping to my feet. "What are you doing?"

He sat, crossing his long legs and reclining on the grass. "I'm simply keeping your unconscious, angry, brooding self company. Honestly, brooding is quite ugly on you. You shouldn't wear that emotion."

I hissed a breath. "Thanks for letting me know. I'll be sure to brood more often."

His eyes flickered, a question lingering behind the many layers of his expressionless face. "What happened earlier? Between you and the Lord of the Crimson Plane?"

I leveled my gaze, not wanting to give him any information.

"Staying quiet, are we?" Tatum smiled, a single black rose spinning between his fingers. Where did he get that? "Well, I'm glad. Your voice is so grating I find it rather annoying."

Balling my hands into fists, I tried to prepare a worthy attack. "Then you won't protest my silence." He was baiting me. I crossed my arms, taking a few steps to the water and dipping my bare feet in. Stars floated all around me, dancing over the lake and fleeing to the gemstone mountain in the distance. This place was getting more and more detailed every time…

"Honestly, a love-sick immortal is the absolute worst."

"I'm not love-sick!" Fire built in my veins. "And I'm not an immortal."

"You imbecile, you are. To both. It's written all over your face." Tatum rolled his eyes. "You can't hide it."

"Who are you calling an imbecile—"

"You, Meris." Tatum turned to mist and reappeared beside me. *Was that new?* "You keep missing everything. You're missing all the clues. All the hints. All the signs."

"What signs? What am I missing?"

His grin was feral and refined all at once. "I cannot tell you. Either you open your own eyes, or someone else will have to."

"Why can't you tell me?"

"Destiny, perhaps? Call it what you want, I simply know if I tell you, things would crumble."

The dream shattered, and the rising morning sun shone through my window. Setizar wouldn't be getting such a pretty sunrise since he was facing west. He should be seeing this.

Wait. Why was I thinking about that? I couldn't be feeling this way toward him… I promised myself I wouldn't.

I breathed out, trying to shake what Tatum had said.

A hollow sound filled the air, and my heartbeat quickened. I knew who just entered the room.

Keep it together, Meris…

I turned, looking at my intruder. Setizar. He smiled, slipping his hands into his coat pockets. He looked… he looked so healthy.

"Meris." He bowed. "I've come to mend your wounds."

I released a weak laugh. "Feeling better?"

"Much." He pulled off his coat, draping it on the chair near my bed and began rolling his sleeves up. "This is quite the view." His eyes were on mine, a gentle smile across his lips.

"It really is." I couldn't tear my gaze from him. There was something about him this morning... something *different*. There was no way to place it, but—he was almost twice as magical as before.

He sat behind me, fingers caressing my wings. "I'll need you to direct me to your injuries, please."

I nodded, pointing to the mangled bone on the tip of my left wing. "There..."

His starlight tipped fingers glided over the wound, stitching it back together. Warmth and ice spread over my body. "Where else?"

I pointed to my back. The open backed top should've showed the burn the icy snow left along my skin. His hands pressed against my injuries, healing them quickly. I could feel his breath on my neck... his hands on my spine... my mind was buzzing.

I couldn't do this.

My heart hurt. I was a stupid, stupid girl for falling like this. For opening myself to the creature who was holding me hostage, holding me against my will to do something for his people... for himself.

But I couldn't help it. I couldn't help the way my heart fluttered when he was near—when he was touching me. "Setizar..."

"Yes, Meris?"

I couldn't love him. I needed to stop these stupid, adolescent feelings. I should've known better than this. "How much did you love Alecto?"

He froze; his palm rested against my shoulder. "More than you can imagine. Every day I hope my Alecto will come back." His voice caught. "But every day I realize she won't come back, and I should accept it. I shouldn't be obsessed over bringing her back—over her death and her absence—and I should be more concerned over what happens to everyone else, not an event that happened nearly two decades ago."

I felt lighter, but also awful. "Jinn must not age." I laughed, trying to change the subject.

"No," he chuckled. "We don't age like humans. You've probably figured that out by now." His hand finally returned to my wings. "Well,
would you look at this."

I gasped. Small feathers protruded from my wings like pale freckles.

"Metamorphosis, my dear." Gently, he thumbed at the plumage, his
smile something between wonder and sadness. "I suppose it's just a matter
of time now."

"A matter of time?"

He paused. "A matter of time before you become what you are destined to be." He stood from the bed, looking out the window. "You have
quite a view in here."

My heart stuttered, beating madly Setizar offered me one last look of
deviance before vanishing into mist.

30

The day was a blur, between the endless meetings, verbal fist fights, and countless glasses of wine. I could still hear Eira and Aurel going at it, hashing out everything from which season should host the Season's Ball to who was to blame for a crime committed over a hundred years ago, while Feng and I sat in a secluded corner.

I liked Feng, despite her offish personality and unflinching honesty, we got along well. I felt as if I'd known her all my life.

"You really should take up a poetry," Aurel snipped, his silver eyes sliding over Eira. "You have a way with words."

"Flattery from you is like drinking wine with a fly in it." Eira shoved her hands into her pockets, her white boots blending into the snow-hued floor. "It's never good."

Setizar snickered.

"Something funny?" Aurel snapped.

"No, no not at all. Please, don't stop on my account," Setizar said, his eyes locking with mine for a half second. They danced with mirth and mischief, smiling at me before returning to Aurel. "I enjoy listening to Eira verbally pummel you."

"I could physically pummel any of you."

Feng's laugh was a grating bark. She kicked her feet up on the chair nearby. "Want to put your words where your mouth is?"

"Are you implying they're not?" Aurel stood from his seat, gold skin gleaming in the winter sun.

"I'm implying that if you think you can, then you won't have any problem sparring with me in the courtyard."

"You have the advantage. We are in *Winter*. I'm a Summer creature."

"Is Summer creature a synonym for weak sphinxling? Because it sounds like it."

Aurel grunted, rolling his shoulders. The white shirt he had on a moment ago vanished, replaced by gold armor in the shape of wings crossing over his chest. "Lead me to the courtyard then, North Wind."

She flashed him a deadly smirk. "With *pleasure*."

— ℂ —

"Dear Aether, he's going to get himself killed," Setizar whispered into my ear, his voice gilded with a laugh. "The question is, how long will he last before she flattens him?"

"Is she really that good?" I watched as Lhysa waved a hand over the snow-drenched courtyard, turning it into a spring oasis. A mixture of summer and winter.

"She is. Alecto and her used to spar for hours on end, and though Alecto was the best warrior there was, Feng still beat her most days." He offered me a forced, unusual smile. "Barring the use of magic, that is. Aurel doesn't stand a chance."

Eira and Lhysa joined us below the balcony. "I give him four minutes," Lhysa muttered.

"Generous," Eira said, her ice-white eye leveling on the make-shift arena. "I give him two."

"What if she chooses to toy with him?" Setizar asked, his grin turning malicious. "I give him six minutes, tops, if that's the case."

"What does the winner of the bet get?" I asked, looking between the three.

Setizar's laugh warmed my cold bones. "Watching Aurel suffer is enough for me."

Eira cackled, nodding. "I second that."

Lhysa shook her head. "I shouldn't be agreeing with *either* of you."

"And yet," Setizar slid his hands into his pockets, leaning against the nearby banister, "you are."

"He drives me up a wall. Seeing him bested by someone will be satisfying." Lhysa lifted her head, as if trying to retain some semblance of benevolence. Everyone in this area appeared to have some form of resentment toward the sphinx. I wonder what he did to irritate them.

Feng raised her hand, pulling a sword from the sky. A whirlwind pounded into the open area, lifting a smile to her black-stained lips.

Aurel made a similar gesture, yanking his weapon from raw sunlight. Something about the way he did that seems out of character...

"Aurel is a mixed-breed," Eira whispered to me. "The son of a Sun Lord and a sphinx. A powerful mixture, but a weak child. It just goes to show that sometimes Terrestrial and Ethereal magic don't mix well."

I watched him, studying him. Was that why he tried so hard? To compensate for what he thought he didn't have? For what everyone thought he couldn't do?

The air hollowed. Feng brought her wind-bound sword down, sending Aurel hurtling backward. Light gleamed around us, shattering the atmosphere with radiant beams. Molten wings flared from Aurel's back, sun-licked and pure. My jaw dropped. *He's winged?* They weren't delicate membranes and plumage tinged like mine. They appeared like solid ore, made of gold itself.

Auburn light glinted from his reddened sword, and he hurdled toward Feng. She pivoted and cleaved the sky with a blood-freezing screech. Aurel dropped his sword, his wings trembling back into him as he covered his ears. We covered our ears, too. Waves of sound became visible as she neared him, that ear-splitting noise growing louder.

"We are almost at two minutes!" Eira laughed, shaking her head.

Aurel raised his hands in defeat, blood dripping from his ears. Silence followed.

"Pointless, honestly. All this build-up for Aurel to be humiliated?" Lhysa clicked her tongue and left. "We shouldn't have wasted our time."

— (—

I walked through the halls alone, trying to understand my own thoughts and feelings. The spar played over and over in my head. The moves, the imbalance of skill and power... it repeated and repeated.

Despite how much Setizar and Aurel didn't like each other, Setizar was the first at the injured sphinx's side, mending the wounds inflicted on his ears. Just another thing that made me feel so strongly about Setizar. Why did he make it so easy to love him?

I paused.

Love.

Did I just admit that to myself?

I weaved around the corner, and smacked my forehead into Aurel's still armored chest. "Meris! In a hurry to go somewhere?"

I absently rubbed my brow, shaking my head. "Not really."

"Then you don't mind if I walk with you?" He smiled, and the sandy-brown hairs of his short beard caught the light.

"Not at all." I returned his grin, and we continued walking down the hallway together. "How're you feeling?"

He shrugged, extending his arm for me to take. "My pride hurts more than my body, but my ears are still ringing."

I looped my arm around his, keeping my eyes on the ice-hued ground below. The snowflake arches above looked to be made of glaciers, though the inside of the castle was a comfortable temperature. "What do you know about the Veil?"

"That dark void out at the base of the mountain?"

I managed a tight nod, unsure if I should have asked.

"There's not much we know about it, other than it's been spreading these past seventeen years. It was a small patch of black forest once, now it's an endless sea of shadows and lightning. We think it's where magic has died."

I looked out the window, inhaling a long, unsteady breath. "Do you think it will go away when I bring magic back?"

Aurel stayed silent for a moment, his eyes filling with embers of uncertainty. "We can only hope."

31

The white world outside the carriage turned to orange and red as the Crimson Plane surrounded us.

My toes burned inside my slippers, so I pulled them off my feet and set them on the bench beside me.

Setizar sat across from me in the carriage, his eyes glued to a book Feng had lent him. "You must be really interested in whatever is in that book," I said, trying to make sense of what was written on the spine.

He nodded slowly.

Great. He's only half-paying attention. "You know, I find that you are a decent fellow," I mumbled.

Another slow nod.

"You're caring… and good humored."

He responded with a non-committal, "That's nice to hear."

I leveled my gaze, rolling my lips together. "And, you're extremely attractive. The best looking man—thing I've seen while in this realm… well, in any realm, really."

His eyes locked with mine, glittering with a thousand mischievous stars. "I knew it was just a matter of time before you admitted it."

I threw my slipper at him, only to have him catch it.

"A little extra feisty today, I take it?" He grinned, tossing the projectile back at me. "Excited to be going home?"

I began to nod, but stopped myself. This wasn't my home. "I would, if I were actually going home."

His expression darkened, reaching his eyes. "We will find the portal."

I already knew about the portal, and I knew when it would open. Tatum told me. I just needed to know when the next full moon is. But if I left, would I be able to find both Setizar's Box and my sister in two days? Would I have to pick one or the other like I've been told?

I breathed out, resting my head against the cushioned seat. The bump and drag of the road under us made me remember Mae. I missed her. There's so much I wished to ask her... so much I needed to tell her.

"Have you given thought to what kind of dress you will be wearing to the ball?"

My eyes snapped to Setizar. He was busy rolling a pen between his fingers. "What?"

"The ball. It's in a few days. Cerie should have everything arranged."

I'd completely forgotten. "No." I scratched my neck. "I don't even know where to begin."

Setizar swatted the air. "I'll request the greatest tailor in this realm to come, then. He will aid you."

I swallowed my unease with the light mountain air. "What's this tailor like?"

"He's...hyper, so don't get too overwhelmed. I think you'll get along just fine. Don't let yourself get worried."

I nodded. "When's the ball?"

"Five days. On your birthday."

I sighed, snatching my slipper from the ground and slipping it and its companion on my feet. "What will you be wearing?"

He grinned. "A suit which will definitely provide the shock I wish to see on your face."

"Wear periwinkle and rose, then I will be shocked."

"Don't tempt me," he said, a wry tone plucking his tone upward. "I doubt either of those colors would look bad on me."

Sadly, I had to agree.

— ☾ —

"Meris!" Cerie's screech was something between glee and horror. "I heard about everything! Are you alright? Did Setizar maim you?"

"Excuse me?" Setizar slipped his arm around her waist, lifting her off the ground and keeping her from grabbing me. "Did you just accuse me of *maiming* this beautiful creature?"

"Let me go!" she grunted, kicking her tiny hooves. "Monster. I need to make sure she's in one piece!"

"I shall lock you in the tower, my blue maiden." Setizar offered me a wink, tightening his arms around Cerie. "Unless you take that back."

"Do you see what he does?" Cerie narrowed her eyes, ceasing her wriggling. "He manipulates!"

"I finesse, those are two different things."

"That's just a synonym for manipulate." Cerie elbowed him in the ribs, resulting in a muffled *humph*.

I laughed.

"Meris, stop laughing. This isn't very entertaining." Cerie huffed. "I'm mad at the both of you for leaving me here while you went to Redrim!"

I paused. "Why?"

"Because," she shot a pointed glare at Setizar, one that could kindle the heat of a thousand suns, "he always becomes so drained afterwards and you knew nothing about the process! It was stupid, inconceivable—"

"We didn't have a choice." Setizar placed his hand on her white head before drawing a finger up her horn. "Perhaps it was for the better. You know Inanna hurts you."

Cerie groaned, shaking his hand away before rubbing her horn. "I still don't like it."

"Now that we have that settled." Setizar stood before me, bowing. "Meris, let's go eat. I'm famished, as I'm sure you are as well."

"I'm getting there." I slipped my hand into his, my heart beginning to beat faster as his skin touched mine. "What are we eating?"

"Depends on what's prepared."

The way his eyes cut into me made me wonder if there was more he wished to say.

32

I slept in. I knew I did. The tailor was supposed to be there in the afternoon, but I was certain I had time to get ready.

Stretching out my numb legs, I lifted my arms to embrace the sunlight. Wait. Sunlight?

I glanced at the clock chiming in the corner. One? My pulse quickened as the afternoon wind trickled through my open window. I leaped out of bed, scrounging up a decent pair of pants and shirt before scurrying into the lavatory. Why didn't I wake earlier?

Closing the door in a fit, I faced myself in the mirror. I looked like death chewed me up and spat me out. Dark bags tugged at my eyes, followed by my odiously pale complexion. What was this? I released a growl. Three red dots formed a triangle on my chin, and one was on my cheek. It looked angry and aggravated. Of course. It was where everyone in the realm could see it.

My wings tightened as my frustration built. So having magic didn't keep the spots away… *perfect*. I washed my face and pulled my hair up into a bun, not bothering to do anything with it. I had enough to worry about.

As soon as I stepped foot out of the lavatory, my bedroom door swung open.

The man from the town—the flaming pumpkin-headed man—entered. "Ah!" He made a sweeping bow which looked to be part of a dance. "My lady. A pleasure to see you again."

I nodded quickly, not entirely knowing why he was here.

"Are you ready to prepare your dress?" His hollow, triangular eyes squinted as a smile spread over his face—or, what I assumed to be a smile. He was a carved pumpkin, after all, who's alive and on fire.

Wait. *He's* my tailor?

"I've brought my suitcase, hoping we can find the suitable garment material with your preferred color." He clapped his hands and two faery boys came in, keeping their poppy-red eyes turned down, hauling a large trunk between them.

"I'm sorry." I scratched my head. Why did I have to sleep in? I looked a mess! "What's your name?"

He froze. The fire encasing his head flickered slightly. "Jack, my lady. Jack O'Lantern."

Really. That was his name?

He flipped open the trunk. "What are you envisioning?" His eyes locked with me, or more importantly, all of me, as if assessing what would need to be done. "I think we should choose something that will accentuate those wings. Something simple, but enough to wow the spectators."

"I'd rather be… hidden." I thought hard, focusing on my wings. "I'd rather blend into the crowd instead of stand out."

He looked at me, his eyes narrowing. "It's your ball, my lady. You don't wish to stand out, at least a little?"

I shook my head. Well, I did in a way. Who didn't want to be looked at and admired? But the possibility that it would turn out horribly for me outweighed anything else. "I'm certain."

He shrugged, thin fingers pulling fabric from the trunk. "Take your pick."

There were some that were as black as midnight, not even catching the afternoon light. Some were ethereal white and red and silver swatches, so bright and flashy that I couldn't seem to picture myself in them.

Finally, I held up a swatch. It was a muted gold color, earthy, but shimmered in a way that made it seem to be coated in magic. It draped over my fingers like warm water, soothing and perfect.

"Like that one?"

I nodded.

"Good!" His gaze still seemed unconvinced by my defiance in wanting to stand out. "Do you want it in a different color? Perhaps black, or red—"

As much as I loved the idea, I thought those colors would be too bold. I shook my head, assuring myself that I've made the right choice.

Jack sighed heavily, but he didn't pressure me with anything else.

I was nervous about his flaming head near all this fabric—what if he caught something on fire?

"Miss?" he said, poking my rib. "Can you please stand on that stool while I take your measurements? I need to get this right."

I nodded. "Of course." My head was in a haze. It was probably because of the late hour I slept. I didn't even pay attention to him as he measured and chatted. I couldn't help but think of Setizar... of his arms around me when we laid in his bed within the Northern Kingdom of Winter. The way his fingers weaved through my hair, as if they were meant to be there... as if he knew exactly where to stroke to calm me. I could listen to his soothing, accented voice till I died.

Oh, I was a fool! Why did I keep forgetting that he was my captor? That he only needed me to break this curse and then I was a discarded rag...

But my stomach still fluttered when I thought about him. When did this even happen?

"...and of course she just vanished!"

"What?" I blinked. Did I miss a whole story? "Who did what?"

He looked at me, clearly not pleased that I ignored his whole tale. "Well, aren't you a good listener. I was just speaking about how ridiculous this whole situation is. We don't even know if we can trust you to get the Box, or that you can even open the Box. A gamble our Autumn Lord is making." Jack exhaled, losing his patience, I believe. "If Alecto were still living, the curse on Setizar could be broken and everything the Silver Queen did would be void, since it's rumored that Alecto is the only one who would be able to open the Box which has sealed the Lords' powers away."

Now that was new.

"Anyway, she was a true queen!" He placed his thin, twig-fingers over his heart—if there was even a heart there. "A beauty among creatures. Fire in the darkness of our world. Warmth in the cold!"

Obsessed much? "Do you know how the Silver Queen killed her?"

Jack paused, tapping where his chin should be. "No. No idea. The only one who would know that is her sister, and she's been missing for as long as Alecto has been dead. So, I have no answers." He stood, plucking a paper from the box and scribbling something down. Measurements perhaps.

His thin, squared shoulders rolled forward a bit as he hunched over whatever he was doing.

"Why was Alecto so…important?" I had to ask, I had to know the answer.

He threw his head back in dramatic display of his displeasure. "Really now!" He made a small mark on the paper, then folded it. "She was the High Queen of the Day! It is a place, the Afterworld for us weary Yamirians, in a sense. You see, when a creature dies, it goes to the Afterworld and lives the rest of eternity there. All creatures except the furies, mind you. The furies are immortal and therefore cannot die unless they give their immortality away. They are simply reborn." My mind went blank. "Well, unless killed by the blade of a Midnight Traveler blessed by the Stars. But that is a rare thing to find, but the only thing able to kill an immortal. Stab an immortal with that, and they're dead forever."

"Is that what happened to Alecto?"

He huffed, a small puff of smoke escaping his carved lips. "Really now. I told you I don't know what happened." He yanked the paper up and flapped it in the air. "Well, I must be going. I will have your dress finished and shipped here as soon as possible."

"When did Setizar send for you?"

"Always asking so many questions! Am I a teacher now? Is this a lecture? I should be paid better." He closed the trunk with a resounding click, brushing off some dust from the lid. "Just a few days ago, if you're truly that desperate to know. He said he wanted the dress prepared before your birthday, for the ball of course."

I nodded.

"Well, good day." Jack bowed at the waist. "And, if you want to get rid of," he pointed to his chin, as a silent reference to my face, "those, you should use witch hazel and clary sage. It works wonders on the skin."

Before I could reply, he was gone.

I frowned at his retreating back. If Alecto was the only one who could open the Box, then how would I do it?

33

The clock struck two. After Jack's visit, I spent the rest of my day looking for Setizar, or clues, neither of which I found. I'd lost several hours of sleep already, and my head hurt, but I couldn't sleep.

A hammer crashing against my skull would be more pleasant than this throbbing pain.

I stumbled out of my bed, grabbing a drink of water. What did this mean? What did everything mean? What if finding Megaera was the clue? What if she was the missing piece to this puzzle?

My stomach turned molten, boiling and readying its assault. I drank the water. The cold liquid cooled my insides, washing over my heated organs and bringing a form of relief.

How would I open the Box if only Alecto could? How? My head hurt too much.

A hollow sound filled the air, and I turned. Setizar sat on the couch in my room. Well, he showed up now and not earlier when I had all the good questions to ask him. I'd almost forgotten most of them.

He leaned against the arm, resting languidly along the velvet-red cushion. His coat pooled around him, and the little sapphire buttons on his navy-blue shirt glinted in the low light of the room. "Meris, I heard you weren't feeling well."

I crossed my arms. "Where were you earlier? No one knew where you went."

His flash of a white smile was layered with mystery and secrets. "When did the headache come on?"

"How did you know—"

"I can see it in your eyes." He exhaled, shaking his head. "You get this look in your eyes, it's like an eye-wince—" He stopped. "Everyone does it."

I groaned, kneading my temples. "I just want it to end. Maybe if I bash my head against the marble."

"And ruin my interior?"

I cut him a glare I hoped looked as feral as I wished it.

He smiled. "Come here, Meris. I can't do anything about headaches, but I can help ease that tension in your shoulders. I think your heavy wings are causing it."

"If I could control these things!" I hissed. It was honestly getting worse and worse by the second. "Either way, what can you do about it?"

"Sit here, and you'll see."

I shuffled over to the couch and sitting beside him. His cool fingers glided over the hot skin along my neck, pressing against the knotted muscles. It hurt, but in the best way.

A moan escaped my lips as I leaned into his palm, my head lightening. "The tailor came today…"

"Oh?" He didn't sound shocked at all, not that I expected him to. "How did it go? I'm sorry I couldn't make it."

"Liar."

He chuckled, and it was the only answer I needed. He was doing something secret that he clearly didn't want me to know about.

"He said some interesting things about Alecto." I chose my words carefully, not wanting his easy demeanor to change.

Too late. He stiffened just at the name. "What did Jack say?"

"He said she was a queen, and that she was the only one who could break your curse." I angled my head. "Which makes me wonder—"

"Why I said you are the one to help me?" he mumbled, fingers trailing down my spine. "Things are complicated. I promise I'll tell you when the time is right. I'll tell you every detail you need to know. But now... it's not time."

"Why?" I snapped, fully facing him. "Why not now? What makes you think I'm not ready?"

"Meris—"

"No!" I stood, not caring that my back tightened at my sudden movement, or that my head was pounding viciously. "Tell me. Tell me everything."

"I can't, Meris!" Setizar raised his voice, then buried his head in his hands. "You don't understand. I can't tell you yet." He looked up at me with eyes like clear-cut diamonds reflecting the blue and purple light in the room. "This? I never wished for anything to happen this way. But here we are. We are here, stuck in this state of touch and go. If I told you now, you wouldn't take it well."

"Why? What makes you think that?"

Rage slithered across his face. "Enough. I can't tell you, and that's final."

"Then you have no business being in my room." I raised my head. My wings, half-covered in feathers, did nothing to aid me in my attempt to look menacing. I must have looked like a freshly hatched chick. Not that I cared too much. I was too frustrated to care.

He raised his brow, crossing his arms. "As you wish, *all mighty one*. I will be gone. Enjoy the rest of your night." And with that, he vanished into thin air.

Great.

Clapping echoed behind me. "Well done! Honestly, I didn't know you had that in you. Really showed him who's boss."

Tatum. Of all the times he had to show up, it'd be now. "What are you doing here?"

"Oh, just watching the show. You are highly entertaining. I can't believe he stayed as long as he did."

I rolled my eyes, falling face-first into bed. "Leave me alone."

"You're as dense as a frozen bucket of water." Tatum flicked my temple, and my headache worsened. "How many hints do you need?"

I reached out to grab him, but he danced out of my reach.

"Really, now?"

"Just leave!" I wanted to sleep... to forget everything. I couldn't think straight tonight. Everything was confusing, and *nothing* was making any sense. Why couldn't this just be easier?

"I'll leave, Meris." Tatum leaned down, his lips against my ear. "But you will have to beg for me to appear again. Remember, I'm only here to help. You're the only one who can see or hear me, and you're also the one pushing me away."

"I don't ever want to see your wretched face again, understood? You cause nothing but trouble, and you ruin my sleep." I swatted at him. For a moment I thought a look of sadness flitted across his face.

"Remember. You will have to *beg* for me to return."

Then, he faded into shadows.

Perhaps I was too harsh on both of them.

PART FOUR
WEEK THREE IN YAMIRA

34

The thrum of rain beat against the glass windows, matching the rhythm of the aching pulse in my head and wings.

After rolling out of bed, I shuffled to the lavatory. So many things seemed to have gone wrong and, for some reason, last night's disagreement with Setizar and Tatum seemed like the worst part. I shucked off my clothes and dipped into the already drawn bath, trying to navigate my focus on washing myself.

I leaned into the magic water, my stiff muscles relaxing until my wings bumped either edge of the tub. *Great. Just, great.*

Focus. *Focus. Focus on the wings...* bringing them inward, hiding them in my skin.

My back heated, and just like that, the burning sensation ceased and my body felt lighter, yet heavier at the same time. "Aether!" I shouted, plugging my fist into the water. "Why! Why am I here? This is the third week and I'm no closer to anything!" I wanted to cry. Frustration pillowed in my chest and slithered into my throat.

Mae must be terrified. She'd lost Julna, and now me. She had no one left. I failed her—

Warm tears streamed down my face. There was no winning against this. No beating the life that was destined to choke me to death. My insides were dead, and breathing was painful. Tears weren't enough. I hurt... and I didn't even know what was hurting. Everything within me was writhing...

wanting to be free.

I splashed my face, washing myself off in hopes of feeling better. My eyes stung still, as if the weight of my failure alone was drawing out my tears. I knew there must be more to it. More to this ache and despair. With a long breath in, I pushed those thoughts to the back of my mind and clambered out of the tub to dry off.

Failure. Failure.

I slipped on my black shirt, tying the back strings securely.

You'll never be good enough. You let everyone down.

The smell of green tea and citrus filled my nose as I massaged the lotion on my arms, still trying to distract myself.

A powerful creature? Liar. You're still powerless.

No.

I clenched my fists, the lotion slicking my palms. Fire flickered around my knuckles, sizzling the oil.

A few steps and I flung open my balcony doors. Would it be so bad to test myself? To spread my wings and fly?

You can't do it.

The storm raged around me; my wings tore from my back, shielding my eyes. Lightning struck in the distance, its web-like fingers splintering through the dark skies.

My wings opened, stiffening against the wind and rain.

You're a fool.

I was born with *wings*. I could do this.

Go ahead and die. That's all you're good for.

I hissed a breath. My wings were taut, my every muscle constricting. Something pounded against my chest. Was that my heartbeat?

I clambered onto the ledge, the wind picking up as I did. I was so far from the ground… I could see the tips of the trees.

A hand pressed against my back. "Don't jump, Meris."

Setizar?

His words alone were enough to make up my mind, to escape this voice in my head. "Watch me." And I leapt from the ledge.

Wind pelted my body, pushing me upward. Limbs stiffened and reflex took over. Setizar's shouts were barely audible over the screaming wind.

I was flying!

Rain and mountain air rushed around me, lifting me higher and higher still. Coils of courage weaved through me, lifting my sinking spirits.

The autumn world below, drenched in a hue of mist and gray from the crying sky, looked like a painting. A moving, delicate painting.

Like the painting Aurel made.

My wings wavered for a half second, and I began plunging downward. Rain pelted my face, my arms—I was a feather, weighed by a brick.

Not now.

I didn't want to die!

Fire burst around me, and I plummeted into a pool of water.

Up was down... down was up. The water held a hand over my mouth and nose. I couldn't breathe. My body was too stunned. Too unsure.

A hand gripped mine, yanking me up.

I was breathing? No, coughing, actually. Water spilt out of my lips, spewing all over my savior—

"Aurel?" I screeched, blinking. Oh no.

"Well, now we're both drenched." He gave me a dazzling smile. "You're lucky I'm on my way to Setizar's palace now, otherwise I am certain you would've drowned." He looked down. "You need to get changed or you'll catch a cold."

I offered him a half grin, shivering from head to toe. "Thank you."

"What were you doing up there?" He braced his hands on his hips, looking up at the sky. He was rather soaked, like me, but not as bad. A horse and carriage were just off the side of the road, waiting patiently for his return.

"I wanted to see if I could fly."

He released a loud laugh, his eyes bright. "That's a very interesting thing to do, and something completely in your character." He gestured to the carriage, his brow raising. "Need a ride back?"

I nodded and swallowed a frozen shiver. "How far are we from the castle?"

"*Palace*," said a voice behind me. Setizar. And judging from his tone, he was *not* pleased.

"And here I didn't think you would show up so far from your nest." Aurel crossed his arms. I was not in the mood for their banter.

Setizar clicked his tongue, clearly not in the mood for this either. "You're about a mile away from the palace, Meris. Congratulations. You learned how to mist." His eyes flicked Aurel's direction. "You aren't supposed to be here for another week."

"That's about three days later than the ball."

"I intended on you missing it."

"I know." Aurel grinned. "Which is why I'm early."

Setizar's cat-like eyes narrowed, anger and irritation weaving through his gaze. Thunder cracked and lightning splintered the heavens into a thousand pieces. "Meris, if you want to head back with me, then take my hand. If you want to ride back with Aurel, then stay here with him."

Despite everything, I wanted to get back. I wanted to stay with Setizar, to feel the warmth of a fire and sip a cup of tea. The dunk in the cold water and plummet from the sky reentered my thoughts. Shivers wracked my body, and gooseflesh rose on my arms. I slipped my hand into his, and his expression turned from rigid to soft. He gave my hand a gentle squeeze, dipping his head so his lips were by my ear.

"Thank you," he whispered. There was more to this than just their banter. There was more under all these layers.

Wind and mist swirled around us, and I could only catch a second glance at Aurel. His hands were in his pockets as water dripped down his white shirt, clinging the fabric to his broad shoulders, allowing the hints of his tribal-like tattoos to show through. Long, wet hair clung to his amber-hued skin.

Despite it all, it was his eyes that gave me pause. Gray like silver waters and unflinching stone, and yet, the shade of sorrow and freshly shed tears.

I could no longer see him.

We'd misted back to the palace.

35

I stumbled as the mist ended, dumping us in my room.

"You—" Setizar froze. His eyes were a conflict of rage and worry. "You could have *died*! What demon possessed you to jump from the balcony?"

"I…" What could I say? That something in me said I couldn't? Said I wasn't worth anything? That I wanted to prove to the voice that I could jump and take flight. "I can—"

"No!" He clenched his fists. "No, you can't. You can't. I can't lose…" He stopped himself from whatever he'd been about to say. "You aren't ready to fly yet. You aren't ready, period."

"Who made you the judge of that?" I stepped closer, closing the gap between us. "You may be my captor, I may be indebted to you, but don't you think for a second that I will roll over. I'm not that kind of person."

"You're a child," he ground out. "You couldn't defeat me in the woods, you can't hold your own in combat, you can't even read the texts here without my help! What makes you think you can do anything without knowing more? What makes you think you can jump out a *window* and not get hurt? I can't always be here to save you, Meris. If you die, we all *die*."

"I'm no child," I said, inches away from his face. Heat radiated off my skin, billowing from my body. "And I think I can save myself."

His eyes froze in mine, layers of words melting in his red and gray eyes. "I'm not saying you won't be able to. I'm saying don't be so rash. If you die, or if you get hurt, I don't know what I'd do." His words were cold on my skin, slithering down my spine like caressing fingers.

"I think you should leave my room." I lifted my head, trying to ignore the nagging guilt and anger prickling around my heart.

"This is my home." His smile flickered with amusement. "Keep that in mind."

"I know full well this is your home. Now, if you would," I gestured to the door behind him "leave."

"Funny." He crossed his arms. "You just said you know this is my home, yet the way you spoke makes me think you don't believe that."

"You're the one flipping from hot to cold." I leaned against the bed-post.

"I'm the one...?" Frustration returned to his face, cutting his jawline and furrowing his brows.

"Fed up with me yet, Setizar?"

"I'm getting there."

"Why don't you just let me go?"

"Not happening." His eyes solidified, appearing like solid blue opals. This was the first time I'd seen them like that, and somehow it filled me with dread. "I'm not letting you go until this curse is broken."

Five days. The portal would open and I would leave. For good. "I know." I slackened my body. Chills shivered up my spine, and my teeth chattered.

"Good." Setizar exhaled. What was wrong with him? Ever since Eira's castle he'd been on edge... borderline skittish. "I'll leave you be, then. Brunch is to be served soon. Don't be late."

"Don't count on me attending."

His back was to me, but I could tell he stiffened. "So, we're back to square one?"

"Yes." I crossed my arms. "I regret ever leaving it."

— ☾ —

I kicked the bedpost, a stab of pain shooting through my foot in the process. I screeched, wanting to throw something. What's wrong with me?

It was my house as much as it was his.

I froze. Why would I think that? That made no sense. I needed to calm down. There has been too much going on, and I just needed to breathe and get a handle on everything. I was losing my mind.

Maybe I should just go to brunch and try and smooth things out. I'd flown off the handle, granted he should probably apologize. For what? I didn't know.

Alright. I was just being petty. I slipped out of my still wet clothes, frustrated with myself. Wait—

Aurel.

He hadn't seemed the least bit phased by my wings, or me fire-balling through the sky and into the water. Why? Why didn't he even ask any questions? It seemed so… unlike him.

How would I know it was unlike him?

I shook my head and slipped on a sleek black evening gown. My hair was still somewhat wet, even after I dried it, so I quickly braided it.

It only took me a few minutes, but I was down the corridor and working my way to the dining hall.

Opening the doors, I braced myself for the pointed looks and questioning gazes.

"Ah," Aurel smiled. "Didn't I tell you she would come down?" His eyes narrowed. "And she looks absolutely stunning."

Setizar didn't bother to look at me. "You have a way with words, Aurel. I imagine your subjects sit along your throne and scribble them down on parchment."

"How did you know?" Aurel grinned. "They do so enjoy reading my sacred words to themselves before they go to sleep."

"Masochists." Setizar huffed. "Is that a way to assure nightmares?"

I barely succeeded in not rolling my eyes. Well, this was going to be so much fun.

Aurel gestured to a seat beside him. "Come and sit. I promise I won't treat you like this unholy pig does. Honestly, have you thought more about staying in Summer with me?" He leaned forward, grinning like a bear. "Best part: It's better than here."

"Anywhere seems better than here right now."

Aurel breathed in, opening his mouth as if to speak, but Setizar cut him off.

"Meris. I will be walking the grounds later. I wish for you to accompany me."

Aurel scrunched his nose, his eyes darting between Setizar and me.

"I think we should spend some time alone, and clear things up."

"Does this mean you're finally going to tell me that thing you said you weren't?"

Setizar's laugh was dry and humorless, an airy thing woven from stars and sea foam. "No."

I half wanted to jump up and knock him upside the head, the other half of me wanted to turn my heel and not look back.

"Let's eat first. No one should make decisions before breakfast." Aurel patted the seat beside him with a bit more passion than before. "Bad decisions are made on an empty stomach."

"Shut up, Aurel," Setizar barked through his teeth. "Why don't you slither back to Summer and roast in the sun."

"Why would I roast myself when you do it so well?"

Setizar was speechless.

"One for me." Aurel looked at Cerie standing in the corner, her hooves crossed. "What does that make now?"

She shook her head. "I don't keep count like you do."

"Then start. I have one, Setizar has zero."

36

The way my heels clicked against the floors sounded like shards of glass clattering against marble. The little stars were nowhere to be seen, and my nerves writhed along my skin. "So, are you going to tell me everything?"

"No. But I do wish to regain our friendship," Setizar said in a voice coated with smoke and honey. "We've made too many strides... bonded too much to fall back to what we were when you first arrived."

"You're forgetting," I ran my hands through my hair, loosening my braid, "I'm still your prisoner."

"You're not a prisoner, Meris. You have no chains, and you do not serve me. But you're safer in my home. Here you need not fear the world. Yamira is dangerous—"

"So is my world!" I clenched my fists, wind peeling through the dark hallway. "The danger there may not be a hungry beast in the woods every twenty seconds, but the people are just as dangerous. They make you feel safe and then tear you apart. They make you wish they were a creature that peeled your skin off your bones." I shook my head. "You don't know."

Silence rippled through the space forming between us. A mortal wound festering. If it were bleeding, I would feel better. But it wasn't. It leaked from somewhere in my soul, killing me slowly.

"No, I don't know." Setizar stood inches away. "And I don't expect you to ever tell me. I am still a stranger to you." His voice dripped with an emotion I couldn't quite place. "Remember I'm doing this for everyone. You can't go home unless we figure this out, together."

He didn't know Tatum told me everything I needed to escape this world. The full moon was the night of the ball.

"Let's try this again, then?" Setizar dipped his head, smiling. "I'm Setizar, welcome to my home. You're my honored guest, and you'll be treated as such."

I couldn't help the smile. He had that power lately… to make me smile even when I was angry at him. "You're the absolute worst jinni I've ever had the displeasure of meeting."

"The worst jinni you've ever had the displeasure of meeting…" His chuckle was sultry and winsome, holding innocence and guile all at once. "Let's hope I can hold that title then. I don't wish for anyone to best me."

I nodded. "I will admit…" It hurt to say. "I overreacted a bit. There was no reason to lash out like that with you when you really are trying to help." Why did I feel like an emotional wreck?

"No. Don't apologize. I have been a tad overbearing. I'm sorry."

I smiled, allowing myself to take his arm. "Forgiven." We began to walk down the halls.

"Want to go somewhere with me?"

"Where?"

He smiled, a lilting mystical thing spreading between us and tightening around my heart. "A secret."

— (—

The doors opened and the solarium's peculiar magic washed over me. "Here?" I asked, testing the limits of the room. "Why did you bring me here?"

"Because it's a very special place to me." He shrugged off his coat and it turned to mist and starlight. "I'm sure you've come in here before."

I nodded, allowing myself to explore the solarium more. My fingers grazed the soft leaves of the glowing willows. "I have. It was an...experience."

"Why do you say that?"

"I went for a swim right in the middle of the magical pool."

I expected a laugh, a mocking comment, or ridicule. Instead, he simply said, "Then let's jump into the water."

I laughed, looking around the trunk of the glowing willow. Setizar leaned against the tree, looking at me as if I was the only thing in this world. "You're mad."

That grin returned as he twined his fingers with my own. The touch sent shivers down my spine. "I can't help that, Meris," he whispered. "Madness is my sanity."

I rolled my shoulders. If I jumped from a balcony, I could jump into a magical pool. "Fine. But I need proper swim clothes if you expect me to do this."

He laughed, shaking his head. "Why worry? Why not just... jump?"

"I'm in a dress!"

"You'll look like a mermaid."

I glared.

"An angry mermaid."

I slapped his arm, unable to withhold my smirk. "Fine. I'll beat you into the water."

Before I could move, he caught my hand. Mist and air exploded around me, as did Setizar's mischievous laugh. We dropped a few feet, and the water rushed over my body.

"Jerk!" I shouted, regaining my bearings.

Water slicked his dark hair to his face, framing gleaming amethyst and emerald eyes. "I believe we tied. Both hit the water at the same time."

"You cheated." I laughed, leaning my head into the water. Prismatic ripples swirled around my arms and fingers, licking my skin with forgotten memories of carnival treats and red roses. "I shouldn't trust you."

"Why would I cheat to tie?"

A laugh bubbled out of my mouth, uninhibited by anything. "You'd prefer tying rather than losing, I believe." I lifted my head again, catching him staring. "What?"

"I was just thinking…" He swam nearer, so close I could almost touch him. "You really do look like an angry mermaid."

I splashed the water toward him, laughing as he turned. His face scrunched up as he failed to avoid the projectile droplets. "You really wish to play dirty?"

"No, but your face was priceless," I said as I struggled to stay afloat.

He laughed, looping his arm around my waist. His eyes were limned with starlight, emanating pure rays of memory and life. "Tell me something, Meris?" he whispered, pulling me closer. "Tell me this isn't going to end in disaster. Tell me this will work out and that it isn't pointless. I don't care if it's a lie. I don't care if you don't mean a single word. Just tell me that we will fix what's been broken." His voice simmered with pain as tears rolled down his cheeks.

And, despite the happiness and peace I felt then, tears were falling down mine.

The magic of the pool. The happiness which breaks your heart.

I pressed my forehead against his, our tears reflecting the light of the glowing willows. "We will win, Setizar." My heart shuddered, cracking against my bones. This was the second time I've been this vulnerable around him. "This isn't pointless." It took everything in me to add, "We aren't pointless."

His eyes locked with mine, gleaming with tears and magic. They were the blue of sorrow, and the gold of promise. His copper-hued skin, wet from the water, was contoured by shadows and turquoise light.

"Tell me something, Setizar?" I closed my eyes, gripping tighter to his neck as I pressed my forehead harder against his. "Please tell me you didn't make a mistake. Tell me I'm not a gamble, or a random roll of the dice. That I won't break my own heart?"

Something warm pressed against my cheek; the fluttering softness of a kiss that set my body alight. "You aren't a mistake, Meris. This isn't a gamble. You're much, much more than a random roll of the dice." I opened my eyes. His brows were furrowed, and his voice dripped with sincerity. "And I'm not lying when I say it. I believe every word. You were born to do great things. You were born to free the universe and tame the fiery mountains."

I breathed in. He smelled of autumn and spices, the scent of a creature who could break my heart and walk away without a hint of regret. But I would let him. If he chose to take my heart and toss it into a fire, I would let him.

I would let him make promises and break them.

I would return to him; love him even if he loved someone else. I would do that, from afar if needed. Because, here in this pool, I realized it. I realized how much I belonged to him, how much my heart yearned to be tangled with his.

Our breath mingled together, twining in the air and tangling like the threads of fated yarn. Our lips were inches away, a small tilt of our heads could bring them crashing together. Temptation gripped me around the throat. I wanted to fall into him and devour the warmth he ignited within me.

"We should get out." I pressed against his chest, pushing myself away from him and gripping the ledge.

The tears didn't stop. They continued to drip slowly, assuredly, down into the water.

But this time, it wasn't prompted by the magic of the room.Because these tears are coiled with the pain in my heart, the ache in my chest.

I loved Setizar.

37

The rain dripped down my bedroom window pane like small beings conjured from dreams. My breath fogged the glass, blurring my view, mirroring my hazy memories.

"Come on!" A female voice, so similar to my own, said. It was ghost-ly, like the memory of a voice. *"Hurry, Setizar, or you'll miss it!"*

"Darling, what am I going to miss? You haven't filled me in yet."

The female's laugh was all I heard, and Setizar was all I saw. He was so happy, so at ease. There was a smile on his face, and a glimmer of love in his eyes.

This was frustrating. I was seeing things that weren't even real. This place was messing with me. I needed to leave before I didn't know what was up and what was down. A shadowy veil draped over my emotions and reality.

Could I leave Setizar, though?

"I'm so confused!" I dropped to my knees, pressing my back against the mute-gray wall. "I don't understand."

Rogue hands wrapped around my waist, jarring me. I opened my eyes, but no one was there. Aether. What was happening to me?

Just a few more days, I reminded myself. Just a few more days.

Just a few more days.

I pushed off the floor, my back burning. Why couldn't I make heads or tails of this whole situation? My room was coated in a dull blue light, like a clouded winter sky.

Three taps at my door jarred me once more. "Yes?"

Aurel's head popped into the room. His smile glittered like diamonds, washing the chamber in warmth. He was a summer day entering a chilly autumn evening, dispersing the cinnamon aroma with the scent of sea breeze and sun.

"Meris. How're you doing?" He shoved his hands into his pockets, his expression turning from jovial to concerned.

"I'm fine."

His eyes narrowed. "You say that, but you don't mean it."

I crossed my arms. "And you think you know what I do and don't mean?"

"I'm just concerned for you—"

"Why?" I felt myself unraveling. "Why are you concerned? We only spoke briefly. We spent barely enough time to become acquainted. Why would you be concerned about a stranger?"

The muscles in his jaw feathered, his eyes solidifying into a terrifying shade of iron-gray. "At least one thing remains the same."

His words tore my anger in two, leaving only a bleeding mess of confusion. "What?"

Aurel turned away from me. In the low light of the room, I could see his tense muscles. He was... retreating.

"Aurel—"

"Rest, Meris." He turned his head and smiled at me. It was so...familiar. As if this very scene had played in my mind before. Before I could question it further, the door clicked closed, and I was alone.

— ☾ —

One more day and I'd be attending a ball.

"Meris," Setizar said. I forgot he was here. He was leaning casually against the windowsill, looking out into the rainy autumn evening. I'd not seen him that casual—as if he had prepared to go to bed and changed his mind last minute and slipped on a velvety green dressing robe. "You've been awful quiet. Something amiss?"

Should I tell him of all the odd things happening? The strange feeling I get when I'm near him—as if I've known him all my life and yet he's a complete stranger? "No." I released a sigh laden with my suppressed feelings. "I'm just tired."

A slither of emotion crept over his features but vanished just as quick as it came. He nodded. "I'll ask Cerie to help you to bed tonight. After everything, I'm sure you could use the company of another female."

I tried not to laugh. He had an interesting way of speaking and communicating. "Alright, thank you. I'll see you tomorrow."

A subtle smirk lifted his lips. What was he thinking? What was running though his mind to make him smile like that?

A shrill cold fluttered over my spine, wrapping around my body like a frozen blanket before a fluttering warmth spread through my veins. "Setizar." I breathed in, trying to find a smidgen of courage. "I think something was wrong with Aurel today."

"Something is always wrong with Aurel, actually he is wrong. He's been wrong ever since—" He stopped himself, as if processing what I said. "What happened?"

"He came in my room."

"He what?" Setizar's eyes shivered a hue darker. "If he—"

"Aurel just wanted to check on me!" I couldn't let him keep talking. I needed to make sure he knew what happened. "But it was strange. Like we both knew more than we were saying to one another, but neither of us were actually saying it. It's like he knows me better than he's letting on."

Setizar leaned back against the wall, his body relaxing. "Why do you think that?"

"I don't know." My fingers trembled. My wings wanted to pop back out. Maybe I was just overthinking.

Setizar pushed himself off the wall, shoving his hands into the deep pockets on either side of his robe. His slippered feet shuffled against the marble floors as he mumbled something under his breath. The silence that took over the room was agonizing. "Well, perhaps a good night's sleep will do you good."

I nodded, looking out into the hall. "Alright." I took a few steps, catching sight of Cerie outside the sitting room. Her sun-bright eyes smiled as she extended her hand to me.

I took it, and we began our walk.

"He seems concerned," Cerie said, her voice trailing off. "Did something happen?"

I released a breath, shrugging. "I'm not sure." Everything was so foggy, so uncertain. I came into this world wanting one thing and one thing alone. Now I didn't know what I really wanted...

38

My wings tore through my shirt and woke me with a start.

Great.

I struggled, sitting up and trying to readjust myself. Every bone burned. My back was a series of stressed knots. Why did everything hurt so much?

Sighing, I shucked off my torn shirt and the rest of my clothes, readying to climb into the tub and wash the ache of my joints away.

"Morning, Meris—"

Seeing Setizar standing by the door, I screeched. "Get out of my room!"

"My house."

My wings curled around me, covering whatever skin I could. "Excuse me for wanting privacy!"

Setizar chuckled.

What a menace.

"Well, I came here to tell you breakfast is ready."

"You could have knocked."

"Like you are ever doing anything remotely interesting." He snapped his fingers, and a new outfit appeared on the foot of the bed. "An early birthday present."

I glared.

He raised his hands, backing up. "Fine, fine. I'm leaving. Will I see you at breakfast?"

"Yes."

A bright smile erupted on his face. It wasn't like Aurel's smile, warm and scorching like a summer afternoon, but gentle and calm, sparking joy in my heart like an autumn morning. "Thank you." Then he was gone, encased in a purple mist.

I exhaled a long breath and grabbing the clothes he put down. It was similar to the first outfit I wore when I arrived, but different. Slimming and beautiful, yet somehow it showed a bit less skin.

Two, long sheer pleats of red fabric fell from the waist, nearly kissing the floor. Under the skirt the trousers, skin-tight and black, shimmered with diamond dust.

I pulled on my shirt. The back was open for my wings. The sleeves were similar the sheets of sheer fabric on my pants, sewn into the black tunic. The outfit was stunning. I quickly combed through my hair, braiding it off to the side.

Finally, I slid into the black slippers, brushed my teeth, and began my trek to the dining hall. Why was Setizar seemingly so excited about me joining him for breakfast?

Something must be different about today.

The stars erupted below my feet, filling me with joy. I hadn't seen them like this in a few days. They were brighter today—more alive.

Something clattered down the hall, and I looked up. Four servants scurried along... *Wait. Servants? Did he hire people?*

I rushed to the dining hall, unsure what was happening. Pressing my hands to the door, I breathed in, readying myself for whatever awaited me. The doors flung open at my touch, and bright sunlight poured through the windows. "Ah! Meris!" Aurel stood, as did the invisible man I'd met in Nightmore with Jack.

He tipped his top hat, and I could only see his monocle and mustache. "Hello again, my lady."

I bowed, forgetting the man's name or if he ever mentioned it to begin with.

"Ah." Aurel cleared his throat. "This is Sir Libby. He is the Master librarian in Nightmore."

"Indeed," Libby said with a lilt in his voice, placing the hat back on his invisible head. "I have come at the request of lord Setizar. He wishes for me to help organize the guests and be sure none with foul intentions sneak in." He waved his hand, gesturing to something. "I have eyes and ears all around this place. I'm positive we shall have no issue the entire night."

I blinked. "Thank you."

Libby nodded, turning his attention back to Aurel. "Now, what were you saying to me about—"

"Ah!" Aurel threw his hands up, sliding them behind his head. "It's honestly nothing. We should get eating. Where's Setizar?"

This was so strange... the way Aurel was acting was far more unsettling than most things the past few weeks. Libby appeared uneasy as well. Or, at least I thought so. His shoulders were tight and his entire posture shifted, turning curious. "Well, I shall have to be going. Come along." He made a quick gesture with his hand, and a dozen footsteps echoed around me. Invisible beings like him?

The room turned silent as soon as Libby left, only Aurel, Cerie, and I remained.

"Where's Setizar?"

Aurel shrugged casually, raising a brow. His eyes were a hue of steel and iron. "Don't know, and I don't care."

"What?"

He smirked. "I wanted to make a good impression on Libby. He's a rather big deal in Nightmore. I don't want to get on his bad side."

I sat across from him, resting my elbow on the redwood table. "Aren't you supposed to be all charming?"

His eyes flicked to Cerie. "I suppose some are immune to my charms."

"Maybe if you were just yourself, like you were when you were painting me."

He blinked. "What?"

"When you were painting me. You were completely yourself."

His eyes narrowed, and he shook his head. "Most don't appreciate sincerity, Meris. They have an idea of what they want, and I give it to them. Nothing in between."

"Why are you trying to impress those who don't want you for who you are?"

This was the first time that I'd seen Aurel confused. It spread over his features, withering the light away from his eyes. "Because I don't even know who I am."

His voice dripped with a foreign, yet so familiar pain. Perhaps I should change the subject, to put him at ease. "So, what's Libby? I've never seen an invisible being before."

"Perhaps that's because they're invisible."

A laugh and groan escaped my lips. "Hilarious."

"I think so." He smiled, shifting in his seat and grabbing his tea. "Libby is a Fae. There's many species. The northern Fae look rather human, the southern Fae look very much like plants, while the eastern Fae have skin as dark as midnight and eyes as bright as fire. All of these, of course, once had two forms…but that has been lost since the Silver Queen had attacked."

"So, that means Libby is a—"

"A Fae from the western territory." Aurel gulped down his tea, licking his lips after he put the cup back down. "They're rather secretive, and we have yet to speak to their ruler. Not that they bother us. Libby is one of the few who's left his people and adapted to our society."

I nodded slowly. "I have a strange question."

Aurel raised an eyebrow, and he leaned forward on his elbow. "I'm listening."

A bit eager, but alright. "I've been… hearing and seeing things lately.

I'll hear someone's voice in the halls, and see flashes of images. Like fractured memories. I can't make sense of it."

Setizar's cut-glass accent echoed in the hall as he stepped into the room. "This is the first I've heard of this."

The air chilled between the three of us.

"You experienced a Memory Wraith. Creatures living in Nightmore that bend reality and dreams." Setizar slid into a seat, his eyes flickering. "Not uncommon, but interesting that they would visit you."

I slumped back. "Why would it make me remember something that isn't my memory then?"

"Simple. It's trying to show you something you need to know." Aurel cleared his throat. "And I believe the things you are seeing? Those are Alecto's memories."

39

It was raining again.

I stood along the edge on the balcony outside my room, feeling the gush of wind and spray of water on my face. What could a Memory Wraith want to tell me? Setizar had explained a bit about them during one of our 'history' lessons. They were a lesser faery with limited powers, and that it'd be best if I avoided speaking with them. The wind cut through my garments, chilling my bones.

I couldn't help but feel—empty. As if something important was missing.

One day. One day until the ball and my escape.

I couldn't do this. I couldn't leave Setizar…

"Well," Tatum said. I spun around to find his shadowy figure perched atop the railing. "Seems like you are in a predicament."

"I thought you said I'd have to beg to see you again."

"I was being dramatic." Tatum slid from the edge, his arms crossed. He looked different, somehow. Why did he look more like a shadow and less solid? "Time is running out, as you can sense. I overheard that wonderful conversation at breakfast—"

"You mean me being spectacularly awkward?" I tried to soften my tone, but it came out more biting than I'd wanted.

"Something along those lines." Tatum exhaled. "Do you not remember what first prompted you to come here to Yamira?"

"My debt."

"No, think a little afterward."

I scratched my head, stalking back into my room. "I don't know."

"Think, Meris." Tatum was just behind me, his figure more of an ominous mist than anything. What did he want me to remember? What was he after?

"I woke up, found a book, and fell into the world after following a rabbit-like rabbit."

A smile spread over Tatum's face. "Good. We are getting somewhere. The book. Do you still have it?"

I nodded, taking a few steps to the writing desk. "In here."

"Open it."

I did. It plopped open, sending dust scattering from the pages. "Okay, well, what now?"

"This is a special volume, one that guides you to the thing your heart truly desires. Flip the pages." Tatum rested his hand on my shoulder. He was becoming more corporal to me. First he flicked my temple, and now I felt the weight of his hand on my shoulder. I doubted that was a very good thing. Perhaps I should speak to Setizar about it.

I did as he said, flipping through the book and letting myself browse the once again blank pages. I was doing this for what seemed like an eternity, until I stopped. A sentence began scrawling itself out on the paper, becoming words I could read. "What's this?"

"Read it."

"Memory Wraiths: Creatures of the darkness, a friendlier species. Can't recall an important event? Forgot a memory which was dear to you? Find a Memory Wraith and for a price they'll help you on your journey to remember everything you need." I looked at Tatum, shrugging off his hand. "And?"

"You don't understand, do you?" He raised a brow. "Well then, I recommend finding a Memory Wraith so they can clear everything up. They appear in the darkness of the cool forest. Tonight is not the time to find them." He looked toward the rain which was still coming down in torrents. "Tomorrow night. You will look for the Wraith tomorrow night."

I scowled. "What are you trying to say? Why do I have to find the Wraith?"

"If you wish to understand, you must dig deep. You must speak with a Wraith."

"Why can't you tell me?" I angled my head, trying to understand him and his riddles.

"If I told you, the alignment of the future would be shattered. I'm doing this for a purpose."

I paced. Purpose, *indeed*! If only he'd tell me what I needed to know, I wouldn't have to bother him.

"Really, Meris. I explained it, why are you complaining?"

"I'm not!" I balled my hands into fists, whirling around to face him.

"I can hear your thoughts."

I scowled. "No you can't."

"I can indeed, and yours are very loud. I can't rest properly."

"How come I can't hear your thoughts?" I asked, hoping to get more than a vague and insulting response.

"Because unlike you I can mute my thoughts and keep them to myself. Quite a nifty trait. You should attempt it at some point."

"You should stop being a jerk." I released a breath. "What will I learn from the Memory Wraith?"

"Many things. You will have to ask the right questions, otherwise the Wraith will not give you the answer you wish. Bargaining with a Memory Wraith is something different. You'll need to prepare yourself. They can choose what memory to take in exchange for showing you one."

My mouth dried. "What do you mean?"

"I mean be careful. Don't recall anything important before bargaining. They will want the memory they think is important to you."

I sat down, pinching my nose. This was all too much too soon. "Let's make a memory. I need one to exchange, right? What memory would be useless to me, but seem precious to a Wraith?"

"Now you're using that brain of yours." Tatum grinned, and I gave him a foul gesture. "Call that little unicorn and have her come here with some tea. We can begin your new memory now."

I rang the bell, a cold sweat dripped down my spine. How could I do this? I would need to be actively thinking about the tea while I spoke to the Wraith. What did the Wraith even look like?

"They're invisible." Tatum picked at something on his shoulder. "You won't be able to see one until it decides to be seen." He picked a monocle from his coat pocket, placing it in my palm. The glass was cool to the touch, while the copper edging made it seem heavier than it should've been. "There will be several at the ball, courtesy of Libby, but they are under strict orders to not make any deals. No bargains. If any steps out of line, he will know, and honestly not even I wish to be on that fae's bad side."

"Alright, so I can't see the Wraith... so how will I make it show itself?"

"Trust me, a bargain with you is enough to pull all the Wraiths from the cracks of this world."

I opened the door as someone knocked. It wasn't Cerie. It was a girl with grass green skin and hair like fresh picked dandelions. "You rang, Miss?"

I nodded, unsure why Cerie hadn't been the one to show. "I'd like some tea? Raspberry."

She narrowed her olive-hued eyes, a solid pupil a shade darker than her skin, that stretched from edge to edge. "I'll bring it up right away."

The door clicked behind her and I turned back to Tatum. "One or two cream?"

His smile was refined and canine. "I prefer mine black."

40

Cerie fussed over my dress, fastening the last few buttons. "You're absolutely breathtaking," she said, fixing the folds of the garment. My wings spread outward, every tip of the white feathers were hued a gentle red color. This dress—I'd never worn a dress like it before. When Jack brought it back, I couldn't believe it was the same dress we agreed on.

A gossamer cape draped from either shoulder, flowing downward, covering some of the gilded, opalescent swirls. The garment twisted into a flat knot at my waist, hugging my hips and thighs before splitting at the knees, flowing outward until it kissed the black marble floor. Every inch shimmered in the light of the firefly lanterns, catching Cerie's admiring gaze.

A warm voice filled the chamber. "You look beautiful, Meris."

I turned to find Setizar leaning against the tall obsidian pillar dressed in a satin suit. It tapered in at all the right places to extenuate his statuesque figure. The beautiful, sharp lines of his face were illuminated by starlight, cutting into my heart and bleeding my emotions out into a fountain. "You look alright as well." I pinched the fabric of my dress, unsure of what to do.

"Thank you. But…" He looked me up and down. "There's something off about your outfit. Perhaps it's the color?"

Jack appeared around the corner, his flaming head illuminating the cold hall outside my room with a warm yellow glow. "I agree. The gold doesn't compliment her skin." He spun around, twining his thin, twig-like fingers along the dress. "You wish to remedy this?"

"I'll need you to help me," Setizar said. "I can only do so much with the terrestrial make of the dress."

Jack smiled. "Well, I can do both. I think I know exactly what you want."

"Meris," Setizar lowered his voice. "May we alter the dress?"

There was a tug within me, urging me to say the words I should have said to Jack when I picked the color. "Yes. You can alter the dress."

Wait. Was Jack a... a fae?

He pulled fire from his head, holding it in his white-gloved hand. The warm flames reached out and wrapped around me, stroking the gown, charring it black. The bottom of the garment became a glowing red color, fading into the darkness of the rest of the dress. Stars flickered within the folds of black, resembling a night sky.

"You're not called the best dressmaker in all of Yamira for no reason." Setizar's smile was woven with sweet dreams and broken hearts, colliding with my soul like a shattering sunset. I wished I could watch him smile like that forever. "You can do anything."

I swore Jack blushed at that. "Well," he said, straightening his tie. "I must be going. I can't leave the Lady of Winter waiting."

"Of course," Setizar bowed. His hand shimmered as a glove appeared on top of it. "Eira would be sour."

Jack exited my room, leaving Setizar and me alone. "So," I said, clearing my throat and taking in his appearance one more time. His suit matched the new make of my dress. The iridescent gold swirls tapering around my waist shifted to black opal, glittering brighter the closer I got to him. "Was this your plan all along?"

"When I saw the color you chose, yes." Setizar stepped closer, tilting his head. "I'm not lying when I say you look beautiful." He held out his hand, a small box appearing. He flipped it over, extending it to me so I could take it. "I think this will suit you well."

Hesitant, I reached for the box. The hinges made a squeak as I flipped open the lid—my breath caught in my throat.

A necklace, simple in make, hung on a delicate silver chain. The gem was shaped like a flower, changing hues as if fire lived within its depths; a whole world thriving under the surface of the ruby. A flutter of a heartbeat stumbled in my chest, as if a memory had suddenly resurfaced in my emotions.

His eyes were soft, enough to shatter whatever ill-will I had toward him in the past. Something shuddered through me as he took the jewel and looped it around my neck. The subtle brush of his hand against my skin, the lingering stare, and the delicate way he adjusted the gem made my heart beat uncontrollably.

It wasn't fair. Why did I have to feel this way about him? Why did he have to love someone who died years ago?

"You look stunning."

"So you keep saying." I smiled at him, my chest wracked with guilt and wish. I wished—what did I want? What was it I was wishing for?

"No." He took my hand gently. "I said you look beautiful, then I said stunning. You should be listening."

I laughed, nodding. "You look... you look really handsome tonight."

A flicker of delight pulled his lips upward. "Thank you." No snappy remarks, no underlining innuendo, just a thank you. He bowed, placing a kiss to the back of my hand between my pinky and ring finger.

My heart stopped, and a pleasant pain zipped through my stomach.

"Meris Vahla," Setizar said, his thumb gliding over my wrist. "Will you do me the honor of being my dance partner tonight?"

I swallowed. "I—" My voice trembled. "I don't know how to dance."

He didn't seem surprised. At all. Almost as if he were expecting that response. Nevertheless, he inclined his head and gestured to the door. "Then, I will do my best to make it look as if you know exactly what you are doing."

The doors swung open, and we walked down the halls into the main area. My heartbeat quickened.

Thump.

Thump.

Thump.

The heavy pounding in my breast imbued my emotions with an ineffable discomfort. The sweet smell of fresh baked bread, caramel apples, and cinnamon, mixed with blooming roses and lavender pierced through the corridors. It was a magical scent, lifting my stumbling spirit. I turned to Setizar, his face a series of sharp lines softened by emotion.

"Happy birthday, Meris." He winked at me, his smile a contagious mixture of beauty and fire. "Ready yourself for the attention. You are more beautiful than you realize."

The doors swung open and I gasped.

The familiar glass-like floor reflected the blue and gold light, dancing off the ground and onto the walls and pillars. People—or, creatures rather —lounged and danced and talked in various areas of the large room.

Everyone was so different. So beautiful. Females with silver skin, males with hair as azure as the sky, and beings that didn't look human at all or rested somewhere in between. All breathtaking, all...perfect. Somehow it filled me with pride, seeing everyone gathered there, standing below the curved archways and moonlight drenched windows.

Eira and Feng were the first two I recognized. Eira's warm honey skin contrasted with her jet black hair and white dress, while Feng's tautly-braided platinum hair and gold-pleated garments looked more like she was ready for war and not a ball.

Then, drifting through the crowd was Aurel. His hair was pulled up, while his shiny silver suit looked like he stole it from Setizar's closet.

Lhysa. I remembered her vividly from Nightmore and Eira's castle, and even then her pure beauty was something I needed to stop and admire for a moment. Her dandelion yellow dress and dark skin were a magical combination. Blue flowers speckled her black hair, bringing out the honey-gold of her eyes.

Setizar tugged at my arm, rousing me back to the moment. A symphony of claps erupted around us, weaving a thread around my heart. Everyone stopped, their eyes landing on Setizar and me. Searching, hopeful, as if somehow we were sovereigns walking up to our throne.

This attention, the feeling of hundreds of eyes on me, watching and waiting and anticipating, was something I doubted I could get used to.

The hum of the forest flute surrounded us, wrapping its lilting arms around my body in a harmonic embrace. It was a haunting sound, one which only legends spoke of. A curl of melodies, shuddering emotions, and forgotten memories flooded the room. Setizar's eyes flicked to mine, causing a shade of crimson to eddy on my cheeks.

"Are you ready?" he asked, dipping his head and turning me to begin the first dance of the night. He bowed gracefully, one arm in front across his stomach, the other behind his back.

The violins began, slow and hopeful, adding to the enchantment surging through the ballroom. Soon, the entire orchestra began to play as a chorus of voices joined.

I curtsied, and the beads on my dress sounded like thousands of glass chimes clinking together. The way he looked at me caused heat to erupt through my body. Aether, why did I have to feel this way? Why did his presence make me want to shrivel and die, yet burst and come alive?

Setizar guided my hand to rest on his neck, while the other was carefully nested in his own. The smell of autumn nights and cloves surrounded me as he dipped his head down, lips against my ear. "Tonight, you are a queen."

I exhaled, feeling my breath against his body. "I'm nowhere near being anything like a queen."

His fingers wrapped around my waist, guiding me gently. Somehow, I felt as if I knew what to do. How to dance. How to embrace the flow of music and waltz. "You will always be such to me. No matter what happened, no matter where you came from, you will be nothing less than royalty in my eyes." His eyes lit a shade brighter. Something in his look told me he wished to say more... to speak something else, yet wouldn't allow himself.

He spun me outward, and my wings twitched open as stardust and ocean mist escaped the floor. I was as light as a feather; my body weightless as it returned to Setizar. This boomerang effect—I would keep coming back to him, wouldn't I? Even if I left tonight, if I slipped through the portal, I would simply return.

My heart fluttered again as his hand rested on my waist.

I was a stupid girl. Why did I fall for him? Why did I do this to myself?

He guided me through turns, the hem of my dress brushing against the floor.

Dozens of other dancers joined us, flooding into the main area as the song began to shift. A lively, more regal song played, nothing like the haunting melody just a moment ago. A piano's keys were gently stroked, accompanying the strings and flute.

Then, like the strike of a match, the tone was dark again, as if an omen had been cast over the enchantment. Everything flickered for a moment. The same scene, yet not. It was as if I stood between two worlds, in two different bodies, watching a mirror image. One was beautiful, bright and magical, while the other was forbidden, dark and cursed.

There were two of us.

One Setizar looked at me with calm dignity, a spark of joy fluttering over his face—the other, a horrid frown slashed his features, sapping away the ethereal life I knew to be him. What was happening?

Where was I?

My hand gripped tighter as the crescendo heightened. The beating of my heart became painful. I struggled for an even breath.

"Meris?" one Setizar said.

"Alecto?" said the other.

Stop. *Stop.*

Fire crackled in my veins, thrumming toward my hands. My skin heated, pulsing and warming. "What's happening?"

Voices. So many voices assaulted me from both worlds. Laughter and screams. Questions and answers. Taunts and worry.

Nothing is as it seems.

The voice spoke again, piercing my thoughts with that agonizing sentence I'd heard several times since I arrived.

Louder.

Louder.

More pressing.

Nothing is as it seems.

My head…

Everything hurt.

"Meris!" Setizar grabbed my arms, both figures of him reacting differently. Where was I? What was happening? One was screaming for help, the other was very nearly cradling me in his arms.

"Alecto!" the other Setizar screamed.

Aether, what was wrong? Why was this happening?

A clock ticked, flicking the seconds away. Drums pounded, tribal and wanting.

Then, it stopped.

Everyone was staring. The music stilled, and Setizar was studying me with a death-white expression. His voice was raspy, a delicate balance between tearing and shattering. "I think we need to talk." He pushed me toward the far east wall, our shadows cast a dozen directions by the multiple chandeliers. The ball was muted behind the glass doors as Setizar slid them closed. "Meris, I think it—"

"What happened in there?" I spun. "What was I seeing?" My voice was cracking. *I* was cracking. This had finally become too much for me to bear. Tatum sighed somewhere near, but I didn't care.

"I didn't see whatever it was you saw, but I can explain some things."

Setizar gestured to a seat. "I need to go back and tell you what happened to Alecto—"

"Screw Alecto!" I was done. "I don't care! I'm seeing things that I've never seen before in my life. Feeling things I've never felt before. There's so many questions, and you're nowhere near answering any of them!"

The doors opened and closed with a resounding clank. "You're right." Aurel stood near the entrance. *"Alecto."*

Fire flickered in my fists. "What?"

Aurel leaned against the marble railing, throwing his head back and laughing. "You don't have the guts to tell her, do you?" His eyes cut to Setizar, who took a step back. "Afraid you're going to scare her away? Afraid that after eighteen years of waiting, it'll only end in your own undoing?"

"Shut up, Aurel," I shouted, then turned back to Setizar. "Explain this."

The seconds passed like the sand in an hourglass. My breath stilled in my throat, and the world around me slowed to nearly nothing.

Setizar looked to the ground, his expression hidden from me. "Meris, *you* are Alecto."

41

My heart stopped.

They truly were mad. Had they thought this the whole time? Did they really think I was Alecto? "This is absurd." I had my own memories. My own childhood. My own home.

Still, there was a nagging thought. A question dangling over me. What if I was?

No. Absolutely not. There's no possible way. Even with magic, you couldn't *die* and come back.

Tatum cleared his throat. "Well, do you think you should find that Memory Wraith? It's the only way to know for sure."

I hissed a breath. Setizar and Aurel were staring at me—one with horror strewn through his flickering lavender eyes, one with no emotion at all past the stone-cold gray gaze.

Setizar reached his hand out to me. "Alecto—"

I stepped back. "Stop!"

"Please..." His voice was a cracked plea.

An invisible knife dragged along my emotions. I could've dealt with him loving someone else, dealt with him pining after his dead love. But this? This was a new pain. He'd never seen me for who I was.

Fire exploded around me, hissing in the autumn night air. The sound of porcelain snapping resounded, cracking in my ears. Wind and a thunderclap surrounded me. Instinctively, I closed my eyes. Ice bit into my skin, no longer fiery and warm.

I was standing in the middle of a frozen forest, my dress singed, completely alone. Alone. *That is what I will always be.*

Darkness eddied around me, coiling threads of loneliness through my heart. Something in me splintered, crackling like the flame in my veins. Another flash of light surrounded me, and I was fireballing away, a wisp of smoke and fire.

The world stilled and a mixture of cold and autumn wind pelted my skin. My heartbeat was so faint, so fragile, that I believed I was dying. I looked around, finding the icy woodland to my right, and an autumn nightmare to the left.

A shadow appeared in the corner of my eye, swirling into a figure. "Well, you've done it this time."

Tatum. As if my loneliness wasn't enough to handle, I had to carry a conversation with Tatum. "Where am I?"

"Somewhere along Winter's border." Tatum made a motion to flick a snowflake from his coat. "I never thought you'd turn into another raging fireball and fly away like an angry phoenix."

"How do I get back?" I stepped closer, the heat kindling in my veins again.

"You would have to *augue* back."

"*Augue?*"

"What you just did. It's the furie version of misting. I'm sure no one but me knows the proper term."

My nails bit into my palms as I balled them into fists.

"This is a perfect opportunity to find a Wraith, don't you think?" He smiled, that white grin unnerving me to the core. "Come along."

I leveled my glare, but followed him nonetheless. "How am I supposed to do anything? I forgot the book back in my—in the jinni's palace."

"You needn't worry," Tatum said as a glimmer of light shuddered at his fingertips. "I already assumed some random catastrophe would occur. You won't need it as long as I'm with you."

"You are worse than the jinni." I lifted my foot, stepping over a fallen log and nearly tripping over my ballgown. The snow crunched under my heels.

"Please." Tatum chuckled, shaking his head. "You're in love with that jinni, and you know it."

I froze. "No I'm not."

"I'm in your head, remember?" Tatum turned, his shoes hissing along the ground. "You can't lie to me."

My throat swelled, burning and stiffening. "So what? He's crazy, and he thinks I'm his dead wife."

"You are, you stupid thing!" Tatum sighed. "We will find the Memory Wraith, you will ask it your questions, and see for yourself."

"What?" I stumbled a step back. "Oh, Aether. You're out of your mind, too."

Tatum grabbed my wrist, pressing me against the tree. How was he doing this? Wasn't he in my head?

"Of course I'm in your head." Tatum's lips were against my ear. "But I'm also very, very real to you. Now, if you continue being useless I may just go back to my cozy mirror so I don't have to deal with your constant chattering."

I grabbed his throat and spun him around, twisting my hand free from his clutches. "Don't you *dare* touch me."

He smiled. "Your instincts are well intact. Too bad your brains were fried during reincarnation."

"Shut your mouth and bring me to the Memory Wraith." I shoved him forward, my body wracked with shivers and tingling nerves. The adrenaline—or perhaps anxiety—had gotten to me.

The sound of Tatum's feet along the snow unnerved me to no end. I couldn't make sense of him. How could he be more corporal now than earlier? What gave him this ability?

A shiver crawled up my spine, and horror nipped at my heart. He, too, believed I was Alecto. Did I bear such a resemblance to her? "Tatum?" I looked up at his shadowy figure. "Why do *you* think I'm Alecto? What's the reasoning behind it?"

Tatum kept walking, weaving through the fir trees and aspens. A collection of snow and leaves fell from above, mingling with each other in a way that appeared a bit more than magical. "There are no more furies in Yamira. The last of the race left in this world, Alecto, died as Biodru the Emberfang sealed the gateway to the realm of the Day forty years ago. When Alecto came back, the hunt for the furies once again began, and that is how she met Setizar." He released a long sigh, angling his poppy-red eyes across the sprawling landscape of autumn and ice. "The Silver Queen, who wished to kill magic, betrayed us. But she didn't account that Alecto was an immortal. Death isn't the end as it is for those who are ageless such as your precious jinni and the others. Alecto was unmade and made again. *Reborn.*"

I tilted my head, wrapping my arms around myself. The wind carved icy daggers into my back, making the walk even more agonizing. "That still doesn't explain why you think I'm Alecto."

Tatum's laugh sounded like the snapping of branches in a storm. "Because I knew you. I knew Alecto. You see, when a furie dies and they are unmade and reborn, the memories of their past life would appear as a dream, or a premonition, if at all. Without those memories kept safe within a furie's artifact, they'll forget all they once were."

I didn't want to believe him. I didn't want to have been killed in the past, not once, but twice, and have come back.

"Alecto and her sister were the last furies to ever *walk* Yamira in the past forty years. Why do you think you so happen to be a furie? That you look *identical* to Alecto; that your powers are the same as hers—scorching and brighter than a morning star?"

I shook my head. "Well I can't remember a thing, so it's rather hard for me to believe what you're saying is true."

"You lost your artifact." Tatum shrugged. "Which is why the Memory Wraith can help, at least with a little. Don't worry, I shall be at your side in case anything goes amiss."

"Well that's comforting."

"Sarcasm is your least attractive quality, I recommend keeping that under wraps."

"You'll be asking me to defy who I am, and I am fairly certain you don't want that, do you?"

Tatum's laugh became guttural. "You are just as feisty as I remember."

I flicked the snowflakes from my shoulder, fighting the chills that overtook my body. "Where will we be able to find a Memory Wraith?"

"Only a little longer. They'll scent your desperation."

As soon as he spoke, a whisper wrapped around me. *"You wish to make a deal?"* The voice came from every angle, every corner of the forest.

Tatum smiled. "Ask it to show itself."

I swallowed. "Show yourself. I wish to bargain."

A creature of rotting flesh, gray and brown in places, stood before me with a cutting grin plastered on its face. Its hands were the talons of an eagle, curved and spiked, dripping with yellow ooze. Its nearly decayed nose hung off its skull by a thin vein. I smelled it… like a dead body mingled with swamp water.

I stepped back, gagging.

A robe of powder white, frayed and torn, draped over its hovering form. *"Bargain?"*

"My," Tatum growled, his voice slippery. "You are starved, aren't you?"

The creature didn't acknowledge him. Perhaps because I was the only one who could see him. I cleared my throat. "You're starved, aren't you?"

The creature clicked its decomposing tongue. *"Very."*

I swallowed the fear and disgust lodging in my throat. "You are a Memory Wraith?"

It nodded, cape levitating behind it and dancing in the hollow wind with a snap. It was an uneasy sound, one like that of an unstable flag withering in a storm. *"Yes. I am."* It looked at me with its calculating, hollow white eyes. Could it even see me? *"You wished to see me."* Its voice was dripping, heavy with metal and liquid. *"What do you need?"*

I straightened my back; the cold drove fangs into my skin. "I need to remember who I am. If I had a life before this one."

The clicking of dry bones clattered below its skin as the Wraith tilted its head. *"You don't need me to tell you, do you?"* It smiled, reaching out a talon. My body shuddered at the touch of the creature. *"Yes, I am hungry. But I can feast on the memories of those who do not need them."*

A jolt of electricity pounded into my body, my veins turning red and glowing below the surface of my white skin.

A beautiful castle by the seaside.

A dance at a ball.

A kiss—

Setizar's kiss...

Love. Passion. Pain.

Memory upon memory. Wings, fire—it was all clicking into place. *"Alecto, the first of the furies,"* the Wraith said, still stirring up memories I had forgotten.

My world swirled darker. The memories grew more intense; more vivid. I remembered standing—Alecto, standing—beside a waterfall, clad in fighting leathers, a sword in my hand, angled at Setizar. His laugh and his smile... it hurt. It was so full of happiness. So full of joy.

Not even a hint of pain.

"Alecto, love, why do you insist on training me?" He pulled his sword, clumsy. I thought it was quite clumsy... and adorable. *"I'm obviously a horrible student."*

I laughed. "Because maybe you'll need it one day." I slashed the air, and he released a muted yelp, dodging my attack. "You can't hope to ever win a battle when you run away, darling."

"I'm a peaceful creature. I don't like fighting." Setizar took a step back, straightening himself again. *"I'm not a warrior, like you."*

"I know." I grabbed his shirt and stared into his eyes. So pure, perfect, tinted like a rainbow of pinks and blues. Mischief pulsed up in my heart and—

I'd stabbed him?

He buckled back in pain. "Aether!" He put his hand to the injury—no blood. "That hurt like a—"

"You should've killed me when you had the chance," I whispered, pressing the tip of my sword under his chin. Aether, he was perfect. "I'm trying to show you that you can't trust anyone. You need to make the kill before they kill you."

"Not everyone wants to kill you, Alecto." Setizar stood, grabbing my right hand. "I certainly could never do it."

Doubt flickered in my heart. What had I experienced before that made me think like that?

The scene changed. Before me was a dark forest, shrouded in mystery. A figure stood in a sliver of shadow, but her figure was someone I knew.

"Inanna."

Her blood-red lips parted into a smile, flashing teeth akin to pure alabaster stones. Her eyes, her face, it was beautiful. She looked like the haunting spirit of a wavering home, bidding lonely travelers into her laced arms. "Well, Alecto... Whatever brought on this change?"

I lowered my weapon, angling my head. "I don't want to do this anymore."

The memory shattered with a blood-curdling scream. The Wraith crumbled down, its skin whiter than the snow around me. A hollow cry resounded as Tatum hissed through his teeth behind me. A crack of lightning split the sky, followed by a deafening screech.

I stumbled a step back—electricity streaking through my body as I looked at the broken figure of the Memory Wraith. Standing above it, with jowls dripping blood, was a creature strewn of my worst nightmares.

An ogarak.

42

I jumped back, evading the teeth gnashing at my head. My wings spread behind me, though I quickly tucked them away.

The ogarak was on me. Hands gripping my wrists, hurdling us into a nearby tree. Pain tore into my back, splintering up my spine. Everything was upside down. A beat of my heart thrummed in my ear.

I had no weapons.

Setizar's words echoed in my mind. *You are a weapon—*

Fire welled in my heart. Everything was slow... sedated. Nothing was pulsing. Nothing was moving. Time suspended.

Then it sped up, just as my fist erupted in flames. The ogarak flew backward, hurdling through the air. The smell of burning reptile pounded in my nose as I gasped.

The ogarak bounded toward me again, every sharp feature—every fang and claw—on display.

I closed my eyes.

A memory flashed; *a shield made of fire, pillowing upward, like a wave crashing against the darkening skies.*

The memory flooded into reality—a pulse of power extruding from my veins outward. The ogarak screamed as its body crashed into my shield and didn't stop. Burning, melting flesh and all, the ogarak continued through my shield.

I tried harder, concentrating all my thoughts to keep it up. The harder I pressed my powers, the more the ogarak clawed and scraped.

One finger jabbed out, ripping into my skin and fracturing the shield. It disintegrated as blood swept down my arm. Pain, fiery hot and winter cold, squeezed into my skin. I inhaled; icy wind filled my lungs. The ogarak raised one claw over its head, bloodlust filling its eyes. No. This was not where I died.

I screamed, my wings unfurling from below my skin, and I vaulted into the sky. The creature's claws narrowly missed me.

But I'd forgotten. The Ogarak also had wings.

A plume of dust and snow exploded from around its deathly carapace as it hurdled into the heavens, snatching my foot. I screamed. The dead weight of the creature dragged me downward. Fire and ice shattered around me as we continued to fall. My wings went limp.

I kicked at the ogarak. My heel dug into its claw, but didn't do much good. Blood spurted from the wound I'd created, but he held tight until we were inches from the ground.

I cracked my wing against the cold snow. Everything was white. Tears stung my eyes. I couldn't feel anything but pain. Pure, unadulterated pain.

There was no movement.

The ogarak wasn't moving, either. Was it dead?

"Well this is *messy*."

Inanna?

My bleary eyes couldn't focus on anything. I only heard her voice through the crackling sound in my ears.

"You killed one of my creatures, *Alecto*..."

I wanted to throw my fist into her face. There were two people warring inside of me. One was Meris, the other... Alecto. But how? I still didn't understand.

"The veneer Setizar put on you was impressive. I had no idea." The crunch of bones resounded and I screamed. My wing! Aether, my *wing*!

"Oh, you look as though you are in pain," Inanna cooed. "Unfortunately, this is just the beginning. You broke a law of Yamira. You're bound to the magic. Never, *ever* attack one of my creatures."

Rage boiled in my stomach. "It attacked me."

"Impossible. It would never do that." Her smile was feral. I couldn't take my eyes off the way her lips angled into a red, scythe-like curve.

"You ordered it to attack me, didn't you?" I hissed, pain climbing through my bones once again. "You wanted this to happen."

"Oh?" She shrugged, her dark dress bleeding into shadows. "It's a shame. I used to like you before you betrayed me. Don't you remember that?" She knelt beside me, her hand grasping my chin and tilting it up.

"What are you talking about?"

She released me, recoiling and pressing her fingers together as if she'd touched something utterly putrid. "Lost some memories, have you?" The way she said it told me she knew about my loss of memory; about everything. "You and me? We were going to remake Yamira. We were going to tear down the useless laws and backwards thoughts of the Lords and rulers. But then, you betrayed me. You fell in *love*." Her laugh was thin and hollow. "You befriended the others, getting in their heads, but then? When you met Setizar? You fell. You fell like someone had clipped your wings mid-flight. His docile, weak nature won you. I saw it happen. He wouldn't hurt a fly, and so you turned to them. You worked with—" She clenched her fists, anger blooming red splotches on her cheeks. "You undid *everything*!" She pulled her veil off her face, and horror streaked through me.

Scars marred the top half of her forehead and brows, while one eye was beautiful—a gorgeous blend of amber and red—the other was white with a raging, angry scar across the lid.

Red.

So much red—and screams.

I did that to her?

"We were going to make Yamira a better place. A place where creatures wouldn't fear one another. But you taught me one thing." She pulled out a knife, pressing it against my neck. "The strong survive. You shouldn't bother looking after others. It's useless."

"Inanna—"

She pressed harder. The blade bit into my skin. "I don't want to hear it. You will come now to Redrim and pay for what you have done. And you better pray to the Aether that you survive."

I swallowed.

"No."

Setizar?

We turned. He stood in the middle of the icy forest, his clothes in disarray, as if he had been through a storm coming here.

Just behind him was Cerie, her golden eyes illuminating the darkness.

"If one is willing to take the punishment, the sin against the law will be given to them, freeing the offender. You abide by this rule, Inanna. Do not pretend you don't know it."

My heart shattered. "No."

Setizar looked at me, a wry smile forming on his lips. "Don't fight me on this, please."

"I won't let you." I groaned, pushing Inanna off me and standing beside him. My wing was limp and mauled, leaving a trail of blood in the snow. "I can't."

"She's right," Inanna cut in. "I won't let you take her place."

"It's a law, Inanna. You created it." Setizar looped an arm around my waist, pulling me closer. "I will take her place. I will take the punishment. She walks free."

Inanna's fingers curled into a fist. "You're out of your mind."

His grip tightened around me, tugging me so close that there was no separation between us. "I most definitely am."

Inanna's good eye narrowed. "Fine. You have two minutes while I make the preparations to hold a jinni." She stopped, a black abyss forming between two trees. "Don't run. You know the consequences."

"Indeed." Setizar watched as she vanished, then turned back to me.

His eyes softened. Everything about him seemed unsettled. "Meris—"

"I remember," I said. "I—I don't know everything, but I remember enough. Enough to apologize."

He shook his head, fingers trailing down my broken wing. "You're hurt."

"It's my fault for running away." I shivered as his thumb glided over my broken bone, mending it. "I should have stayed."

"You were overwhelmed. I used to do the same thing when I first met you, if you remember." He smiled, a red flush covering his face.

No. He couldn't be sent to Redrim to be punished. I wouldn't allow it. No one should be going. This was a trap. "I can't let you take my place."

Setizar cupped my face, looking into my eyes. "It's the law until the curse is undone. You must undo the curse. Find Jack and Libby. They will help you once you retrieve the Box." His eyes slid over mine again, as if he was taking me in one last time. "Once the Box is opened, you will be able to bless the seasons again, and we will tear down Redrim and its horrors for good, just like we planned."

"We… planned?"

His smile fluttered between sorrow and joy. "You will remember, given time. Jack or Libby will fill you in completely. Just hurry. When the portal opens, go into the human realm and do what you must."

The portal. So he knew? Despite it all, he knew my plan?

"Come with me."

"I would die." He narrowed his gaze "Since it was my magic which was taken, I will become unraveled and turn to dust before your eyes in the human realm. Why do you think I haven't ventured there?"

My heart was breaking and twisting, torn in a thousand different directions. I couldn't do this to him. I couldn't leave him with Inanna. I'd seen the little torture she inflicted on him—and she enjoyed it! I couldn't let that happen again. "Setizar—"

"Go." He released me from his hold. "Go, and go quick."

Cerie rested a hand on my shoulder, pulling me further from Setizar.

"No! I can't leave him. I can fight Inanna!"

"Meris," Cerie murmured. "You aren't restored enough to fight Inanna. Give it time."

"We don't have time." I shook her hand off. "*He* doesn't have time!"

Setizar stiffened. He wasn't a fighter. He wasn't born a warrior. He was doing this for me—for everyone. "I love you, remember that. No matter who you are, or what you decide to call yourself, I will never stop loving you."

Two portals opened, one on the right of Setizar, one to the left of me. Dark as night beside him, bright as a sunny day beside me. Inanna stepped out of the abyss.

"Setizar I—"

A hand pulled at me, yanking me left. Blazing yellow sunlight rolled over me, and I shut my eyes. My body felt shattered—warped and gnarled like a puzzle put together wrong—as I re-entered Inder; my veins froze with magic and power. My mind was a mess of confusion and nerves as I steadied myself again. Somehow, the jump between worlds left my mind utterly upside down, like a bat hooked to the ceiling of a cave.

I breathed in and out, rolling my shoulders. The world around me was drenched in green and golden light, somehow so muted compared to the world I was in just a moment prior. Pink and purple flowers popped up around me, lacking the luster of the ones in Yamira.

It struck me like a blow to my face. "No." I stood, spinning around and facing Cerie. "You didn't let me finish!"

"We *had* to leave. Inanna appeared."

I crumbled, my skin prickling from the sudden heat. My insides were cold and frigid. "I didn't get to tell him... tell him I love him too."

Cerie leaned down beside me, her blue skin changing hue. Everything about her dulled as she became utterly human. Her white hair dripped to blonde, her skin became the shade of desert sands, and her horn vanished like mist over a morning lake. Her eyes, however, remained that same magical sun-lit gold. "Meris, you will see him again. We don't have much time. If we stay here for too long we will forget all that had to do with magic. We must conserve the magic you have. Don't use it all up, or you will risk forgetting everything."

I nodded, tears still rolling down my cheeks. When I looked back up, more than just Cerie and I stood in the meadow.

PART FIVE
RETURN TO INDER

43

S oldiers.

More than a dozen of them stood around us with armor made of dragon scales, layered in a serpentine fashion. Their bronze helmets glinted in the early sunlight, with a different animal motif atop each spire. In their hands were spears, each pointed at me.

"State your name," one growled, pointing his finger at me.

"Well," Cerie breathed. "This isn't good."

The men looked at her. "State your name."

I stood. "Meris Vahla."

The guards looked at each other. Something in their demeanor seemed uneasy. Perhaps it was because two women were sitting in their field, in ballgowns, and one had a heavy wool coat on in the middle of summer. "We must bring you to the governor."

My heart fluttered. "Governor?"

They nodded, one grabbing my arm, the other grabbing Cerie's. "You're in Yeodo. Do you not know where you are?"

"Sirs, me and my dear friend were robbed!" Cerie squeaked as the man tightened his grip. "I'm glad you found us."

The men looked less skeptical and more confused at that. "Well," one said, scratching his neck. "Come along. We're a few miles away." He looked at my arm, the wound from where the ogarak attacked. "What happened?"

"As my friend said," I lifted my head. "We were attacked."

The soldiers nodded. "We will find you aid quickly and get you out of the sun."

— ☾ —

The countryside was stunning, in its own non-magic way. Everything was so green, contrasting against the purple mountains in the far distance. The guards surrounded us, heavy armor clanking with every step.

"Meris," Cerie whispered, her fingers drawing an idle circle on my wrist where the bracelet still rested. I could barely hear her voice over the clanking armor. "I have no clue what to do in this world."

"That's the least of our concerns," I whispered, patting her arm. "I have to find the Box and return to the portal before the full moon ends."

She nodded, looking at the loud guards.

"But how will we find it?"

Cerie's grin was shudderingly beautiful as she pulled something from the folds of her coat. "You need to do some studying."

I stifled my gasp of surprise as she placed the codex in my hands. The ornate cover glinted in the daylight. "What am I looking for?"

"A way to find magical objects in a world without magic." Cerie slipped her arm around me, guiding me away from one of the soldiers who was getting a little too close for comfort.

Tatum's voice filled my mind, tapping on the walls of my nerves. *"You must be careful here, Meris."*

I nodded, keeping close to Cerie. The hollow clank clank of armor grated against my nerves.

We traveled for what seemed like forever until the city, all pale cream stone, came into view. Just along the outskirts of the capital was a road, which we walked down.

It was late afternoon, and the sun had drifted so low beyond the mountains that the land below was washed in a pale orange light.

Tatum's figure appeared. "Look, Meris." He pointed his finger in the direction of a house. Wherever they planned for us to go, I hadn't expected this. It looked like the Palace of Ka'zor from Yeodian legends. The cream stucco walls pillared up to the orange bricks, mingled with red and blue ceramic tiles. Along the sides of the building were designs of creatures. One was a man whose legs were made of mist, his arms and neck bound in chains, bowing before the figure of a woman. A mermaid and a pirate clung to each other, lips pressed in a kiss as bubbles peppered the surrounding painting. Fire painted the portrait of wings above the fifth window; a figure wrapped in shadow and night presented the sultana with a small orb of light.

There were many others of the same style.

"Where are we?"

Tatum looked at me, a nervousness surfacing in his gaze. "I thought that would be obvious? We are at the Ka'zor."

I swallowed. But that was impossible, was it? *The* Ka'zor wasn't for just anyone to walk into.

"Of course not. You're special," he said, weaving his fingers around my wrist. His touch was cold, rolling up and down my spine in gentle, soothing waves. He leaned down, his lips brushing against my ear as he added, "The governor, I'm sure, wants to know everything. If you make yourselves as small as possible, he won't bother you. You just need enough time to perform whatever location spell is needed for the Box."

I nodded.

The shell-lined pathway leading up to the Ka'zor crunched below our feet. What were these images? What did they mean?

"History. Look closely… the Yeodians love to display every moment in history here on the walls of the Ka'zor." He sighed. "If I remember correctly, there are more inside."

I didn't know if I wanted to see more of these. I stepped on the pavement, looking at the ground. The entire route leading to the portico was made of shattered marble. Hues of turquoise, red, orange, and yellow speckled the ground. The doors opened, leading into a massive foyer. As Tatum said, the paintings continued inside. I gazed at the mythical creatures, the statues, and the small images. The chained mist-man was everywhere. "What is that?" I asked, pointing to him.

Cerie followed my gaze. "Sadistic."

Guards stomped their spears against the golden marble floors, silencing her. "The governor wishes to see you."

Well that was fast.

We bowed and followed the man in a red robe into the next room. The ceiling stood high above, supported by pillars and tall windows. Brightly colored birds chirped from where they perched in the trees and foliage about the chamber, singing along with the bubbling fountain in the center of the room.

A man in his early thirties, with long black hair and calculating brown eyes, sat near the fountain, a smile stretched over his features. "Welcome, travelers, and have a seat. Where's my wife?" He pointed to a nearby glass table, angling his head behind me. "Ah! Julna, come meet our guests."

44

Every bone in my body shook. Emotions raged within me; anger, joy, confusion. It couldn't be *my* Julna. She wouldn't marry a wealthy lord and not look for me and Mae, would she? She wouldn't make us suffer while she lived in luxury.

She rounded the corner, her velvety brown hair rippling down her shoulders in delicate waves. I wouldn't forget that innocent face and thin-lipped smile.

My Julna.

It was torture. I wanted to grab her, say hello, and catch up on the years we'd been apart. Yet a bitter tang surfaced on my tongue. She forgot about us. She could've saved us.

She stopped, eyes hardening into two dark stones. "Meris?"

I stood, bowing curtly. "Julna."

The governor looked between us, confusion sweeping over his face.

Get in line, stranger. We're in the same boat.

"How did you get here?" She regained her former, smiley demeanor. "Oh, Farelyn, this… this is my sister, Meris."

The governor, or Farelyn, furrowed his brows. "You never mentioned a sister."

"You're being silly, of course I did. Why wouldn't I?" Julna perked up, only her eyes revealing her less than joyful state. "And who's this?"

Cerie's eyes narrowed. "I'm her friend. Meris, this is your sister?"

I nodded. Julna was acting strange now. What was going on? I needed questions answered, and I needed Farelyn out of the room for that to happen.

Julna sat in front of me, her smile forced. "Dear, I'd love to talk with my sister. Catching up on the time we haven't been together would make me very happy."

Farelyn waved his hand. "Of course."

Julna touched her fingers to her forehead and bowed, tugging at my arm. "Meris?"

I stood with her, and she led me from the room through winding orange and teal halls. Shimmering glass doors were propped open. Everything was so ordinary now, things I would've died to see before seemed unimaginably dull after being in Yamira. We walked through the doors, entering an opulent garden. Hedges, which could have been taken from a painting, lined golden bricked pathways.

I gazed lazily over the yard as Julna's coral dress danced in the soft breeze. "How did you get out of that hellhole?" She looked at me, dark eyes narrowing.

"I owe a debt. I have a few weeks to repay it. If I don't, I'll be sold to the highest bidder, or Mae will have to pay my fine."

Julna's breath was ragged. "What brought you here?" She grabbed my wounded arm with trembling fingers. "What happened to you? Who's that girl?" Willows draped weeping limbs over the blue water as it bubbled against the grassy bank. Hummingbirds fluttered from flower to flower as butterflies, the colors of Setizar's eyes, flew gently in the air.

Setizar.

Nausea rolled through my stomach. I needed to get him back. What was Inanna doing to him? I knew she was doing it partially to spite me—

Julna pulled me to my knees and dipped my arm into the water, washing off the dried blood and dirt. "Meris?"

I blinked. "You wouldn't believe me if I told you."

"Try me." She smiled gently, dipping her fingers deeper into the water and splashing the cool liquid on my wound. "I need to know what my twin sister has been up to these past years."

I shook my head. "Other than serving under the Gathbred's iron rule? I've been living in… another realm." I released the codex from under my arm, placing it on my lap. "Julna, we aren't human."

Her eyes remained unblinking. *Great.* I should have waited. I'd overwhelmed her. I could see it on her face. The rigid lines, tight lips, everything was telling me she was trying to process my insanity.

"Meris—"

"I know." I stood, shoving the book to the ground. "I know I sound insane, like I've finally snapped. But I swear everything I'm saying is true. If you don't believe me, then meet me here tomorrow night."

"Meris," Julna shouted, or at least *her* way of shouting. It was more like a strained yelp. "I can't leave this house."

I froze. "What?"

"I'm staying here."

I breathed in, shaking my head. "I can bring you somewhere—"

"No." She shook her head adamantly. "I can't do that to him." Her face paled, her bright ruby lips dulling.

"Does he love you?" I asked, nearing her.

She paused, her neck stiffening as a ring of emotion flickered in her eyes. "He married me, didn't he?"

"Julna," I grabbed her arms, "does he *love* you?"

Her eyes glazed over, glimmering with tears. "Of course he does."

Despite what she said, in my heart I knew that he didn't, but I could save her. And she wouldn't have much of a choice come tomorrow. Oh, Aether please let this plan work. Otherwise, I was certain Julna would destroy me. "Alright, I won't pester you about leaving." I bit my tongue, not wishing to say anything that would give me away. If she knew I was going to kidnap her—save her, really—she would definitely be more alert.

Julna nodded. "Let's get you changed into some clean clothes."

— ☾ —

Evening settled over Yeodo before I saw Cerie again. She slammed the door closed as a plethora of curses began to pour from her mouth. She was nearing the end of her frustration, but she couldn't seem to speak clearly. "He might as well claim to be the Aether!"

"Farelyn?" I leaned on the bed, trying to get comfortable in the dress Julna had given me. I couldn't. I was used to the clothes in Yamira. "He's worse than all those beautiful words you just spoke?"

Cerie grinned, pouring herself a glass of water. Her face was ashen. "I need to go to sleep. I'm exhausted after dealing with that... piece of work."

I laughed.

"Really! He proposed I become part of his harem several times."

"I didn't know he has a harem..."

Cerie waved my comment off. "Of course he does. What self-righteous, wealthy man doesn't? And I had to *repeatedly* set him straight and tell him that a relationship of that sort, in any shape or form, is repulsive to me."

"Are you really opposed to romance?" I snagged a grape from the plater, tossing it into my mouth.

"Well, not to the extent I expressed to Farlyn. I would love to spend the rest of my life with someone I love, but... there are aspects of a relationship that appall me. So, I simply live my life as a blissful unicorn, unattached to any person aside from my friends and family."

The word friend sent a jolt of pain through me.

I couldn't handle having shards of memory, only feeling the knowledge lingering outside of my grasp and not being able to touch it. I wished I could just remember everything.

"Alecto! For the gods' sake, please stay still." Tatum stood in the dark room with a frustrated grin along his lips. "You won't be able to perform

these spells if you don't pay attention."

"But I don't wanna!" My voice was so... squeaky. Small. "Why do I have to listen?"

Tatum knelt. "Because until you learn to become a warrior, until you are two times as smart, as strong, as resourceful as the males in this land, you won't stand a chance."

"But you're a male."

"Dear child, remember I exist outside those confines." He lifted my head with his index finger. "And I am not the one who draws those lines."

"I don't understand." I tried to fix my eyes on his, but he looked away.

"The creatures of the realm, whether they are male, female, human, or monster—they all only see one thing. Power. Power is the universal language. You possess enough power to shatter the foundations of this realm. You are one of the most powerful creatures to ever be born. I'm simply trying to show you control."

"Does that mean I'm more powerful than you?" The hopeful tone in my voice was embarrassing. Did I actually speak like that?

Tatum laughed and threw his head back. "I said born. I was not born... I was made."

I didn't understand, but he proceeded to hold out his hand, and I placed mine in his. It was so small. My wings twitched behind me.

"Now, to give magic, you must think very, very hard about the source. What do you see your magic as? What does it look like? Now, slice a small sliver from that, and move it through your body. You need to focus."

I blinked. Tatum was staring at me. The same way he had in the vision, except he wasn't as tall as he was in my memory. Or, perhaps it had been me that was small. "Alecto?"

I closed my eyes. I couldn't speak to him while Cerie was in the room. She'd think I'd lost my mind.

A fiery mountain erupted in my mind against the dark skies. A vision of brilliant orange against velvet heavens. It billowed upward, cascading cinders and ashes like an angry god. I couldn't take my eyes off it.

It was beautiful.

I walked forward, my feet heavy. A lone rock sat at the base of the mountain, glowing brighter than fire. I scooped it up in my hands, surprised to find it was cool to the touch.

The vision flickered to darkness, swirling back to reveal Tatum again. "If you remembered that, do you remember who I am to you?"

I shook my head. Unfortunately I didn't remember that part.

"Are you alright, Meris?" Cerie asked.

Tatum's expression softened. "All is not lost." He shrugged off his coat, placing it on the chair.

"Yes," I said, raising my head. "I'm fine, Cerie. I'm just... worried."

Tatum's brow quirked upward, and a wry smile played at the corners of his mouth. "Little liar."

I blinked. *Shut up, Tatum.*

His fingers danced atop my palm, taunting me to break and speak in front of Cerie. "Are you going to tell her you have me in your head?"

"Cerie," I rolled my shoulders. "I have a proposal."

"Didn't we just talk about how I don't want a relationship?"

I smiled. "Cerie, I'm being serious."

Her eyes were alight, brightening as she leaned forward. "I just wanted to see you smile again. Alright, what's your plan?"

I cleared my throat, quickly glancing at Tatum, who leaned in the corner, a wisp of shadow and darkness. *Please don't ruin this.* "We should kidnap my sister."

45

"A bsolutely *not*," Tatum said.

I ignored him.

"What?" Cerie was as shocked as I expected. "Kidnap her?"

"Yes."

"I don't think you've thought this through."

I shook my head, raising my brow. "I can't leave her with Farelyn."

Tatum was the one to speak this time. "But she is his wife," he said, leaning against the bureau. "How do you suppose you will make this work? You need to leave her behind...something isn't right about kidnapping her."

I grinned, pulling the codex out from under the bed and plopping it down. The pages fluttered as I flipped the leather-bound cover open. "I found a spell here. I'll find the Box and replicate it using an illusion spell."

Cerie gaped at me as she ran a hand over her face. "This could possibly end very, very badly if we're found out."

"It's a risk I'm willing to take."

Tatum growled, his voice dripping with unknown promises. "The Box is in the trophy room of the Ka'zor. You will be able to snatch it at any time, but there's plenty of guards. It won't be easy to take."

"I think we can do it, Cerie."

Tatum barked a laugh. "You should really leave Julna here."

I focused my mind, speaking to Tatum. *You're just a ray of sunshine, aren't you?*

"I try to think of all the outcomes. Stealing the Box comes at a cost one way or another."

Are you the embodiment of doom, or is sarcasm a foreign language to you?

He laughed. "There are certainly more options than that." He raised his head, motioning toward the window. "Meris, you're making a mistake—"

Focusing, I shoved a wall of magic toward him, pushing him away. He vanished, my head was pounding mercilessly in response.

— ☾ —

I guided Cerie down the halls. "I saw this." I gestured to the door at the far end of the corridor. The gallery. I supposed it would be guarded. With all the precious items there, the governor would be an idiot to leave it unattended.

"Well," Cerie whispered in my ear. "What now?"

"I need to get in there."

"I'll make sure you're not bothered."

I inhaled, trying to ready my nerves and head down the hall. The golden marble floor reflected my figure, reminding me of the dance floor—

The ballroom.

A fist tightened around my heart, squeezing tight and stirring agony in my bones. I needed this spell to work.

The copper archways led me through the hall of blazing light. I pressed against the doors, my fingers finding the looped handle. The barrier creaked open, wood hissing against iron hinges. As suspected, there were two guards posted in the room. They didn't even look at me, but I wasn't going to try and steal the Box until I was sure they couldn't see what I was doing.

The Box.

It sat just beyond my reach in a glass case. I could smell the magic on it, seeping out through the container. The Box was coated in it. Eerie, beautiful, yet full of unsettling promises. The mist man was on the outside of the Box, etched into the gold, as well as a skull, a sun, and strange writing on the top. It had an ethereal glow to it, pulsing with danger and enchantment.

The guards shifted, their attention grabbed by Cerie. She'd entered the room, gazing incredulously at a few more risqué images before insulting them and the men.

The two guards turned their backs to me.

The moonlight trickled in like an invisible beast breathing down my neck. I pushed against the glass case.

I stood in a room filled with shadows. Neither the floor nor ceiling was visible. "How do I make it look like I'm here when I'm not?" I asked, my hands glowing.

Another version of Tatum appeared in the memory. I was taller. Older. I could hear it in my voice. "You must concentrate on the object," he said. "You need something to take its place, momentarily. You can use your fire as a substitute, but I recommend a real object. A stone, a tree, whatever you need."

"I think about it, and it happens?"

Tatum smiled, his grin so pure against his dark skin. "Essentially."

The memory faded as the voices in reality grew louder. A debate had begun to take place. I swallowed my fear and pulled out a hairpin, focusing on replicating the small Box. A pulse of power extended from my hand as I lifted the case, and replaced the artifact with my hairpin. A mirror image took its place, flickering like the surface of a too-hot fire.

I shoved the Box, which was about the size of my palm, into my dress pocket as I glanced in Cerie's direction. She was so dedicated to swaying the men's opinions, her gestures wild and crazed, that I almost thought she truly held those opinions about the artist.

I breathed in. The illusion stayed secure. But my legs wobbled, my knees weakened.

The spell had drained in my power.

"Oh, dear." Cerie was at my side, her arms looping around my waist. "Are you alright?"

I shook my head. "I feel faint." Not a lie. It was also an excellent excuse to get out of this room and back to our own.

"Thank you for the chat, gentlemen. I need to bring my friend to her room."

The soldiers bowed their heads, keeping their predatory gazes on Cerie, as if they knew something now that they didn't before.

It couldn't be this easy, could it?

46

The clock struck midnight and my body felt as if a thousand pounds rested atop every muscle. The world spun, and I had yet to regain my footing completely. "Well?"

"Your magic is draining. You have enough to mist once, but anything more is deadly." Cerie was flipping through the codex as she paced my room, her eyes narrowed.

"No, I mean, when can you perform the mirror spell on Julna?"

Cerie didn't miss a beat. "I can't perform the mirror spell on your sister. My magic doesn't work like that."

A jolt of shock rumbled through my veins. "What?"

"I can't. I'm a unicorn, not an illusionist."

I groaned, kneading my temples. "Fine. I'll do it then."

She stood, tossing the book on my lap. "Absolutely not! You saw what that *small* mirror spell did to you in the gallery. If you tried to do a full-sized illusion, you might deplete yourself."

"Leaving her isn't an option."

"Meris—"

"No!" I stood, balling my hands into fists. The raging light from the nearby oil lamp caused my shadow and Cerie's to twine together in the darkness, melting into something similar, yet foreign. "I'm not leaving her."

"The fate of Yamira and Inder rests on you bringing *that*"—she point-

ed to the object in my hand—"back and setting Setizar free. Do you remember where he is? Have you forgotten he took *your* place in Redrim?"

"I haven't." I took in a sharp breath, trying to ease the knot in my
chest. "Why do you think I'm doing this? I could leave, steal my sister
away and survive here in Inder. But I'm stealing a stupid Box for him! I
don't even know who I am anymore, Cerie. I see me—but it's not me. A
child who I was once, but I don't remember. It's almost like it's someone
else's memory. How do you think that makes me feel?" I shook my head,
my breathing unsteady. "I love Setizar. I know he meant something to who
I was before, and I feel it now. The connection. I want to save him, not
only because I love him, but because I should be the one in Redrim. I
should be the one under Inanna's blade. I owe him a debt. But I also owe it
to my sister to save her as well."

Cerie nodded, her posture changing as she releases an uneasy, labored
breath. "Then we'll save your sister."

I jumped and grabbed her, hugging her tight. "Thank you."

"It doesn't mean I feel good about any of this. I have a really, really
bad feeling."

— ☾ —

I found Julna in the courtyard, drenched in a subtle blue light, twisting the
ring on her finger.

A cup of steaming tea rested on the table in front of her as she sat by
candlelight. Not that she needed the candlelight since the moon was bright
enough to take a long walk and not worry. A book rested in her hand, and
her head was angled so she couldn't see me. I knew the guards were locat-
ed everywhere, but if I did this right, I would have her and be in the field
in no time.

I had to augue. With a sharp breath in, I began to walk her way. The
blue light was a cold, weeping color, the kind that invited and warned at
the same time. I crept closer, staying as quiet as possible.

A twig snapped below my right foot. Great.

"Meris?" Julna looked at me, her smile appearing. "What're you doing up?"

"I wanted to talk with you." I slid closer. Would she call for the guards? Was I safe?

"Alright." She gestured beside her. "What do you want to talk about? Ah, I suppose that's a silly question to ask." Her face flushed and she closed her book, flipping the cover face down. "Maybe we should start simple."

"Yeah." I just needed to touch her. Grab her hand. It was as easy as that, right? "Julna, what if—"

She shook her head. "No more talk about the other land, please." She grasped my hand. I felt wrong about doing this to her. Ripping her away from what she knew. "I'm going to call for a doctor and see if the stress has gotten to your head."

I bit back every pointed word I wished to bark out and instead thought about Cerie—where she was in the field, waiting and pacing, fingers clasped around the Box and codex, no doubt. I thought deeper—about the portal, about Setizar, about Yamira . Fire burst around us and light flashed in my vision. Spots of red and black danced in the corners of my eyes and wind whipped at my body.

Julna screamed.

Slowly, I looked around. My heart sank so low in my gut that I couldn't seem to form words. We didn't go far, in fact, I saw the Ka'zor still standing ominously in front of us like an undaunted titan.

A thousand lifetimes flashed before my eyes as it dawned on me. I failed. My knees wobbled and my arms went limp. Languid light illuminated Julna's disoriented features for only a half second before everything shifted. Her brows were a series of tight lines, tracing her anger.

"What was that!" Julna screamed, balling her hands into fists. I couldn't have her screaming. This wasn't good. "Meris!"

"Please, be quiet?"

She shook her head, arms flailing in the air as she spun to face the

Ka'zor. "Help! Guards! *Help!*"

47

My pulse pounded through my veins. Nerves made my teeth chatter, and chills rolled up and down my spine. I wasn't ready for this. Fear writhed in my chest, squeezing my lungs and stunting my breathing. I couldn't stand.

Everything became bleary. Every sound, every light, every smell, every touch burned my skin, my ears, and my eyes. I couldn't move without pain searing through my body and the smell of metal bombarding my nose.

Julna was shouting something beside me, but I couldn't hear it over my thundering heartbeat.

Soldiers.

The beat of soldier's feet marching toward us rattled my nerves, the clap of their armor too loud.

"Halt!" the men yelled. I couldn't do anything.

My wings spread out, opening like the arms of the Reaper. I was choking.

My heart beat.

Once.

Twice.

Silence.

Arms wrapped around me, and I looked up, meeting a flash of poppy-red eyes. Tatum?

"Alecto." He rolled his shoulders, a frown pulling at his lips.

What was he doing?

Fire exploded around me and Julna. It was warm, like sunshine—and dark like the night sky above us. My knees knocked against each other as it stopped again.

"Remember, Alecto—" Tatum kneeled down, a gentle smile on his features. "You should never view anything in this life as random. Everything happens for a purpose."

"Why?" Pressure formed around my leg and I looked down. Leather boots? He was tightening my leather boots. Right. I was about to go into battle.

"If you believe things are random and without purpose, then what is the point in learning? What is the point in life? There is a beginning, an end, and most importantly," he pulled a sword from his side, placing it in my hands, "there is a middle. What we do with that middle affects the ending."

I nodded. "Is this the middle then?"

He smiled. It was a wicked thing, between care and mischief. "No. This is the beginning."

With a sigh, I sheathed my sword at my side. His eyes stayed locked with my own, flickering with answers to my many questions. "I'll be sure to make this a beginning worthy of your approval."

Tatum patted my head; such an informal gesture, one that warmed my heart. "Try to stay alive, Alecto. Things would be rather complicated if either of us die."

"Well, I'm not dying." I grinned. "So you're the one likely to pass first. And if you die, I will have to raise you until you're old enough to remember everything again." I lifted my brow, muscles taut as my wings snapped open.

Tatum laughed, taking a step toward the stairwell. "There's already a plan in place, but thank you for thinking of me."

"What's the plan?"

He paused, tapping his chin. "Perhaps if you paid more attention in your studies, you would have heard me explain it all."

I balled my hands into fists. "Do you mean to tell—"

Screams.

So many, many screams echoed around me. Slivers of shadows slithered along the ground. Julna was laying on the ground, her body limp. She was unconscious. Was that her screaming? Or was that something in my memory?

Click.

Click.

Click.

The ticking of a clock chimed somewhere in the surrounding air. Just off to the left, a strange white figure appeared. The rabbit.

"You're late." He tilted his head to the side. Those giant black eyes seemed to be looking at me. Searching my soul for something.

What did he want?

"You're late." His voice wasn't coming from his mouth, but from my head. Inside my head. He spoke in my mind.

I staggered to my feet, scrambling to Julna and pulling her up. Aether, she was heavy! My hands were full just holding my sister up off the ground. "Help?"

The creature tilted its head, as if I'd confused it.

"I can't do this on my own."

Soldiers barked orders in the distance, shouting to one another to do something. I couldn't focus on anything—just on the small being that stood in front of me. It stepped closer, the watch swinging back and forth on its neck.

Tick.

Tick.

Tick.

My dull heartbeat stuttered into a gallop. I spun, my body balking at the motion. "Tatum!"

He was on the ground, his chest slowly rising and falling. His skin was muted against the silver moonlight.

"What's happening?" I whispered.

"I used all my magic. I can no longer stay..." His voice dripped with pain. A fissure broke in my soul, ripping the emotions out of my body. "I couldn't save you, Alecto. I promised you." He grabbed my hand, but our fingers didn't touch. He could no longer touch me. "I suppose this is my way of making it up to you."

No. No one should vanish this way. "Tatum, stay with me. Wait a little longer! We can get you through the portal—"

Shouts and echoes reverberated in the skies. The soldiers were searching for us. "Go. You can make it into the portal." He pointed toward a nearby tree. In the winking twilight, the lamp and codex were visible. "Remember me."

"I can't leave you here."

"You can't pick me up," he whispered, voice was something between agony and worry, "And I can't stand."

"Tatum—"

He coughed, shudders of smoke and shadow flickering from him. "Go."

Hot tears stung my eyes. I didn't even know who he was, who he was to me, or who I was to him. I only wished to know, to give him that. To let him know I remembered him.

But, I couldn't. I couldn't remember anything but fragments. This was my fault.

I should have listened to him.

I was a stupid girl, wasn't I? So blinded by what I wanted that I forgot there were others involved. Tatum's breathing was uneven. Every second passed like a thousand, pouring down on the moment with shards of glass.

"Alecto." Tatum's eyes squeezed shut. "Break the glass." His voice was a strangled, hissing thing, barely audible.

"What?" I heard nothing but ringing in my ears.

I shouldn't have been standing then. Not with this pain in my body—in my heart. Who was he to me? His figure shuddered. A shadow swept over the ground, and, as the languid light vanished, so did he.

PART SIX
RETURN TO YAMIRA

48

Following the rabbit was like reflex. I had Julna, and Cerie had the codex and the Box. I wasn't sure why I trusted such a creature to guide us back into the realm, but somehow I did. Watching it, I realized the small creature was something else entirely. How it did what it did, I didn't know. The creature must not be bound by magic.

We dropped through the portal. Wind and rain ripped at my body like the claws of an angered fiend. I could barely keep my eyes open. Everything was so harsh, so brutal—

Water, as icy and frigid as the first time I arrived in Yamira, greeted me. We plunged down, down, down into its biting depths until my wings were numb and aching.

Up.

I swam upward as did Julna, who must have woken from the shock. Her struggle was only momentary, lasting a half second as she realized we were underwater. She locked her arm with mine and we both paddled upward, kicking against the current and breaking through the surface. The air was frosty, coating my lungs in bitter ice.

"What—" she gasped, her breath uneven. "Where are we?"

I urged her to the bank, our clothes sticking to our freezing bodies. "We are in Yamira. No one is going to hurt you—"

"Why!" Julna's blue lips quivered. Every ounce of energy she had seemed to be in her exclamation. "Why did you do this?"

Why was she asking me this? She'd been sold to Farelyn. She was still a version of a slave. "To save you." I couldn't make sense of her reaction.

"No!" She stood, legs wobbling, and grasped a nearby branch for support. The sharp thorns of the tree pierced her skin, digging into her flesh like a dagger. Fresh blood bloomed along her palm, dripping into the snow. It was morning here, and the sun bathed fresh yellow light on the white earth, illuminating the drops of crimson beside Julna. "No, no!"

I staggered a step back, my mind a gray void. "What?"

"Why?" Her voice crumbled, breaking off bit by bit. "Why would you do this to me?"

"What? You—"

"Stop!" Julna screeched. "Make it stop! Bring me back!"

I shook my head. "I—I can't do that. The portal is closed."

She fell.

Blood smeared on her beautiful face as she cupped it with her hands. Sobs wracked her body, her shoulders convulsing as she cried. What had I done?

— ☾ —

The walk was slow and agonizing, every step weighed down by lead. Julna was as silent as the grave beside me, Cerie was shivering worse than us, and the rabbit was nowhere to be found.

I was so *stupid*! Why did I do this? I should have listened to Cerie and Tatum. I should've left Julna and made my way back to Yamira with the Box in hand. He would still be here, helping me along the way. Instead? I *killed* him.

I killed him and ruined my sister's life.

It was all my fault.

Something snapped in the corner of my eye. Bright and glowing, like the embers of a still kindling fire. I turned, craning my neck over a large bush. "Jack?"

He bowed, an open gash of a smile spreading over his face. "Yes?"

"What're you doing here?"

He flicked a snowflake from his shoulder, how it got there with his flaming head, I didn't know. "Well you see, a small rabbit told me."

Just as he spoke, the rabbit appeared beside him. "You're late."

Jack slid his hands into his trouser pockets. "Well, well, well." He pivoted his body around, looking at Julna. "Who's the guest?"

"Oh!" I turned to her, smiling. "This is my sister."

Jack's eyes narrowed. "Is it now? You look nothing like Megaera."

Julna straightened. "Who?"

I stood between them, my breath ragged. "Jack, she doesn't know everything."

He seemed unconvinced. "We have the Box and the codex. Now all that's left is to rescue our beloved Lord."

I stopped, fingers trembling. "How are we going to do that?"

"Ah!" Another voice joined in, stepping into the area. Sir Libby, the invisible man. "That part will be bloody difficult and easy to botch. Since we know Inanna won't abide by the law, we'll have to get *into* Redrim and not get caught."

"Libby," Jack's voice was low and gruff, grinding against my bones like shards of metal. "You can't be scaring them."

"I doubt Alecto is frightened of anything."

Not true, but alright.

Jack turned, looking up at the bright skies darkening with clouds. His black eyes settled on me, Julna, and Cerie. "You three look wretched. If we start moving, I will begin drying you off. Come on, Libby." Jack released a ball of fire in the air, which split into three parts, licking our outfits with warmth. Steam wafted up into the air, floating into the sky and mingling with the clouds.

"Rightly so." Libby tucked his cane under his arm, walking behind Jack. "Alecto, Cerieandria the Unicorn, and..." Libby paused, as if pondering what he was going to say. "And, sister."

Seemed like Jack wasn't the only one who didn't believe me about Julna.

"Why don't you or Libby believe Julna is my sister?"

Jack looked at me, lowering his voice as Libby began to tell Julna about the world. "She looks very different. However, Megaera was a reclusive creature, and not many saw her. But I did. You look a shade different too, but otherwise you look relatively the same. I can't be the judge, but something doesn't settle with me."

I looked at Julna, who had scooped up the rabbit in her arms and was listening intently to everything Libby was saying to her. There was no possible way she wasn't my sister. If she wasn't in my past life, she was now. I couldn't expect him, or anyone else, to understand that.

"Aether!" Libby gasped, still as a painting. If it weren't for the monocle, I wouldn't have known where he was looking. "Really now, Jack?"

"What?"

"You aren't exactly whispering. The entire frozen wasteland can hear you."

Jack crossed his arms. "Then you better keep your voice down, Libby. I'm sure Feng can hear your wheezing voice on the wind."

49

Hunger pinched my stomach. Every aching bone begged me to stop and rest, however, the fact Setizar was in Inanna's clutches pushed my tired body onward.

"How far?" I looked at Libby, my wings beginning to weigh heavier than lead.

"Until what?" Libby's monocle reflected my face. I looked absolutely horrid. "Until we die, or until we rest?"

"Until we get to Redrim."

"Ah." Libby rubbed his fingers together. "Until we die, then. Well, I suppose a half day journey. Shame none of us can portal."

They bickered, and late afternoon pulled crooked shadows along the path, promising darkness and death. A jumble of emotions and thoughts bombarded my mind, ranging from mundane to horrific.

My stomach gave me nothing but pain, reminding me I haven't eaten—and Julna hadn't either. And yet my sister remained cautiously quiet, rather undisturbed by Jack and Libby's less-than-optimistic conversation. She was subdued, holding tight to the rabbit as if it was her last line to her sanity.

I didn't blame her.

I pulled her into this world, and she was in the company of a winged girl, a unicorn, an invisible man, and a living pumpkin. I should've been smarter and listened to Tatum.

Aether! I wished he was still here.

"Alecto," Tatum said, his eyes shrouded in the darkness. "Do you know who I am?"

"Of course I do." I slipped my sword into its sheath, casting him a sideways glance. "Why do you ask?"

"Because I have a feeling one day you'll forget me, and you won't remember who I am to you and how much you mean to me."

I laughed. It seemed silly, that question. "And what do I mean to you?"

His hands were warm as they wrapped around me, his arms tightening about my waist. "You mean the cosmos to me, Alecto. You're my—"

"Alecto!"

Everything around me became unbearably bright as the light of the surrounding world bombarded my eyes. "What?"

It was Jack, his face utterly displeased. "We lost you there. Are you alright?"

"Of course." My hand found its way to my chest; the rhythm of my heartbeat felt like an angry drum. Why didn't I remember who Tatum was to me?

A hollow formed in my gut, growing until it spread through my entire body.

"We must stop at Lhysa's place." Libby tipped his hat to me. "Just in time too… I'm certain we're all famished and exhausted."

I knew I was, and my magic had yet to recover. I could feel the strain, the magical muscles Setizar talked about, I'd never felt so internally exhausted in my life. I used too much in too short a time without the proper preparation. I frowned. "We aren't going to Redrim?"

"We can't get there." Libby shrugged delicately. "Unless Lhysa opens a portal for us to get through, we cannot step foot on Redrim."

My breath stilled in my lungs. I should've guessed as much;. we were traveling along the line between Eira's plane and Lhysa's territory. I resigned myself to this inconvenience. As soon as we met with Lhysa, I was sure we'd be on our way to rescuing Setizar.

Taking in a deep breath of the sugar and citrus air, a calm overtook me. Spring had never been so sweet. Birch trees with clover-green leaves marked the beginning of a golden sand pathway. The light danced between the foliage, casting speckles of magical afternoon sunlight along the earth.

"Well?" Libby stabbed the end of his walking cane into the ground. "I must say I'm very surprised Inanna hasn't sent an army of ogarak to come and kill you, Jack. Very impressive."

"She won't send an army." Jack's voice was a whisper on the spring wind, adding a level of anxiety to my nerves. "She will send one of them."

We went still. Even Julna, who hadn't spoken a word other than to the little rabbit, gasped. Only birds and the echo of a bubbling brook nearby filled the silence.

"The leviathan. Stars, I hate those." Setizar's voice tightened as he *emphasized his words. His entire torso was made up of toned, copper muscle, gleaming in the sunlight. Sweat drenched his body.*

"What is so important about this leviathan?" I angled my weapon at him, the blade pointed at his abdomen. "How is it different than any other creature?"

"Because," he lowered his voice, a sultry mix of rumbling tones and accent. "You can't just kill it. You need to—"

"No!" Jack's yell cut through my memories.

No! What was Setizar going to tell me?

"I'm positive the *north*-west route is the way to go. I can't believe you think it's strictly west."

Libby clicked his tongue. "You are not the one who has studied cartography for years on end."

"You've never traveled this path for years on end, you invisible doorknob."

"Invisible doorknob?" His voice rose in pitch. "I'll show you a thing or two that a doorknob certainly couldn't ever do."

"Both of you!" I said, my laden wings lightening as the swell of magic began to fill my veins. "Just pick a route and let's go. I can't have you arguing. It won't aid us in any way, shape, or form."

Jack and Libby exchanged a pandering glance at each other—well, Jack did and I was certain Libby was making a similar face. "Fine." Jack dipped his head. "Lead the way, oh mighty Sir Libby, renown cartographer."

"You wretch." Libby's voice was coated in disdain, filling my mouth with an unsavory taste.

50

My eyes couldn't focus on anything. Not after I heard it the first time.

Screams.

Setizar's screams.

Flashes of images conjured up in my mind, his body torn, blood dripping on the flagstones. Everything was dark in the vision—cold. I wanted to vomit, my insides turned upside down. Inanna grinned as she tortured him. I wanted to cut off her face.

I didn't care who she was. No one—not even the Aether himself—had a right to torture Setizar. Fire crackled along my knuckles at the thought of it. The muscles in my back constricted.

I wanted to tear Redrim down with my bare hands.

Libby must have picked up on my anger since he'd kept his distance. Jack, however, stayed closer.

"I know what it's like." He looked at me, hollow eyes seeking mine. Fire danced in their depths, raging and smoldering gently with a passionate flame. "To burn everything you touch. To be feared. It's a creature of its own making. We have no control over the fire, it has control over us."

I offered him a half smile. "I don't want the fire to be in control."

He laughed, his spindly hand resting on my shoulder. "You learn to accept it. I remember when you were the most feared and revered creature in the entire realm. Every inhabitant in Yamira either loved you or respected you."

"What happened?"

Jack shook his head. "No one knows. There's several rumors, one that Inanna assassinated you and your sister. Others believe the Silver Queen cursed you along with the rest of the realm."

"Do you know why no one can remember who the Silver Queen is?"

Jack's voice was strained. "I have no idea, no one does. There are simply myths and legends about her. Anyone who ever *actually* had contact with her can't seem to remember her face or her voice. She's the tale you tell your children at night when you want them to behave. Sadly this legend is very real. When we use the Box, doubtless she will be summoned. It's part of the curse. The spell she placed on the Seasons, if they ever regain their powers, she would appear to right it once more—this time to bring blood and darkness. To finish what she started."

My breath caught in my throat. "We should be prepared." I looked at Julna. "We should leave her with Lhysa. She can't be brought into Redrim. She's not a fighter."

"I agree." Jack nodded. "We don't need any distractions."

The purr of the wind caressed my neck—

"What are you doing?" Setizar laughed, his fingers trailing down my spine.

I fought back my own laugh as I hid the paper in the desk drawer. "Nothing…"

"Lies. Tell me what you're up to, you mischievous furie." He smiled against my skin; his lips pressed against my bare shoulder.

"Can't I surprise you?" I tried to move my body to look at him. His hands gripped my waist, keeping me secured in place. "Stuffed up jinni."

His laugh had fingers, caressing my spine and stomach. "Resulting to insults now?"

I straightened my body. "Of course."

His hands moved slowly from my waist, arms twisting around me. "Well." His breath was hot against my skin, his chin resting along the nape of my neck. "If it pleases you to insult me," his amethyst eyes flashed with mischief as a feline smile spread over his lips, "then please, continue. I will be your verbal punching bag."

I swiveled, grabbing his head. "Good thing I love you and don't mean a single thing outside our banter."

His eyes searched mine, two dimples forming on his cheeks. "You don't need to explain that. I already know."

"And we continue for how long?" Libby groaned. "Do you even hear yourself?"

Why were they always interrupting my memories? It was like a shattered mirror, never fully seeing it all. Fragments that made no sense.

"Where is the mirror?"

"Why do you want to know?" Setizar leaned back in his chair. "Are you curious?"

"Just a tad." I slid into the sofa across from him, angling him a look I hoped would have driven my point across.

Setizar grinned, his head angling to the side. "I'm sure you got Aurel to spill many dirty secrets because of that."

My heart beat so fast I forgot it was beating at all. "What?"

"You don't think I know what you did to my closest friend? What you mean to him?" Setizar stood, fire welling in his eyes. "Why do you want to know where the mirror is?"

I stood, my own voice trembling. "Don't do this."

"You used me, Alecto." He stepped closer. "You wove yourself into everyone's lives, just to find that mirror."

"You don't know! None of you understand what you did. Why did you do that?"

"We did that because it's dangerous. We had to make the best choice." Setizar shook his head. "Don't worry about the mirror. It's safe."

"Give it to me. You had no right."

A hand tugged at mine, and I turned. A woman, but her face was shrouded. All I knew was she asked to go outside. But, I couldn't hear her speak.

Setizar nodded. "We will discuss this later, Alecto."

"Despite everything, I didn't use you. I love you. I have a mission, and my mission is to find and make sure that mirror is safe. That he's safe." I grabbed Setizar's arm. He didn't fight me. "Do you understand?"

"I prayed to the Aether you would say that."

I smiled, hugging him. "I'll explain it all. And once I do, you'll see why I needed to do this."

Aether. What was I doing? Something inside me told me I knew. The mirror—Tatum's mirror.

"Break the glass."

Is that how I could bring him back?

I turned to Julna, to the rabbit happily trotting beside her. As soon as I got Setizar back and we returned to the Crimson Plane, I would break the mirror. I just prayed I did it right.

A giant structure rose over the tree line, gleaming in the waning sunlight. The edifice was a bright yellow color, surrounded by vibrant gardens. Lhysa's palace. It was so beautiful. The gardens varied in colors, from deep purple to white lilies. The entire field was mostly treeless, grass rolling along the valley like a tumultuous sea.

"We'll stop here," Jack said. "We must attempt to bargain with the Lady of Spring, otherwise our entrance into Redrim will be more complicated."

"Isn't she just opening the portal for us?" I sidled up to him, angling my body so the wind didn't blow me over.

"No." Jack tilted his head. "And you can't walk to Redrim, either. It's an island. There are only three ways there. Flying, which only the furie can do, boat, which is extremely dangerous, or portal. The latter only the daemon and numina can do."

"Numina—" I inclined my head, memories stirring. "The light side of the daemon. Creatures made of stars and sunlight."

Jack chuckled. "Good. Glad to know your memory is returning. Slowly, but returning. Lhysa is a numina, and the last of her kind." His tone was sorrowful, aching.

"How long have you known her?"

He laughed. Something bitter was on his tongue as he said, "Long."

It clicked. I knew the sound of that voice and the way the vowels dripped out as if coated in blood from the still fresh wounds of affection. "How long have you loved her?"

His head dropped, his shoulders slumping. The act was so defeated, as if he was holding onto every last ounce of control he could muster. "For as long as I can remember. But she would never notice me. I'm a fae, and she's a numina. We can't mix."

"Why?"

He flashed me a pointed gaze. "Because, that's how it's been, and will always be. We can't break our own species rules."

"Yes you can." I slid into his view, returning his pointed stare with one of my own. "I'm a furie, and Setizar is a jinni. If we can make it work—"

Jack's laugh was grating and rough. "Look at me, Alecto. Look at my face. Look at what I'm made of." He pulled back his leather gloves, revealing the twisted limbs of vines. "Would you love someone like me? The Silver Queen stole our ability to change forms. Now I'm just limbs and vines, and can never be anything more."

My heart sank inside, swirling and twisting. "Yes." I grasped his hand, looking into his face. "I would love someone like you. If a person loves someone only for how they look, then what does that say about them?"

He shook his head, the fire around his skull diminishing slightly. "I only cause pain. Fire and flesh do not mix. It's for her safety."

I couldn't help but feel he didn't entirely mean what he said.

51

Flowers bloomed from Lhysa's aura. It was the deep gold color of royalty and refinement, flickering between tangerine orange and honey yellow. She could spark the beginning of spring just by her presence. The hem and drooping sleeves of her lemon-hued dress danced in the wind as the silver beads along her neck reflected the light. She turned her black eyes to us, glittering like a thousand diamonds in a twilit night.

"Lhysa." Libby placed a white-gloved hand over his heart and bowed. "Lady of Spring."

Lhysa's eyes narrowed on each of us, her fingers knitting together. "What brings you to my sector?"

"We're on a mission," Jack began. "We—"

"Inanna took Setizar, and I plan on getting him back." I stepped forward, my body tensing. "But we need your help."

A muscle feathered in her jaw. "Oh?" She arched a brow upward into her coiled bangs. "And when did she take him?"

"Four days tomorrow," Cerie said, trotting forward and handing me the satchel with the Box and codex. "Before we make any rash decisions, I'd like to return to the Crimson Plane, my lady, if you would allow it, and prepare the place for my lord's return."

Lhysa's expression fluttered slightly, but she nodded. A second later sparks appeared, flickering to the left of us and spiraling into a large gateway.

Cerie stepped through, and the gateway closed.

Jack pressed a hand to his chest. "Lhysa, she remembers."

Lhysa froze. "Oh, do you remember *everything*?" She spun to face me, that golden aura changing to a nettled red. "Tell me, do you remember the Silver Queen?"

I took a step back. "What?"

"Lhysa." Jack stepped between us. His tall figure loomed over me. "Please?"

Irritation flickered in her eyes, but she gestured to the house, silver nails gleaming in the evening sun. "Come in and eat. Rest however long you need, and I will think about opening a portal to the land of nightmares."

"Think?" I pushed past Jack, balling my fists. "*Think*? Setizar is in Inanna's clutches right now! We don't have time to—"

"Would you rather me answer you now and say no?" Lhysa snapped. "Or can I have time and discuss this with my council?"

"Of course," Libby said, pulling at my arm. "We apologize for the inconvenience, my lady. Thank you for your generosity and kindness." He poked my shoulder as he guided Julna with his free hand.

Lhysa dipped her head. "My guards will escort you to your rooms and ensure there are no issues."

As she spoke, four men in dark robes and black veils approached. I followed them silently, wishing someone would say something. I couldn't take my eyes from their weapons. Two had staffs, the shade of blood and obsidian, with dual knives soldered together on either side, forming a spear. The other two had sabers.

I had only heard of those sorts of swords in tales, never seen one before me. They were far more imposing in person with their curving metal and razor-thin edges.

The guards remained ghost-quiet, not even their feet made a noise against the chalky gravel path. I would have enjoyed the view if it weren't for the situation. It was lovely; the palace sat on a lush riverside bordering a sprawl of hills. Golden domes sat along the various spires like fallen suns. It screamed beauty, and yet felt muted without Setizar being there. Without him being *safe*.

The guards led us up curling staircases made of pearly marble, glimmering with flakes of opal and diamond. Gold railings curved up toward the vaulted ceilings, glistering like a tawny ocean. When we reached the landing, Libby tugged gently at my elbow, keeping me close. Perhaps he could sense my rattled nerves around the guards.

Another set of stairs and we entered the hall. Crown molding, ornate and appearing to be made of ivory, decorated the border between the walls and roof.

Two guards escorted Libby and Jack farther down the hall, while the two with the sabers escorted Julna and me to a pair of glassy doors made of frosted crystal. I couldn't see anything on the other side of the door, yet there was an illusion that made me think I could.

It was stunning.

The door opened, and I entered a powder-blue room with four open doors leading to an outside balcony. I turned to the guard, but he was gone before I could thank him.

I shrugged off the pack Cerie had given me to hold the Box and codex and placed it on the dresser. The floor was covered in snow-white carpet, greeting my weary feet with plush softness.

The bed was anything but ordinary, with ornate white and blue covers and seashell pink pillows. Four spires protruded from the posts, nearly touching the ceiling. An extravagant blue veil was strewn from pillar to pillar, covering the bed in a muslin canopy.

A pang of guilt spidered through my stomach. Setizar was in Redrim, and I was here in Lhysa's palace.

It wasn't fair. I should have been the one taken to Redrim.

I shrugged off my dress and walked into the bathing chamber. I needed to wash Yeodo off me and somehow wash the memories into place. I needed to remember *something* other than small fragments.

I willed my wings into my back as I dipped into the water. The mixture was something between warm and cold, refreshing my mind while soothing my nerves. It was milky looking, allowing my body to vanish below the water.

"Well, I didn't know this would happen, but I'm not opposed."

Setizar?

I looked up. He was translucent, his black hair falling over his forehead, arms bound behind his back—white shirt soaked in blood. "Setizar!" I nearly jumped out of the tub, much to his apparent amusement.

"Don't get out." He released a pained, hollow laugh.

"How are you doing this? Are you injured?" I fought the need to try and touch him, but I knew that was pointless.

"I'm injured, but recovering. Inanna wants me to be healed before—" His words trailed off, and he looked at me. "Are you well?"

I couldn't answer him, not when he was hurt and I was absolutely fine. "I'm coming to get you."

His eyes widened. "Meris, *no*."

"Yes! I'm not going to leave you in her clutches, and if you think I'm going to stand by while you—"

"There's something much bigger at stake here. I don't know what, but your memories are key." His eyes flickered a shade, changing to a dull gray. "I love you."

"Setizar—" Before I could say another word, he was gone.

I didn't care if there was something bigger at stake. I didn't care if I brought the universe to its knees in the process. I was rescuing him.

52

As soon as I got out of the tub, I fell into bed and slept until morning. My dreams were silent and dark—like I lay in the middle of a blackened lake, watching the cosmos flicker to death. I didn't feel rested when the first light of the sun sliced through the open balcony, casting a delicate blue light on my bed from the veils.

The clamor of swords rang below my windows, and curiosity took hold. I slid out of the curtained bed and walked toward the balcony. A soldier stood with a weapon in hand, wearing nothing but loose trousers. His dark skin gleamed in the early light, like the dew on a newly budded flower. In front of him, with her back to me, was a woman, her sword held deftly between herself and the soldier.

She was good, whoever she was.

I squinted, hoping to get a better look at her. Long, flowing chestnut locks were braided neatly on the crown of her head.

Julna?

My breath snagged. When did she learn to fight like that?

I leaned forward a bit more, my stomach pressing against the mezzanine railing as I tried to watch their spar.

Well it wasn't so much of a spar as it was a dance. Julna was as evasive as a serpent, and her opponent was as quick as a hummingbird. Slashes of silver light reflected off their swords, cutting through the dew and mist coating the garden. The hill was drenched in golden sunlight, conflicting with the green hues.

"I see you're awake." I didn't flinch hearing Lhysa's voice behind me. "Enjoying the spar?"

I offered her a partial glance. "I don't know where she learned to fight like that."

"You and Megaera were fierce warriors. The strongest in the realm." Lhysa stood beside me, touching her fingers to the sheer honey-hued veil covering her nose and lips. "Do you remember *everything*?"

"No, I don't." I looked at her, really taking in her appearance. She was beautiful. Her dark skin and hair glowed as hints of gold appeared under the surface. Her eyes were darker than a pirate's soul, but far more enchanting than diamonds.

She rested her hand on mine, the clink of her jewelry chiming against each other as she did so. "No one will speak to you about this, but we can't remember what happened the day you died. Our memories are as broken as yours. We're depending on you to remember what we cannot. I've tried to break the curse myself, hunting for remedies and bargaining with others, but it's useless. As a part of the Silver Queen's spell, we forgot about her aside from her name. If she was ever in our midst, we won't recall it."

"Why tell me this?" I leaned against the railing, facing the doorway.

"If you can remember, then there is a chance you can shatter her spell completely. Returning us to our full power is one thing, but it comes at a cost. Once we return to our previous states, so does the Silver Queen." Lhysa pulled a note from her gown, pressing it into my hands. "I found fragments of her spell. Loopholes." She pointed to the letter, and I began to unfold it. "She bargained with an ancient creature, sealing the deal within the Box. Her powers were stripped from her, as was ours, locked away in the Box until they're returned to us. But—" She swallowed her words.

"What? What is it?"

Her eyes were cutting. "In order for us to get the powers, you must take them in, and you mustn't allow anything to distract you. If you're distracted, then the balance of the powers will tip...and at that point, anyone and anything could take them. It's all written here."

I glanced at the paper, reading every word. "So we will only do this in a room where you, me, Eira, Feng, Julna, Setizar, and Aurel are present."

Lhysa looked wary, but nodded. "If it goes right, we will restore this realm to what it was before."

Every nerve in my body balked at the thought. Something wasn't right. "So, does this mean you made your mind up about the portal?"

Lhysa's eyes smiled. "Perhaps I did. Perhaps my council is averse to the idea, and perhaps this afternoon I will be practicing my magic, as usual, and inadvertently open a portal to Redrim."

I smiled. "Perhaps I'll have to watch your practice."

— (—

Jack stared at me over the breakfast table. He'd taken a few bites of his food, but otherwise he didn't do much else than read the contents of the letter. Libby was the talkative one, exploring all the details of the plan, while Julna remained utterly silent, not even touching her breakfast.

The rabbit was sitting beside her. I was discomforted by how it remained at her side, not deigning to leave her for a second.

"Well!" Libby clapped his hands, leaning his elbows on the table. "We retrieve Setizar, and Lhysa will portal us back to the Crimson Plane?"

"That's the plan we have gone over four times already," Jack snapped, slicing his gaze to the invisible man.

Libby straightened his collar. "I simply wish to be on the same page. Nothing's wrong with that, is there?"

"No, but stop repeating the same thing over and over." Jack pressed his fingers to the sides of his flaming head. "It's giving me a headache."

"This entire ordeal is giving me one," I said, leaning back in my seat and crossing my legs. "Every time I think I know what I'm supposed to do, something else is added."

"I can see how that would be exhausting." Jack stretched, angling his head toward Libby. "Mind if you come with me, Sir Libby? I have a few things to find."

"Of course." Libby stood, bowing to me and Julna. "I will see you later."

The two strode out of the room, leaving me alone with my sister. She was as quiet as ever. But I wanted to know how she'd learned to fight like she was earlier. "So—"

"I don't feel up to speaking, Meris." Julna dabbed her mouth and stood.

"No." I slammed my hand down on the table. "You've been avoiding speaking to me since we first came here."

"Maybe because it's your fault that I'm here," Julna said, her voice taut. "Ever think about that?"

I froze. No. I was tired of holding my tongue. "No, Julna. I need you to speak to me."

She shook her head, trying to brush past me.

"Julna, stay."

Her steps faltered, and she paused. "I just want to go back to where I was, when you were Meris and I was Julna. I don't like this new reality, the memories…" She glanced out the window. "I don't like this at all."

I nodded. "I didn't either. I wanted nothing more than to go back home. But now… I can see this is where I'm supposed to be."

Her eyes wavered, emotions swimming in her eyes. I didn't know what she was thinking or feeling. "How much do you remember?" she asked. "Of this life, here, before we were… us."

"Not much, I'm afraid." I leaned against the cold marble pillar, my back embracing the chill. "It's all… pieces."

She released a long breath, combing a hand through her wavy hair. "Well, I suppose pieces are better than nothing."

I closed my eyes. "So where'd you learn to fight like that? The way you were fighting this morning?"

Julna's laugh was as delicate as butterfly wings. "It came to me before the sun was up. I asked the guard outside my room if he would be willing to spar with me, and he was happy to oblige."

I offered her a smile that felt somewhat forced. "Like reflex?"

"Yes." Julna sputtered something between a sob and a laugh. "I suppose that's what it is."

I looped my arms around her, hugging her. "I promise, once I rescue Setizar," the words twisted my heart, plunging a guilt-ridden dagger into my stomach, "we can go back home, and return to life before."

"Really?" Julna's eyes fluttered up to mine, tears pooling at the corners. "Truly?"

"Yes." I winced at my own promise. But, she was my sister. She mattered more to me than anything.

She slackened, finally returning my embrace. "Good."

— ☾ —

The portal was a mist, venturing into a land of white nothingness. Lhysa stood beside it, her eyes beckoning the warnings which never passed her lips. Warnings we all knew.

Julna was beside me, her face paler than before. "Be careful."

Jack gave her a reassuring nod, looking at Libby who, aside from his monocle and mustache, was completely invisible.

It was just the three of us.

"Well, my lady, are you ready to rescue your beloved?" Jack smiled.

"Yes." I breathed, adjusting my suit. I was clad in flexible fighting leathers with metal plates across my shoulders, spine, and forearms. There were two flaps in the back for my wings in case I needed them. It felt strange. This suit wasn't something I was used to, but somehow it felt right. "Are you sure this will work?"

Jack waved his hand, handing me a hooded coat. "Lhysa will be able to see everything Libby sees for the next hour. Anything after that, the spell wears off. So, we need to find Setizar before the hour's end, or we risk being closed in Redrim with no escape."

A hollow formed in my heart as Jack and Libby took a step forward. Aether, I wasn't ready for this.

But whether I was ready or not, we stepped through the white-nothingness into the dark, scarlet-drenched world of Redrim.

53

My head spun. Up was down, down was up, and the sound of a thousand screams filled the atmosphere. I fell to my knees, resting my back against a fallen monument.

Jack's fire was a shade darker, a shade closer to black than I thought was natural, making him appear grim. Everything around us was an unearthly hue, dripping in red.

"Alecto?" Jack looked at me, his eyes narrowing. *Alecto.* I was still not used to that name. "Ready?"

I nodded, gesturing to the surrounding area. "Lead the way."

Jack stood, taking a step toward the looming mountain in the distance. Perched atop, exuding horror and anger, stood a citadel with gleaming red windows shaped like clocks. I followed Jack, glancing over my shoulder to be sure Libby was there. Our shoes were silent against the stone bridge, drowned out by the swelling, blood red river as it thundered into the distance. The ground below vibrated and whirred, making every step unsteady.

The windows of the threatening building reflected the sun, which seemed to be hiding behind the moon in an eternal eclipse.

Jacks steps were deliberate. Fear took hold, sinking frozen claws into my heart. I flinched at the smell of blood; the rusty, metal scent dripped into my nose.

"Jack?" I could see his head from a mile away. How was this going to work? "Your head."

He looked at me. "Worried about my light?" He gave me a devilish smile, fanged by the sharp rows of carved teeth. "You know why I'm here, right?"

"To help me?"

Jack's smile grew. "To be a distraction."

My heart stuttered a step. "What?"

"Take the eastern block, downward. There'll be a route to the dungeons. I'm certain he's in there." Jack pulled a key from his pocket, pushing it into my palm. "This key will unlock his binds. She most likely has him in power-dampening cuffs."

"Jack." I grabbed his arm, searching his face. "Please be careful."

He made a sweeping bow, a mocking gaze falling on me. "I suppose you remember nothing then. Very few seem to anymore."

Libby touched my shoulder, perhaps sensing my reluctance to let Jack go. "Allow him to do what he must."

I stared. I stared and stared, not able to move my limbs—my feet were as heavy as rock. Jack was still walking, nearly vanishing past the gated walls as I stood, frozen as ice. Rings of fatigue swirled over me, and I finally turned and looked at Libby, or, at least what I could see of him.

"Come along, Al—Meris."

I struggled out a breath, grasping the hand he placed in mine. Our heels clicked softly against the stone pathway toward the wall that stood like a sentinel of darkness and doom over us. "Where are the guards?"

"Inanna doesn't post guards outside. She assumes no one would dare set foot in Redrim on purpose. The ogarak are mere lackeys, doing the dirty work like pawns in a game."

My teeth chattered as a chill rolled down my spine. Every ounce of my energy was used to push onward, weaving around the falling boulders and rocks that litter the pathways. Libby guided me through the main entrance, opposite the direction Jack decided to take.

"He won't make himself known unless it's needed. I fear it will be.

With the amount of creatures crawling through Redrim, I'm surprised that we haven't run into any yet," Libby whispered.

The archway was ink-black, with two, withered looking and aged statues carved into the walls. They stared at me with hollow gazes and open mouths. Dripping from their lips was a liquid—dark crimson and congealed. It slithered down their gnarled fingers onto swords, the hue of dried bones and ash, tinting its ancient path scarlet and brown. I held my breath, daring to glance off the side of the bridge toward the red river.

We entered the gatehouse, blurred by darkness. The smell of metal ravaged my nose, splintering my consciousness. I was seeing double of everything. "Libby, are you getting... dizzy as well?"

"No." His fingers grasped my shoulder, his voice a rasping growl. "Are you alright, Meris?"

I made a quick nod, pushing forward. The eclipse light shed an unearthly color on the outer ward, which was as still and silent as death. Even the cobblestone, glittering with wetness, appeared frozen in time. There was no wind. No... *nothing*.

"The guardhouse is just up the path. We must be careful and not draw attention." He hissed a breath between his teeth for emphasis, making sure I stayed quiet.

The dark obsidian gleamed in the light as we ascended the path. I held my breath. Clatter and noise and the clanking of armor or steel-goblets, resounded from the building beside us. The silhouettes of ogarak were cast on the frosted windows, enhancing their animalistic appearances.

The horns on their chests were the most unnerving. I tugged my hood tighter over my head, trying my best to blend into the darkness around. Our steps were silent, and we walked up to the portcullis without issue.

The iron grate closed off our path, sealing the gateway. On either side, gibbets swung, with twin rotting corpses inside. It smelt of death and nightmares. "Aether!" Libby cursed, his monocle shattering light on the road.

"Well," Tatum said, his fingers weaving between the bars. "You're in a

bind."

"Hilarious."

"You sound cocky." Tatum waved his hand, and the cell shrunk. The bars kissed my face, grazing my bound hands and wings. "I don't like cocky."

Something snapped over my mouth and panic bloomed in my chest. Anxiety begun to take hold.

My heartbeat slowed.

Once.

Twice.

No. I knew how to get out. I knew the magic. I twisted my hand, snapping my thumb out of socket. Pain pulsed up my arm as I pulled it free, but not without injury. Scrapes peppered my wrist and hand from the iron. I grabbed whatever was clasped over my face, ripping it free. Tears stung my eyes, one trickling down my cheek. "Souvrir."

Iron clanked, falling limp at my sides as the door swung open.

Tatum's eyes gleamed with pride. "Well done."

"Well?" Libby's monocle was inches from my face. "We could try climbing—"

I shook my head, raising my arm. "*Souvrir.*"

The distinct hiss of metal and iron turning roused his attention. "Well," he said, amusement dancing in his voice, "that wasn't expected. Where did you learn that?"

"I... remembered it."

Libby's tone was no longer amused, but skeptical. "That is ancient magic forbidden by the Seasons."

"Why?"

He remained quiet, a cane appearing in his hand. "Because, that sort of magic is never free. It steals from one, giving to another, but the cost of the exchange is high. Don't use it again... I fear it won't end well."

I swallowed the fear and began following him once again.

The steep mountain slope was to the left, curling with the pathway which led up. To the right was the wall, overlooking a land of darkness, and the sea of raging red beyond.

The citadel rested just at the top of the mountain peak. Where had Jack gone? "We won't be going up there." Libby pressed his cane to my stomach. "Not until you tell me something."

"What?" Irritation built in my gut, festering around the area he pressed his cane.

"Where did you learn that spell?"

"I told you, I remembered it."

"No memory attached to it?" The way his words came out were clipped—jagged almost. Was this an interrogation?

"No." I didn't know why I lied. Something inside me said this wasn't something Libby needed to know. A secret I should keep. "I wish I did."

I couldn't tell if he believed me or not. The cane was still pressed flush against my body. Agonizing seconds dragged by.

His cane dropped and vanished. "Very well. Let's continue."

I released a breath of ease, fog swirling around me. We needed to hurry.

We followed the curve of the wall to the left, gently sloping upward, easing along the trail toward the castle at the top.

Another archway led us into a city of sorts. Redrim felt ghostly until now; the town was practically teeming with life. Ogarak, and creatures I'd never seen before, were bustling back and forth. Four females, which looked like Wraiths, stood in a secluded corner next to an alleyway, whispering to each other.

I saw a sign hanging in the distance, a little marker letting me know what this place was named: Tophet. *Death Valley.*

Fire flickered in one of the windows of a nearby tavern, casting a warm glow on the chilled cobblestone. The roar of the crowd around us was different than the silence earlier. Growls, grunts, laughter, roars, whimpers… everything was a form of agony or jeering.

I'd lost sight of Libby completely; panic stuttered in my heart.

A hand wrapped around my wrist, and I turned. No one.

"Meris," Libby's voice was lower than a whisper, so low I could barely hear him. "Up the street. Make no contact." He tugged at my arm, and I let him guide me. Weaving through the creatures of the night was not easy; not making any form of contact with them was even harder. I needed to keep my head down.

Something brushed me from behind, and I fought the urge to look back.

I pushed onward until we hit the outer rim of the town, my heart beating faster than anything. My breathing was ragged, and I tried to steady my nerves.

A hand wrapped around my waist, too low for comfort. "Who's this?"

I spun this time, facing whoever it was. The word entered my mind, dredged up from some unknown memory.

A leviathan.

His dark hair fell like paint down his shoulders, slicked back from his face. Eyes, tumultuous and dark as the raging ocean, stared into mine as a cruel smile slit his mouth. "I've not seen you around."

I took a step back, only to have his nails dig into my hip.

"Try and get away, and there'll be a bit of a problem." He leaned in, pulling a lock of my hair from under my hood out, twining it around his finger. "Alecto."

There was a loud snap, and he flew backward. "Run!" Libby shouted.

My feet began to move before I realized it. Adrenaline pushed me up, my legs heated like molten lava.

The leviathan grabbed my hand, shoving me down. My body collided with the slick cobblestone. Pain erupted in my right cheek, collarbone, and breast. My arm was limp."Tag." His voice pierced the air around me.

I thrust my leg up, but it did next to nothing. He tightened his grip, pushing me down harder, his foot pressed against my spine.

"Not nice, Alecto," he growled. "I heard if you break a furie's spine, the wings will fall out. I also heard—" He pressed harder against my spine, my body crunching. I screamed, my voice raw in my throat. "If you cut the wings, it's twice as painful as cutting anywhere else. How about I do that?"

He knelt on my back, his hand gripping my face. My jaw popped from his grip, and tears stung my eyes. Pain riveted me, shuddering through my body.

"Oh, I love that look." His eyes hardened, turning into solid spheres of sea-black. "The helplessness."

I closed my eyes. Breathe. *Breathe.*

As quick as I could, I grabbed the dagger at my side and clipped his hand. Blood oozed. He reeled back, releasing a howl of pain. Anger flashed over his face, flickering into rage as he too drew a weapon.

A small scythe made of the purest steel.

I stumbled to my feet, drawing my short-sword. I was not ready for this.

The scythe plowed through the air. I barely escaped the blow, careening to the left.

It wasn't enough to escape his foot.

His boot connected with my jaw. Blood filled my mouth. White spots streaked my vision, confusing me.

The leviathan made another jab at me with his scythe, and I dodged. He slashed the other way, and I barely managed to parry the deadly blow with my sword.

His hiss echoed up and down the path, curdling my blood. "Is that all you have?" He spat on the ground, eyes gleaming. "The great, powerful Alecto, resorting to childish tactics."

"I seem to be doing pretty good. Not dead, am I?" I widened my stance, readying my weapon again.

He laughed. "Because I don't want you dead. I want to drain you."

I launched myself at him. Light fractured along the ground as our weapons collided.

"Have you seen him lately?" the leviathan asked, his scythe taut against my sword. "We cut into him this morning. Oh how he yelled, *begged* for us to stop…"

I screamed, pulling my sword back.

"And you should have seen how much fun we had. I'm surprised he's even alive after what our goddess did to him."

My wings tore out of my coat, filling the surrounding area. "I'm going to end you."

"There we are!" He brandished his scythe, lips curling into a feral grin. "Now I see those beautiful wings. Which one should I clip first? Right? Or left?"

"Neither." Fire curled up my weapon.

He was upon me in a second.

I slashed my sword up, blocking an attack, but his other hand was faster; he drew a dagger while I was distracted, driving the blade toward my wing.

I swung my wings out, catching the wind within the feathers and sailed backward several yards. But, not before I thrust my blade into his skin.

He growled.

Two ink-black wings dripped from his back, looking too much like that of a bat. I could see every vein—every inch of gray-brown membrane in the wings. His eyes snapped to mine, and my breath caught. He looked more animal than anything. He released a loud screech, claws gleaming from the tips of his nails. Horror streaked through my body as the wound I'd inflicted swelled and healed in a second.

A smile. A simple, bloodcurdling smile rose on his deathly features. "Finally."

54

His body was marble against mine; heavy muscle collided with fragile bone and flesh. The sound of bone cracking filled my ears.

But I didn't feel pain.

A loud, echoing wail reverberated the earth, and the leviathan stumbled back, his wings engulfed in flames.

My bleary eyesight barely took in Jack's figure, striding up the pathway. Two fireballs rested in his gloved hands. The dark cloak billowed behind him, as if they were wings and he would meet the leviathan in the heavens.

The leviathan cursed, his eyes leaking silver tears. "*You!*"

"Glad you recognize me." Jack angled his heel on the leviathan's ankle, making a sharp-right twist. Again, the snapping of bones resounded around us, like a butcher cutting into the carcass of a freshly slaughtered chicken. "I remember the last time we met." He knelt beside the leviathan, one fireball flickering out.

"I recall that day with fondness," hissed the leviathan. "If you've come for justice and revenge, you will not find it here. I won't beg for mercy like your sister."

Jack's fire flickered brighter, tendrils of smoke raging up into the sky.

"It was fun, dismembering her piece by piece, listening to her scream and suffer. You were there, remember?"

Jack's fist to his face only made the creature laugh.

Bile crawled up my throat. Jack had to watch that. Feel that. Remember that.

"I should have finished the job and killed you." The leviathan's breath was ragged, though he smiled like a demon. "I still have time, don't I?"

"Don't bet on it." Jack took a step back, his smile cutting. "Alecto, go. I have him."

I stumbled up, with the aid of someone. *Libby*. He must've done something to bring Jack here.

"Meris," Libby whispered. "If you would augue, I would do so now. Please. Think of the top of this hill."

I couldn't just leave Jack here. Fire flickered around his fingertips as he stared down the creature.

There would likely be more.

And I thought he knew it. He had that look—the look I saw in the village market. The look I saw when I was Alecto. The look I saw when I looked in the mirror.

The look of someone standing up against the world when it's against them.

Fire rolled around my body, spiriting me and Libby away from the ensuing battle.

However, we weren't on the top of the hill. We were somewhere below in a dark citadel, buried deep within the heart of Redrim.

A tall pair of beaten copper doors blocked our path, standing like a pair of sentinels. A coil of heat wailed through the chamber, beckoning us to step across the threshold. Libby gingerly placed his hand on the barrier, testing its resistance. To my surprise, they swung open easily. We walked inside a strange labyrinthine hall lit by red-hued lanterns wreathed in smoke. The corridors reeked of death, plunging daggers into my nose.

Chains rattled, and I managed a glance at Libby.

"We're here."

He became more visible; a leather coat appeared, along with trousers and calf-high boots. Somehow, in battle clothes, he still looked completely gentleman-like. "Where do you think they're keeping him?" I asked, glancing around us.

"In the back where they held the southern fae."

"Held?"

Libby looked at me, his monocle reflecting the burning red glow of the lanterns. "Jack thinks they're still alive, but I know they're gone. He is the last of his kind."

My heart twisted. "Shouldn't we be protecting him? Shouldn't we do something?"

"He's harder to kill than you think." Libby began walking, his steps taken in tandem with mine. There was something dry and withering in his voice, something I couldn't place.

Every cell was empty. Dried clumps of blood caked the walls, torn bits of flesh hung from hooks, and bones—snapped or shattered—were strewn along the black stone floors. The remnant of torture left behind. My stomach hardened as we continued down.

The hall ended, and I turned to my left.

The sound of rattling drew my attention to a dingy corner. Setizar.

His arms were chained above him as blood dripped down his chest. A small, pained sound escaped his lips as he opened his eyes, casting a squinting look in my direction.

Aether.

I fumbled, searching for the key in my pocket. Metal, warm from being against my body, greeted my fingertips. I yanked it out, pressing it into the door. The key snapped, falling out of the door.

"Aether!"

Libby materialized beside me. "Oh, blast me for this." Libby pressed his hands against the locks, breathing in. "Do you have a pin?"

I peeled off my cloak, snapping the clasp and handing it to him. "What're you doing?"

"Picking the lock."

"You pick locks?"

He snapped the clasp, unhooking the thin springs. "Yes."

"Where did you learn that?" I muttered, trying to calm my raging heartbeat.

"I did have my humble beginnings." The locks clicked and the door swung open. I nearly toppled over in relief and panic, hurrying into the small cell.

Setizar stirred slightly, his eyes a vacant gray. "Meris?" He nearly smiled, though it was weak.

I fitted the key into the chains, and they sprung open. My heart beat harder than before. "We're getting you out, alright?" I looked at Libby, searching for his help.

Setizar leaned in, his fingers wrapping around my neck. "There's no way I can get out of here. I am paying your debt. I need to stay—"

"No, you've paid the debt. I should have killed Inanna in the forest and not let you get taken."

"You couldn't. You aren't restored."

"I'm getting there." I kissed his forehead, and emotions pounded through me, the impulse feeling like the first right thing I'd done in the past three weeks. "Don't argue. We need to get you out. I have the Box."

His eyes shuddered lavender. "What?"

Libby looped his arm around Setizar's torso, lifting him up. Setizar groaned. "Yes, my lord. We will restore everything in due time."

I slipped my arm around Setizar as well, and together, Libby and I helped him down the hall. The candlelight was low, and I could barely make out the surrounding area. Our feet nearly slipped on the slick cobblestone.

A hollow scream echoed around us, along with the sound of a metal door slamming.

Light flickered, and Libby became seemingly uneasy. "Come along, Meris. We must hurry if we wish to make it back to Lhysa in time."

Setizar moaned, his face chalky. "Inanna said something to me, Meris, but I didn't understand it. She always speaks in riddles."

"We're going to get you home." I brushed a strand of his hair out of his eyes, trying to maintain my balance while doing so.

"She said we're doing what she wants, that we're only passengers on a ride which we think we have control over." Setizar's knees began to buckle, and Libby cursed as he adjusted his grip. "Maybe this, you rescuing me, is part of the plan. Maybe fate would have been different if you didn't save me."

I shook my head. "Inanna can't know the future, or what we'll do next."

"You're right. But I can't shake the feeling…" Setizar winced, his eyes flicking toward Libby.

"What feeling?"

Setizar stiffened. "Feeling that we're pawns, and we're doing exactly what she wants us to."

— ☾ —

We stumbled up the stairs while trying to help Setizar. Time was flaking away.

"Where's Jack?" I spun, looking up at the sky. There was nothing but shadow and ember. "Libby?"

His monocle faced the opposite direction. "He's not here."

"What?"

"Come. Lhysa will be creating the portal if it's safe—"

Light shattered in front of us. Sunshine, the scent of white-tea, and warmth spread around us as we stepped through the portal.

We collapsed in Lhysa's garden.

She was coated in a layer of blood, but not her own.

"Where's Jack?" I stumbled to my feet, looking around. "What happened?"

"I had to step in." Lhysa's voice was gruff, emotionless. "He...he will be fine. He just needs some time, and he'll be back to normal."

"Let me—"

"No." She made a quick motion with her hand, as if cutting the air. "You need to bring Setizar to the Crimson Plane. I have sent messengers to Aurel and Eira letting them know to meet us there. Sir Libby?" Her eyes connected with the half-invisible man. "Will you stay here with Jack?"

He made a sweeping bow. "Yes, my lady."

Lhysa nodded, looking at me and Setizar. "Time to return the Lord of Autumn to the Crimson Plane."

55

Tatum's fingers curled around my neck, tightening. "Remember, Alecto..." His breath was fire against my skin. "You are your worst enemy."

I slammed my elbow into his abdomen, swinging my sword. He parried my blow, eyes gleaming. The air in the garden stilled, freezing like the frost-tipped mountains in the far distance.

"Don't doubt yourself."

"I'm not!" I threw my foot forward, only to have him slap it away like it was nothing. Anger coiled around me, rising into the air.

"You're losing control." Tatum stood, his head cocked to the side. "Calm down."

"I am calm." My wings tore out of my back.

"Clearly." He taps my left wing, fingers caressing the feathers. "Be careful. Your wings are a powerful weapon, but they can also be your downfall. If something decides to clip them, the pain itself may kill you."

"You're right." I breathed in, bracing my hands on my hips. "What would I do without you?"

"You'd get me back, of course." He smiled, craning his neck upward. "Well, looks like it's time—"

I splashed cold water on my face. The memories were returning more frequently, and most of them involved Tatum. He knew something...

something I needed to know. Tomorrow morning, I would do exactly what he'd said.

I would shatter the mirror.

Slipping on my robe, I exited the bathing chamber and into the evening-soaked bedroom.

"Meris?" Setizar walked into my room, dressed in simple black trousers and sleeveless tunic. Ever since Cerie put that colored salve on him, he'd healed extremely well. Even after a few hours, most of his injuries had disappeared.

"Setizar." I pressed the sleeve of my robe against my face, wiping the lingering drops of water away, and walked over to where he stood. "How're you feeling?"

"Like we're in a trap." He raked his hand through his hair. I wasn't used to seeing him on edge with rattled nerves. However, the way he looked now, standing in a web of moonbeams, nearly made me forget the danger. I wanted to stare at him, drink in his every feature until I was dizzy from it.

I shook the thoughts away, willing myself to look him in the eye. "If it's a trap, we'll just have to expect everything. Assume someone will try and kill us."

His hands found my waist, filling my body with assuring warmth as he tugged me closer and wrapped his arms around me. His fingers tangled in my hair, as though he expected I'd vanish. "Even each other?"

"If you want to." My heart twisted, fighting the words which slipped from my mouth. I drew back slightly, gently tracing the small scars peppering his arms and shoulders. Remnants of the brutal bruise on his temple had nearly vanished from sight, as had the cut on his cheek. The large wound on his chest had healed, though it still looked sensitive. "But I'd rather think that out of everyone who'll be in the room, you'd have my back and I'd have yours."

He lowered his voice as he leaned in closer, those sunset eyes glowing. "I will always believe you have my back." One hand trailed up my spine, gently caressing where my wings should be. "And I will always have yours."

"I know you do. You've proved this." I moved closer, so close that there was nearly no space between us. "You've proved it from the past, to the present."

His fingers danced along the back of my neck, eyes settling on my lips. There was a heated look in those eyes, something like a fire over the horizon of a cold winter morning. The way his skin brushed against mine was a version of agony. I only wished to draw nearer. To envelop myself in him and this feeling of utter peace and completion.

"May I?"

I smiled. "May you what?"

"You're a demon, you know that?"

"What a lovely way to seduce a woman, you're making great headway."

His laugh was guttural. "May I kiss you?"

I nodded, twisting the fabric of his shirt between my fingers. My heart beat spiked, my body began to burn. "You may."

He smelled like the dawn of an autumn day—the beautiful combination of mystery and shadow, of cloves and honey. His lips hovered an inch away from mine. Taunting, perfect.

Waiting. Nervous, perhaps? Unsure?

Every nerve in my body stood to attention, alert and expectant. He kissed me; his lips soft, barely a feather of a touch against my own.

"Not too bad?" he whispered, a small smile curving his mouth.

I didn't respond. Instead, I kissed him back. He was sugar and night mist made of forgotten dreams. It was irresistible. My brain was a mess of blurred emotions and fractured memories.

I slipped my arms around his neck, devouring every second of the kiss. I wished it could last forever.

His hands grabbed my waist, drawing me closer. His lips left an aching burn on mine. There was barely a second before we kissed once again, and

I sucked in a breath, unable to settle my nerves. "I need you to tell me one thing, Setizar."

"Anything."

"Why me? Why did you wait all this time? Why did you choose to marry Alecto—me, I mean. Why?"

He smiled as his fingers slid over my jaw, lifting my chin a fraction. "Because, you crashed into my world like a fiery demon. You bombarded my world and... changed me. You made me want to be different. There's no way I wouldn't wait for you. If you left now, I'd wait. I'd wait for as long as it took for you to return. I wouldn't have married you if this wasn't what I would have chosen."

My emotions and heart beat in tandem. "Then let's be different and make this right. Let's make the world a better place—together."

"And how should we begin?" He raised a brow, fighting off the smirk lifting the universe into his eyes.

My stomach fluttered. "I suppose... by you listening to me instead of me having to obey you every waking moment of the day."

"Not that you ever did to begin with." He chuckled, a deep, sensuous laugh which curled autumn tendrils into my stomach. "Now that we've established the hierarchy..." Setizar kissed me once more. It was like kissing time and magic... like dancing with the embodiment of darkness and light. Like kissing the obsidian nothingness of the future, and the solid stone of the past. A fleeting memory became tangible.

The memory of our vows, said below the weeping orange willow gilded in starlight and sunshine.

The memory of *us*.

PART SEVEN
RESURRECTION DAY

56

The gentle caress of sunlight fell over us. Setizar and I had laid in bed, his arm looped around my waist as he'd spoken of the memories I couldn't conjure on my own. The past I couldn't remember.

He'd told me of the day we first met, when he'd been forced to attend a meeting with Eira and Feng. That was when he saw me.

Well, more like the first time I'd insulted him.

I supposed that's how we always started. An insult. Hate to love. Cold to hot. That was us.

The exhaustion of the week came crashing down on me not long after midnight, and I fell asleep in Setizar's arms.

Somehow, between the night of reminiscing and my confused dreams, it was getting harder to remember who I was and what I was supposed to do. What was I doing? I felt like I was missing something very, very important, yet I couldn't pin-point it. It was lingering just out of my grasp, taunting me.

— ☾ —

We stood at the edge of the gardens, Lhysa looking far more irritated—far more grim—than usual. "Is everyone ready?"

I looked at Julna who was clutching the rabbit creature in her arms. I swore she hadn't separated herself from that thing since we first arrived. And the rabbit hadn't made any attempt to leave.

I wasn't sure what that meant for the rest of us.

"We're ready," Setizar said, holding the codex in his hand.

Lhysa raised her arm, making a wide gesture to her left. White sparks erupted from the surrounding area, lighting up the garden around us. A moment later, Eira, Feng, and Aurel walked through portals, dressed for war.

Eira's long, black hair was tied up, gently blowing in the wind, allowing her piercing blue eyes to show. Feng smiled at me, her black lips parting into a vicious grin. Her gold armor shattered rays of sunlight onto the cobblestone pathway. Aurel's bare chest was covered by golden armor in the shape of two wings, x-ing over his torso, connecting at the nape.

What were they expecting to happen?

Aurel bowed, grinning. "It's been long since we've had our powers." His eyes flicked to Julna, a ravaging look passing over his face. "Well, hello."

Julna tilted her head up and ignored his attention. Aurel flashed an amused smirk.

"Well," Lhysa looked around the garden, smiling gently. "At least you took my words to heart, Setizar. The flora looks absolutely stunning."

A flicker of pride fluttered over his face as he accepted her compliment. "Thank you, Lhysa. I had an excellent teacher."

"Flirting? In front Meris?" Feng said, her words clipped. "I would think you knew better."

Setizar made a sweeping bow, mischief rolling over his entire body. Whatever he was about to say would not go well. "Of course you wouldn't know the difference between flirting and simple compliments, North Wind, since you rarely receive either."

There it was. Feng went for her sword, and I braced for the impending fight.

"You two," Eira's frozen tone cut through the heated moment. "Stop. Setizar, why do you need to annoy her? And Feng, you are not allowed to mortally wound Alecto's jinni. She wouldn't take very kindly to that."

"What if I almost mortally wound him?" Feng looked at her sister, but Eira held firm. Feng stood down.

Aurel clapped his hands, the gleaming black onyx arm-cuffs absorbing the light. "Let's get this over with."

"I couldn't agree more." Setizar tugged my arm, and we entered the home. We followed him up the spiraling staircase toward the western side of the palace. My heart was pounding furiously, beating in my chest like a rabid animal, trying to claw its way out of my body.

This was really happening.

Our shoes made a clicking sound against the marble, shuddering against the interior of the palace walls. The stars fluttered to our feet, clustering around Setizar. Some flocked to me, some lingered around Eira and Feng; dozens of stars trailed behind Aurel and Lhysa, and yet none were around Julna.

Perhaps it was the way she was standing, tucked into herself and holding tight to the rabbit.

We entered a large, windowless chamber. The walls were without plaster, and the floors were without stars. A force surrounded me as I stepped through the barrier, pushing against me.

Setizar made a waving gesture, and the invisible barrier ceased its opposition. "We will be safe here from any outside forces. If Inanna shows up, she'd have to come through the door."

Cerie's hooves echoed in the chamber as she bowed. "Everything is ready." She smiled gently, her burning eyes locking with mine. Something about the look told me she was worried.

Worried for us all.

"Shall we get started?" Setizar tilted his head, and they each stood in a different section of the annular room. Julna was behind Setizar, and Cerie was behind me.

I grasped the Box out of the bag, looking up at Setizar. His face hardened, and he nodded.

We exchanged the items. He gave me the codex, and I gave him the

Box. My insides were shaking, and my mouth was a desert. I couldn't take a steady breath as I opened the book and searched for the spell.

It took a moment, but I found it.

It wasn't a spoken spell, rather, a concentration one, like what Tatum showed me all those years ago. Taking the magic from one thing and placing it into another.

This shouldn't be too difficult, right?

I placed the Codex back into the bag.

I couldn't do this.

I couldn't do this.

With a sharp breath, I pressed the tip of my finger against the lock. Blood bloomed at the tip, and I closed my eyes.

There was a loud snap; the sound of a small metal plate moving. The world around was drenched in blue light; as if we were deep under water floating in the nothingness of time and space, breathing air reminiscent from the days of old. My skin crawled as I sank further and further down.

Streams of cerulean light poured in from angles as silver particles drifted in their glow. They tasted like magic. Potent, powerful magic constrained by metal and gold. I couldn't shake the unease washing over me; pumping in my veins a version of apprehension I hadn't felt before.

Everything went dark except for a glowing ball of blue light. It pulsed, drawing me closer. Waves of emotion pressed into my heart, drowning my ability to think clearly.

My hand touched the ball of light and pain ricocheted through my arm. I couldn't let go.

Focus—*focus*!

The pain throbbed through me. I could barely focus on anything but the sting. *Push it out, Meris. Absorb and give.*

I saw Setizar's power; it was the shade of passion and amethysts, with ebony shadows dancing in the center. I needed to give this to him—to that orb of magic pulsing in the far distance. Sparks of green and gold light scattered from my fingertips as silver stars congregated around my body.

Mist exploded around me. The roar of a thousand waterfalls pounded in my ears, hissing and screeching along broken shards of glass.

Meris.

Meris.

The orb called my name. Beckoning me toward it. To give myself over; to give my own power away.

No.

I pulled myself back, using every ounce of energy to hold onto my power while the other magic poured into Setizar.

The world cracked. The earth below my feet shook. Tremors wrapped around my legs, and I struggled to keep my balance. Dizziness spilled into my stomach, turning my world upside down.

A disembodied, animalistic screech rang out above me. The world went dark once again.

57

Sunlight. A second ago I was in a tumultuous realm, now I stood in Yamira with golden sunlight caressing my sweat-streaked face.

Cerie held Setizar up, her arm looped around his waist. He looked more beautiful than ever. There was a glow to him, something unearthly and yet I was drawn to it like an insect to light.

"Meris." Setizar smiled, looking at me. "You did it."

"How long before we can receive the magic?" Aurel asked, his feet tapping against the floor.

"Just a moment." Lhysa clicked her tongue. "Meris needs to regain control before she can gift them to us."

Aurel grunted, obviously impatient. Eira and Feng turned, speaking to each other in low, cautious tones, but I couldn't make out a word.

I faced Cerie. "You did well, Meris." She released Setizar, who had halfway pushed himself away from her. "Soon, we'll be able to join the worlds together again."

A slash of darkness rippled through the room, followed by a cry of pain. My heart stopped. Julna stood behind Setizar, and in her hand—a dagger. It dripped with blood.

Setizar's blood.

He crumbled to his knees, face ashen, expression hollow.

My sister's eyes locked with mine, no longer the warm mahogany I knew so well, but fiery red. The color of rage and hatred. "I told you. You should've left me on Inder."

58

I stumbled back, the magic roaring inside my body.

"Why?" Blood coated my hand. It was difficult to even look up at Julna...no, her name was Belenia. "I...I trusted you."

Her lips curled upward. "Alecto." She grabbed a fistful of my hair, tugging it back. "You could've helped me. You could've helped me kill magic. Now that you know, I can't have you talking to anyone about it. If they find out? I'm done."

The taste of metal surfaced on my tongue, dripping from my lips. "If I die, Belenia," I pulled out my own weapon, thrusting it into her heart, "I'm taking you with me."

Panic swept over me, crashing into my heart as I relived the same scene–the same betrayal. However, there was a difference. Here she was my sister, and I wasn't the one she'd stabbed with a dagger.

My world shattered. The place where the magic had been was emptied, and I nearly dropped to my feet. "The Silver Queen."

She tilted her head up, eyeing me like a predator.

No one in the room moved. "Why?" I asked as icy fingers drew up my spine.

"You don't remember, do you?" Her eyes sank into slits, darkening along the edges as she held the blood-soaked dagger up in the air. "Everyone else?" She pressed the tip of the blade to her finger, smearing the blood on her skin. My stomach hardened, every nerve on edge. Alert.

Pounding along with my raging pulse. "Do you remember? Do you remember what I'm going to do?"

Everyone remained deathly quiet.

"Well, if you don't, you will soon enough."

A dark mist encased the room, pouring into my nostrils with a smoky vapor. My body lifted; everything was upside down, disoriented. Shouts and yells echoed around me, and a sooty fist wrapped around my lungs. I couldn't breathe.

Aether.

My wings tore from my back, giving me an inch before I was pinned against the wall again. I managed to thrust them outward, wind rushing around the feathers, forcing the smoke away in small, whirling surges.

Smoke.

"Aurel! Can you clear that?"

He muttered a curse. Then, after long, agonizing seconds, the smoke cleared. Aurel, Lhysa, Eira, Feng, and Cerie were pinned against the ceiling with me.

Julna—Belenia—was gone.

I screamed, pushing against whatever magic that had me tacked to the roof, and I glided down.

Setizar.

He was so pale. Aether. How could I reverse this? How could I save him?

Tatum!

I stood, throwing open the door and plunging down the hall. Shadows licked my feet as I ascended the stairwell, trying to pull me into the darkness of despair. No. I wasn't giving up hope. Not yet.

I hurried under the iron beams which vaulted the ceiling. The membranous wings were eerily similar to how mine once looked.

The dragon-like beasts in the floor seemed to rebuke me through starlit eyes. I shook off the feeling inside as I stepped into the frozen room. The tall chandelier cast no light, and that same phantom wind tousled the crystals. I followed the sliver of moonlight—moonlight during the day? Right. I'd forgotten this room was something different.

I found the mirror. It hung on the wall in the same place as last time I entered.

Break the mirror. Tatum's words were as clear as when he'd first spoke them.

I peered around the room, searching for something—anything—to throw at the glass. Nothing but dust, cobwebs, and darkness greeted me. Frustrated, I looked back at the mirror. Something lurked behind the reflective surface. Something which beckoned me toward it.

Break the mirror.

I grabbed the mirror frame, yanking it off its mount. The glass squeaked against my fingers, hissing along my skin as it dropped down. The edge of the frame clicked against the marble floor, cracking the side of the mirror. My pulse quickened as the glass toppled over.

Please, let this work!

Magic reverberated, pealing through the air with the sound of thousand chimes crashing into one another as the mirror shattered. Echoes from the past whispered in my ears, caressing my neck with promises. What the promises were, I didn't know.

I looked to where I'd tossed the mirror, narrowing my eyes at the figure standing there.

Tatum.

"Took you long enough."

"I was busy." I looked him in the eye. His dark form, licked with shadows and icy-fury, seemed different... strange and unknown. "I need your help."

— ☾ —

We entered the room where I'd left Setizar and the others. Eira's honey-gold skin was blanched, and even Aurel looked ill.

Lhysa looked at me. "He's fading."

I hurried to Setizar's side, grabbing his hand. "Hey," I muttered, pushing the hair out of his eyes and trying to read his expression. "You're going to be alright."

He strained a smile, yet his face was so pale, so lifeless. "Keep fighting." His fingers wrapped around my neck, his thumb gliding along my jawline. "I love you."

"I'm not who you needed." Tears stung my eyes, pain festering in my gut. "I wish I could have been everything you wanted—"

"Meris." He looked into my eyes. Time stilled. "I love you. Not just who you were. You. Your past. Your present. Your future. I will always love you."

Tatum, where are you? "Setizar, just… hang on. You're not going to die."

"I'll find you in the Day."

"Don't do this to me."

His eyes shuddered to a muted gray, and fear splintered in my chest. Something shredded my insides, tearing me apart.

"No!" I gripped him tighter. I couldn't move. There was so much still unsaid between us. So much I needed to tell him, to give him, to *live* with him. "Setizar, no! Come back." Fiery tears streamed down my face, dragging claws down my cheeks.

He didn't deserve this. He deserved the universe, the worlds beyond and the fractured beginning.

He deserved a lifetime of happiness.

Tatum appeared.

Everyone took a step back, while Cerie stood frozen.

"You," Eira muttered, her spine stick-straight. "How are you here?"

"I was here to help…" he said, placing his fingers on Setizar's neck.

"But, I'm sorry...I'm too late."

"Bring him back!" I grabbed his coat, tugging him to me. "Bring him back!"

"There's no way, not unless a life is exchanged. A life for a life."

I scowled. "Then how are you alive?"

"I never truly left the mirror." He smiled, as if right now was the time for smiling. For gloating. "If someone here is willing to take his place, then be my guest."

Everyone was frozen. Statues of wonder and shock.

"I'll do it." I placed my hand on Setizar's chest. There was no heartbeat... nothing. "I'll take his place."

"Oh?" Tatum took a step toward me, his eyes gleaming. "You would take his place in the chamber of death?"

I nodded.

His grin became predatory. "This is... irreversible."

"I understand."

"There's no coming back... ever. No one comes back from the dead."

I lifted my head, angling my body. "Isn't that what irreversible means? Do it."

"Stop!" Aurel's voice cut through the air, his eyes flicking from me to Setizar. "Alecto, I can't let you do this." He glanced at Tatum, his shoulders tightening. "This'll work? No tricks?"

"No tricks."

"Aurel—"

He stepped forward, grabbing my shoulder and cutting me off. "The worlds need you, Alecto. Allow me to do this exchange. I owe it to him." There was a strain in his voice—a pain that tore through me.

"Aurel!"

Feng and Eira grabbed my arms, pulling me back. I pushed against them, fighting their hold. This was for me to do. This was my choice. I couldn't let Aurel do what I was supposed to do. And something in

Tatum's face told me this was what he wanted.

He pulled out a candle from the darkness around him, grinning. "Light this end of the candle, Aurel, with your magic. I will be able to do the rest."

Waves of cold rushed over me, followed by unbearable heat. I continued to struggle against Eira and Feng, but between them, they had me in a tighter hold than I'd ever been in before.

Seconds dripped by. Aurel raised his finger, light flickering out the tip.

"Aurel, *stop*!" I screamed. "Please!"

The candle lit, and the world shifted. Shadows became darker swallowing the light v. It was too late to stop him now—too late for the exchange to be hindered. The fire was sucked into the black wax, dripping from Tatum's hand. It liquified further, turning into something golden and iridescent. With every second that passed, more color drained from Aurel's face.

He looked at me, the healthy golden glow nearly gone. "Tell him I said he better use my life right."

Yet... there was nothing. Nothing happened.

Aurel's gaze flicked to Tatum, his usually healthy skin a sickly shade of white. "What did you do?" He stood, grasping Tatum by the collar. "What did you *do*?"

Tatum cocked his head, his eyes slithering into a sickly shade of green. "You idiot. You can't bring anyone back from the dead. Didn't I say that already?"

Fire welled up in my veins. "What?"

Tatum vanished from the wall, appearing before me as nothing more than shadow. "You should know this, Alecto. This was the plan, after all. When you're ready to join me once more, just call my name. If you choose these," he looked at the lords and ladies in the room, "lesser beings? Expect a war. You have two days at best." His laugh echoed around us, cleaving the air like a death chime. "Now, if you excuse me, I need to find Inanna. We have some work to finish."

59

Time and space stilled. Not even the birds made a sound as the rest of us neared Aurel. My stomach coiled in hatred. I looked at Setizar, his face ashen. I crumbled, dizziness taking over.

No. No, this couldn't be happening.

Waves of pain washed over my body, drawing claws over my heart. The fire in my veins quelled, frosted over. The beat of the stars in the hall went silent, no longer humming their ethereal music.

Nothing.

His smile, the one strung from starlight and magic, flickered from my mind. His sunset eyes vanished from memory, leaving only a vague illusion of what it was. His voice, a mix of lilting notes and soothing melodies, slipped from my grasp.

I didn't want to forget him like this.

The lagoon of pain swelled, surging through my soul with icy torment. I would give everything… *anything*…

The thump of my heart was uneven. My breath was ragged in my lungs. This couldn't be the end. This wasn't the end.

The world was hollow, empty without him here. Silence never felt so loud. I slipped my arms around him, closing my eyes. Trying so hard to remember everything about his voice, his laugh, his eyes.

"Don't leave me." Tears fell down my cheeks, boiling, searing my skin with pain. "Don't leave. Don't leave…"

"We need to fight," Cerie mumbled, her voice broken.

"How?" Eira snipped. "We are in the same situation as before, only worse! We lost Setizar, and Aurel's magic is gone. We couldn't fight Inanna and her army before, what makes you think we can fight her, Tatum, *and* the Silver Queen?"

I flashed a cutting glare at the place where Tatum had stood. Tatum. Tatum was the Changeling. "We knock one pawn off the board at a time. There's more at stake here than we realize."

"We will destroy the hierarchy of Yamira by knocking one pawn off the board at a time, and rebuild it. An empire. A perfectly balanced empire." Tatum slid into a seat, his grin vicious. *"First we must sever the connection to the humans. Those beasts wouldn't allow any of this to happen with their knowledge. Take magic away from them and they will forget. Then we will be their salvation."*

"How will this work?" I leaned my elbows on the counter top. *"We still have the Seasons to deal with."*

Inanna appeared, her white face unmarred—beautiful. "This is where Belenia comes in." *She turned, facing a silhouette in the corner.*

"How can a mutt help us?" I snapped, my eyes narrowing.

"For your information," Belenia closed the gap between us, a dark fire flickering in her eyes, *"this mutt can do one thing very, very well."* She handed me a small, ornate box. *"I can give you the tools to take their magic."*

"Without all their magic, they will be rendered weak," Inanna said. *"With this, they'll become dependent on my armies, and I will be able to keep them under my thumb. Their magic is strengthened when they change the season, so they will crawl to me like flies to honey."*

"Where do I come in?" I leaned against the counter, looping one ankle over the other.

"You will gain their trust and then you'll need to take blood. We need a drop of blood from each season lord and lady for the box to work. The goal? Gain their trust, gather them together for one grand event, and Be-

lenia will take their magic."

I nodded. "When their magic is taken, then what? How do we sever their connection from the humans?"

Tatum took a step closer. "Once the magic is taken, it will close the gateways."

I nodded, while the others in the room snickered. I leveled my glare toward them. "The only reason I'm helping you is because of Tatum. I don't like this plan, nor do I agree completely, but if Tatum believes this will herald change, so be it."

Tatum clapped. "Perfect. There's only one way to seal the passage-ways...and that will take a lot of work on my end." He took a step toward the door.

My memory flashed again.

"Tatum was found by the Seasons." Inanna leaned over the fire, her eyes smoldering. "They locked him away in a mirror. He can't escape..."

"They can do that?" I stopped sharpening my blade, looking up at her. "He's the reason they have any magic to begin with! Why would they do that?"

"Because the Seasons will do anything to stop what scares them. Tatum scares them. They must suspect what he wants to do."

"You mean take back what is rightfully his? What their ancestors stole from him?" Anger billowed in my chest. "How does this affect our plan?"

"It affects it greatly. You'll have to get close to the lord of the Crimson Plane. Very, very close. He'll need to trust you with the whereabouts of the mirror. Be careful, Alecto." Inanna looked me in the eyes. "He's a power-ful being. The most powerful of the jinn, and the only threat to the Changeling."

I laughed, sheathing my blade. "Then I'll make sure to be thorough."

She shook her head. "Just don't die. If you die, then we'd need to find a Dastamen rabbit."

I laughed inside. She didn't know I could come back, that I didn't need a mythical rabbit to help me return from the dead.

"Those are just legends. Those rabbits can't help bring back the dead."

"You'd be surprised to know how many legends are true."

My breath caught between my lungs and throat. The rabbit! I spun, looking in the rabbit's direction. The clock ticked gently around its throat.

"You're late."

"I know." I neared the creature, lifting the clock from around its throat. No wonder Jul—Belenia kept it so close. If she died, this would've helped bring her back.

I took the clock and placed it around Setizar's neck, looking at the rabbit. "What do I do now?"

The rabbit trotted near me, nuzzling my hand with its tiny nose. "You're late."

I glanced at the clock. It had this moment—this second. I grabbed the timepiece and turned the knob backward. Farther and farther.

To when we arrived earlier.

"Exchange," said the rabbit, eyeing me with eyes darker than midnight, yet brighter than the evening sun. "Immortal becomes ageless. You give him your life immortal, you will become ageless. Death, should it find you, will keep you."

That wasn't even a question. "What're we waiting for?"

The rabbit bowed, kneeling its front leg against the stone floor as it dipped its head low. "Then, you are no longer late."

Color rushed to Setizar's cheeks, to his face. Light surfaced in his eyes, gleaming brightly. The color of the universe trapped within a sunset. "Setizar!" I wrapped my arms around him. "I thought—"

He chuckled, tugging me close. Seconds slipped by like an eternity, allowing me to drink in his life, the feel of his heart beating against me, and the smell of autumn lifting from his skin.

His eyes cut to the rabbit, softening. The rabbit laid there, limp, breathing shallow, its tiny body immobile. A deflated moan escaped its small mouth, whiskers twitching as its large black eyes glazed over.

I scooped it up, holding it close. It's fur was silk against my fingers, and it was so…weak. "What do I do? How do I stop this?"

"You can't. He existed to give others a chance in life." Setizar's fingers gently stroked my hair.

Pain stung my chest as I looked at the small rabbit. Its eyelids fluttering closed. It was so light in my arms. Tears stung the corners of my eyes as it stopped breathing.

The lightness in its body vanished.

Setizar took the rabbit from my hands. He was so gentle, placing the creature on the ground. "No animal should die." He smiled softly, tugging me into his arms, and a small wave of relief speared through me. "We will make this right, Meris. We will."

I knew we would, but at what cost?

60

I slammed the book on the table, fire slithering up my arms like twin serpents. "We're no closer to finding how to stop them than before."

"And Tatum stole whatever was left of Aurel's magic," Feng snapped, picking at her nails with a four-point shuriken. "I believe we're one step backward, not in the same place."

"I'm not a slab of meat without my powers." Aurel pulled his hair up, tying it behind his head.

"You're a slab of meat with your powers." Feng grinned. "But at least you could contribute something. Now you're a useless slab of meat."

Eira released a long sigh. "Useless is a strong word. He can still do basic things, like get us water."

"I'd worry it was contaminated." Feng tossed the metal star, sending it across the room and piercing a nearby bookshelf.

"My shelves!" Setizar griped. "Does no one have respect for property."

Feng grinned. "I hold tight to my opinion."

Lhysa remained silent as she leaned against the window. The patter of rain clicked against the glass pane, making me wonder what was going through her mind.

Aurel released a loud huff, sitting on a chair and kicking his feet up on the table. "I wouldn't get you water even if you were dying in the desert, Feng."

"I wouldn't drink it even if you brought it."

"Feng," Eira growled. "Stop. You would."

"Throw me in the desert and see. I'd die."

Aurel laughed. "Because I wouldn't bring you water."

Setizar rolled his eyes, leaning back in his seat. "If you think Feng would be interested in you, Aurel, I recommend looking at her past relationships. You're not her type."

Aurel's laughter rumbled in my chest. "If her type is a weak, shriveling piece of mortal flesh, then you'd be right."

"Still not close," Feng snapped.

"What then?" Aurel's tone turned almost serious, though the twinkle in his eyes said otherwise.

Eira grunted. "When do you think they will attack?"

"Give them a few days. They need to rally their armies… and come up with a plan," Setizar said. "I'll keep reading. Eira, can you send a message to the surrounding militia?"

"You mean—" Feng dropped her star. "You're calling the elves?"

"They're our only chance."

"Elves are *elves*. They don't side with anyone, especially Seasons."

"We're their only hope at keeping what they love." Setizar's coat rustled as he moved. "If elves love anything, it's familiarity, and they'll fight tooth and nail to ensure that stays put."

Everyone in the room became silent. The dripping of water on the outside pavement was thunderous in comparison.

Eira bowed. "Give me four hours."

"Aurel." Setizar turned to the sphinx, his eyes softening. "There will likely be many wounded. Work with Feng and see if you can bring your healers."

Aurel eyed Feng warily. "Alright."

Feng chuckled. "Yes, *King* Setizar."

"Lhysa." Setizar's eyes snapped to her, ignoring Feng completely.

"How long before Jack and Libby arrive?"

"A few more hours, so I've been told. Jack is still recovering, but he's nearly ready to make the journey through the portal."

Setizar nodded and bent over his books once more.

— ☾ —

I sat in the kitchen with Lhysa and Cerie, nursing a small cup of tea. The rain pattered relentlessly against the windows, sending droplets sliding down the frames.

"Never take this off." A woman stood nearby, her long, black hair coiled into several braids. "If you lose the ring of your creation, you won't be able to remember everything..."

I looked up from sharpening my blade.

The realization pounded into me like a drum.

Megaera. My sister.

Lhysa stirred her tea, her eyes locked on the berry pink liquid. "I fear this may end in a way we aren't prepared for."

I struggled in a breath, the memories mixing with reality.

"Unless a miracle happens, we're more than doomed." Lhysa shrugged.

"Mae," I said, shaking my head. "You're paranoid."

"I'm cautious."

Mae?

My stomach knotted. Megaera. Mae...Oh, Aether! Why hadn't I seen that?

Cerie and Lhysa looked at me. Cerie's upturned brow and Lhysa's pursed lips told me they wished for me to explain my sudden expression change. The screeching howl of a distant horn told me there wasn't time.

"The Redrim horn," Lhysa muttered. "They're here. They're here earlier than we thought."

I stood and dashed down the halls, my pulse thick in my throat. Every second pounded in my body like the tick of a clock before an execution. The distant wail of the horn echoed in the darkened heavens. White reflections of lightning shattered across the floor, and the stars vanished. Every stroke of the lingering seconds burned in my skin, devouring my body. My wings tore from my back as I stopped in the middle of the corridors.

Belenia.

Her grin was taunting as she angled her head toward the room where Setizar had died. "I see you used the gift I left you."

"You expected us to use the rabbit?"

"Of course." She pulled her straight hair upwards, tying it behind her head. "But I didn't expect you to do it so quickly. So heartless."

Flames licked my arms and tears sprang into my eyes. This was my sister. No matter what the past life was, we still had this life—this closeness.

"You see, when you died, I didn't realize what I was up against. A furie is the last of the immortals. So I had to be smart. I had to find a way to strip you of your immortality, to keep you from sprouting back like a weed." She stepped closer, and wings sprang from her back. Wings like mine, though hers were cloaked in a heavenly-silver glow.

And she vaulted, crashing into me. The world around us spun as she portaled us. The palace shuddered into something else entirely. Lightning thrashed over the deadened forest, breathing death into the atmosphere. I couldn't focus my eyes. Everything was a blur—a swirl of black midnight and shadows. The caw of the raven was the only sound I heard, although somehow muted.

The Veil.

"Well," Julna's voice stabbed me. "I hope you understand."

"I don't understand." My voice trembled, like a song gliding across a sour note. "Why did you do it?"

"I did what I needed to do." Her eyes hardened. "To make the end goal a reality."

"Why are you helping Tatum?"

"You think I'm helping him?" She laughed; a bitter, poisonous cackle. "Well, I suppose you would." Her figure was a mixture of shadows and fabric, lifeless and threatening. "I wish to kill him—and the seasons. To take the magic and destroy it completely. There will no longer be predators and prey—only equals. The strong will survive, not the blessed. Magic is evil, Alecto. Magic is something no one should possess. Not even the Stars we call creators."

Two opposites. The Silver Queen wished to destroy magic and free the humans, while Tatum wished to absorb all the magic and control them.

Yet I had the feeling they both wanted me dead.

"Julna, don't do this."

"You don't get to call me that. Julna died the second we landed in Yamira." Her eyes flashed with a dangerous glint. "I remembered *every-thing*. I remembered you aren't my sister. I remembered why I exist—my past and future. I remembered who I am."

"And is that bad?" I ventured a step closer, my fingers trembling. "We have a chance to rebuild this world together—"

"Your version and mine differ." Julna's eyes narrowed. "We would never agree. I tried to convince you once, and it ended with our deaths. It's not meant to be."

"Despite this, despite our past," I took another step, my stomach hardening, "you will *always* be my sister. I would die for you…"

"You don't mean that." She flinched slightly, tendons in her neck stiffening.

"I do." I meant it. I would take an arrow for her… the sharp claw of an ogarak to the gut for her. No matter what, she was my sister. The life we lived before didn't change that. "I wouldn't say it unless I meant it."

"Then you're a fool." Her words were like a blow to the stomach, cutting into my flesh. "Because I would enjoy watching you die."

It was as if my heart was torn out of my chest, thrown on the forest floor, and stabbed. I stumbled back a step; blood curdled in my veins. The pain bloomed in my breast, spreading over my bones and tendons like fire. I couldn't see outside my burning vision. "Then do it. Kill me."

She pulled a blade. Her smile was an angled thing, twisted and so unlike Julna. "Don't blame me, Alecto. You were always destined to end like this, at the end of my blade, and I was destined to be alive, to end magic."

I swallowed the thickness in my throat. "Maybe this is your second chance. Maybe you were given another chance in life—"

"No." She angled her sword, her smile evaporating. But she didn't run me through. Her arm trembled, making the sword waver.

Her eyes found mine, mahogany again, reminding me of what she was once...

"Maybe I'll let you suffer here." She took a step back, sheathing her sword. "Why kill you when the creatures of the Veil could kill you instead?"

"Julna—"

"That's not my name!" Silver magic curled around her arms, sizzling up her fists and crackling at her knuckles. "It was never my name."

Shadows licked at her heels as she strode through the opening into the Veil and vanished.

My heart shredded into a thousand pieces, tearing apart bit by bit. Hope splintered and vanished in front of me.

A thundering roar cleaved the air, jarring me to a presence within the dark forest. Massive claws pressed against the bark of the shade-trees as the enormous serpentine body slithered into view. Its scales were as black as coal, dripping with inky-wetness onto the earth. Wings made of shadow and nightmares spread high overhead as it craned its neck closer, angling it to the side as violet eyes locked with mine.

"Furie," it breathed, its voice a mixture of a thousand beings speaking through one entity. "Fire bringer."

I readied myself, fear pulsing through me.

A dragon.

My tongue was made of cotton, drying my throat as the beast's yellow teeth began to show themselves. It spoke in a low tone, coursing through my bones with magic. "I have been waiting for you."

My legs weakened. I was about to die.

"We have been waiting for our queen to return."

My mind numbed. "What?"

Indigo fire spun through its nostrils. "We have spent many years waiting for you, our High Queen of the Day. The Dark Swan."

I stumbled, my back pressing against a tree. Other creatures entered the clearing, their figures a mixture of horrors and imagination. "I'm not a queen."

"You are Alecto. Daughter of Time and Earth." The dragon's eyes flared into a furious fire. "The creature of chaos stole you from us, and caused you to forget your destiny. Rumors spread of the dangers here. That death only comes to those who visit our forest." Its wings folded close, tucking against its scales. "Many have come nevertheless. They sought the true legend."

Two wolf-men bound into view, their hairy bodies covered in red cloaks. They drew a circle around me, etching three smaller ones within. A line extended outward, pointing north. The circle in the earth glowed silver, shooting beams of light up around me. Beyond the light I saw land— farms and villages spreading across a beautiful countryside. At the end of it was a gleaming castle made of gold crystal and white stone.

"This is your land. Knowledge of this place has been forgotten, and we have kept it hidden from those who would wish to plunder it." Creatures which looked like Jack tended farms, interacting with women made of shadows and men with skin as transparent as a stream. "It has been safe, locked from those who should seek its power until you were to open the gateways once more."

My wings trembled. "How many lives have I lived?"

A dazzling stream bubbled off the side and the scent of fresh-picked lemons prickled my nose. Sugared lemons. "Many lives, my queen." The dragon's tail flicked to the side. "All but one has been lived to rewrite your first life."

"And which life is that?"

The dragon's teeth flashed through the beautiful scene. "This one."

61

With the magic of the dragon, my memories returned. I couldn't explain it… the *feeling* of remembering everything. Remembering who I was—where I came from. That I wasn't alone. That I wasn't just the last of the furie.

The tangled yarn of memory snapped tight, the timeline no longer intertwined with each other.

This was who I was: Alecto, High Queen of the Day, and the first furie created by the Stars. I had died many times in my years, and found only one love who I have returned to more than once—a love I would never abandon.

I was raised in my last life by the Changeling, Tatum, in his attempt to take back what the Stars took.

And he'd nearly won.

Fire crawled over my feathers, charring the white plumage silken black, the tips of each feather dipped in the red of anger—the red of revenge. I needed to find Tatum and end this once and for all.

To end his immortal life and unmake him.

Spreading my shadowy wings, I snapped them down, and ash rose from the ground. The tree's dark leaves burst to green, and the coal-hued wood rippled to rich mahogany. Sunlight penetrated the clouds overhead, shining down on the lush forest floor. A gateway formed in the clearing made of crystal and gold, sun streaming from the arch. My kingdom laid just beyond the barrier, ready for my return.

Biodru breathed in, their eyes narrowing. "You wish not to return?"

"Not yet." I closed my eyes, pressing my hand against the gateway. Armor, as black as the midnight sky, appeared on my body. "Not until the rest of the realms are safe."

Biodru smiled a fangy grin. "That is my queen." Their body pulled into view. "What is your command?"

I looked into the portal I'd opened, to the glittering beyond calling my name. "How long would it take for you to assemble the army?"

Biodru cocked their head. "An hour at most."

"Good." I turned, facing south. "Speed them along. I will do what I can in the meantime."

Biodru's form shifted, and they turned into a humanoid creature—a leviathan. "Remember, My Queen." Their voice lowered. "Remember who you are fighting."

I nodded. Yes, I remembered all too well.

Tatum, otherwise known as the Changeling, was a creature bound between heavens and earths. A being of everything and nothing. I was right to be afraid of him. He was the emptiness willing to be filled.

Tatum and I went back—far, far back. Back to the first time we'd met when he'd tried to steal my powers and it killed me.

The next time, he'd raised me. He'd called me his own…

And I'd loved him like a father.

Spreading my wings, I took another breath in. The air was stiff and cold with impending war. I leapt, my wings grasping the wind and propelling me upward. Lighting cracked in the distance, rolling over the horizon like a creature damning the world.

Inanna's army would be right behind us.

Over the rumble of thunder screams and screeches echoed—the sound of a thousand ogarak in the air. I clutched my sheath, checking my weapon. With a deep breath in, I augued.

Fire burst around me, wrapping along my arms and legs as I shot through the atmosphere. Light, darkness, and stars wrapped with fire.

It stopped, and I was flying above Setizar's palace, above the sprawl of lush gardens and wintery maze. It was as still as death. I folded my wings, dropping like an arrow. And just before I hit the ground, I opened them again.

Leaves swirled into a spiral, lifted into a maelstrom of autumn fury as I drifted to a landing, crunching the foliage below my boots. The world was as silent as the grave; not even the wind made a noise as I began walking down the uneven cobblestone steps toward the entrance. Ice nipped at my heels, dread blooming in my chest.

I continued forward, ebony armor glinting in the scattered sunlight. Flowers began to wither as I walked past, coating the garden in a deathly emotion. Light shuddered around me as I threw open the door, washing the area in shattered light. The clank of my armor against the marble floor bounced off the walls, rippling through my skin and bones like a chorus.

A clock ticked in the corner someplace, the seconds marked by the click of the gears. Time flickered in my muscles, pressing hard against my armor.

"Meris?" Setizar's figure filled the doorway; his wide shoulders gilded in amethyst plates which looked like stones, pleated together and folded to cover his body. *His* armor. Of course he would wear something so beautiful.

My pulse raced, flooding my stomach with butterflies. I could die a thousand times, and no matter how many times I did, I would still find myself loving him.

Because in every life I had, I'd loved him. From afar—a girl wide-eyed and bewildered by the mythical creature—to close up, stealing kisses in between the tresses of the weeping willow. And I wouldn't allow myself to lose him again.

Together we'd change the realms and *free* magic, as it once was. No more hiding in the shadows of the past. Tatum wanted to strip this world of magic and control everyone. Inanna wanted to do the same. Julna—Belenia—she wished to take magic and destroy it all.

I wanted us all to be whole once more. To become the united realm we could be. Where the gateways were open and magic flowed freely. I took a step toward him, closing the space between us.

"You look fierce," he said, looking me over. "I like the old look."

I smiled, angling my head. "Same to you."

Seconds bled by, dripping between us like sand in an hourglass. "Meris, if this is the last minute we ever have together..." He took my hand in his, taking in a long, audible breath. "I need to tell you—"

"I love you." I tightened my grip, tugging him closer. Our armor clanked together, scraping metal and gemstone like the raw grate against my heart and lungs.

"Exactly." His eyes searched mine. "I love you too, Meris. Maybe in another life we could have lived without war, or death."

If this was the last moment we had, then I was going to remember him the best I could. I would etch this moment in my mind. I wouldn't forget him.

"You better go," I whispered after hearing the distant howl of the ogarak. "We need to win this war, Setizar."

"We *will* win this war. One way or another. We will win."

The way he said it, with reassuring clarity, made me wonder what he was up to. "Setizar..."

A grin spread on his face, and he took my hand. "I think you need to see a pet project of mine."

"Now isn't the time to be showing me your pet project, there's a war outside."

"You're going to enjoy this thoroughly." He tugged at my arm, leading me through the labyrinth of his palace, up toward the east wing. *The east wing.*

Guilt poured into my heart, and a stuttering panic surged upward in my gut. Where was he taking me?

We entered the obsidian darkness, stopping atop the glimmer of starlight below. The beasts—feral gigantic tigers bred with dragons and darkness—were frozen below, claws out and fangs bared, made only of thousands of tiny stars.

With Setizar standing beside me, looking down, the creatures began to slowly move, releasing growls which vibrated the floor below.

They were *alive*.

The wings above moved, slithering from iron to starlight and dissolving into the air around. Shadows wavered, flickering and shuddering gently as the beasts moved steadily upward. Light flashed, followed by a hissing explosion. The sensation of pickaxes driving into my ears shot pain through my skull. Heat licked at my skin. Screams cleaved the air.

Silence.

A screeching ring.

My eyes adjusted to the wreckage —the once splendid east wing of the palace wrapped in destruction.

I couldn't breathe. My skin was taut against my bones, crawling up my muscles like electricity. Wind lapped at my unbound hair, spinning as a chaos of air peeled through the now destroyed palace.

Setizar.

I stood, pulling my sword despite the protest of my body. "Setizar!" I yelled, looking around. "Setizar!"

"Here, Meris." He stood mere feet away, unharmed, with an expression of glee on his face. His eyes were locked onto something behind me, to the source of the ethereal glow washing though the area.

I spun, standing face to face with two beings made of stars and night. Their bodies were translucent, like water or crystal, with only starlight etching out their figures. Wings, like those in the hall, were bound to their backs, made entirely of stardust and dreams. The hulking tiger creatures regarded me for a still moment, eyes like black holes, holding a mystery within their gazes.

"Meet the twins, Vega and Rigel, my own magical guardians gifted to me by my parents. I've worked long and hard, and finally got them wings."

I gazed at them. "They're…"

"Perfect, almost." Setizar smiled, though his expression darkened as soon as a silvery light exploded in the sky above. "That was a leviathan blast. Inanna's army is here."

I turned heavenward. Something akin to a thousand bats flying through the air met my vision. "We need to find Tatum." I ignited my sword, fire billowing upward and licking the blade with smoldering heat.

Setizar took a step back, raising his hand for Vega and Rigel. "I should have taken more precautions against the Changeling's escape."

I slid closer, angling my head. "However you and the Seasons accomplished trapping him, I would like to know."

His grin cut through me. "Get me my powers back and I'll show you how I did it. Otherwise, right now I'm good for nearly nothing."

My tongue became a desert. "You can still mist, right? In case of danger?"

"Of course."

"Good. Stay safe. Your powers will return." Fire burst around me. Starlight, sunlight, and echoing darkness clambered along my skin.

I flew in front of the ogarak army; a sea of thousands upon thousands of red carapaces and fangs. Their wings clapped against the air like flags in a fierce storm.

This ended today.

62

*T*here were once rumors about the High Queen of the Day. Tales the humans would tell their misbehaving offspring. They said her wings are those of darkness and shadow, ready to bring death. She would kill with a gleam in her roguish eyes, thirsting for the blood of those who disobeyed their parents. This, of course, wasn't true. Only the men who kill and harm the innocent—those are the ones she judges." Biodru's eyes slid toward me, bright and burning. "Remember, My Queen, you cannot allow yourself to forget who and what you are. Do not forget why you have breath in your lungs, a beating heart, and fire in your soul."

I watched Biodru carefully, holding my tongue. Perhaps they sensed my reluctance to speak.

"Alecto, the reason you have those things is because you were chosen to change the worlds."

Anger swelled in my chest, and a burst of fire exploded around me. The fire illuminated the heavens like the brand of an angered god. Searing. Brutal.

Hundreds of ogarak screamed, falling from the heavens, while others swarmed.

I readied my weapon, my fingers trembling as I angled the sun-licked sword. A clap of roaring thunder broke on the horizon, signaling another wave of enemies. Power ripped through the sky, and I pivoted, throwing a fiery shield around me. It connected with a dozen Ogarak, frying their leathery wings. The air smelled like smoke and burnt hair.

My head lightened.

The source of the power–Biodru–cast rings of fire down the ogarak's ink-black scales. Their eyes, as violet as vervain, rippled across the ogarak.

Behind the Emberfang's massive body was the furie army, armed to the teeth and shining like newly-birthed stars. Beside them, Vega and Rigel unfurled their star-mist wings and vaulted into the fray.

A wave of darkness and light—furie against ogarak, led by the dauntless Biodru. The Emberfang's enormous talons tore through dozens of the enemies like paper, igniting any that dared touch their inky scales with indigo flames.

Claws pierced my shield, and I prepared myself again. As the bloodthirsty creature plunged through, I flung myself atop the ogarak, thrusting my blade through its eye. Brains splintered through its skull, followed by dark blood and the smell of burning flesh.

I careened my body sideways, throwing the hilt of my blade into the jaw of an opposing ogarak. A loud pop ricocheted through the atmosphere.

A claw drove at me, nearly clipping my wing. The slow-thudding pulse in my neck grew stronger as I swung my sword through the air, severing the head from the ogarak's body.

Another beat of my heart, and a thousand arrows soared up from the forest below, striking the creatures around me. A resounding screech of pain flung from their mouths, followed by red and gray foam. Poison. The elves were poisoning the ogarak.

Eira and Feng walked from the wood. Eira wore her fighting leathers, while Feng stood in her scale-like dress with a glimmer in her black eyes. The scales shifted, clinging to her form in the shape of armor. A cruel, wicked type of armor that could frighten legions of warriors.

With a banshee scream, Feng hurdled herself into the air. Eira stood ready at the base of the road, sword drawn.

Ice slicked the wings of the surrounding ogarak. No flapping. Only immediate death.

I looked in Feng's direction, offering her a smile. "Fe—"

Chains wrapped around my ankle, pulling me down. Heavy, icy shards flooded my body. A torrent of wind pushed against my wings, keeping me from stopping my sudden descent.

I was only yards above the forest, my knees weakening. A weight collided with my breast, strangling my breath.

"Hello again." A figure materialized, his smile a cutting mixture of brutality and wickedness.

Tatum.

Wings, as gilded and golden as Aurel's, flapped behind him, reminding me of what he did. A slimy sensation slithered along the crook of my neck as he suspended us both in mid-air.

I wriggled, heaving my elbow into his face. His grip loosened, and I dropped once more, plummeting down. Useless against the pull, I willed my wings into my body. My back connected with the limb of a tree, breaking my armor where I collided.

Something tore into my skin, ripping my flesh. Icy-heat seared through me.

Another bone-crushing drop, and I was face-first on the forest floor.

"Look at you." A laugh rang around me. "Struggling. It's unsightly."

Pressure formed in my stomach as a heel pressed against my back. Black spots tore into my vision.

"I've never thought you beautiful like the ballads paint you out to be. A fierce, sun-wreathed warrior." Tatum's voice bit into me as his boot was thrust into my ribs. I yelped. "The *great* Alecto. High Queen of the Day, bringer of hope, keeper of the eternal flames, rumored to be the most breathtaking creature in the galaxies. You're far more jagged...more... sharp. A weapon. It's why I cared for you once...and if I am honest, a small part of me still does. I wish to end this war fast, so call off your furie army and surrender, and neither you nor your people will be harmed. I only want what was taken from me."

I knew better than to trust him...to trust anything coming from his forked tongue. "No."

"You have never been able to defeat me, Alecto. I'm your inevitable demise. The itch you can't scratch. The wound which keeps bleeding. You will keep trying to kill me, to end me, but you fail. You *keep* failing."

"My failures don't define me or my future." I breathed. Focus... *focus*. "But I learned more from being a human than I ever learned as a furie." Fire flickered below the leaves around me.

"You're right. I fail. I keep failing." I staggered to my feet, fresh blood dripping down my back. "Perhaps I'm destined to die." A smile pulled at my lips. His eyes were void—soulless. Every edge of his face screamed his true nature. His true self. I felt my rage—the freedom shuddering through my bones and skin. "But if I go down, you will go down with me."

I snapped my fingers. The explosion erupted before he realized it. The shattering of a thousand leaves, combusting like bombs, threw him back and into the nearest aspen. His screech ripped into my marrow, curdling my blood.

I stepped closer, fire swirling over my arms as I knelt beside him and gripped his throat, pressing him into the ground.

He smiled, his breath cold against my heated skin. "But could you die knowing Setizar would die too?"

I faltered.

His knee connected with my stomach, throwing me off, and he gripped my throat. My armorless elbow scraped against the foliage, burning my arm.

"You just keep coming back like a luckless coin." He pinned me up against the nearby tree. My back burned, fresh pain blossomed in my spine, bits of bark digging into the gashes.

Fire spread over my palm, and I thrusted my hand into his chest. He flew backward—vanishing. I gasped for breath, looking around for my sword.

Fiery red electricity flooded the area, spidering up the trees and singeing the earth. The Changeling walked into the area once more, now a wisp of a shadow in the shape of a hound. Tendrils curled up from his mane and vanished in the dark air around. He bared his teeth, and red eyes flashed. "Make this easy, won't you?"

Fire swarmed up my fists, coating my forearms in an orange glow. A dance with death.

"You can do better than that, Alecto." His wolfish smile spread as wings peeled out from behind his back. "There are ghosts of our past which plague us. There are whispers from the future we hear. Then there are the nightmares..." Tatum's figure began to elongate, limbs twisted and talons showing.

The red moon rose. A tribal drum reverberated in the distance as the war continued on.

"Meris," Tatum crooned. "*Meris...*"

My heart stuttered. I couldn't speak. Fear clutched me, and the taste of blood surfaced on my tongue.

Tatum lifted his hands, the rocks and trees around us shivering. "Terrestrial magic, remember?" My mouth dried. Hundreds of stones propelled toward me. I barely put my fiery shield up in time.

The stones piled against the fire-screen, blackening my vision and shrinking my shield down. Blood pumped in my veins and lava dripped from my fingertips. I was straining myself. I could barely breathe, my oxygen was slowly slipping away.

"Before you die," Tatum said. "Let me make sure you know a few things." A wicked, crescent-moon smile peeled over his face, revealing jagged teeth. "No matter where you went in the human realm, I could always see you. Your every move was dictated by me. The treats, the little gift of the codex, the rabbit showing you the way."

Everything stopped.

"The Silver Queen being taken away, and even when that boy took your ring. The ring that would have allowed you to remember all your past life the moment you entered Yamira."

Red blurred my vision. Something popped in my ears, swirling with memories.

"Every second of your pathetic life on Inder was guided by my hand, to bring you here. And now look, you're broken. You've been broken. Once I kill Belenia, this world can be as it once was." His laugh mingled with a thousand screams, a thousand pained shouts in the distance.

My bones hardened as I yelled. The rocks mixed with raging lava. My limbs lengthened. My skin turned to basalt and magma. It pooled around me, dripping from my hair, my fingers, my back. "No," I growled. "You will never win this."

I thrust my hand out and my powers collided with his, washing over his terrestrial magic with something far more scorching, far more violent.

"I may be broken." I stepped closer, my flames roiling around the stones he was hurdling my way. I lifted my arm once more, creating an arch of magma. It reached toward the heavens, washing over a battalion of ogarak. "But that's part of being human."

Their screams were swallowed by the molten earth.

This was me. Every broken, weak, ugly part. It made me who I was. I smiled, and lava dripped from my stony body.

Tatum launched toward me, and I threw another wave of fire at him. Ripples of power hummed, screeching as it collided with him. He slammed into a tree, his yells cleaving me in two, tearing into my wounds bit by bit.

I threw another wave of fire into him; the howling expanse of my power pounding against his body. "I'm not a puppet."

He released a low, mirthless laugh, though the crunch of his bones twisted it into screams.

I grabbed his arm and threw him into the center of the forest.

He barked in pain, scrambling to rise. "You cannot kill me. I will simply come back…I'm immortal, just as you once were."

Then, the world slowed as a hollow sound filled the air.

Erecting from within Tatum's chest was a blade—a blade as black as midnight writhed in inked, midnight magic.

He doubled forward, blood spurting from the wound.

And behind him stood a small, familiar figure.

Belenia.

Her eyes locked with mine, a silent threat as her smile curled upward. She pressed her hand against Tatum's wound as his eyes, wide and filled with horror, stared into the darkening skies. Flecks of multicolored magic pulled from him, swirling into Belenia. "You wouldn't have been able to kill him. Not without this," she said, twisting the blade with a sickening crunch.

"You—" I spat, lava dripping from my lips. "This is what you wanted?"

"Well, I suspected he'd have killed you first." She pulled the sword from Tatum's body, driving it deep into his skull. His body twitched before going still. "Well, I suppose I just need to finish the job."

My pulse thickened.

"Have you ever wondered about the source of magic?" She sheathed the still-dripping weapon. "With *your* magic I will have collected enough power to find that source. Enough power to find the Stars and slay them, therefore ending it *all*. If you give up your power, Alecto, I will show you mercy. You will return to the life you knew before. Setizar can join you as a human. You can be happy as I wipe this world clean from magic. Clean from all those *tainted* by the wicked thing. There will be no pain to those who vanish because of it, and the world will be equal. Don't you want that?"

"Why would I want that?" I gripped my stomach. "Why would I want to alter what is created? Why would I want millions dead?"

Her teeth flashed. "Because it's not good enough."

"Nothing is good enough. Even if you banish magic, things will still be in disarray. Things will still be unbalanced and without equality. We have to make do. We have to embrace our differences and live in harmony—"

"Your version of harmony is oppression." Belenia took a step toward me. "I was raised by a furie mother and a daemon father. Do you know what that was like?" She held out her hands. "Do you know what he did to her? To me? He used magic to punish us. The seasons did nothing when my mother came to them. The courts dismissed her. She was killed three days later for trying to undermine him with *this* blade."

My heart sank.

"And you wish to keep a corrupt system like that in place? You wish to allow the weak and the magical beasts to intermingle?" Her words were laced with venom. "You want to bring such a thing back?"

"Evil will always be within the hearts of everyone." I took a step closer. "Furie. Numina. Daemon... *human.*"

Her eyes narrowed.

"I've seen it... witnessed it. I've been subject to its evil. We can either learn or become bitter." I lifted my hands, my volcanic body returning to flesh. My armor clamped over me as the rocks melted into skin. "Help me make this world a better place with magic... not without it. We can help the humans—"

"No!" Belenia screeched. "I'd rather die than help you restore magic."

I raised my head. I needed to find a way to weaken her—

My wings sprouted from behind me and I offered her one last look. "Then so be it. If you want my magic?" Fire pillowed around me. "You're going to have to tear it from my soul."

I augued.

The garden—the maze. I needed to get to the maze.

Focusing my energy on the memory of the strange fountain in the center of the garden, I appeared there. The snow was still fresh on the ground, and I spun.

"What are you doing here, pretty?" The Hag stood before me, her ragged form hovering inches over the ground. "Come to give me your youth?"

I looked around, taking in the crisp whiteness of the surrounding maze. "I need your help"

Her eyes widened as she grinned. "Oh? And why would I help you?"

I angled my head at the Grimhildr. "I need your help to defeat some-one… someone who wishes to destroy magic. If you try and turn on me, everyone will die, and you will be reduced to nothing. Understood?"

Her cackle was dark and grating. "Understood. Who is this creature?"

"She will be here soon. Allow me to distract her. When we near the fountain, I need you to dig your claws into her skin."

The Grimhildr vanished with one last demonic chuckle. "As you wish, My Queen."

I breathed in. The distant clash of weapons and screeching cries of pain reverberated through the air, chilling me to the bone. This had to work. If it didn't, then we were done for. The armies would be lost—the cause would be lost—*everything* would be lost.

Belenia appeared in the middle of the garden, her eyes narrowed. "Are you trying to hide in a maze?"

"Something like that." I stepped back. "This is your last chance. Please… please don't make me do this."

"I'll never make that deal, Alecto."

I set my jaw. "My name isn't Alecto. It's Meris." I flapped my wings, kicking snow up into a torrent. With a snap of my wrist I ignited the sur-rounding area in a sea of flames. Mist encased the maze.

I willed my wings into my back. I couldn't hear anything other than the howling wind and the clamor of the battle in the distance, mingling with the roar of a dragon. Purple light flashed above us as Biodru released a breath of fire.

"Nice party trick," Belenia said inches behind me.

I augued, reappearing on the other side of the fountain. Her frustrated grunt cleaved through the misty air. "It's much more than a party trick."

"I can see." Belenia was behind me again, but this time her sword was ready.

I spun, kicking the blade from her hand.

She grabbed my head, pressing me into the wall of the hedge. I saw the battle. "Watch as your beloved Setizar dies. Watch as Biodru fails you. Watch as your choice to refuse me kills everyone you love. Watch as magic kills them as it did my mother."

I could no longer see her. I saw the battle—I saw Inanna and Setizar. He careened his body to the side, blocking Inanna's attack.

Biodru spread their wings, shifting into a leviathan just feet away from the two battling.

Ogarak swarmed the area, converging on the both of them.

The vision vanished with my scream. I spun and thrusted a fiery dart of magic into Belenia.

Her body slammed against the nearby fountain, her pained shriek cutting into me.

Belenia stood, blood trickling down her neck. Fury danced in her eyes, like smoldering coals. "So, this is what we've become?"

"I didn't want this." My heart was ready to give. This was the last thing I wanted... to lose her.

The hag's arms wrapped around Belenia's neck, stealing her breath from her lungs as fresh gore split from her jugular.

I couldn't watch.

My heart shattered.

I couldn't block out her scream—her plea for help clawed into my ears. Her curses to my name bruised my soul.

I'd never forget this.

Never forgive myself for this.

I turned my gaze to Belenia, slumped on the ground. Her breath was uneven as I plucked her sword up from the ground. Everything was numb. "Give up, please, Julna." I knelt beside her, pressing my fingers to her wound, trying to stop the bleeding. "There's still time. Give up and we can fix this... *together*."

Her hollow gaze flickered with hatred. Her words were garbled, a whisper holding onto her last breaths of life. "I told you I would rather die."

Needles stung my heart. "I love you." Tears pricked my eyes, my finger trembling as her blood coated my hand. "You were, and always have been, my sister. No matter what…" I couldn't see. My vision was blurred. "Please—"

"Never. You were *never* my sister." She was weak; her skin as white as the snow around us.

I pressed my hands against her wound, healing it and remembering what Setizar had said.

"A Grimhildr's claws infect." He looked at me. *"If I were to allow this to sit, you would turn to stone before the hour is up. If anything other than a powerful, cunning jinni tends a wound like this, the process would be sped up. You would be stone in seconds."*

I poured more of my power into healing…

"No!" Belenia screamed, a garbled sound. Her legs, arms, torso… they were already enveloped in stone.

Bursts of color shot from Julna's healing wound, streaking into the heavens. The atmosphere was thick with magic, pulsing into the sky.

The Season magic would find their true hosts within a heartbeat.

Her eyes hardened. She was stone.

I choked on my tears, looking over my sister's face. I'd spent so many years trying to find her, only to lose her—to be the one who killed her—to have her hate me in the end.

Fire erupted around me, singeing the garden and scorching the earth as I screamed.

Above, the ogarak army had diminished, giving way to hundreds of winged leviathans.

The war wasn't over.

Starlight, as white and pure as an angel's wings, speared through the sky.

Another spire of light burst in the heavens, this time coiled with darkness and mist.

Setizar.

He couldn't take on the leviathan army. Not without fire—

A burst of red shuddered through the sky as small bombs made of flame and madness exploded, wrapping fiery fingers around the leviathans' wings.

Jack.

They were dropping like flies.The Seasons' magic returned, and not a moment too soon.

Silence rang in my ears, and I crumbled. The war was ending and the Seasons were restored. Nothing remained but to put Inanna in her place and take control of her army. Well, whatever army she had left.

Fresh tears blossomed in my eyes, hot and horrid. I didn't care that ice had begun to lick at my body. I didn't care that blood dripped from my wounds.

I didn't care if I was dying.

We did it. We won.

But at what cost?

The smell of autumn winds and cloves flooded my senses. A hand pressed against my back, healing the wound in an instant. "Meris?"

Setizar.

I turned, looking up at him. His eyes shimmered like a sunset, glowing brighter than a thousand stars. "I will never be forgiven for what I've done."

His arms wrapped around me, tugging me close. "I know you did what you could."

"No." I buried my face in his chest. "I didn't."

63

"My Queen," said a slender faced unicorn, very different from Cerie. His skin was a deep indigo hue, and his eyes were as green as fresh spring leaves. "Biodru requests you to finish the battle report."

I nodded, sliding back into my chair. It'd been six days. Six days since the battle.

I slid the paper back in front of me, snatching the ink and pen from the left corner of the desk, and resumed my writing.

We won the war. The elves and the furie army, led by Biodru, overwhelmed those from Redrim, forcing them back to their island. Their surrender was sealed when Setizar brought Inanna before the Seasons, bound in her own power-dampening chains. She is safely locked away in a dungeon in Eira's sector.

Setizar's palace is nothing but ruins within a blood-soaked battlefield; however it has begun fixing itself. Word came from the elves that the beasts of the forest are already making their way there to collect the bodies and feast.

We did our best to pull the fallen from the battlefield, but our death count is still being calculated.

I dropped the pen, shaking my head. I couldn't keep reliving it.

My eyes were heavy as I pushed myself away from the desk and plopped into my bed. The room was beautiful, but everything seemed to be dark and muted in my eyes. Earthy wood floors, red as vintage wine, complimented the white gold walls. The ovular chamber opened out into a balcony which wrapped around to the adjoining chamber, allowing endless sunlight to pour in. The muffled sounds of the city danced into the room, followed by the smell of fresh citrus blossoms and honey.

The world outside was even more grand, and yet I couldn't bring myself to get out of the Palace. Biodru had come and called several times, only to be met with Setizar's warning to leave and give me time.

Time wouldn't heal this.

Nothing would heal losing Julna, no matter her end...no matter what she did.

The door creaked open and Cerie stepped in. Her blue skin had a glow to it, different than before. "How are you?"

"Not well." I lifted my head. "Any word?"

"Yes." Cerie settled into a seat beside me. "The Seasons are here and ready. We just need you to open the gateways."

I shifted, my limbs taut and sore. I should be happy. We would be washing the land of the plague, healing the humans, and freeing slaves. I would be able to see Mae—my real sister again. Thank her for all she did and all she sacrificed.

And yet I couldn't heal from this bleeding wound. This emptiness inside my heart. If I could go back and heal what was broken—fix what was done—I would. But the past was in stone, and I stood here in the future without Julna.

"We've made the announcement as you wished, that you will no longer be addressed as Alecto, but Meris." Cerie gently placed her hand on my shoulder, her sun-lit eyes fixing on mine. "Your dress is ready as well. Do you need anything else? Something to eat?"

I shook my head. "No, I'm not hungry." I barely pulled myself out of my bed, gripping tightly to the gold railing. Shadows lapped away at the light as I crossed the chamber. My head was a mess of emotions. I couldn't sort through this.

It was too much.

"Alright. I'll send Jack and he'll help you with the finishing touches of your gown." Cerie breathed out, her eyes narrowing on me. "You did everything you could."

"I keep telling everyone that I didn't. I could've saved her." I looked toward the doorway. "Wouldn't you feel the same way if you had to kill someone you viewed as a sister?"

"It was either her life, or the life of millions. You made the hard choice for everyone. What you did was selfless, Meris. Please know that none of us blame you or accuse you." Cerie bowed her head and turned her heel.

She left the room, yet the accusation remained.

No one needed to blame me or accuse me.

Because I did.

— (—

Jack finished the last tie, eyeing the garment. "It's splendid!"

I managed a weak smile, looking into the mirror he placed in front of me. The dress was a deep galaxy blue, studded with a thousand diamonds twirling around and climbing up the skirt. The bodice faded to black, embracing the sapphires that studded the breast of the garment and trailed up the collar. A blue and black gossamer cape billowed down my shoulders, caressing the floor like mist.

"You look like a queen..." Jack whispered as he placed a crown made of crystal on my head. A single light, like a tiny star, floated above the center spire of the piece. His smile was bright as he bowed. "My Queen."

I couldn't fight the smile. "I wish the conditions were different."

"We all do." He extended his arm to me, and I took it. "Time will heal the wounds the war inflicted."

I nodded slowly, looking outward. "Will it?"

"Of course." He patted my hand, guiding me toward the door. "For now, we must open the portals and show the realm who you are. The High Queen of the Day who understands humanity, who understands the wielders of the magic, and ultimately, a queen who cares."

"I feel as if you're describing someone else entirely." I walked with him, down the halls and toward the grand stairwell. "I don't feel at all like the same creature who came here."

"Because you aren't," Setizar whispered, taking Jack's place. His suit was tailored to compliment mine. Deep blue with hints of purple laying below the surface. The gleam in his eyes was brighter than any star, sun, or light I'd ever seen. "You came into this realm a strong woman, and now you're leaving as an even stronger, braver, fiercer, kinder one."

Tears sprang into my eyes.

"And it's not flattery, Meris. No matter how many times we meet, you become stronger. You become more like the fire you hold inside."

Our heels clicked against the marble as we descended the stairwell. I could melt into Setizar, and not care about the past or future.

The shadows of the alabaster statues stood like sentinels along the glittering gold floor, mingling with Setizar's and my own. "I'm not ready for this," I whispered, clutching tighter to his arm.

Setizar smiled at me, placing his hand on mine. "I'll be right beside you. If you took on an army of ogarak and defeat the Changeling, you can open the portals to Inder."

I released a breath, nodding. He was right. I needed to calm down.

A battalion of furies stood outside the palace doors, ready to act at my command. Their wings gleamed white and gold, matching the hair, their spears, swords, arrows, and other weapons strung at their sides or on their backs, just within arms reach.

Biodru stood in leviathan form, a smile spreading across their pale face. "Welcome back, My Queen." They bowed, followed by the hurrah of the troops.

My heart stumbled.

At the end of the lane, leading out into the field, stood the other three Seasons. Eira, Lhysa, and Aurel. They were dressed in their finest attire, with a handful of guards and captains at their side. Feng offered me a devilish smirk and a sweeping bow. The others followed.

Libby held the Codex in his hands, standing before a large stone arch. "Are we ready to greet the humans after all this time of separation?" he asked, his voice clean and clear.

We nodded.

He placed the codex down, flipping open the leather cover. "A drop of magic on these pages will aid you in breaking open the gateways, Meris."

I blinked, my heart pounding as I readied my magic. Lhysa stepped forward, placing her hand on the pages. The parchment glowed a vibrant green at her touch, then yellow at Aurel's. Setizar stepped forward, his palm covering the page and changing the hue to purple. Eira was next, and the entire volume erupted in a white light.

I stepped toward the Codex. Magic pulsed from the document, drawing me closer. Warmth enveloped my palm as I pressed it to the paper. Its hue shifted, burning a vibrant red. Light erupted into the sky, splintering across the atmosphere with the colors of our magic, tearing a hole in the heavens.

Shards of severed sunlight crashed down, spiraling around me and shuddering into my veins. It was a pure, untamed version of magic. I waved my hand, willing the pulsing waves toward the archway. The portal flickered.

I saw Yeodo.

"All the gateways are opened," Libby announced, which resulted in a deafening cheer from the thousands surrounding us.

Setizar stepped beside me, a flicker of a smile pulling at his lips. "Meris," he whispered, holding out his hand for me to take. "Shall we make a grand entrance?"

I nodded, slipping my hand into his as we stepped into the portal. I thought of home, of the small cottage we owned on Inder. The world around us shifted, as though we walked into water and emerged dry on the other side.

Nothing had changed.

I looked at the cottage, my heart blossoming with excitement. Setizar's laugh echoed behind me as I lifted my skirts and dashed toward the front door. It wasn't very queenly, but I couldn't allow another moment to pass.

I pounded on the wood, heart hammering just as violently. What if she was taken? What if she got sick? The seconds that passed felt eternal.

Locks clicked and the handle turned. The door creaked on its hinges as it opened, and Megaera's face showed through the crack. Her gasp was loud, and she stumbled a step back upon seeing me. I supposed this was shocking. I had shown up at our front door dressed like a queen.

"Meris?" Mae whispered.

I nodded, so many emotions flooding my heart that I didn't know where to start or what to say.

Her eyes roamed over my outfit, settling on the crown perched atop my head. "What happened?"

"More than you may be able to take in." I held out my hand, stepping aside so as to reveal Setizar standing on the other side of the fence. "Do you remember anything from before?"

She shook her head. "Before what?"

I looked down, seeing the ring still hanging on her neck. Libby told me that would possibly take some work. "May I have that?"

She looked down, partially unable to take her eyes off Setizar standing yards away. "Of course." She unhooked the necklace, placing it in my hand. Powerful magic pulsed from the pendant, wishing to be released.

I obliged it.

Pressing my thumb against the gem, I willed my own magic into it, and vibrant blue light erupted, bursting into a star above us then colliding with Megaera's aging body. She gasped, stumbling back and nearly falling.

I grabbed her, yanking her into my arms before she could hurt herself.

Seconds ticked by. The birds ceased their chirping; insects stopped their chattering. Only silence and the whisper of wind was heard.

Slowly, I let Megaera go. Her face was relieved of lines and age, eyes as bright as the sky above. "You—"

I nodded.

"We won?"

"We won, Meg."

EPILOGUE

I slid the parchment closer, dipping the quill into the glittering black ink again before pressing it against the paper.

After I released Megaera, Setizar and I paid a visit to the Gathbreds to pay the debt. The looks on their faces were of pure horror. I've never seen anyone so terrified in all my years. It was particularly satisfying seeing Lady Gathbred practically gobble as she searched for words to say to us.

Chester Gathbred wasn't humbled in the least from our presence. I don't think even the end of the realms could have fazed him. He said he should have tried harder to make me his wife, but said that I looked like a demon, which didn't bode well with Setizar.

"You know, Meris..." he'd said, "how would you like a pet rat? I'm certain there's a spell or two that could turn this child into one. Wouldn't take much since he's nearly there."

Chester couldn't get in a word without being verbally pummeled, and I could barely hold in my laughter. However, I still forgave them, which amounted to baffled faces and confused whispers. He still has my ring. I don't think I'll ever get it back, but I also don't need it anymore.

As far as the plague, Aurel and his people worked tirelessly and came together with a cure. Jack and Lhysa seem to be closer now than before. I suppose only time will tell what becomes of them... though I have my hopes.

Cerie is still working for Setizar, happily moving between the Day and the Crimson Plane using the portal Lhysa and I concocted.

Feng is traveling through Inder, inspecting the prisons and armies, trying to bring back chivalry and true knighthood. She's doing a very good job, I believe.

Eira is back in her sector, fairly unchanged aside from the fact that she promised to keep the snow out of Setizar's newly replanted garden. He's very proud of it.

Setizar, well, he visits as often as he can. Though we're married, I wish to say our vows once more. To solidify everything. Our ceremony is to be held on the solstice of the next season. Yes, the winter solstice.

Adventure seems to lurk around every corner when he's around, even though he wishes to only stay tucked away in the library and read all the days of his life. Let's hope the human poets and authors will continue to inspire him as the tale of the pirate and the mermaid, which is currently enrapturing his mind and emotions.

As for me? I'm still learning how to work with the humans and their rulers. Magic was foreign to them not too long ago, so the leap it is taking to embrace it is immense. We've been met with some opposition by the northern kingdoms, but otherwise only open arms and willing hearts have greeted us—"

Fingers wrapped around my wrist, keeping me from writing down another line on paper. "My love," Setizar purred in my ear. "I think you left out a good bit about me."

"Oh?" I angled my head, looking at him. "What did I leave out, exactly?"

He grinned, pressing a kiss to my neck. "How much you love me, how much I love you, how I would die for you... just a few things."

I grabbed his shirt, tugging him closer. "You're full of it."

"I'm full of a lot of things." His voice dipped into a deep growl. "I can show you a few other things that I'm full of, if you have a few hours to spare. I've recently discovered an interesting lagoon just north of here that I'm certain would capture your attention. "

"I'm rather busy giving my report to Biodru and all."

Setizar chuckled. "Didn't you already send a letter to your benevolent second-in-command?"

"Yes. But I forgot a few things."

"Another hour and I'll give you some more things to tell them of." His kiss sealed my mouth, hindering a response.

"Fine," I whispered, looking into his eyes. "You have two hours."

He bowed his head, eyes lit with excitement. "Yes, your majesty."

ACKNOWLEDGEMENTS

I began writing this book in 2019, not sure where it would go. I decided to have fun—to create something that I didn't need to worry about—and it became one of the most important books I've ever written. Though the story changed from its original conception to what it is now, the message is still there.

However, this book wouldn't have been possible without my cheerleaders, my writer family, and the friends who encouraged me throughout this entire process.

First off, a huge thank you to Josh Langlois, who was with this story through every step and every change. I don't think this book would have been possible without your encouragement and your enthusiasm. Some days were so much harder than others, but your constant excitement about each (at the time, very crummy) chapter that I wrote was one of the only things that kept me going.

Phoebe Ross, who tore into my book with claws of love and provided me with so much insight, your ability to take a step back and draw lines from beginning to end gave me perspective on what I needed to work on.

Benét Stoen, who fangirled over each character and gave me an in-depth analysis into what each chapter needed, you have no idea how much you helped with this story and its every moving part. It's now a well oiled machine.

To my writer family, Dave, Kathleen, Brandon, and Kim, your sprints, open conversation, and second pairs of eyes helped me so much throughout this long journey.

Of course, I couldn't do this without my amazing beta readers! Philippa P., Josh R., Laura R., Charlotte S., David A., J.C. Scraba, Emma C., you were the lifeblood to the revisions that made this book into the final ring of publication war. There's no way I could have navigated the final steps without your input!

Lastly, but of course not least, thank you to you, reader, for picking up this book and giving it a chance.

ABOUT THE AUTHOR

J.M. Ivie is a U.S. based graphic designer and author. Her passion for writing stems from her life-long love of reading and telling stories to her younger siblings. When she isn't writing, she's drawing, reading, playing with her all too-rowdy Labrador retriever, or baking things that aren't good for those trying to maintain the semblance of a good diet.

SCAN THE CODE
For the Spotify Playlist of Dark Swan!

SETIZAR

Her red hair was damp, clinging to her neck as she lifted her chin and closed her dark eyes. She was a queen who knew nothing of her royalty and yet appeared for all the world in control of the invisible crown she bore. Alecto.

I'd waited years, and there she stood, mere feet away, dancing to the music of the North. Did she know that music was a homage to her? Did she know that song was written about how she'd sacrificed herself for Yamira?

The music grew louder, and she drifted about the room like a wraith, carried by the chiming music, while I watched from the shadow of the doorway.

I loved her. With every passing moment, every passing breath I took, the secret I'd held so tightly to grew harder and harder to keep. How terrible would it be to tell her? To reveal all the mysteries she was likely wondering about?

No.

No, she wouldn't take it well. She already seemed to think me insane, or at least partially there.

The pulse of her magic hummed in the air and crackled across my skin like kindling flames. It called to me. It wanted to be awoken, wanted to open its angry, monstrous eye and emerge from the cocoon she kept it in.

And I wanted to help it along, though that would be utterly impossible. My magic didn't speak to hers as hers did to mine. She would need to awake the beast that slumbered inside her, not I.

A flash of her drying hair had my attention sliding back to her face, and the slight limp in her step alerted me of the wound she likely still had.

She stilled, and I knew I'd overstayed my silent spectating.

"Well," I muttered, leaning against the doorframe. Her body went rail-straight, and her eyes snapped to mine. "All washed?"

There was a flash of fire in those ever-dark eyes as her brows twitched. Was she fighting a glare?

It was hard to withhold my smile, but somehow I managed. Before I could fail in my attempt to seem impassive, I gestured to a chair, hoping she'd stay cordial.

She sat without a word, though her crossed arms did let me know she wasn't entirely happy with the situation.

I slid my hands into my pockets, trying to make sense of the woman before me. She'd fought me at every turn, every small choice and word, and yet...yet she was complying? Was she up to something nefarious? I wouldn't put it past her. She always had a way of catching me off guard.

"Meris," I said, trying to keep my voice from betraying my unease. "Roll up the right pant leg, please."

She rolled her shoulders, eyes darting from my mouth to my eyes to my head, likely plotting something.

Surprisingly, she did as I'd asked and rolled up the pant leg.

Aether, what in the name of the Stars was she up to?

I gently took her leg and set it in my knee, unfurling the bandage I had with me. "This is a nasty cut," I said, looking at her. Aether, she was beautiful. The smattering of freckles on her face, the halo of fire-limned lashes around those dark eyes—

I dropped my gaze back to her leg, trying to set my mind straight. Quickly, I pulled a small vial out of my coat before reaching through the veil of mist to retrieve a cloth from my room. "You'll have to take it easy for the next few hours while it heals."

I could feel her eyes on me, burning the top of my head.

I poured some of the vial on the cloth, pressing it gingerly to the wound.

She gasped, gripping the chair arm.

"I'm sorry." I looked at her. Just that sound from her...the undertone of the pain. I didn't want to hear that again—not from my hand nor anyone else's. "I'll try to be gentler."

She opened her mouth, but no words came out. She shook her head, then seeming to find her voice, said, "It just stings a little."

"I don't often tend wounds, so please... let me know if any of this hurts."

I could take her pain away. I'd done it before, though it always seemed to backfire on me. But I could better clean her cut if I weren't focusing on keeping her level of pain to a minimum.

Steeling my nerves, I focused my attention on the wound—on the feeling of pain she'd experience.

It filtered to me. Slicing through my veins and splintering my bones.

"How is there no pain?" Meris asked.

A wave of nausea washes over me. Would I vomit right here? On her? Stars, that would not only be embarrassing, but would break the magic link on us. Would she feel the pain if the link broke? Or would she still be numb?

I finished, waves of sickness easing as I wrapped her leg neatly with the bandage. "All better?"

She nodded. "Thank you."

I smiled. "Would you like to go somewhere with me?"

"Where's my lecture?" She scowled, seeming doubly confused when I use my magic to fetch her slippers from her trunk. "Where are we going?"

"Is that a yes, then?" I stood. "Because I won't take you unless you say you want to go."

She groaned and narrowed her eyes. A long moment of silence stretched between us, and each heartbeat had me tensing. What was she thinking?

"Alright. I want to go."

Thank the Stars she agreed. "Then, my lady, allow me to take you to the destination." I hold my hand out to her.

She returned to looking skeptical. "Can I trust you?"

It was a good question, likely one which had an obvious answer. Of course she could, but the words that left my mouth were what she likely expected. "You probably shouldn't."

Her beautiful, star-bright smile was worth it. And the moment she slipped her hand into mine, the ability to mist wasn't as difficult as it had been before.